Dear Reader,

Thank you for participating in Harlequin's fiftieth anniversary celebration! I hope you enjoy *Love by Degree*, which was originally published in 1987. Although I wrote this book many years ago, it's one that holds a special place in my heart. If you feel I depicted living with teenage boys realistically—well, there's a reason. It was at this time in my life that all four of my own children were in their teens. I swear hormones ricocheted all over our house!

I'm grateful to be part of the Harlequin family of authors and for the opportunities given to me throughout the years to grow and mature as a writer. The truth is, I read Harlequin romances long before I became a novelist myself. I know readers love their Harlequin novels, too. These not-so-simple love stories have touched our lives for fifty years now. They've taught many of us to dream, and to look forward to the future with optimism and hope. They've helped us find the true heroine buried deep inside ourselves, and define what it is to be a true hero.

If this is your first time reading Renee Roszel, you're going to enjoy her stories. I certainly do, and I'm grateful to have my book published with hers.

Thank you again—and happy 50th anniversary to all of us.

Debbie Macomber

HARLEQUIN · CELEBRATES

FIVE DECADES OF ROMANCE

LIMITED COLLECTOR'S EDITION 2 IN 1

DEBBIE MACOMBER

LOVE BY DEGREE

RENEE ROSZEL

BOARDROOM BRIDEGROOM

HARLEQUIN®

TORONTO • NEW YORK • LONDON
AMSTERDAM • PARIS • SYDNEY • HAMBURG
STOCKHOLM • ATHENS • TOKYO • MILAN • MADRID
PRAGUE • WARSAW • BUDAPEST • AUCKLAND

ISBN 0-373-83409-8

HARLEQUIN 50th ANNIVERSARY LIMITED COLLECTOR'S
EDITION VOLUME 1

Copyright © 1999

The publisher acknowledges the copyright holders
of the individual works as follows:

LOVE BY DEGREE
Copyright © 1987 by Debbie Macomber

BOARDROOM BRIDEGROOM
Copyright © 1998 by Renee Roszel

Look us up on-line at: http://www.romance.net

Printed in U.S.A.

Table of Contents

Love by Degree
Debbie Macomber

CHAPTER ONE

THE MELODIOUS SOUNDS of a love ballad drifted softly through the huge three-storey house in Seattle's Capitol Hill. Ellen Cunningham hummed the catchy Neil Diamond tune as she rubbed her wet curls with a thick towel. These late-afternoon hours before her housemates returned were the only time she had the place to herself, so she'd taken advantage of the peaceful interlude to leisurely wash her hair. Privacy was at a premium with three men in the house, and she couldn't always count on the upstairs bathroom being available later in the evening.

Twisting the fire-engine-red towel around her head, turban style, Ellen walked barefoot across the hallway toward her bedroom to retrieve her blouse. Halfway there, she heard the faint ding of the oven timer, signalling that her apple pie was ready to come out.

Automatically she altered her course and bounded down the wide stairway, humming as she went. Her classes that day had gone exceptionally well. She couldn't remember ever being happier, even though she still missed Yakima, the small apple-growing community in central Washington, where she'd been raised. But she was adjusting well to life in the big city. She'd waited impatiently for the right time—and enough money—to complete her education, and she'd been gratified by the way everything had suddenly fallen into place during the past summer. Her younger sister had married, and her "baby" brother had entered the military. For a while, Ellen had feared that her mother might suffer from the "empty nest syndrome," so she had decided to delay her education another year. But her worries had been groundless, as it turned out. James Simonson, a widower friend of her mother's, had started dropping by the house often enough for Ellen to recognise a romance brewing between the two. The time was finally ripe for Ellen to make the break, and she did it without guilt or self-reproach.

Clutching a pot holder in one hand, she opened the oven door and lifted out the steaming pie. The fragrance of spicy apples filled the huge kitchen, mingling with the savory aroma of the stew that simmered gently on top of the stove. Carefully, Ellen set the pie on a wire rack that rested on the counter. Her housemates appreciated her culinary efforts and she enjoyed doing little things to please them. As the oldest, Ellen fit easily into this household of young men; in fact, she felt that the arrangement was ideal. In exchange for cooking, a little mothering on the side and a share of the cleaning, Ellen paid only a nominal rent.

The unexpected sound of the back door opening caused her to swivel around sharply.

"What the hell?" The open doorway was dominated by a man with the most piercing green eyes Ellen had ever seen. They reminded her of emeralds caught in the sunlight, flashing now, and intense. She noticed immediately that the rest of his features were strongly defined and perfectly balanced. His cheekbones were high and wide, yet amazingly his face remained lean and appealing. His mouth was twisted in an unspoken question and his forehead was pleated in a thick frown, narrowing the intense eyes.

In one clenched hand he held a large leather suitcase, which he slowly lowered to the kitchen floor. "Who are you?" He spoke sharply, but it wasn't anger or disdain that edged his voice; it was genuine bewilderment.

Ellen was too shocked to move. When she'd whirled around so suddenly, the towel had slipped from her head and covered one eye, blocking her vision. But even a one-eyed view of this stranger was enough to intimidate her. She had to admit that his impeccable three-piece business suit didn't look very threatening— but then she glanced up at his glowering face again.

With as much poise as possible, she raised a hand to straighten the turban and realised that she was standing in the kitchen wearing washed-out jeans and a bright white bra. Grabbing the towel from her head, she clasped it to her chest for protection. "Who are you?" she snapped back. To her chagrin, she realised she must have made a laughable sight, holding a red bath towel in front of her like a matador before a charging bull. This man reminded her of a bull. He was tall, muscular and solidly built. And she somehow knew that when he moved, it would be with effortless power and sudden speed. Not exactly the type of man she'd want to meet in a dark alley. Or a deserted house, for that matter. Already Ellen could see the headlines: Small-Town Girl Assaulted in Capitol Hill Kitchen.

"What are you doing here?" she demanded in her sternest voice.

"This is my home!" The words vibrated around the walls like claps of thunder.

"Your home?" Ellen choked out. "But...I live here."

"Not any more you don't."

"Who are you?" she demanded a second time.

"Reed Morgan."

Ellen relaxed her defences. "Derek's brother?"

"Half-brother."

No wonder they didn't look anything alike. Derek was a lanky, easy-going nineteen-year-old, with dark hair and equally dark eyes. Ellen would certainly never have expected Derek to have a brother—even a half-brother—like this glowering titan.

"I—I didn't know you were coming," she hedged, feeling utterly foolish.

"Apparently." He cocked one brow ever so slightly as he viewed the velvet perfection of her bare shoulders. He shoved the heavy suitcase out of the doorway, then sighed deeply and ran his hands through his hair. Ellen couldn't help making the irrelevant observation that it was a dark auburn, thick and lustrous with health.

He looked tired and irritable. He obviously wasn't in the best frame of mind for any explanations of why she was running around his kitchen half-naked. "Would you like a cup of coffee?" she offered congenially, hoping to ease the shock of her presence.

"What I'd like is for you to put some clothes on."

"Yes, of course." Forcing a smile, Ellen turned abruptly and left the kitchen, feeling humiliated that she could stand there discussing coffee with a stranger when she was practically naked. Taking the stairs two at a time, she entered her room and removed the blouse from the end of the bed. Her fingers were trembling as she tried to do up the buttons.

Her thoughts spun in confusion. If this house was indeed Reed Morgan's, then he had every right to ask her to leave. She sincerely hoped he'd made some mistake. Or that she'd misunderstood. It would be difficult to find another place to share this far into the school term. And her meagre savings would be quickly wiped out if she had to live somewhere on her own. Ellen's brow wrinkled with worry as she dragged a brush through her short, bouncy curls, still slightly damp from washing. Being forced to move wouldn't be a tragedy, but close enough to one that she was understandably apprehensive. The role of housemother came naturally to Ellen. The boys couldn't so much as boil water without her. She'd only recently broken them in to running the vacuum cleaner and the washing machine without her assistance.

When she returned to the kitchen, she found Reed leaning against the counter. His hands hugged a ceramic mug of steaming coffee.

"How long has this cosy set-up with you and Derek been going on?"

"About two months now," she answered, pouring herself a cup of coffee. Although she rarely drank it she felt she needed something to occupy her hands. "But it's not what you're implying. Derek and I are nothing more than friends."

"I'll just bet."

Ellen could deal with almost anything except sarcasm. Gritting her teeth until her jaw ached, she replied in an even, controlled voice. "I'm not going to stand here and argue with you. Derek advertised for a housemate and I answered the ad. I came to live here with him and the others and—"

"The others?" Reed almost choked on his mouthful of coffee. "You mean there's more of you around?"

Expelling her breath slowly in an effort to maintain her calm, Ellen boldly met his scowl. "There's Derek, Pat and—"

"Is Pat male or female?" The sheer force of his personality filled the kitchen. But Ellen refused to be intimidated.

"Pat is a male friend who attends classes at the university with Derek and me."

"So you're all students?"

"Yes."

He eyed her curiously. "Aren't you a bit old for the college scene?"

"I'm twenty-four." She wasn't about to explain her circumstances to this man.

The sound of the front door opening and closing directed their attention to the opposite end of the house. Carrying an armload of books, Derek Morgan sauntered into the kitchen and stopped cold when he caught sight of his older brother.

"Hi, Reed." Uncertain eyes flew to Ellen as if seeking reassurance. A worried look pinched the boyishly handsome face. Slowly, he placed his books on top of the counter.

"Derek."

"I see you've met Ellen." Derek's welcoming smile was decidedly forced and looked as brittle as old parchment.

"We more or less stumbled into each other." Derek's stiff shoulders relaxed as Reed straightened and set the mug aside.

"I didn't expect you back so soon."

Momentarily, Reed's gaze slid to Ellen. "That much

is obvious. Do you want to tell me what's going on here, little brother?''

"It's not as bad is it appears."

"Right now it doesn't look particularly good."

"I can explain everything."

"I'm hoping that's possible."

Nervously swinging her arms at her sides, Ellen stepped forward. "If you two will excuse me, I'll be up in my room." The last thing she wanted was to find herself positioned between the two brothers while they settled their differences.

"No, don't go," Derek said quickly. His dark eyes urgently pleaded with her to stay.

Almost involuntarily Ellen glanced at Reed for guidance.

"By all means, stay." But his look wasn't encouraging.

A growing sense of resentment made her arch her back and thrust out her chin defiantly. Who was this... this unnerving male to burst into their tranquil lives and raise havoc? The four lived congenially together, all of them doing their parts in the smooth running of the household.

"Are you charging rent?" Reed demanded.

Briefly Derek's eyes met Ellen's. "It makes sense, doesn't it? This big old house has as many bedrooms as a dorm. I didn't think it would hurt." He swallowed nervously. "I mean with you being in the Middle East and all. The house was...so empty."

"How much are you paying?" Reed directed the question to Ellen. That sarcastic look was back and Ellen resisted the urge to give him the good tongue-lashing he deserved.

"How much?" Reed repeated when she hesitated.

Ellen knew just from the way Derek's eyes widened that they were entering into dangerous territory.

"It's different with Ellen," Derek hurried on to explain. "She does all the shopping and the cooking, so the rest of us—"

"Are you sure that's all she provides?" Reed interrupted harshly.

Ellen's gaze didn't waver. "I pay ten dollars a week, but believe me, I earn my keep." The second the words slipped out, Ellen wanted to take them back.

"I'm sure you do."

Ellen was too furious and outraged to speak. How dared he just barge into this house and immediately assume the worst? All right, she'd been walking around half-naked, but she hadn't exactly been expecting company.

Angrily Derek stepped forward. "It's not like that, Reed."

"I discovered her prancing around in the kitchen in her bra. What else am I supposed to think?"

Derek groaned and cast an accusing look at Ellen. "I just ran down to get the pie out of the oven," she asserted in her own defence.

"Let me assure you," Derek said, his voice quavering with righteousness. "You've got this all wrong." He glared indignantly at his older brother. "Ellen isn't that kind of woman. I resent the implication. As far as I'm concerned, you owe us both an apology."

From the stunned look on Reed's face, Ellen surmised that this could well be the first time Derek had stood up to his domineering older brother. Her impulse was to clap her hands and shout: "Attaboy!" With an immense effort she restrained herself.

Reed wiped a hand over his face and pinched the bridge of his nose. "Perhaps I do at that."

The front door opened and closed again. "Anyone here?" Monte's eager voice rang from the living room. The sound of his books hitting the stairs echoed through the narrow hallway that led into the kitchen. "Something smells good." Skidding to an abrupt halt just inside the room, the tall student looked around at the sombre faces. "What's going on? You three look like you're about to attend a funeral."

"Are you Pat?" Reed asked.

"No, Monte."

Reed closed his eyes and wearily rubbed the back of his neck. "Just how many bedrooms have you rented out?"

Derek lowered his gaze to his hands. "Three."

"My room?" Reed questioned.

"Yes, well, Ellen needed a place and it seemed only logical to give her that one. You were supposed to be gone a year or so. What happened?"

"I came home early."

Abruptly stepping forward, her fingers nervously laced together, Ellen broke into the tense interchange between the two men. "I'll move up a floor. I don't mind, really." The third floor of the older house had once been reserved for the servants. The rooms were small and airless, but sleeping there was preferable to suffering the wrath of Derek's brother. Or worse, being forced to find somewhere else to live.

Reed responded with a dismissive gesture of his hand. "Don't worry about it. Until things are straightened out, I'll sleep up there. Once I've taken a long, hot shower and gotten some rest I might be able to make some sense out of this mess."

"No, please." Ellen persisted. "If I'm in your room, then it's only right that I move."

"No," Reed grumbled on his way out the door, waving aside her offer. "It's only my house. I'll sleep in the servants' quarters."

Before Ellen could argue further, Reed was out of the kitchen and halfway up the stairs.

"Is there a problem?" Monte asked, opening the refrigerator. He didn't appear particularly concerned, but then he rarely worried about anything unless it directly affected his stomach. Ellen didn't know how any one person could eat so much. His build was strong and lithe, and he never seemed to gain weight, but if it were up to him he'd feed himself exclusively on pizza and french fries.

"Do you want to explain what's going on?" Ellen pressed Derek, feeling guilty but not quite knowing why. "I assumed your family owned the house."

"Well...sort of," he hedged, sinking slowly into one of the kitchen chairs.

"It's the *sort of* that worries me." She pulled out the chair across from Derek and looked at him sternly.

"Reed is family."

"But he didn't know that you were renting out the bedrooms?"

"He told me this job would last nine months to a year. I couldn't see any harm in doing it. Everywhere I looked there were ads for students wanting rooms to rent. It didn't seem right to live alone in this house with all these bedrooms."

"Maybe I should start looking for someplace else to live," Ellen suggested reluctantly. The more she thought about it, the harder it was to see any other solution now that Reed had returned.

"Not before dinner," Monte protested, delivering a loaf of bread and assorted sandwich makings to the table.

"There's no need for anyone to leave," Derek returned with defiant bravado. Three thick lines marred his brow. "Reed will probably only be around a couple of weeks before he goes away on another assignment."

"Assignment?" Ellen questioned, her curiosity piqued.

"Yeah. He travels all over the place—we hardly ever see him. And from what I hear, I don't think Danielle likes him being gone so much, either."

"Danielle?"

"They've been practically engaged for ages and... I don't know the whole story, but apparently Reed's been putting off tying the knot because he does so much travelling."

"Danielle must care a great deal for him to be willing to wait." Ellen watched as Monte spread several layers of smoked ham over the inch-thick slice of Swiss cheese. She knew better than to warn her housemate that he would ruin his dinner. After the triple-decker sandwich, Monte could sit down to a five-course meal—and then ask about dessert.

"I guess," Derek answered nonchalantly. "Reed's perfect for her. You'd have to meet Danielle to understand." Reaching into the teddy-bear-shaped cookie jar and helping himself to a handful, Derek continued. "Reed didn't mean to snap at everyone. Usually, he's a super brother. And Danielle's all right," he added without much enthusiasm.

"It takes a special kind of woman to stick by a man that long without a commitment."

Derek shrugged his shoulders. "I suppose. Danielle's got her own reasons, if you know what I mean."

Ellen wasn't sure, but she didn't press. "What does Reed do?"

"He's an aeronautical engineer for Boeing. He travels around the world working on different projects. This last one was somewhere near Saudi Arabia."

"What about the house?"

"Well, that's his, an inheritance from his mother's family, but he's gone so much of the time that he asked me if I would live here and look after the place."

"What about us?" Monte wanted to know, revealing his concern for the first time. "Will big brother want us to move out?"

"I don't think so. Tomorrow morning I'll ask him. I can't see me all alone in this huge old place. It's not like I'm trying to make a fortune by collecting a lot of rent."

"If Reed wants us to leave, then I'm sure something can be arranged." Already Ellen's mind was working. She didn't want her fate to be determined by a whim of Derek's brother.

"Let's not do anything drastic. I don't think he'll mind once he has a chance to think it through," Derek murmured with a thoughtful frown. "At least, I hope not."

Later that night as Ellen slipped between the crisply laundered sheets, she wondered about the strange man whose bed she occupied. Tucking the thick quilt around her shoulders, she battled down a wave of anxiety. Everything had worked out so perfectly that she should have expected something to go wrong. If anyone voiced objections to Reed's renting out bedrooms, it would probably be his almost-fiancée. Ellen sighed apprehensively. She had to admit that if the positions were reversed, she wouldn't want the man she loved sharing his house with another woman. Tomorrow she'd check around to see if she could find a new place to live.

ELLEN WAS SCRAMBLING EGGS the following morning when Reed appeared, coming down the narrow stairs that led from the third floor to the kitchen. He'd shaved, which emphasised the lean chiselled look of his jaw. His handsome face was weathered and everything about him spoke of health and vitality. Ellen paused, her fork suspended in midstroke with raw egg dripping from the tines. She wouldn't call Reed Morgan handsome so much as striking. He had an unmistakable masculine appeal that wouldn't go unnoticed by the female population. Apparently the duties of an aeronautical engineer were more physically demanding than she'd suspected. Strength showed in the wide muscular shoulders and lean, hard build. He looked even more formidable this morning.

"Good morning," she greeted him cheerfully, as she continued to beat the eggs. "I hope you slept well."

Reed poured coffee into the same mug he'd used the day before. A creature of habit, Ellen mused. "Morning," he responded somewhat gruffly.

"Can I fix you some eggs?"

"Derek and I have already talked. You can all stay."

"Is that a yes or a no to the eggs?"

"I'm trying to tell you that you don't need to worry about impressing me with your culinary efforts."

With a grunt of impatience, Ellen set the bowl aside and leaned forward, slapping her open palms down on the countertop. "I'm scrambling eggs here. Whether you want some or not is entirely up to you. Believe me, if I was concerned about getting on your good side, I wouldn't do it with eggs.''

For the first time, Ellen saw a hint of amusement touch those brilliant green eyes. ''No, I don't suppose you would.''

''Now that we've got that settled, would you like breakfast or not?''

''All right.''

His eyes boldly searched hers and for an instant Ellen found herself regretting that there was a Danielle. With an effort, she turned away and forced her concentration back to the mechanics of cooking breakfast. This man's potency, his sheer intensity, was making her cautious.

''Do you do all the cooking?'' Just the way he asked made it sound as though he were already criticising their household arrangements. Ellen bit back a sarcastic reply and busied herself melting butter and putting bread in the toaster. She'd bide her time. If Derek was right, his brother would soon be away on another assignment.

''Most of it,'' Ellen answered, pouring the eggs into the hot skillet.

''Who pays for the groceries?''

Ellen shrugged, hoping to give the appearance of nonchalance. ''We all chip in.'' She did the shopping and most of the cooking. In return, the boys did the majority of the housework.

The bread popped up from the toaster and Ellen reached for the butter knife, doing her best to ignore the overpowering presence of Reed Morgan.

''What about the shopping?''

"I enjoy it," she stated simply, putting two more slices of bread into the toaster.

"I thought women all over America were fighting to get out of the kitchen."

"When a replacement is found, I'll be pleased to move aside." She wasn't comfortable with the direction this conversation seemed to be taking. Reed was looking at her as though she were some kind of museum piece.

"Leave it to Derek to stumble onto another Betty Crocker."

Ellen wasn't amused. She liked to cook, but that didn't make her an antique. As it turned out, the boys needed someone who knew her way around a kitchen, and she needed an inexpensive place to live. Everything had worked out perfectly and she wasn't about to let Reed ruin it now.

She carefully spooned the cooked eggs onto one plate and piled the toast on another, then carried it to the table, which gave her enough time to control her indignation. She was a modern woman who just happened to fit into the role of surrogate mother to a bunch of college-age boys. All right, maybe that made her a little unusual these days, but she enjoyed living with Derek and the others. It helped her feel at home, and for now she needed that.

"Aren't you going to eat?" Reed stopped her on her way out of the kitchen.

"I'll fix myself something later. The only time I can count on the bathroom being free in the mornings is when the boys are having breakfast. That is, unless you were planning to use it?"

Reed's eyes narrowed fractionally. "No."

"What's the matter? You've got that look about you again."

"What look?"

"The one that pinches your lips together as if you aren't pleased about something and are wondering just how much you should say."

The tight expression relaxed into a slow, sensual grin. "Do you always read people this well?"

Ellen shook her head. "Not always. I just want to know what I've done this time."

"Aren't you concerned about living with three men?"

"No. Should I be?" She crossed her arms and leaned against the doorjamb, almost enjoying their conversation. The earlier antagonism had disappeared. She'd agree that her living arrangements were a bit unconventional, but there weren't any strings attached and was mutually advantageous.

"Any one of them could fall in love with you."

With difficulty, Ellen restrained her laughter. "That's unlikely. They see me as their mother."

The corners of his mouth formed deep grooves as he tried—and failed—to suppress a taunting grin. Cocking one thick brow, he did a thorough inspection of her womanly curves, pausing at the full swell of her breasts.

Hot colour flooded her pale cheeks. "All right—a sister. I'm too old for the boys."

Monte sauntered into the kitchen, followed closely by Pat. Typically, Pat carried a basketball under his arm. Ellen sometimes wondered if he slept with it as well. "I thought I smelled breakfast."

"I was just about to call you," she told the two and slipped quietly from the room, wanting to avoid a head-on collision with Reed. And that was where this conversation was going.

Fifteen minutes later, Ellen returned to the kitchen. She was dressed in cords and an Irish cable-knit sweater; the soft dark curls framed her small oval face. Ellen had no illusions about her looks. Men on the street weren't going to stop and stare, but she knew she was reasonably attractive. With short, dark hair and deep brown eyes, she considered herself boringly average. Far too ordinary to hold the affection of a man like Reed Morgan. One look at Ellen, and Danielle would feel completely reassured. Angry at the self-pitying thought, she grabbed a pen and tore out a sheet of notebook paper.

Intent on making up the shopping list, Ellen was halfway into the kitchen before she noticed Reed standing at the sink, wiping the frying pan dry. The table had been cleared and the dishes were stacked on the counter, ready for the dishwasher.

"Oh," she said, sounding a little startled. "I would have done that."

"While I'm here, I'll do my share." He said it without looking at her, his eyes avoiding hers.

"But this is your home. I certainly don't mind—"

"I wouldn't be comfortable otherwise. Haven't you got a class this morning?" He sounded anxious to be rid of her.

"Not until eleven."

"What's your major?" He'd turned around, leaning against the sink and crossing his arms over his broad chest. He was the picture of nonchalance, but Ellen wasn't fooled. She knew very well that he wasn't exactly pleased about her living in his home, and she felt he'd given his permission reluctantly. She suspected he

was even looking for ways to dislike her. Ellen understood that. Reed was bound to face some awkward
questions once Danielle discovered there was a woman
living in his house. Especially a woman who slept in
his bed and took charge of his kitchen. But that would
change this afternoon—at least the sleeping in his bed
part.

"I'm majoring in education."

"That's the mother in you coming out again."

Ellen hadn't thought of it that way. Living with the
boys hadn't made her matronly. Reed simply felt more
comfortable seeing her in that light, she decided. She'd
let him, if it meant he'd be willing to accept her arrangement with Derek and the others. Besides, he probably wouldn't be around long and then the happy
household could go back to its comfortable existence.

"I suppose you're right," she murmured as she began opening and closing cupboard doors, checking the
contents on each shelf, and scribbling down several
items she'd be needing the following week.

"What are you doing now?"

Mentally, Ellen counted to ten before answering. She
resented his overbearing tone, and despite her earlier
resolve to humour him, she snapped, "I'm making a
grocery list. Do you have a problem with that?"

"No," he answered somewhat gruffly.

"I'll be out of here in just a minute," she said, trying
hard to maintain her patience.

"You aren't in my way."

"And while we're on the subject of being in someone's way, I want you to know I plan to move my
things out of your room this afternoon."

"Don't. I doubt that I'll be here long enough to
make it worth your while."

CHAPTER TWO

SO REED WAS LEAVING. Ellen felt guilty and relieved all at the same time. Derek had told her Reed would probably be sent on another job soon, but she hadn't expected it to be quite this soon.

"There's another project Boeing is sending me on. California this time—the Monterey area."

Resuming her task, Ellen added several more items to the grocery list. "I've heard that's a lovely part of the state."

"It is beautiful." But his voice held no enthusiasm.

Ellen couldn't help feeling a twinge of disappointment for Reed. One look convinced her he didn't want to leave again. After all, he'd just returned from several months in the Middle East and already he had another assignment awaiting him in California. If he was dreading this latest job, Ellen could well imagine how Danielle must feel.

"Nonetheless, I think it's important to give you back your room. I'll move my things this afternoon." She'd ask the boys to help and it wouldn't take long.

With his arms crossed over his chest, Reed lounged against the doorjamb, watching her.

"And if you feel that my being here is a problem," she went on, thinking of Danielle, "I'll look for another place. The only thing I ask is that you give me a couple of weeks to find something."

He hesitated as though he were considering the offer, then shook his head, grinning slightly. "I don't think that'll be necessary."

"I don't mind telling you that I'm relieved to hear it, but I'm prepared to move if necessary."

His left brow rose a fraction of an inch as the grin spread across his face. "Having you around does have certain advantages."

Ellen hesitated. "Such as?"

"You're an excellent cook, the house hasn't been this clean in months and Derek's mother thinks you're a wonder with these boys."

Ellen had briefly met Mary Morgan, Derek's mother, a few weeks before. "Thank you."

He sauntered over to the coffeepot and lazily poured himself a cup. "And for that matter, Derek's right. This house is too big to sit empty. I'm often out of town, but there isn't any reason why others shouldn't put it to good use. Especially with someone as…domestically inclined as you around to keep things running smoothly."

So he viewed her as little more than a live-in housekeeper and cook! Ellen felt a flush of anger tint her cheeks. Before she could say something she'd regret, she turned quickly and fled out the back door on her way to the local grocers. Actually, Reed Morgan had interpreted the situation correctly, but it somehow bothered her that he saw her in such an unflattering light.

ELLEN DIDN'T SEE REED again until late that night. Friday evenings were lazy ones for her. She'd dated Charlie Hanson, a fellow student, a couple of times but usually preferred the company of a good book. With her heavy class schedule, most of Ellen's free time was devoted to her studies. Especially algebra. This one class was getting her down. It didn't seem to matter how hard she hit the books, she couldn't understand the theory.

Dressed in her housecoat and a pair of bright purple knee socks, she sat at the kitchen table, propping her legs on the chair across from her. Holding a paperback novel open with one hand, she dipped chocolate-chip cookies into a tall glass of milk with the other. At the unexpected sound of the back door opening, she looked curiously up from her book.

Reed seemed surprised to see her. He frowned as his eyes darted past her to the clock above the stove. "You're up late."

"On weekends my mommy doesn't make me go to bed until midnight," she said sarcastically, doing her best to ignore him. Reed managed to look fantastic without so much as trying. He didn't need her gawking at him to tell him that. If his expensive sports jacket was anything to judge by, he'd spent the evening with Danielle.

"You've got that look about you," he grumbled.

"What look?"

"The same one you claim I have—wanting to say something and unsure if you should or not."

"Oh." She couldn't very well deny it.

"And you wanted to tell me something?"

"Only that you look good." She paused, wondering how much she should say. "You even smell expensive."

His gaze slid over her in a slow inspection. "From the way you're dressed, you look to me as though you'd smell of cotton candy."

"Thank you, but actually it's chocolate chip." She

pushed the package of cookies in his direction. "Here. Save me from myself."

"No, thanks," Reed murmured and headed toward the living room.

"Don't go in there," Ellen cried, swinging her legs off the chair and coming abruptly to her feet.

Reed's hand was on the kitchen door, ready to swing it open. "Don't go into the living room?"

"Derek's got a girl in there."

Reed continued to stare at her blankly. "So?"

"So. He's with Michelle Tanner. *The* Michelle Tanner. The very girl Derek's been crazy about for the last six weeks. She finally agreed to a date with him. They rented a movie."

"That doesn't explain why I can't go in there."

"Yes, it does," Ellen whispered. "The last time I peeked, Derek was getting ready to make his move. You'll ruin everything if you barge in there now."

"His move?" Reed didn't seem to like the sound of this. "What do you mean, 'his move'? The kid's barely nineteen."

A soft smile turned up the edges of Ellen's mouth. "Honestly, Reed, you must have been young once. Don't you remember what it's like to have a crush on a girl? All Derek's doing is plotting that first all-important kiss."

Reed dropped his hand as he stared at Ellen. His eyes narrowed and seemed to focus on her mouth. Then the glittering green eyes skimmed hers, and Ellen's breath caught somewhere between her throat and her lungs as she struggled to pull her gaze away from his. Reed had no business giving her that kind of look. Not when he'd so recently left Danielle's arms. And not when Ellen reacted so profoundly to a mere glance.

"I haven't forgotten," he murmured. "And as for that remark about being young once, I'm not exactly over the hill."

This was ridiculous! With a sigh of annoyance, Ellen sat down again, swinging her feet onto the opposite chair. She picked up her book and forced her eyes—if not her attention—back to the page in front of her. "I'm glad to hear that." If she could get a grip on herself for the next few days everything would be fine. Reed would leave and her life with the boys would settle back into its routine once again.

The sound of the refrigerator opening and closing drew her gaze. She watched as Reed poured himself a glass of milk and then reached for a handful of chocolate-chip cookies. When he pulled out the chair across from her, Ellen reluctantly lowered her legs.

"What are you reading?"

Feeling irritable and angry for allowing him to affect her, she deliberately waited until she'd finished the page before answering. "A book," she muttered.

"My, my, you're a regular Mary Sunshine. What's the matter—did your boyfriend stand you up tonight?"

With exaggerated patience she slowly lowered the paperback to the table and marked her place. "Listen. I'm twenty-four years old and whole light-years beyond the age of boyfriends."

Reed shrugged. "All right. Your lover."

The air caught in her lungs, strangling off a reply. She hadn't meant to imply that at all. And Reed knew it. He'd wanted to fluster her and he'd succeeded.

"Women these days have this habit of letting their jaws hang open," he said pointedly, staring at her. "I suppose they think it looks sexy, but actually, they resemble beached trout." With that, he deposited his empty glass in the sink and marched briskly up the back stairs.

Ellen closed her eyes and groaned in embarrassment. He must think her a world-class idiot, and with good reason. She'd done a remarkable job of imitating one. She groaned again, infuriated by the fact that she found Reed Morgan so damned attractive.

Ellen didn't climb the stairs to her new bedroom on the third floor for another hour. And then it was only after Derek had paid her a quick visit in the kitchen and given her the thumbs-up sign. At least his night had gone well.

Long after she'd turned off her reading lights, Ellen lay staring into the silent, shadow-filled room. She wasn't in the least sleepy, and the mystery novel no longer held her interest. Her thoughts were troubled by that brief incident in the kitchen with Reed. Burying her head in the thick feather pillow, Ellen yawned and closed her eyes. But sleep still wouldn't come. A half-hour later, she threw back the covers and grabbed the housecoat from the end of the bed. Perhaps a glass of milk would help.

Not bothering to turn on any lights, she took a clean glass from the dishwasher and pulled the carton of milk from the refrigerator. With her drink in her hand, she stood at the kitchen window, looking out at the huge oak tree in the backyard. Its bare limbs stretched upward like skeletal hands, silhouetted against the full moon.

"I've heard that a woman's work is never done, but this is ridiculous."

She nearly spilled her milk at the sudden sound of Reed's low voice behind her. She whirled around and glared at him hotly. "I see there's a full moon tonight.

I wonder if it's safe to be alone with you. And wouldn't you know it, I left my silver bullet upstairs.''

"No woman's ever accused me of being a werewolf. Several other things," he murmured tightly, "but never that."

"Maybe that's because you hadn't frightened them half out of their wits."

"I couldn't resist. Sorry," he grumbled, reaching for the milk carton.

"You know, if we'd stop snapping at each other, it might make things a lot easier around here."

"Perhaps," he agreed reluctantly. "I will admit it's a whole lot easier to talk to you when you're dressed."

Ellen slammed down her empty glass and spoke through clenched teeth. "I'm getting a little tired of hearing about that."

But Reed went on, unperturbed. "Unfortunately, ever since that first time when I found you in your bra, you've insisted on overdressing. Do you always wear socks to bed?"

"Usually."

"I pity the man you sleep with."

"Well, you needn't worry…" She hesitated and expelled a lungful of oxygen. "We're arguing again."

"So, you're suggesting we stop trading insults for the sake of the children."

An involuntary smile touched her full mouth. "I hadn't thought to put it that way, but you're right. No one's going to be comfortable if the two of us are constantly snapping at each other. I'm willing to try if you are. Agreed?"

"All right." A smile softened Reed's features, harsh and shadowed in the moonlight.

"And I'm not a threat to you and Danielle, am I? In

fact, if you'd rather, she need never even know I'm here," she suggested casually.

"Maybe that would have been best," he conceded, setting aside his empty glass. "But I doubt it. Besides, she already knows. I told her tonight." He grumbled disparagingly something else that she didn't catch.

"And?" Ellen coaxed.

"And," he breathed, "she said she doesn't mind in the least, but she'd like to meet you."

This was one confrontation Ellen wasn't going to enjoy.

THE FOLLOWING MORNING, Ellen brought down her laundry and was running the washing machine and the dryer before Reed or the others were even awake.

She grumbled disparagingly as she tested the iron with the wet tip of her index finger and found that it still wasn't hot, although she'd turned it on at least five minutes earlier. This house was owned by a wealthy engineer, so why were there only two electrical outlets in the kitchen? It meant that she couldn't use the washer, the dryer and the iron at the same time without causing a blow-out.

"Damn," she muttered, setting the iron upright on the padded board.

"What's the matter?" Reed asked from the doorway leading into the kitchen. He ambled over to the coffee-pot and poured himself a cup.

"This iron."

"Say, Ellen, if you've got some ironing to do, would you mind pressing a few things for me?" Monte asked, walking barefoot into the kitchen. He paused at the refrigerator and took out a slice of cold pizza.

"I was afraid this would happen," she grumbled, still upset by the house's electrical problems.

"Ellen's not your personal maid," Reed interrupted harshly. "If you've got something you want pressed, do it yourself."

A hand on her hip, Ellen turned to Reed, defiantly meeting his glare. "If you don't mind, I can answer for myself."

"Fine," he snorted and took a sip of the hot coffee.

She directed her next words to Monte, who stood looking at her expectantly. "I'm not your personal maid. If you want something pressed, do it yourself."

Monte glanced from Reed to Ellen and back to Reed again. "I'm sorry I asked," he mumbled on his way out of the kitchen. The door was left swinging in his wake.

"You said that well," Reed commented with a soft chuckle.

"Believe me, I was conned into enough schemes by my sister and brother to know how to handle Monte and the others."

Reed's gaze was admiring. "If your brother is anything like mine, I don't doubt it."

"All brothers are alike," she said. Unable to hold back a grin, Ellen tested the iron a second time and noted that it was only slightly warmer. "Have you ever thought about putting another outlet in this kitchen?"

Reed's returning glance revealed surprise. "No. Do you need one?"

"Need one?" she flared. "There are only two for this room. It's ridiculous."

Reed scanned the kitchen. "I hadn't thought about it." Setting his coffee mug aside, he shook his head. "Your mood's not much better today than it was last night." With that remark, he quickly left the room, following in Monte's footsteps.

Ellen unconsciously tightened her grip on the iron as the frustration worked its way through her. Reed was right, of course. She was behaving like a real shrew and she really didn't understand why. But she was honest enough to admit, at least to herself, that she was attracted to this man whose house she occupied. She realised she'd have to erect a wall of reserve between them to protect them both from embarrassment.

"Morning, Ellen," Derek said as he sauntered into the kitchen and swung his lithe frame into a chair. As he emptied a box of cornflakes into a huge bowl, he casually announced, "Say, I've got some shirts that need pressing."

"If you want anything pressed, do it yourself," she fairly shouted.

Stunned, Derek blinked twice. "Okay."

Setting the iron upright, Ellen released a lengthy sigh. "I didn't mean to scream at you."

"That's all right."

Turning off the iron, she joined Derek at the table and reached for the cornflakes.

"Are you still worried about that maths paper you're supposed to do?"

"I'm working my way to an early grave over it."

"I would have thought you'd do well in maths."

Ellen snickered. "Hardly."

"Have you come up with a topic?"

"Not yet. I'm going to the library later, where I pray some form of inspiration will strike me."

"Have you asked the others in your class what they're writing about?" Derek asked as he refilled his bowl, this time with rice puffs.

Disgruntled, Ellen nodded her head. "That's what worries me most. The brain who sits beside me is doing hers on the probability of solving Goldbach's conjecture in our lifetime."

Derek's eyes widened. "That's a tough act to follow."

"If that overwhelms you, let me tell you about the guy who sits behind me. He's doing his paper on mathematics during World War II."

"You're in the big league now," Derek muttered with a sympathetic shake of his head.

"I know," Ellen lamented. She was taking this course only because it was compulsory; all she wanted out of it was a passing grade. The quadratic formula certainly wasn't going to have any lasting influence on her life.

"Good luck," Derek offered.

"Thanks, I'm going to need it."

After straightening up the kitchen, Ellen changed into old jeans and a faded sweatshirt. The jeans had been washed so many times the blue was nearly gone. They fit her hips so snugly she could hardly slide her fingers into the pockets, but she hated the idea of throwing them away.

She tied an old red scarf around her hair and headed for the garage. While rooting around there for a ladder a few days earlier, she'd discovered some pruning shears. In the backyard she'd noticed several overgrown bushes that needed trimming and she decided to tackle those first, before cleaning the drainpipes.

After an hour, she had a pile of underbrush large enough to be worth a haul to the dump. She'd have one of the boys do that later. For now, the drainpipes demanded her attention.

"Derek," she called as she pushed open the back door. Her faced was flushed with exertion and a light film of perspiration wet her upper lip.

"Yeah?" His voice drifted toward her from the living room.

Ellen wandered into the room to discover him on the phone. "I'm ready for you now."

"Now?" His eyes pleaded with her as his palm cupped the telephone mouthpiece. "It's Michelle."

"All right, I'll catch Monte."

"Thanks." He tossed her a smile of appreciation.

But Monte was nowhere to be found, and Pat was at the YMCA shooting baskets with some friends. When she stuck her head into the living room again, she saw Derek still draped over the sofa, deep in conversation. Unwilling to interfere with the course of young love, she decided she could probably manage to climb onto the roof unaided.

Dragging the aluminium ladder from the garage, she speculated that she might not need Derek's help anyway. She'd mentioned her plan earlier in the week, and he hadn't looked particularly enthusiastic. But when it came to chores, none of the boys were eager volunteers.

With the extension ladder braced against the side of the house, she climbed onto the roof of the back porch. Very carefully, she reached for the ladder and pulled it to that level before extending it to the very top of the house.

She manoeuvered herself back onto the ladder and climbed slowly and cautiously up.

Once she'd managed to position herself on the slanting roof, she was fine. She even took a moment to enjoy the spectacular view. She could see Lake Washington, with its deep-green water, and the spacious grounds of the university campus.

Using the brush she'd tucked—with some struggle—into her back pocket, Ellen began clearing away the leaves and other debris that clogged the gutters and drainpipes.

She was about half finished when she heard raised voices from below. Pausing, she sat down, drawing her knees against her chest, and watched the scene unfolding on the front lawn. Reed and his brother were obviously embroiled in a heated discussion—with Reed doing most of the talking. Derek was raking leaves and didn't look the least bit pleased about devoting his Saturday morning to chores. Ellen guessed that Reed had summarily interrupted the telephone conversation between Derek and Michelle.

With a lackadaisical swish of the rake, Derek flung the multicoloured leaves skyward. Ellen restrained a laugh. From the looks of things, Reed was giving him a good scolding.

To her further amusement, Reed then motioned toward his black Porsche, apparently suggesting that his brother wash the car when he'd finished with the leaves. Still chuckling, Ellen reached for the brush, but she missed and accidentally sent it tumbling down the side of the roof. It hit the green shingles over the front porch with a loud thump before flying onto the grass only a few feet from where Derek and Reed were standing.

Two pairs of astonished eyes swiftly turned in her direction. "Hi," she called down and waved. "I don't suppose I could talk one of you into bringing that up to me?" She carefully braced her feet and pulled herself to a standing position as she waited for a reply.

Reed pointed his finger at her and yelled, "What the bloody hell are you doing up there?"

"Playing tiddlywinks," she shouted back. "What do you think I'm doing?"

"I don't know, but I want you down."

"In a minute."

"Now."

"Yes, *sir*." She gave him a mocking salute and would have clicked her heels had she not feared that she might lose her footing.

Derek burst out laughing but was quickly silenced by a scathing glance from his older brother.

"Tell Derek to bring me the broom," Ellen called, moving closer to the edge.

Ellen couldn't decipher Reed's response, but from the way he stormed around the back of the house, she figured it was best to come down before he had a heart attack. She had the ladder lowered to the back-porch roof before she saw him.

"You idiot," he shouted. He was standing in the driveway, his hands positioned challengingly on his hips, glaring at her in fury. "I can't believe anyone would do anything so stupid."

"What do you mean?" The calmness of her words belied the way the blood pulsed through her veins. Alarm thickened his voice and that surprised her. She certainly hadn't expected Reed, of all people, to be concerned about her safety. He held the ladder steady until she'd climbed down and was standing squarely planted on the ground in front of him. Then he started pacing. For a minute Ellen didn't know what to think.

"What's wrong?" she asked. "You look as pale as a sheet."

"What's wrong?" he sputtered. "You were on the *roof* and—"

"I wasn't in any danger." Her brow wrinkled in confusion as she studied his ashen face.

"Like hell," he shouted, clearly upset. "There are people who specialise in that sort of thing. I don't want you up there again. Understand?"

"Yes, but—"

"No buts. You do anything that stupid again and you're out of here. Have you got that?"

"Yes," she said with forced calm. "I understand."

"Good."

Before she could think of anything else to say, Reed was gone.

"You all right?" Derek asked a minute later. Shocked by Reed's unprovoked outburst, Ellen hadn't moved. Rarely had anyone been that angry with her. Heavens, she'd cleaned out drainpipes lots of times. Her father had died when Ellen was fourteen, and over the years she'd assumed most of the maintenance duties around the house. She'd quickly learned that, with the help of a good book and a well-stocked hardware store, there wasn't anything she couldn't fix. She'd repaired the plumbing, built bookshelves and done a multitude of household projects. It was an accepted part of her life. Reed had acted as though she'd done something hazardous, as though she'd taken some extraordinary risk, and that seemed totally ridiculous to her. She knew what she was doing. Besides, heights didn't frighten her; they never had.

"Ellen?" Derek prompted.

"I'm fine."

"I've never seen Reed act like that. He didn't mean anything."

"I know," she whispered, brushing the dirt from her knees. Derek drifted off, leaving her to return the ladder to the garage single-handed.

Reed found her an hour later folding laundry in her bedroom. He knocked on the open door.

"Yes?" She looked up expectantly.

"I owe you an apology."

She continued folding towels at the foot of the single bed. "Oh?"

"I didn't mean to come at you like Attila the Hun."

Hugging a University of Washington T-shirt to her stomach, she lowered her gaze to the bedspread and nodded. "Apology accepted and I'll offer one of my own. I didn't mean to come back at you like a spoiled brat."

"Accepted." They smiled at each other and she caught her breath as those incredible green eyes gazed into hers. It was a repeat of the scene in the kitchen the night before. For a long, silent moment they did nothing but stare, and she realised that a welter of conflicting emotions must have registered on her face. A similar turmoil raged on his.

"If it'll make you feel any better, I won't go up on the roof again," she said at last.

"I'd appreciate it." His lips barely moved. The words were more of a sigh than a sentence.

She managed a slight nod in response.

At the sound of footsteps, they guiltily looked away.

"Say, Ellen." Pat stopped in the doorway, the basketball under his left arm. "Have you got time to shoot a few baskets with me?"

"Sure," she whispered, stepping around Reed. At that moment, she'd have agreed to just about anything to escape from his company. There was something happening between them and she felt frightened and confused and excited, all at the same time.

The basketball hoop was positioned above the garage door at the end of the long driveway. Pat was attending the University of Washington with the express hope of making the Husky basketball team. His whole life revolved around the game. He was rarely seen without a ball tucked under his arm and sometimes Ellen wondered if he showered with it. Or if the ball was glued to his armpit. She was well aware that the invitation to practise a few free throws with him was not meant to be taken literally. The only 'slam dunk' Ellen had ever accomplished was with a doughnut in her hot chocolate. Her main job was to stand on the sidelines and be awed by Pat's talent. He needed someone to look upon him with appreciative eyes now and then and she fulfilled the role admirably.

They hadn't been in the driveway fifteen minutes when the back door opened and Derek strolled out, his forehead contracted in a tight frown. "Say, Ellen, have you got a minute?"

"What's your problem, my friend?"

"It's Michelle."

Lowering himself onto the concrete porch step, Derek gazed at Ellen with those wide pleading eyes of his.

Ellen sat beside him and wrapped her arms around her bent knees. "What's wrong with Michelle?"

"Nothing. She's beautiful and I think she may even fall in love with me, given the chance." He paused to sigh expressively. "I asked her out to dinner tonight."

"Naturally she agreed. Right?" If Michelle was anywhere near as taken with Derek as he was with her, she wasn't likely to refuse.

The boyishly thin shoulders heaved in a gesture of despair. "She can't."

"Why not?" Ellen watched as Pat bounced the basketball across the driveway, pivoted, jumped high in the air and sent the ball swooshing through the net.

"Apparently Michelle promised her older sister that she'd baby-sit tonight."

"That's too bad." Ellen gave him a sympathetic look.

"The thing is, she'd probably go out with me if there was someone who'd be willing to watch her niece and nephew for her. It has to be an adult so that Michelle wouldn't worry about them."

"That sounds reasonable." Pat made another skilful play and Ellen applauded vigorously. He rewarded her with a triumphant smile.

"Then you will?"

Ellen switched her attention from Pat's antics at the basketball hoop back to Derek. "Will I what?"

"Baby-sit Michelle's niece and nephew?"

"What?" she nearly exploded. "Not me. I've got to do the research for a term paper."

"Ellen, please, please, please."

"No. No. No." She sliced the air forcefully with her hand and jumped to her feet.

Derek rose with her. "I sense some resistance to this idea."

"The boy's a wonder," she mumbled under her breath as she hurried into the kitchen. "I've got to write my term paper. You know that."

Derek followed her inside. "Ellen, please. I promise I'll never ask anything of you again."

"I've heard that before." She tried to ignore him as

he trailed her to the refrigerator and watched her take out sandwich makings for lunch.

"It's a matter of utter importance," Derek pleaded anew.

"What is?" Reed spoke from behind the morning paper he was reading at the kitchen table.

"This date with Michelle. Listen, Ellen, I bet Reed would help you. You're not doing anything tonight, are you?"

Reed lowered the newspaper. "Help Ellen with what?"

"Baby-sitting."

Reed glanced from the intent expression on his younger brother's face to the stubborn look on Ellen's. "You two leave me out of this."

"Ellen. Dear, sweet Ellen, you've got to understand that it could be weeks—weeks," he repeated dramatically, "before Michelle will be free to go out with me again."

Ellen plunked down an armload of cheese, ham and assorted jars of mustard and pickles. "*No!* Can I make it any plainer than that? I'm sorry, Derek, honest. But I can't."

"Reed," Derek pleaded with his brother. "Say something that will convince her."

"I'm out of this one."

He raised the newspaper again, but Ellen could sense a smile hidden behind it. Still, she doubted that Reed would be foolish enough to involve himself in the proceedings.

"Ellen, puleease."

"No." Ellen realised that if she wanted any peace, she'd have to forget about lunch and make an immediate escape. She whirled around and headed out of the kitchen, the door swinging in her wake.

"I think she's weakening," she heard Derek say as he followed her.

She was on her way up the stairs when she caught sight of Derek in the formal dining room, coming toward her on his knees, his hands folded in supplication. "Won't you please reconsider?"

Ellen groaned. "What do I need to say to convince you? I've got to get to the library. That paper is due Monday morning."

"I'll write it for you."

"No, thanks."

At just that moment Reed came through the door. "It shouldn't be too difficult to find a reliable teenager. There are a few families with teenagers living in the neighbourhood, as I recall."

"I...don't know," Derek hedged.

"If we can't find anyone, then Danielle and I'll manage. It'll be good practice for us. Besides, just how much trouble can two kids be?"

When she heard that, Ellen had to swallow a burst of laughter. Reed obviously hadn't spent much time around children, she thought with a mischievous grin.

"How old did you say these kids are?" She couldn't resist asking.

"Nine and four." Derek's dark eyes brightened expectantly as he leaped to his feet and gave his brother a grateful smile. "So I can tell Michelle everything's taken care of?"

"I suppose." Reed's gaze sought out Ellen. "I was young once myself," he said pointedly, reminding her of the comment she'd made the night before.

"I really appreciate this, Reed. I'll be your slave for

life. I'd even loan you money if I had some. By the way, can I borrow your car tonight?''

"Don't press your luck."

"Right." Derek chuckled, bounding up the stairs.

THE DOORBELL CHIMED close to six o'clock, just as Ellen was gathering up her books and preparing to leave for the library.

"That'll be Michelle," Derek called excitedly. "Can you get it, Ellen?"

"No problem."

Colouring books and crayons were arranged on the coffee table, along with some building blocks that Reed must have gone out and purchased that afternoon. From bits and pieces of information she'd picked up, she concluded that Reed had discovered it wasn't quite as easy to find a teenage baby-sitter as he'd assumed. And with no other recourse, he and Danielle were apparently taking over the task. Ellen wished him luck, but she really did need to concentrate on this stupid term paper. Reed hadn't suggested that Ellen wait around to meet Danielle and Ellen hadn't offered. But she had to admit she'd been wondering about the woman from the time Derek had first mentioned her.

"Hello, Ellen." Blond Michelle greeted Ellen with a warm, eager smile. They'd met briefly the other night. "This sure is great of Derek's brother and girlfriend, isn't it?"

"It sure is."

The four-year-old boy was clinging to Michelle's trouser leg so that her gait was stiff-kneed as she loped into the house with the child attached to her thigh.

"Jimmy, this is Ellen. You'll be staying in her house

tonight while Auntie Michelle goes out to dinner with Derek.''

"I want my mommy.''

"He won't be a problem,'' Michelle told Ellen confidently.

"I thought there were two children.''

"Yeah, the baby's in the car. I'll be right back.''

"Baby?'' Ellen swallowed down a laugh. "What baby?''

"Jenny's nine months.''

"Nine months?'' A small uncontrollable giggle slid from her throat. This would be marvellous. Reed with a nine-month-old was almost too good to miss.

"Jimmy, you stay here.'' Somehow Michelle was able to pry the four-year-old's fingers loose from her leg and pass the struggling child to Ellen.

Kicking and thrashing, Jimmy broke into loud sobs as Ellen carried him into the living room. "Here's a colouring book. Do you like to colour, Jimmy?''

But he refused to talk to Ellen or even look at her, as he buried his face in the sofa cushions. "I want my mommy,'' he wailed again.

By the time Michelle had returned with a baby carrier and a fussing nine-month-old, Derek sauntered suavely out from the kitchen. "Hey, Michelle, you're looking good.''

Reed, who was following closely behind, came to a shocked standstill when he saw the baby. "I thought you said they were nine and four.''

"I did,'' Derek explained patiently, his eyes devouring the blonde at his side.

"They won't be any trouble,'' Michelle cooed as Derek placed an arm around her shoulders and led her toward the open door.

"Derek, we need to talk," Reed insisted, his voice tinged with exasperation.

"Haven't got time now. I made our reservations for seven." His hand slid from Michelle's shoulders to her waist. "I'm taking my lady out for a night on the town."

"Derek," Reed demanded.

"Oh," Michelle tore her gaze from Derek's. "The nappy bag is in the entryway. Jenny should be dry, but you might want to check her later. She'll probably cry for a few minutes once she notices I'm gone, but that'll stop almost immediately."

Reed's face was grim as he cast a speculative glance toward Jimmy, who was still howling for his mother. The happily gurgling Jenny looked up at the unfamiliar dark-haired man and noticed for the first time that she was at the mercy of a stranger. She immediately burst into heart-wrenching tears.

"I want my mommy," Jimmy demanded yet again.

"I can see you've got everything under control," Ellen announced, reaching for her coat. "I'm sure Danielle will be here any minute."

"Ellen…"

"Don't expect me back soon. I've got hours of research ahead of me."

"You aren't really going to leave, are you?" Reed gave her a horrified look.

"I wish I could stay," she lied breezily. "Another time, maybe." With that, she was out the door, smiling as she bounded down the stairs.

CHAPTER THREE

AN UNEASY FEELING struck Ellen as she stood waiting at the bus stop. But she resolutely hardened herself against the impulse to rush right back to Reed and his disconsolate charges. Danielle would show up at any minute and Ellen really was obliged to do the research for her yet-to-be-determined maths paper. Besides, she reminded herself, Reed had volunteered to baby-sit and she wasn't responsible for rescuing him. But those marvellous eyes of his had pleaded with her so earnestly. Ellen felt herself beginning to weaken. *No!* she mumbled under her breath. Reed had Danielle, and as far as Ellen was concerned, they were on their own.

However, by the time she arrived at the undergraduate library, Ellen discovered that she couldn't get Reed's pleading look out of her mind. From everything she'd heard about Danielle, Ellen realised the woman probably didn't know the first thing about babies. As for the term paper, she supposed she could put it off until Sunday. After all, she'd looked for excuses all day to avoid working on it. She'd done the wash, trimmed the shrubs, cleaned the drainpipes and washed the upstairs walls in an effort to escape that paper. One more night wasn't going to make much difference.

Hurriedly, she signed out some books and journals that looked as though they might be helpful and headed for the bus stop. Ellen had to admit that she was curious enough to want to meet Danielle. Reed's girl-friend had to be someone very special to put up with his frequent absences—or else a schemer, as Derek had implied. But Ellen couldn't see Reed being duped by a woman, no matter how clever or sophisticated she might be.

Her speculations came to an end as the bus eased to a stop at the kerb and Ellen quickly jumped on for the short ride home.

Reed was kneeling on the carpet changing the still-tearful Jenny's nappy when Ellen walked in the front door. He seemed to have aged ten years in the past hour. A nappy pin was clenched between his teeth and the long sleeves of his wool shirt were rolled up to the elbows.

Reed took one look at her and sagged with relief. "Thank God you're here. She hasn't stopped crying from the minute you left."

"You look like you're doing a good job without me. Where's Danielle?"

He muttered a few words of profanity under his breath. "She couldn't stay." He finished the nappying and awkwardly tugged the plastic pants back into place. "That wasn't so difficult," he said, glancing proudly at Ellen as he stood Jenny up on the floor, holding the baby upright by her small arms.

Ellen swallowed a laugh as she noticed the bunches of material sticking out from the legs and waist of Jenny's plastic pants. She was trying to think of a tact-ful way of pointing it out to Reed when both the nappy and the plastic pants began to slide down Jenny's pudgy legs, settling at her ankles.

"Maybe you should try," Reed conceded, handing her the baby. Within minutes, Ellen had successfully refolded and secured the nappy. Unfortunately, she didn't manage to soothe the baby any more than Reed had.

Cradling Jenny in her arms, Ellen paced the area in front of the fireplace, at a loss to comfort the sobbing child. "I don't know that I'll do any better. It's been a while since my brother was this size."

"Women are always better at this kind of stuff," Reed argued, rubbing a hand over his face. "Most women," he amended, with such a look of frustration that Ellen smiled.

"I bet Jimmy knows what to do," she suggested next, pleased with her inspiration. The little boy might actually come up with something helpful, and involving him in their attempts to comfort Jenny might distract him from his own unhappiness. Or so Ellen hoped. "Jimmy's a good big brother. Isn't that right, honey?"

The child lifted his face from the sofa cushion. "I want my mommy."

"Let's pretend Ellen is your mommy," Reed offered.

"No! She's like that other lady who said bad words."

Meanwhile, Jenny wailed all the louder. Digging around in the nappy bag, Reed found a stuffed teddy bear and pressed it into her arms. But Jenny angrily tossed the toy aside, the tears flowing unabated down her face.

"Come on, Jimmy," Reed pleaded desperately into the din. "We need a little help here. Your sister is crying."

Holding his hands over his eyes, Jimmy straightened and peeked through two fingers. The distraught Jenny continued to cry at full volume in spite of Ellen's best efforts to comfort her.

"Mommy bounces her."

Ellen had been gently doing that from the beginning. "What else?" she encouraged.

"She likes her boo-loo."

"What's that?"

"Her teddy bear."

"I've already tried that," Reed snorted. "What else does your mommy do when she cries like this?"

Jimmy was thoughtful for a moment. "Oh." The four-year-old's eyes sparkled. "Mommy nurses her."

Reed and Ellen glanced at each other and dissolved into giggles. The laughter faded from his eyes and was replaced with a roguish grin. "That could prove to be interesting."

Hiding a smile, Ellen decided to ignore Reed's comment. "Sorry, Jenny," she said softly to the baby girl, "but mine are strictly for decoration."

"But maybe he's got an idea," Reed suggested eagerly. "Could she be hungry?"

"It's worth a try. At this point, anything is."

Jenny's bellowing had finally dwindled into a few hiccuping sobs. And for some reason, Jimmy suddenly straightened and stared at Reed's craggy face, at his deep auburn hair and brilliant green eyes. Then he pointed to the plaid wool shirt, its long sleeves rolled up to the elbows. "Are you a lumberjack?"

"A lumberjack?" Reed repeated, looking puzzled. He broke into a full laugh. "No, but I imagine I must look like one to you."

Rummaging through the nappy bag, Ellen found a plastic bottle filled with milk. Jenny eyed it sceptically, but no sooner had Ellen removed the cap than Jenny grabbed it from her hands and began sucking eagerly at the nipple.

Sighing, Ellen sank into the rocking chair and gently swayed back and forth with the baby securely tucked in her arms. "I guess that settles that."

"Aren't you supposed to heat those things?"

"That's what I thought," Ellen agreed. The silence was so blissful that she wanted to wrap it around herself. She felt the tension drain from her muscles as she relaxed in the rocking chair. From titbits Jimmy had dropped, she surmised that Danielle hadn't been much help. Everything she'd learned about the other woman told Ellen that Danielle would probably find young children frustrating—and apparently she had.

Jimmy had crawled into Reed's lap with a book and demanded that 'the lumberjack' read to him. Together the two leafed through the colourful storybook. Several times during the peaceful interlude, Ellen's eyes met Reed's across the room and they exchanged a contented smile.

Jenny sucked tranquilly at the bottle, and her eyes slowly drooped shut. At peace with her world, the baby was utterly satisfied to be tenderly held and rocked to sleep. Ellen gazed down at the angelic face, and brushed fine wisps of hair from the untroubled forehead. Releasing her breath in a slow, drawn-out sigh, she glanced up to discover Reed watching her, the little boy still sitting quietly on his lap.

"Well, Mother Ellen, you've finally got a baby in your arms," he said softly.

"I guess I do, at that."

"Ellen?" Reed spoke in a low voice. "Did you finish your maths paper?"

"Finish it?" She groaned. "Are you kidding? I haven't even started it."

"What's a maths paper?" Jimmy asked curiously.

Gently rocking the baby, Ellen looked solemnly over at the boy. "Well, it's something I have to write for a maths class. And if I don't write a paper, I haven't got even a hope of passing the course." She didn't think he'd understand any algebraic terms. For that matter, neither did she.

"What's maths?"

"Numbers," Reed told the boy.

"And, in this case, sometimes letters—like x and y."

"I like numbers," Jimmy declared proudly. "I like three and nine and seven."

"Well, Jimmy, my boy, how would you like to write my paper for me?"

"Can I?"

Ellen was more than willing to transfer the task. "You bet."

Reed got out pencil and paper and set the four-year-old to work.

Glancing up, she gave Reed a soft smile. "See how easy this is? You're good with kids." Reed grinned at her in answer as he carefully drew numbers for Jimmy to copy.

After several minutes of this activity, Jimmy decided it was time to put on his pyjamas. Seeing him yawn, Reed brought down a pillow and blanket and tucked him into a hastily made bed on the sofa. Then he read a bedtime story until the four-year-old again yawned loudly and cuddled into a tight ball.

Ellen still hadn't moved, fearing that the slightest jolt would rouse the baby.

"Why don't we set her down in the baby seat?" Reed prompted.

"I'm afraid she'll wake."

"If she does, you can rock her again."

His suggestion made sense and besides, her arms were beginning to ache. "Okay." He moved to her side and gently lifted the sleeping child. Ellen flexed her muscles, unaccustomed to holding them in one position for so long. She held her breath momentarily when Jenny stirred. But the little girl simply rolled her head against the cushion and returned to sleep.

Ellen rose to her feet and turned the lamp down to its dimmest setting, surrounding them with a warm circle of light.

"I couldn't have done it without you," Reed whispered, coming to stand beside her. He rested his hand at the back of her neck.

An unfamiliar warmth seeped through Ellen, and she began to talk quickly, hoping to conceal her sudden nervousness. "Sure you could have. From my point of view, you had everything under control."

Reed snorted. "I was ten minutes away from calling the crisis clinic. Thanks for coming to the rescue." He casually withdrew his hand, and Ellen felt both relieved and disappointed.

"You're welcome." She was dying to know what had happened with Danielle, but she didn't want to ask. Apparently, the other woman hadn't stayed around for too long.

"Have you eaten?"

Ellen had been so busy that she'd forgotten about dinner, but once Reed mentioned it, she realised how hungry she was. "No, and I'm starved."

"Do you like Chinese food?"

"Love it."

"Good. There's enough for an army out in the kitchen. I ordered it earlier."

Ellen didn't need to be told that he'd made dinner plans with Danielle in mind. He'd expected to share an intimate candle-lit evening with her. "Listen," she began awkwardly, clasping her hands in front of her. "I really have to get going on this term paper. Why don't you call Danielle and invite her back? Now that the kids are asleep, I'm sure everything will be better. I—"

"Children make Danielle nervous. She warned me about it, but I refused to listen. She's home now and has probably taken some aspirin and gone to sleep. I can't see letting good food go to waste. Besides, it gives me an opportunity to thank you."

"Oh." It was the longest speech that Reed had made. "All right," she agreed with a slight nod.

While Reed warmed the food in the microwave, Ellen set out plates and forks and brewed a large pot of tea, placing it in the middle of the table. The swinging door that connected the kitchen with the living room was left open in case either child awoke.

"What do we need plates for?" Reed asked with a questioning arch of his brow.

"Plates are the customary eating device."

"Not tonight."

"Not tonight?" Something dark and amusing glinted in Reed's eyes as he set out several white boxes and brandished two pairs of chopsticks. "Since it's only the two of us, we can eat right out of the boxes."

"I'm not very adept with chopsticks." The smell drifting from the open boxes was tangy and enticing.

"You'll learn if you're hungry."

"I'm starved."

"Good." Deftly he took the first pair of chopsticks and showed her how to work them with her thumb and index finger.

Imitating his movements Ellen discovered that her fingers weren't nearly as agile as his. Two or three tries at picking up small pieces of spicy diced chicken succeeded only in frustrating her.

"Here." Reed fed her a bite from the end of his chopsticks. "Be a little more patient with yourself."

"That's easy for you to say while you're eating your fill and I'm starving to death."

"It'll come."

Ellen grumbled under her breath, but a few tries later she managed to deliver a portion of the hot food to her eager mouth.

"See, I told you you'd pick this up fast enough."

"Do you always tell someone 'I told you so'?" she asked with pretended annoyance. The mood was too congenial for any real discontent. Ellen felt that they'd shared a special time together looking after the two small children. More than special—astonishing. They hadn't clashed once or found a single thing to squabble over.

"I enjoy teasing you. Your eyes have an irresistible way of lighting up when you're angry."

"If you continue to insist that I eat with these absurd pieces of wood, you'll see my eyes brighten the entire room."

"I'm looking forward to that," he murmured with a soft laugh. "No forks. You can't properly enjoy Chinese food unless you use chopsticks."

"I can't properly *taste* it without a fork."

"Here, I'll feed you." Again he brought a spicy morsel to her mouth.

A drop of the juice bounced against her chin and Ellen wiped it off. "You aren't any better than me." She dipped the chopsticks into the chicken mixture and attempted to transport a titbit to Reed's mouth. The small piece of white meat balanced precariously on the end of the chopsticks, and Reed lowered his mouth to catch it before it could land in his lap.

"You're improving," he told her, his voice low and slightly husky.

Their eyes met. Unable to face the caressing look in his warm gaze, Ellen bent her head and pretended to be engrossed in her dinner. But her appetite was instantly gone—vanished.

A tense silence filled the room. The air between them was so charged that she felt breathless and weak, as though she'd lost the energy to move or speak. Ellen didn't dare raise her eyes for fear of what she'd see in his.

"Ellen."

She took a deep breath and scrambled to her feet, battling down the frantic beating of her heart. "I think I hear Jimmy," she whispered.

"Maybe it was Jenny," Reed added hurriedly.

Ellen paused in the doorway between the two rooms. They were both overwhelmingly aware that neither child had made a sound. "I think they're still asleep."

"That's good." The scraping sound of his chair against the floor told her that Reed, too, had risen from the table. When she turned, she found him depositing the leftovers from their dinner in the refrigerator. His preoccupation with the task gave her a moment to reflect on what had just happened. There were too many problems involved in pursuing this attraction and they both knew it. The best thing to do was ignore it and hope the craziness passed. They were mature adults, not adolescents, and besides, this would complicate her life, which was something she didn't need right now. Neither, she was sure, did he.

"If you don't mind, I think I'll head upstairs," she began awkwardly, taking a step in retreat.

"That shouldn't be a problem. I appreciated the help."

"I appreciated the dinner," she returned.

"I'll see you in the morning then."

"Right." Neither seemed eager to bring the evening to an end.

"Good night, Ellen."

"Night, Reed. Call if you need me."

"I will."

Turning decisively, she took the stairs and was panting by the time she'd climbed up the second narrow flight. The third floor had originally been built to accommodate servants. The five bedrooms were small and opened onto a large central room, which was where Ellen had placed her bed. She'd chosen the largest of the bedrooms as her study.

She sat resolutely down at her desk and leafed frantically through several books, hoping to come across an idea she could use for her term paper. But her thoughts were dominated by the man two floors below. Clutching a study on the origins of algebra to her chest, she sighed deeply and wondered whether Danielle truly appreciated Reed. She must. Few women would be so willing to sit at home waiting, while their fiancés traipsed around the world directing a variety of projects.

Reed had been so patient and good-natured with Jimmy and little Jenny. When the youngster had climbed into his lap, Reed had read to him and held him with a tenderness that stirred her heart. And Reed was generous to a fault. Any other man would have told Pat, Monte and Ellen to pack their bags. This was his home, after all, and Derek had been wrong to rent out the rooms without Reed's knowledge. But Reed had let them stay.

Disgruntled with the trend her thoughts were taking, Ellen forced her mind back to the books in front of her. But it wasn't long before her concentration started to drift again. Reed had Danielle, and she had...Charlie Hanson. First thing in the morning, she'd call good old dependable Charlie and suggest they get together; he'd probably be as surprised as he was pleased to hear from her. Feeling relieved and a little light-headed, Ellen turned off the light and went to bed.

"WHAT ARE YOU DOING?" Reed arrived in the kitchen early the next afternoon, looking as though he'd just finished eighteen holes of golf or a vigorous game of tennis. He glowed with health and vitality. Reed had already left by the time she'd wandered down to the kitchen that morning.

"Ellen?" he repeated impatiently.

The wall plates were off the electrical outlets and the receptacle had been pulled out of its box, from which two thin coloured wires now protruded. "I'm trying to figure out why this outlet won't heat the iron," she answered without looking in his direction.

"You're what!" he bellowed.

She wiped her face to remove a layer of dust before she straightened. "Don't yell at me."

"Good grief, woman. You run around on the roof

like a trapeze artist, cook like a dream and do electrical work on the side. Is there anything you can't do?''

"Algebra," she muttered.

Reed closed the instruction manual Ellen had propped against the sugar bowl in the middle of the table. He took her by the shoulders and pushed her gently aside, then reattached the electrical wires and fastened the whole thing back in place.

As he finished securing the wall plate, Ellen burst out, "What did you do that for? I've almost got the problem traced."

"No doubt, but if you don't mind, I'd rather have a real electrician look at this."

"What can I say? It's your house."

"Right. Now sit down." He nudged her into a chair. "How much longer are you going to delay writing that term paper?"

"It's written," she snapped. She wasn't particularly pleased with it, but at least the assignment was done. Her subject matter might impress four-year-old Jimmy, but she wasn't too confident that her professor would appreciate her effort.

"Do you want me to look it over?"

The offer surprised her. "No, thanks." She stuck the screwdriver in the pocket of her grey-striped coveralls.

"Well, that wasn't so hard, was it?"

"I just don't think I've got a snowball's chance of getting a decent grade on it. Anyway, I have to go and iron a dress. I've got a date."

A dark brow lifted over inscrutable green eyes and he seemed about to say something.

"Reed." Unexpectedly, the kitchen door swung open and a soft, feminine voice purred his name. "What's taking you so long?"

"Danielle, I'd like you to meet Ellen."

"Hello." Ellen resisted the urge to kick Reed. If he was going to introduce her to his friend, the least he could have done was waited until she looked a little more presentable. Just as she'd figured, Danielle was beautiful. No, the word was gorgeous. She wore a cute pale-blue one-piece outfit with a short, pleated skirt. A dark-blue silk scarf held back the curly cascade of long blonde hair—Ellen should have known the other woman would be blonde. Naturally, Danielle possessed a trim waist, perfect legs and blue eyes to match the heavens. She'd apparently just finished playing golf or tennis with Reed, but she still looked cool and elegant.

"I feel as though I already know you," Danielle was saying with a pleasant smile. "Reed told me how much of a help you were with the children."

"It was nothing, really." Embarrassed by her ridiculous outfit, Ellen tried to conceal as much of it as possible by grabbing the electrical repair book and clasping it to her stomach.

"Not according to Reed." Danielle slipped her arm around his and smiled adoringly up at him. "Unfortunately, I came down with a terrible headache."

"Danielle doesn't have your knack with young children," Reed inserted.

"If we decide to have our own, things will be different," Danielle continued sweetly. "But I'm not convinced I'm the motherly type."

Taking a step backward, Ellen offered the couple a wan smile. "If you'll excuse me, I've got to change my clothes."

"Of course. It was nice meeting you, Elaine."

"Ellen," Reed and Ellen corrected simultaneously.

"You, too." Gallantly, Ellen stifled the childish im-

pulse to call the other woman Diane. As she turned and
headed up the narrow stairs leading from the kitchen,
she heard Danielle whisper that she didn't mind in the
least if Ellen lived in Reed's home. Of course not, Ellen muttered to herself. How could Danielle possibly
be jealous?

Winded by the time she'd marched up both flights,
Ellen walked into the tiny bedroom where she stored
her clothes. She slammed down the electrical manual
and kicked the door shut with her foot. Then she sighed
with anger and frustration as she saw her reflection in
the full-length mirror on the back of the door; it revealed baggy coveralls, a faded white T-shirt and
smudges of dirt across her cheekbone. She struck a
seductive pose with her hand on her hip and vampishly
puffed up her hair. "Of course, I don't mind if sweet
little Elaine lives here, darling," she mimicked in a
high-pitched falsely sweet voice.

Dropping her coveralls to the ground, Ellen gruffly
kicked them aside. Hands on her hips, she glared at her
reflection. Her figure was no less attractive than Danielle's, and her face was pretty enough—even if she did
say so herself. But Danielle had barely looked at Ellen
and certainly hadn't seen her as a potential rival. That
was what frustrated Ellen most.

As she brushed her hair away from her face, Ellen's
shoulders suddenly dropped. She was losing her mind!
She liked living with the boys. Their arrangement was
ideal, yet here she was, complaining bitterly because
her presence hadn't been challenged.

Carefully choosing her light-pink blouse and matching maroon skirt, Ellen told herself that Charlie, at
least, would appreciate her. And for now, Ellen needed
that. Her self-confidence had been shaken by Danielle's

casual acceptance of her role in Reed's house. She didn't like Danielle. But then, she hadn't expected to.

"ELLEN." Her name was followed by a loud pounding on the bedroom door. "Wake up! There's a phone call for you."

"Okay," she mumbled into her pillow, still caught in the last dregs of sleep. It felt so warm and cosy under the thick blankets that she didn't want to stir. Charlie had taken her to dinner and a movie and they'd returned a little after ten. The boys had stayed in that evening, but Reed was out and Ellen didn't need to ask with whom. She hadn't heard him come home.

"Ellen."

"I'm awake, I'm awake," she grumbled, slipping one leg free of the covers, and dangling it over the edge of the bed. The sudden cold that assailed her bare foot made her eyes flutter open in momentary shock.

"It sounds long distance."

Her eyes did open then. She knew only one person who could be calling. Her mother!

Hurriedly tossing the covers aside, she grabbed her housecoat and scurried out of the room. "Why didn't you tell me it was long distance before now?"

"I tried," Pat complained. "But you were more interested in sleeping."

A glance at her clock radio told her it was barely seven.

Taking a deep, calming breath, Ellen walked quickly down one flight of stairs and picked up the telephone receiver at the end of the hallway.

"Good morning, Mom."

"How'd you know it was me?" came the soft, familiar voice.

Although they wrote to each other regularly, this was the first time her mother had actually phoned her since she'd left home. "Lucky guess."

"Who was that young man who answered the phone?"

"Patrick."

"The basketball kid."

Her mother had read every word of her letters. "That's him."

"Has Monte eaten you out of house and home yet?"

"Just about."

"And has this Derek kid finally summoned up enough nerve to ask out...what was her name again?"

"Michelle."

"Right. That's the one."

"They saw each other twice this weekend," Ellen told her, feeling a sharp pang of homesickness.

"And what about you, Ellen? Are you dating?" It wasn't an idle question. Through the years, Ellen's mother had often fretted that her oldest child was giving up her youth in order to care for the family. Ellen didn't deny that she'd made sacrifices, but they'd been willing ones.

Her letters home had been chatty, but she hadn't mentioned Charlie, and Ellen wasn't sure whether she wanted her mother to know about him. Her relationship with him was based on friendship and nothing more, although Ellen suspected that Charlie would have liked it to develop into something romantic.

"Mom, you didn't phone me long distance on a Monday morning to discuss my social life."

"You're right. I called to discuss mine."

"And?" Ellen's heart hammered against her ribs. Already she knew what was coming. She'd known it months ago, even before she moved to Seattle. Her mother was going to remarry. After ten years of widowhood, Dorothy Cunningham had found another man to love.

"And—" her mother faltered "—James has asked me to be his wife."

"And?" It seemed to Ellen that her vocabulary had suddenly been reduced to one word.

"And I've said yes."

Ellen closed her eyes, expecting to feel a rush of bittersweet nostalgia for the father she remembered so well and loved so much. Instead, she felt only gladness that her mother had found another happiness.

"Congratulations, Mom."

"Do you mean that?"

"With all my heart. When's the wedding?"

"Well, actually…" Her mother hedged again. "Honey, don't be angry."

"Angry?"

"We're already married. I'm calling from Reno."

"Oh."

"Are you mad?"

"Of course not."

"James has a winter home in Arizona and we're going to honeymoon here until April."

"April," Ellen repeated, sounding a little dazed.

"If you object, honey, I'll come back to Yakima for Christmas."

"No…I don't object. It's just a little sudden."

"Dad's been gone ten years."

"I know, Mom. Don't you worry."

"I'll write soon."

"Do that. And much happiness, Mom. You and James deserve it."

"Thank you, love."

They spoke for a few more minutes before saying goodbye. Ellen walked down the stairs in a state of stunned disbelief, absentmindedly tightening the belt of her housecoat. In a matter of months, her entire family had disintegrated. Her sister and mother had married and Bud had joined the forces.

"Good morning," she cautiously greeted Reed, who was sitting at the kitchen table already dressed and reading the paper.

"Morning," he responded drily, as he lowered his newspaper.

Her hands trembling, Ellen reached for a mug, but it slipped out of her fingers and hit the counter, luckily without breaking.

Reed carefully folded the newspaper and studied her face. "What's wrong? You look like you've just seen a ghost."

"My mom's married."

"Why the fuss? That should remove an ugly mark from your birth certificate."

"It's not my father."

"Ah, the plot thickens."

"Stop it, Reed," she murmured in a subdued voice. Tears burned in her eyes. She was no longer sure just what she was feeling. Happiness for her mother, yes, but also sadness as she remembered her father and his untimely death.

"You're serious."

"I'm afraid so." She sat across from him at the table, holding the mug in both hands and staring into its depths. "It isn't like it's sudden. Dad's been gone a lot of years. What surprises me is all the emotion I'm feeling."

"That's only natural. I remember how I felt when my dad remarried. I'd known for months that Mary and Dad were going to marry. But the day of the wedding I felt that my father had betrayed the memory of my mother. Those were heavy thoughts for a ten-year-old boy." His hand gently reached for hers. "As I recall, that was the last time I cried."

The emotion filled her eyes and Ellen nodded. It was the only way she could thank him, because speaking was impossible, just then. She knew instinctively that Reed didn't often share the hurts of his youth.

Just when her throat had relaxed and she felt she could speak, Derek threw open the back door and dashed in, tossing his older brother a set of keys.

"I had them add a quart of oil," Derek said. "Are you sure you can't stay longer?"

The sip of coffee sank to the pit of Ellen's stomach and sat there. "You're leaving?" Suddenly she felt as though someone had jerked her chair out from under her.

He released her hand and gave it a gentle pat. "You'll be fine."

Ellen forced her concentration back to the black coffee. For days she'd been telling herself that she'd be relieved and delighted when Reed left. Now she dreaded it. More than anything, she wanted him to stay.

CHAPTER FOUR

"ELLEN," DEREK SHOUTED as he burst in the front door, his hands full of mail. "Can I invite Michelle to dinner Friday night?"

Casually, Ellen looked up from the textbook she was studying. By mutual agreement, they all went their separate ways on Friday evenings and Ellen didn't cook. If one of the boys happened to be in the house, he heated up soup or put together a thick sandwich or made do with leftovers. In Monte's case, he did all three.

"What are you planning to fix?" Ellen responded cagily.

"Cook? Me?" Derek slapped his hand against his chest and looked utterly shocked. "I can't cook. You know that."

"But you're inviting company."

His gaze dropped and he restlessly shuffled his feet. "I was hoping that maybe this one Friday you could..." He paused and his head jerked up. "You don't have a date, do you?" He sounded as though that was the worst possible thing that could happen.

"Not this Friday."

"Oh, good. For a minute there, I thought we might have a problem."

"We?" She arched her brows playfully. "I don't have a problem, but it sounds like you do." She wasn't going to let him con her into his schemes quite so easily.

"But you'll be here."

"I was planning on soaking in the tub, giving my hair a hot-oil treatment and hibernating with a good book." Her gaze fell on the algebra text and she involuntarily grimaced.

"But you could still fix dinner, couldn't you? Something simple like seafood jambalaya with shrimp, stuffed eggplant and pecan pie for dessert."

"Are you planning to rob a bank as well?" At his blank stare, she elaborated. "Honestly, Derek, have you checked out the price of seafood lately?"

"No, but you cooked that Cajun meal not so long ago and—"

"Shrimp was on sale," she broke in.

He continued undaunted. "And it was probably the most delicious meal I've ever tasted in my whole life. I was kicking myself because Reed wasn't here and he would have loved it as much as everyone else."

At the mention of Reed's name, Ellen's lashes fell, hiding the confusion and longing in her eyes. The house had been full of college boys and their shenanigans, yet it had seemed astonishingly empty without Reed. He'd been with them barely a week and Ellen couldn't believe how much his presence had affected her. The morning he'd left, she'd walked him out to the truck, trying to think of a way to say goodbye and to thank him for understanding the emotions that raged through her at the news of her mother's marriage. But nothing had turned out quite as she'd expected. Reed had seemed just as reluctant to say goodbye as she was, and before climbing inside the truck, he'd leaned forward and lightly brushed his lips over hers. The kiss had been so spontaneous that Ellen wasn't sure if he'd

really meant to do it. But intentional or not, he *had*,
and the memory of that kiss stayed with her. Now a
day rarely passed that he didn't enter her thoughts, one
way or another.

A couple of times when she was on the second floor
she'd wandered into her old bedroom, forgetting that it
now belonged to Reed. Both times, she'd lingered
there, enjoying the sensation of remembering Reed and
their verbal battles.

Repeatedly Ellen told herself that it was because
Derek's brother was over twenty-one and she could
therefore carry on an adult conversation with him. Although she was genuinely fond of the boys, she'd discovered that a constant diet of their antics and their
adolescent preoccupations—Pat's basketball, Monte's
appetite and Derek's Michelle—didn't exactly make
for stimulating conversation.

"You really are a fantastic cook," Derek went on.
"Even better than my mother. Why, only the other day
Monte was saying…"

"Don't you think you're putting it on a little thick,
Derek? If you continue like this, my head will begin
to swell."

The teenager blinked twice. "I just wanted you to
know how much I'd appreciate it if you did happen to
decide to do me this tiny favour."

"You'll buy the ingredients yourself?"

"The grocery budget couldn't manage it this once?"

"Not unless everyone else is willing to eat oatmeal
three times a week for the remainder of the month."

"I don't suppose they would be," he muttered. "All
right, make me a list and I'll buy what you need."

Ellen was half hoping that once he saw the price of
fresh shrimp, he'd realise it would be cheaper to take
Michelle to a seafood restaurant.

"Oh, by the way," Derek said, examining one of the envelopes in his hand. "You got a letter. It looks like it's from Reed."

"Reed?" Her lungs slowly contracted as she said his name and it was all she could do not to snatch the envelope out of Derek's hand. The instant he gave it to her, she tore it open.

"What does he say?" Derek asked, sorting through the rest of the mail. "He didn't write me."

Ellen quickly scanned the contents. "He's asking if the electrician has come yet. That's all."

"Oh?"

She made a show of tucking the letter back inside the envelope. "I'll go into the kitchen and make that list for you before I forget."

"I appreciate it, Ellen, honest."

"Sure," she grumbled.

As soon as the kitchen door swung closed, Ellen took out Reed's letter again, intent on savouring every word.

Dear Ellen,

You're right, the Monterey area is beautiful. I wish I could say that everything else is as peaceful as the scenery here. Unfortunately it's not. Things have been hectic. But if all goes well, I should be back at the house by Saturday, which is earlier than I expected.

Have you become accustomed to the idea that your mother's remarried? I know it was a shock. I remember how I felt, and that was many years ago. I've been thinking about it all—and wondering about you. If I'd known what was happening, I might have been able to postpone this trip. You looked like you needed someone. And knowing

you, it isn't often you're willing to lean on anyone. Not the independent, self-sufficient woman I
discovered walking around half-naked in my
kitchen. I can almost see your face getting red
when you read that. I shouldn't tease you, but I
can't help it.

By the way, I contacted a friend of mine who
owns an electrical business and told him the problem with the kitchen outlet. He said he'd try to
stop by soon. He'll call first.

I'm not good at writing letters, but I wanted you
to know that I was thinking about you and the
boys. Actually, I'm pleased you're there to keep
those kids in line. I know I came at you like a
wounded bear when I first learned you were living
in the house. I didn't mean to insult you. Derek
is right, you're not that kind of woman. Problem
is, I'm not sure what kind of woman you are. I've
never known anyone quite like you.

Anyway, the electrician is coming, as promised.
Take care and I'll see you late Saturday.

Say hi to the boys for me. I'm trusting that they
aren't giving you any problems.

                                        Reed

Ellen folded the letter and slipped it into her pocket.
She crossed her arms, smiling to herself, feeling incredibly good. So Reed had been thinking about her.
And she'd bet it was more than the troublesome kitchen
outlet that had prompted his letter. Although she acknowledged that it would be dangerous for her to read
too much into Reed's simple message, Ellen couldn't
help but feel encouraged.

Humming softly, she propped open her cookbook,
compiling the list of items Derek would need for his

fancy dinner with Michelle. A few minutes later, her spirits soared still higher when the electrical contractor phoned and arranged a date and time to check the faulty outlet. Somehow, that seemed like a good omen to her—a kind of proof that she really was in Reed's thoughts.

"Was the phone for me?" Derek called from halfway down the staircase.

Ellen finished writing the information on the pad by the phone before answering. "It was the electrician Reed wrote about."

"Oh. I'm half expecting a call from Michelle."

"Speaking of your true love, here's your grocery list."

Derek took it and slowly ran his finger down the items she'd need for his special dinner with Michelle. "Is this going to cost over ten dollars?" He glanced up, his face doubtful.

"The pecans alone will be that much," she exaggerated.

With only a hint of disappointment, Derek shook his head. "I think maybe Michelle and I should find a nice, cosy, inexpensive restaurant."

Satisfied that her plan had worked so well, Ellen hid a smile. "I thought as much. By the way," she added, "Reed says he'll be home Saturday."

"So soon? He hasn't even been gone two weeks."

"Apparently it's only a short job."

"Apparently," Derek grumbled. "I don't have to be here, do I? Michelle wanted me to help her and her sister paint."

"Derek, my boy," Ellen said softly. "I didn't know you could wield a brush. The upstairs hallway—"

"Forget it," he told her sharply. "I'm only doing this to help Michelle."

"Right, but I bet Michelle would be willing to help you, since you're being so generous with your time."

"No way," he argued disgustedly. "We're college kids, not slaves."

The following afternoon, the electrician arrived and was in and out of the house within thirty minutes. Ellen felt proud that she'd correctly traced the problem. She could probably have fixed it if Reed hadn't become so frantic at the thought of her fumbling around with the kitchen wiring. Recalling his reaction produced an involuntary smile.

THAT EVENING, Ellen had finished loading the dishwasher and had just settled down at the kitchen table to study when the phone rang. Pat, who happened to be walking past the phone, answered it on the first ring.

"It's Reed," he told Ellen. "He wants to talk to you."

With reflexes that surprised even her, Ellen bounded out of her chair.

"Reed," she said into the telephone receiver, holding it tightly against her ear. "Hello, how are you?"

"Fine. Did the electrician come?"

"He was here this afternoon."

"Any problems?"

"No," she said breathily. He sounded wonderfully close, his voice warm and vibrant. "In fact, I was on the right track. I probably could have handled the problem myself."

"I don't want you to even think about fixing anything like that. You could end up killing yourself or someone else. I want you to understand that, Ellen. I absolutely forbid it."

"Aye, aye, sir." His words had the immediate effect of igniting her temper, sending the hot blood roaring

through her veins. She hadn't been able to stop thinking about Reed since he'd left, but two minutes after
picking up the phone, she was arguing with him again.

There was a long, awkward silence. Reed was the
first to speak, expelling his breath sharply. "I didn't
mean to snap your head off," he admitted.

"And I didn't mean to shout back," she answered,
instantly soothed.

"How's everything else going?"

"Fine."

"Have the boys conned you into any more of their
schemes?"

"They keep trying."

"They wouldn't be college kids if they didn't."

"I know." It piqued her a little that Reed assumed
she could be bamboozled by three teenagers. "Don't
worry about me. I can hold my own with these three."

His low sensuous chuckle did funny things to her
pulse rate. "It's not you I'm concerned about."

"Just what are you implying?" she asked, a smile
evident in her voice.

"I'm going to play this one smart and leave that last
comment open-ended."

"Clever of you, my friend, very clever."

"I thought as much."

After a short pause, Ellen quickly asked, "How's
everything your way?" She knew there really wasn't
anything more to say, but she didn't want the conversation to end. Talking to Reed was almost as good as
having him there.

"Much better, thanks. I shouldn't have any problem
being home by Saturday."

"Good."

Another short silence followed.

"Well, I guess that's all I've got to say. If I'm going to be any later than Saturday, I'll give you a call."

"Drive carefully."

"I will. Bye, Ellen."

"Goodbye, Reed." Smiling, she replaced the receiver in its cradle. When she glanced up, all three boys were staring at her, their arms crossed dramatically over their chests.

"I think something's going on here," Pat spoke first. "I answered the phone and Reed asked for Ellen. He didn't even ask for Derek—his own brother."

"Right," Derek agreed. "Reed even wrote her a letter."

"I'm wondering," Monte said, rubbing his chin thoughtfully. "Could we have the makings of a romance on our hands?"

"I think we must," Pat concurred.

"Stop it." Ellen did her best to join in the banter, although she felt the colour flooding her cheeks. "It's only natural that Reed would want to talk to me. I'm the oldest."

"But I'm his brother," Derek countered.

"I refuse to listen to any of this," she said with a small laugh and turned back to the kitchen. "You three aren't even making sense. Reed's dating Danielle."

All three followed her. "He could have married Danielle months ago if he was really interested," Derek informed the small gathering.

"Be still, my trembling heart," Monte joked, melodramatically folding both hands over his heart and pretending to swoon.

Not to be outdone, Pat placed the back of his hand against his forehead and rolled his eyes. "Ah, love."

"I'm getting out of here." Before anyone could argue, Ellen bounded up the back stairs to her room, laughing as she went. She had to admit she'd found the boys' little performances quite funny. But if they pulled any of their romance-brewing pranks around Reed, it would be extremely embarrassing for her. Ellen resolved to say something to them when the time seemed appropriate.

FRIDAY AFTERNOON, Ellen walked into the kitchen, her schoolbooks clutched tightly to her chest.

"What's the matter? You look pale as a ghost," Monte remarked, cramming a chocolate-chip cookie in his mouth.

Derek and Pat turned toward her, their faces revealing their concern.

"I got my algebra paper back today."

"And?" Derek prompted.

"I don't know. I haven't looked."

"Why not?"

"Because I know how tough ol' Engstrom was on the others. The girl who wrote about solving that odd-ball conjecture got a C-minus and the guy who was so enthusiastic about his subject of Mathematics in World War II got a D. With impressive subjects like that getting low grades, I'm doomed."

"But you worked hard on that paper." Loyally, Derek defended her and placed a consoling arm around her shoulders. "You found out a whole bunch of interesting facts about the number nine."

"You did your paper on that?" Pat asked, his smooth brow wrinkling with amusement.

"Don't laugh." She already felt enough of a fool.

"It isn't going to do any good to fret," Monte insisted with perfect logic, slipping the folded assignment from between her fingers.

Ellen watched his expression intently as he handed

the paper to Derek who raised two thick brows and gave it to Pat.

"Well?"

"You got a B-minus," Pat said in a husky whisper, revealing his own surprise. "I don't believe it."

"Me neither." This was what heaven must feel like, Ellen decided, this delicious feeling of relief. She sank luxuriously into a chair. "I'm calling Charlie." Almost immediately she jumped up again and dashed to the phone. "This is too exciting to be real. I'm celebrating."

The other three had drifted into the living room and two minutes later, she joined them there. "Charlie's out, but his roommate said he'd give him the message." Too happy to contain her excitement, she added, "But I'm not sitting home alone. How about if I treat everyone to pizza tonight? The whole works on me."

"Sorry, Ellen." Derek looked up with a frown. "I've already made plans with Michelle."

"I'm getting together with a bunch of guys at the gym," Pat informed her, shifting the basketball from one hand to the other.

"And I told Mom I'd be home for dinner."

Some of the excitement drained from her, but she put on a brave front. "No problem. We'll do it another night."

"I'll go."

The small group whirled around, shocked to discover Reed standing there, framed in the living-room doorway.

CHAPTER FIVE

"REED," ELLEN BURST OUT, astonished. "When did you get here?" The instant she'd finished speaking, she realized how stupid the question was. He'd obviously just walked in the back door.

With a crooked grin, he checked his wristwatch. "About fifteen seconds ago."

"How was the trip?" Derek asked.

"Did you drive straight through?" Pat asked, then added, "I don't suppose you had a chance to see the Warriors play, did you?"

"You must be exhausted," Ellen said, noting how tired his eyes seemed.

As his smiling gaze met hers, the fine laugh lines that fanned out from his eyes became more pronounced. "I'm more hungry than tired. Didn't I just hear you offer to feed me pizza?"

"Ellen got a B-minus on her crazy algebra paper," Monte said with pride.

Rolling her eyes playfully toward the ceiling, Ellen laughed. "Who would have guessed it—I'm a mathematical genius!"

"So that's what this offer for dinner is all about. I thought you might have won the pools."

He was more deeply tanned than Ellen remembered. Tanned. Vital. And incredibly male. He looked glad to be home, she thought. Not a hint of hostility showed in the eyes that smiled back at her.

"No such luck."

Derek made a show of glancing at his watch. "I'm out of here or I'll be late picking up Michelle. It's good to see you, Reed."

"Yeah, welcome home," Pat said, reaching for his basketball. "I'll see you later."

Reed raised his right hand in salute and reached for his suitcase, heading up the wide stairs. "Give me fifteen minutes to shower and I'll meet you down here."

The minute Reed's back was turned, Monte placed his hand over his heart and wildly batted his lashes as he mouthed something about the beauty of love. Ellen practically threw him out of the house, slamming the door after him.

At the top of the stairs, Reed turned and glanced down at her. "What was that all about?"

Ellen leaned against the closed door, her hand covering her mouth to smother her giggles. But the laughter drained from her as she glanced at his puzzled face, and she slowly straightened. She cleared her throat. "Nothing. Really. Did you want me to order the pizza and pick it up? Or do you want to go out?"

"Whatever you prefer."

"If you leave it up to me, my choice would be to get away from these four walls."

"I'll be ready in a few minutes."

Ellen suppressed a shudder at the thought of what would have happened had Reed caught a glimpse of Monte's antics. She herself handled the boys' teasing with good-natured indulgence, but she was fairly sure that Reed would take offence at their nonsense. And heaven forbid that Danielle should ever catch a hint of what was going on—not that anything *was* going on.

With her thoughts becoming more muddled every minute, Ellen made her way to the third floor to change into a pair of grey tailored trousers and a frilly pale-blue silk blouse. One glance in the mirror and she sadly shook her head. They were only going out for pizza—there was no need to wear anything so elaborate. Hurriedly, she changed into dark-brown cords and a turtleneck sweater the colour of summer wheat. Then she ran a quick brush through her short curls and freshened her lipstick.

When Ellen returned to the living room, Reed was already waiting for her. "You're sure you don't mind going out?" she asked again.

"Are you dodging your pizza offer?"

He was so serious that Ellen couldn't help laughing. "Not in the least."

"Good. I hope you like spicy sausage with lots of olives."

"Love it."

His hand rested on her shoulder, warming her with his closeness. "And a cold beer."

"This is sounding better all the time." Ellen would have guessed Reed to be the type of man who drank martinis or expensive cocktails. In some ways, he was completely down-to-earth and in others, surprisingly complex. Perceptive, unpretentious and unpredictable; she knew that much about him, but she didn't expect to understand him soon.

Reed helped her into his pickup, which was parked in the driveway. The evening sky was already dark and Ellen regretted not having brought her coat.

"Cold?" Reed asked her when they stopped at a red light.

"Only a little."

He adjusted the switches for the heater and soon a rush of warm air filled the cab. Reed chatted easily, telling her a little about his project in California and explaining why his work demanded so much travelling. "That's changing now."

"Oh?" She couldn't restrain the little shiver of gladness that came with the announcement. "Will you be coming home more often?"

"Not for another three or four months. I'm up for promotion and then I'll be able to pick and choose my assignments more carefully. Over the past four years, I've travelled enough to last me a lifetime."

"Then it's true that there's no place like home."

"Be it ever so humble," he added with a chuckle.

"I don't exactly consider a three-storey, twenty-room turn-of-the-century mansion all that humble."

"Add four college students and you'll quickly discover how unassuming it can become."

"Oh?"

"You like that word, don't you?"

"Yes," she agreed, her mouth curving into a lazy smile. "It's amazing how much you can say with that one little sound."

Reed exited from the freeway close to the Seattle Center and continued north. At her questioning glance he explained, "The best pizza in Seattle is made at a small place near the Center. You don't mind coming this far, do you?"

"Not at all. I'll travel a whole lot farther than this for a good pizza." Suddenly slouching forward, she pressed her forehead into her hand. "Oh, good grief, it's happening."

"What?"

"I'm beginning to sound like Monte."

They both laughed. It felt so good to be sitting there with Reed, sharing an easy, relaxed companionship, that Ellen could almost forget about Danielle. Almost, but not quite.

Although Ellen had said she'd pay for the pizza, Reed insisted on picking up the tab. They sat across from each other at a narrow booth in the corner of the semidarkened room. A lighted red candle in a glass bowl flickered on the table between them and Ellen decided this was the sum total of atmosphere. The inevitable jukebox blared out the latest country hits, drowning out the possibility of any audible conversation, which seemed just as well since she was beginning to feel strangely tongue-tied.

When their number was called, Reed slid from the booth and returned a minute later with two frothy beers in ice-cold mugs and a huge steaming pizza.

"I hope you don't expect us to eat all this?" Ellen asked anxiously, shouting above the music. The pizza certainly smelled enticing, but Ellen doubted that she'd manage to eat more than two or three pieces.

"We'll put a decent dent in it, anyway," Reed said, resuming his seat. "I bought their largest, thinking the boys would appreciate any leftovers as a midnight snack."

"You're a terrific older brother."

The fast-paced rhythms of the song on the jukebox were fading into silence at last.

"There are times when I'd like to shake some sense into Derek, though," Reed said without elaborating.

Ellen dropped her gaze to the spicy pizza and lifted a small slice onto her plate. Strings of melted cheese still linked the piece to the rest of the pie. She pulled them loose and licked her fingers. "I can imagine how you felt when you discovered that Derek had accidentally-on-purpose forgotten to tell you about renting out bedrooms."

Reed shrugged non-committally. "I was thinking

more about the time he let you climb on top of the roof," he muttered.

"He didn't *let* me, I went, all by myself."

"But you won't do it again. Right?"

"Right," Ellen agreed reluctantly. Behind Reed's slow smiles and easy banter, she recognised a solid wall of unrelenting male pride. "You still haven't forgiven me for that, have you?"

"Not you. Derek."

"I think this is one of those subjects where we should agree to disagree." It astonished Ellen that within the space of a few words they could find something to argue about.

"Have you heard from your mother?" Reed asked, apparently just as willing to change the subject and avoid an argument.

Ellen nodded. "She seems very happy and after a day or two, I discovered I couldn't be more pleased for her. She's worked hard all these years and deserves a lot of contentment."

"I knew you'd soon realise that." Warmth briefly showed in his green eyes.

"I felt a whole lot better just talking to you. It was a surprise when Mom announced her marriage, but it shouldn't have been. The signs were there all along. I suppose once the three of us kids were gone, she felt free to remarry. And I suppose she thought that presenting it to the family as an accomplished fact would make it easier for all of us."

There was a comfortable silence between them as they finished eating. The pizza was thick with sausage and cheese and Ellen placed her hands on her stomach after leisurely munching two narrow pieces. "I'm stuffed," she declared, leaning back. "But you're right, this has got to be the best pizza in town."

"I thought you'd like it."

Reed brought over a carry-out box and Ellen carefully put the leftovers inside.

"How about a movie?" he asked once they were in the car park.

Astounded, Ellen darted him a sideways glance, but his features were shadowed and unreadable. "You're kidding, aren't you?"

"I wouldn't have asked you if I was."

"But you must be exhausted." Ellen guessed that he'd probably spent most of the day driving.

"A little," he admitted.

Her frown deepened. Suddenly, it no longer seemed right for them to be together. The problem was that Ellen had been so pleased to see him that she hadn't stopped to think about the consequences of their going out together. "Thanks anyway, but it's been a long week. I think I'll call it an early night."

When they reached the house, Reed parked on the street, rather than the driveway. The light from the stars and the silvery moon penetrated the tree limbs that hung overhead and created shadows on his face. Neither of them seemed eager to leave the warm cab of the pickup truck. The mood was intimate and Ellen didn't want to disturb this moment of tranquillity. Lowering her gaze, she admitted to herself how attracted she was to Reed and how much she liked him. She admitted, too, that it was wrong for her to feel this way about him.

"You're quiet all of a sudden."

Ellen's smile was decidedly forced. She turned toward him to apologise for putting a damper on their evening, but the words never left her lips. Instead her eyes met his in a slow, sensual exchange. Paralysed, Ellen stared at Reed, battling to disguise the intense attraction she felt for him. It seemed the most natural thing in the world to lean toward him and brush her lips over his. She could smell the woodsy scent of his after-shave and could almost taste his mouth over hers. With the determined force of her will, she pulled her gaze away and reached for the door, like a drowning person grasping a life preserver.

She was on the front porch by the time Reed joined her. Her fingers shook as she inserted the key into the lock.

"Ellen." He spoke her name softly and placed his hand on her shoulder.

"I don't know why we went out tonight." Her voice was high and strained as she drew free of his touch. "We had no business being together."

In response, Reed mockingly lifted one eyebrow. "I believe it was you who asked me."

"Be serious, will you," she snapped irritably and shoved open the door.

Reed slammed it shut behind him and followed her into the kitchen. He set the pizza on the counter and turned to face her. "What the hell do you mean? I *was* being serious."

"You shouldn't have been with me tonight."

"Why not?"

"Where's Danielle? I'm not the one who's been patiently waiting around for you. She is. You had no business taking me out to dinner and then suggesting a movie. You're my landlord, not my boyfriend."

"Let's get two things straight here. First, what's between Danielle and me is none of your business. And second, you invited *me* out. Remember?"

"But…it wasn't like that and you know it."

"Besides, I thought you claimed you were far too

old for 'boyfriends.'" She detected an undertone of amusement in his low-pitched voice.

Confused, Ellen marched into the living room and immediately busied herself straightening magazines. Reed charged in after her, leaving the kitchen door swinging in his wake. Defensively clutching a sofa pillow to her stomach, Ellen searched for some witty retort. Naturally, when she needed a clever comeback, her mind was a total blank.

"You're making a joke out of everything," she told him, damning her voice for shaking. "And I don't appreciate that. If you want to play games, do it with someone other than me."

"Ellen, listen—"

The phone rang and she jerked her attention to the hallway.

"I didn't mean—" Reed paused and raked his fingers through his hair. The phone pealed a second time. "Go ahead and answer that."

She hurried away, relieved to interrupt this disturbing conversation. "Hello." Her voice sounded breathless, as though she'd raced down the stairs.

"Ellen? This is Charlie. I got a message that you phoned."

For one crazy instant, Ellen forgot why she'd wanted to talk to Charlie. "I phoned? Oh, right. Remember that algebra paper I was struggling with? Well, it came back today."

"How'd you do?"

A little of the surprised pleasure returned. "I still can't believe it. I got a B-minus. My simple paper about the wonders of the number nine received one of the highest marks in the class. I'm still in shock."

The sound of Charlie's delighted chuckle came over

the wire. "This calls for a celebration. How about if we go out tomorrow night? Dinner, drinks, the works."

Ellen almost regretted the impulse to contact Charlie. She sincerely liked him, and she hated the thought of stringing him along or taking advantage of his attraction to her. "Nothing so elaborate. Chinese food and a movie would be great."

"You let me worry about that. Just be ready by seven."

"Charlie, listen—"

"No arguing. I'll see you at seven."

By the time Ellen was off the phone, Reed was nowhere to be seen. Nor was he around the following afternoon. The boys didn't comment and she couldn't very well ask about him without arousing their suspicions. As it was, the less she mentioned Reed around those three, the better. The boys had obviously read more into the letter, phone call and dinner than Reed had intended. But she couldn't blame them; she'd read enough into it herself to be frightened by what was happening between them. He'd almost kissed her when he'd parked in front of the house. And she'd wanted him to—that was what disturbed her most. But if she allowed her emotions to get involved, she knew that someone would probably end up being hurt. And the most likely "someone" was Ellen herself.

Besides, if Reed was attracted to Danielle's sleek elegance, then he would hardly be interested in her own more homespun qualities.

A few minutes before seven, Ellen was ready for her evening with Charlie. She stood before the downstairs hallway mirror to put the finishing touches to her appearance, fastening her gold earrings and straightening the single chain necklace that graced her slender neck.

"Where's Reed been today?" Pat enquired of no one in particular.

"His sports car is gone," Monte offered, munching on a chocolate bar. "I noticed it wasn't in the garage when I took out the garbage."

Slowly Ellen sauntered into the living room. She didn't want to appear too curious, but at the same time, she was definitely interested in listening to the conversation.

She had flopped into a chair and picked up a two-month-old magazine before she noticed all three boys staring at her.

"What are you looking at me for?"

"We thought you might know something."

"About what?" she asked, playing dumb.

"Reed," all three said simultaneously.

"Why should I know anything?" Her gaze flittered from them to the magazine and back again.

"You went out with him last night."

"We didn't *go out* the way you're implying."

Pat, with the basketball still tucked under one arm, pointed an accusing finger at her. "The two of you were alone together and both of you have been acting weird ever since."

"And I say all three of you have overactive imaginations."

"All I know is that Reed was like a wounded bear this morning," Derek volunteered.

"Everyone's entitled to an off day." Hoping to give a casual impression, she leafed through the magazine, idly fanning the pages with her thumb.

"That might explain Reed. But what about you?"

"Me?"

"For the first time since you moved in, you weren't downstairs until after ten."

"I slept in. Is that a crime?"

"It just might be. You and Reed are both behaving real strange. It's like the two of you are avoiding each other and we want to know why."

"It's your imagination. Believe me, if there was anything to tell you, I would."

"Sure, you would," Derek mocked.

From the corner of her eye, Ellen noticed Charlie's car pull up in front of the house. Releasing a sigh of relief, she quickly stood and gave the boys a falsely bright smile. "If you'll excuse me, my date has arrived."

"Should we tell Reed you're out with Charlie if he wants to know where you are?" Monte looked uncomfortable asking the question.

"Of course. Besides, he probably already knows. He's free to see anyone he wants and so am I. For that matter, so are you." Walking backward as she spoke, she made her way toward the front door and pulled it open before Charlie even got a chance to ring the doorbell.

The evening didn't go well. Charlie took her out for a steak dinner and spent more money than Ellen knew he could afford. More and more, she regretted having phoned him. Charlie had obviously interpreted her call as a sign that she was interested in becoming romantically involved. She wasn't, and didn't know how to make it clear without offending him.

"Did you have a good time?" he asked as they drove back toward Capitol Hill.

"Lovely, thank you, Charlie."

His hand reached for hers and squeezed it reassuringly. "We don't go out enough."

"Neither of us can afford it too often."

"We don't need to go to a fancy restaurant to be

together," he contradicted lightly. "Just being with you is a joy."

"Thank you." If only Charlie weren't so nice. She hated the idea of hurting him. But she couldn't allow him to go on hoping that she might ever return his feelings. As much as she dreaded it, she knew she had to disillusion him. Anything else would be cruel and dishonest.

"I don't think I've made a secret of how I feel about you, Ellen. You're wonderful."

"Come on, Charlie, I'm not that different from a thousand other girls on campus." She tried to swallow the tightness in her throat. "In fact, I was noticing the way that girl in our third-period class—what's her name—Lisa, has been looking at you lately."

"I hadn't noticed."

"I believe you've got yourself an admirer."

"But I'm only interested in you."

"Charlie, listen, please. I think you're a wonderful person. I—"

"Shh," he demanded softly as he parked in front of Ellen's house and turned off the engine. He slid his arm along the back of the seat and caressed her shoulder. "I don't want you to say anything."

"But I feel that I may have—"

"Ellen," he whispered her name seductively. "Be quiet and just let me kiss you."

Before she could utter another word, Charlie claimed her mouth in a short but surprisingly ardent kiss. Charlie had kissed her on several occasions, but never had she allowed their lovemaking to go beyond the most innocent of exchanges.

When his arms tightened around her, Ellen resisted.

"Invite me in for coffee," he whispered urgently in her ear.

She pressed her forehead against his shirt collar. "Not tonight."

He tensed. "Can I see you again soon?"

"I don't know. We see each other every day. Why don't we just meet after class for a coffee one day next week?"

"But I want so much more than that," he protested.

"I know," she answered, dropping her eyes. She felt confused and miserable.

Ellen could tell he was disappointed just by the way he climbed out of the car and trudged around to her side. There was tense silence between them as he walked her up to the front door and kissed her a second time. Again, Ellen had to break away from him by pushing her hands against his chest.

"Thank you for everything," she whispered.

"Right. Thanks, but no thanks."

"Oh, Charlie, don't start that. Not now."

Eyes downcast, he wearily rubbed a hand along the side of his face. "I guess I'll see you Monday," he said with a sigh.

"Thanks for the lovely evening." She didn't let herself inside until Charlie had climbed into his car and driven away.

Releasing a jagged breath, Ellen had just started to unbutton her coat when she glanced up to find Reed standing in the living room, glowering at her.

"Is something wrong?" The undisguised anger that twisted his mouth and hardened his gaze was a shock.

"Do you always linger outside with your boyfriends?"

"We didn't linger."

"Right." He dragged one hand roughly through his hair and marched a few paces toward her, only to do an abrupt about-face. "I saw the two of you necking."

"Necking?" Ellen was so startled by his unreasonable anger that she didn't know whether to laugh or argue. "Be serious, will you? Two chaste kisses hardly constitute necking."

"What kind of influence are you on Derek and the others?" He couldn't seem to stand still and paced back and forth in agitation.

He was obviously furious, but Ellen was at a loss to understand the real reason for his anger. He couldn't possibly believe those absurd insinuations. Perhaps he was upset about something else and merely taking it out on her, she reasoned. "Reed, what's wrong?" she finally asked.

"I saw you out there."

"You were spying on me?"

"I wasn't spying," he snapped.

"Charlie and I were inside his car. You must have been staring out the windows to have even seen us."

He didn't answer her, but instead hurled another accusation in her direction. "You're corrupting the boys."

"I'm what?" She couldn't believe what she was hearing. "They're nineteen years old. Trust me, they've kissed girls before now."

"You can kiss anyone you like. Just don't do it in front of the boys."

From the way this conversation was going, Ellen could see that Reed was in no mood to listen to reason. "I think it would be better if we discussed this issue another time," she said quietly.

"We'll talk about it right now."

Ignoring his domineering tone as much as possible, Ellen forced a smile. "Good night, Reed. I'll see you in the morning."

She was halfway to the stairs when he called her, his voice calm. "Ellen."

She turned around, holding herself tense, watching him stride quickly across the short distance that separated them. His thumb and forefinger captured her chin, tilting it slightly so he could study her face. Gently, he rubbed his thumb across her lips. "Funny, you don't look kissed."

In one breath he was accusing her of necking and in the next, claiming she was unkissed. Not knowing how to respond, Ellen didn't. She merely gazed at him, her eyes wide and questioning.

"If you're going to engage in that sort of activity, the least you can do—" He paused. With each word his mouth drew closer and closer to hers until his lips hovered over her own and their breaths mingled. "The least you can do is look kissed." His hand located the vein pounding wildly in her throat as his mouth settled over hers. The kiss leisurely explored her lips as he worked his way from one side of her mouth to the other. She felt the full weight of his muscular body against her own, and its heat seemed to melt her very bones.

Slowly, patiently, his mouth moved over hers with a petal softness, an exquisite tenderness that left her quivering with anticipation and delight. Timidly, her hands crept across his chest to link behind his neck. Again his lips descended on hers, more hungrily now, as he groaned and pulled her even closer.

Ellen felt her face grow hot as she surrendered to the heavenly sensations that stole through her like the gentle fog of an early spring. Yet all the while, her mind was telling her she had no right to feel this contentment, this warmth. Reed belonged to another woman. Not to her...to someone else.

Her breath caught as he twisted his mouth away from hers. His laboured breathing was audible. "I was afraid of that," he mumbled.

"Of what?" she asked uncertainly.

"You taste too good. Like cotton candy," he moaned.

Colour seeped into her face. When she'd realised that he intended to kiss her, her first thought had been to resist. But once she'd felt his mouth on hers, all her resolve had drained away. Embarrassed now, she realised that she'd pliantly wrapped her arms around his neck. And worse, she'd responded with enough enthusiasm for him to know exactly what she was feeling.

He pressed his mouth to the corner of her forehead as though he couldn't bear to release her.

Ellen struggled to breathe normally. She let her arms slip from his neck to his chest and through the palm of her hand she could feel the rapid beating of his heart. She closed her eyes, knowing that her own pulse was pounding no less wildly.

She could feel his mouth move against her temple. "I've been wanting to do that for days." The grudging admission came low and taut.

The words to tell him that she'd wanted it just as much were quickly silenced by the sound of someone walking into the room.

Guiltily Reed and Ellen jerked apart. Her face turned a deep shade of red as Derek stopped in his tracks, staring at them.

"Hi."

"Hi," Reed and Ellen said together.

"Hey, I'm not interrupting anything, am I? If you like, I could turn around and pretend I didn't see a thing."

"Do it," Reed ordered.

"No," Ellen said just as quickly.

Derek's eyes sparkled with boyish delight. "You know," he said, "I had a feeling about the two of you from the beginning." While he spoke, he was taking small steps backward, until he stood pressed against the polished kitchen door. "Right on." He gave his brother the thumbs-up sign as he nudged open the door with one foot and hurriedly backed out of the room.

"Now look what you've done," Ellen wailed.

"Me? As I recall you were just as eager for this as I was."

"It was a mistake," she blurted out. A ridiculous, illogical mistake. He had accused her of being a bad influence on the boys and then proceeded to kiss her senseless.

"You're telling me." A distinct coolness entered his eyes. "It's probably a damn good thing I'm leaving."

There was no hiding the stricken look. "Again? So soon?"

"After what's just happened, I'd say it wasn't nearly soon enough."

"But...where to this time?"

"Denver. But I'll be back before Thanksgiving."

Mentally, Ellen calculated that he'd be away another two weeks.

When he spoke again, his voice was gentle. "It's just as well, don't you think?"

CHAPTER SIX

"IT LOOKS LIKE RAIN." Pat stood in front of the window above the kitchen sink and frowned at the thick black clouds that darkened the late afternoon sky. "Why does it have to rain?"

Ellen turned over her sister's letter and glanced up at him. "Are you seeking a scientific response or will a simple 'I don't know' suffice?"

The kitchen door swung open and Derek sauntered in. "Has anyone seen Reed?"

Instantly, Ellen's gaze dropped to her sister's letter. Reed had returned to Seattle two days earlier and so far, they'd done an admirable job of avoiding each other. Both mornings, he'd left for his office before she was up. Each evening, he'd come home, showered, changed clothes and then gone off again. It didn't require much detective work to figure out that he was with Danielle. Ellen had attempted—unsuccessfully—not to think of Reed at all. And especially not of him and Danielle together.

For her part, she secretly wished that she'd had the nerve to arrange an opportunity to talk to Reed. So much remained unclear in her mind. Reed had kissed her and it had been wonderful, yet that was something neither seemed willing to admit. It was as if they had tacitly agreed that the kiss had been a terrible mistake and should be forgotten. The problem was, Ellen couldn't force the memory of his touch from her troubled mind.

"Reed hasn't been around the house much," Pat answered.

"I know." Derek sounded slightly disgruntled and cast an accusing glance in Ellen's direction. "It's almost like he doesn't live here anymore."

"He doesn't. Not really." Pat stepped away from the window and gently set the basketball on a chair. "It's sort of like he's a guest who stops in now and then."

Ellen preferred not to be drawn into this conversation. She hastily folded her letter, slid it back inside the envelope and stood up to leave.

"Say, Ellen." Pat stopped her.

She muttered something disparaging under her breath about almost making a clean getaway. Turning, she met his questioning gaze with a nervous smile. "Yes?"

"I'll be leaving in a few minutes. Have a nice Thanksgiving."

Relieved that the subject of Reed had been dropped, she threw him a brilliant smile. "You, too."

"Where are you having dinner tomorrow?" Derek asked, as if the thought had unexpectedly occurred to him.

Her mother was still in Arizona, her sister had gone to visit her in-laws and Bud couldn't get leave, so Ellen had decided to stay in Seattle. "Here."

"In this house?" Derek's eyes widened with concern. "But why? Shouldn't you be with your family?"

"My family is going in different directions this year. It's no problem. In fact, I'm looking forward to having the whole house to myself."

"There isn't any reason to spend the day alone," Derek argued. "My parents wouldn't mind putting out an extra plate. There's always plenty of food."

Her heart was touched by the sincerity of his invitation. "Thank you, but honestly, I prefer it this way."

"It's because of Reed, isn't it?" Both boys studied her with wide, inquisitive eyes.

"Nonsense."

"But, Ellen, he isn't going to be there."

"Reed isn't the reason," she assured him. Undoubtedly, Reed would be spending the holiday with Danielle. She made an effort to ignore the instant flash of pain that accompanied the thought; she knew she had no right to feel hurt if Reed chose to spend Thanksgiving with his "almost" fiancée. The other woman had a prior claim.

"You're sure?" Derek didn't look convinced.

"You could come and spend the day with my family," Pat offered next.

"Will you two quit acting like it's such a terrible tragedy? I'm going to *enjoy* an entire day alone. Look at these nails." She fanned her fingers and held them up for their inspection. "For once, I'll have an uninterrupted block of time to do all the things I've delayed for weeks."

"All right, but if you change your mind, give me a call."

"I asked her first," Derek argued. "You'll call me. Right?"

"Right to you both."

THANKSGIVING MORNING, Ellen woke to a torrential downpour. Thick drops of rain pelted against the window and the day seemed destined to be a melancholy one. Lazily, she lounged in her room and read, enjoying the luxury of not having to rush around, preparing breakfast for the whole household.

She wandered down to the kitchen, where she was greeted by a heavy silence. The house was definitely empty. Apparently, Reed, too, had started his day early. Ellen couldn't decide whether she was pleased or annoyed that she had seen so little of him since his return from Denver. He'd been the one to avoid her, and she'd concluded that two could play his silly game. So she'd purposely stayed out of his way. A sad smile touched her eyes as she reflected on the past few days. She and Reed had been acting like a pair of adolescents.

She ate a bowl of cornflakes and spent the next hour wiping down the cupboards, with the radio tuned to the soft-rock music station. Whenever a particularly romantic ballad aired, she danced around the kitchen with an imaginary partner. Not so imaginary, really. In her mind, she was in Reed's arms.

The silence became more oppressive during the afternoon, while Ellen busied herself fussing over her nails. When the final application of polish had dried, she decided to flip on the television to drown out the quiet. An hour into the football game, Ellen noticed that it was nearly dinnertime, and she suddenly felt hungry.

Popcorn sounded wonderful, so she popped a small batch and splurged by dripping melted butter over the top. She carried the bowl into the living room and climbed back onto the sofa, tucking her legs under her. She had just found a comfortable position when she heard a noise in the kitchen.

Frowning, she twisted around, wondering who it could possibly be.

The door into the living room swung open and Ellen's heart rate soared into double time.

"Reed?" She blinked to make sure he wasn't an apparition.

"Hello."

He didn't vanish. Instead he took several steps in her direction. "That popcorn smells great."

Without considering the wisdom of her offer, she held out the bowl to him. "Help yourself."

"Thanks." He took off his jacket and tossed it over the back of a chair before joining her on the sofa. He leaned forward, studying the television screen. "Who's winning?"

Ellen was momentarily confused, until she realised he was asking about the football game. "I don't know. I haven't paid that much attention."

Reed reached for another handful of popcorn and Ellen set the bowl in the centre of the coffee table. Her emotions were muddled. She couldn't imagine what Reed was doing at the house with her. He was supposed to be at Danielle's. Although the question burned in her mind, she couldn't bring herself to ask it. She glanced at him covertly through her lashes, but Reed was staring at the television as though he were alone in the room.

"I'll get us something to drink," she volunteered.

"Great."

Even while she was speaking, Reed hadn't looked in her direction. Slightly piqued by his attitude, she stalked into the kitchen and took two Pepsis out of the refrigerator.

When she returned with the soft drinks and two glasses filled with ice, Reed reached out and took one set from her. "Thanks," he murmured, popping open the can. He carefully poured the soda over the ice and set the can aside before taking a sip.

"You're welcome," she grumbled and flopped down again, pretending to watch television. But her mind was spinning in a hundred different directions. When she couldn't tolerate it any longer, she blurted out the question that dominated her thoughts, her voice high and agitated.

"Reed, what are you doing here?"

He took a long swallow before answering her. "I happen to live here."

"You know what I mean. You should be with Danielle."

"I was, earlier, but I decided I preferred your company."

"I don't need your sympathy," she snapped, then swallowed painfully and averted her gaze. Her fingers tightened around the cold glass until the chill extended up her arm. "I'm perfectly content to spend the day alone. I just wish everyone would kindly refrain from saving me from myself."

His low chuckle was unexpected. "That wasn't my intention."

"Then why are you here?"

"I already told you."

"I don't accept that," she said shakily. He was toying with her emotions, and the thought made her all the more furious.

"All right." Determinedly, he set down his drink and turned toward her. "I thought this was the perfect opportunity for us to talk."

Her eyes were clouded with anger as she met his steady gaze. "You haven't said more than ten words to me in three days. What makes this one day so special?''

''We're alone, aren't we, and that's more than we can usually say.'' His voice was strained. He hesitated a moment, his lips pressed together in a thin, hard line. ''I don't know what's happening with us.''

''Nothing's happening,'' she said wildly. ''You kissed me, and we both admitted it was a terrible mistake. Can't we leave it at that?''

''No,'' he answered drily. ''I don't believe it was such a major tragedy, and neither do you.''

If it really had been a mistake, Ellen wouldn't have remembered it with such vivid clarity. Nor would she yearn for the taste of him again and again, or hurt so much when she knew he was with Danielle.

Swiftly she turned her eyes away from the disturbing intensity of his, unwilling to reveal the depth of her feelings.

''It wasn't a mistake, was it, Ellen?'' he prompted in a husky voice.

She squeezed her eyes shut and shook her head. ''No,'' she whispered, but the word was barely audible.

His arms gathered her close to the warmth of his taut, muscular chest. She felt his deep shudder of satisfaction as he buried his face in her hair. Long moments passed before he spoke. ''Nothing that felt so right could have been a mistake.''

Tenderly he kissed her, his lips touching hers with a gentleness she hadn't expected. As if he feared she was somehow fragile; as if he found her highly precious. Without conscious decision, her arms slipped around him as she opened her mouth to his, savouring this moment.

''The whole time Danielle and I were together this

afternoon, I was wishing it was you. Today, of all days, it seemed important to be with you.''

Ellen gazed up into his eyes and saw not only his gentleness, but his confusion. Her fingers slid into the thick hair around his lean, rugged face. ''I don't imagine Danielle was pleased to have you leave.''

''She wasn't. I didn't even know how to explain it to her. Hell, I don't know how to explain it to myself.''

Ellen swallowed down the dryness that constricted her throat. ''Do you want me to move out of the house?''

''No,'' he said forcefully, then added more quietly, ''I think I'd go crazy if you did. Are you a witch who's cast some spell over me?''

She tried unsuccessfully to answer him, but no words of denial came. The knowledge that he was experiencing these strange whirling emotions was enough to overwhelm her.

''If so, the spell is working,'' he murmured, although he didn't sound particularly pleased at the idea.

''I'm confused, too,'' she admitted and pressed her forehead to his chest. She could feel his heart pounding beneath her open hand.

His long fingers stroked her hair. ''I know.'' Gently he leaned down and kissed the top of her head. ''The night you went out with Charlie, I was completely unreasonable. I need to apologise for the things I said to you. To put it plain and simple, I was jealous. I've admitted that, these last weeks in Denver.'' Some of the tightness left his voice, as though the events of that night had weighed heavily on his mind. ''I didn't like the idea of another man holding you and when I saw the two of you kissing, I think I went a little berserk.''

''I...we don't date often.''

"I won't ask you not to see him again," he said reluctantly. "I can't ask anything of you."

"Nor can I ask anything of you."

His grip around her tightened. "Let's give this time."

"It's the only thing we can do."

Reed straightened and draped his arm around Ellen's shoulders, drawing her protectively close to his side. Her head nestled neatly against his chest. "I'd like for us to start going out together," he said, his chin resting on the crown of her head. "Will that cause a problem for you?"

"Cause a problem?" she repeated uncertainly.

"I'm thinking about the boys."

Remembering their earlier buffoonery and the way they'd taken such delight in teasing her, Ellen shook her head. If those three had any evidence at all of a romance between Reed and her, they could make everyone's lives miserable. "I don't know."

"Then let's play it cool for a while. We'll work into this gradually until they become accustomed to seeing us together and it won't be any big deal."

"I think you might be right." She didn't like pretence or deceit, but she'd be the one subjected to their good-natured heckling. They wouldn't dare try it with Reed.

"Can I take you to dinner tomorrow night?"

"I'd like that."

"Not as much as I will. But how are we going to do this? It'll be obvious that we're going out together," he mused aloud.

"Not if we leave the house at different times," she countered.

She could feel his frown. "Is that really necessary?"

A sigh worked its way through her. "I'm afraid so."

Ellen and Reed spent the remainder of the evening doing nothing more exciting than watching television. His arm remained securely around her shoulders and she felt a sense of deep contentment that was new to her. It was a peaceful interlude in a time that had become increasingly wrought with stress.

Derek arrived back at the house close to nine-thirty. They both heard him lope in through the kitchen and Reed gave Ellen a quick kiss before withdrawing his arm.

"Hi." Derek entered the room and stood beside the sofa, shuffling his feet. "Dad wondered where you were." His gaze flitted from Ellen back to his brother.

"I told them I wouldn't be there for dinner."

"I know. But Danielle phoned looking for you."

"She knew where I was."

"Apparently not." Reed's younger brother tucked one hand in the side pocket of his trousers. "Are you two friends again?"

Reed's eyes found Ellen's and he smiled warmly. "You could say that."

"Good. Neither of you have been the easiest people to be around lately." Without giving them a chance to reply, he whirled around and marched upstairs.

Ellen placed a hand over her mouth to smother her giggles. "Well, he certainly told us."

Amusement flared in Reed's eyes, and he chuckled softly. "I guess he did, at that." His arm slid around Ellen's shoulders once again. "Have you been bitchy lately, my dear?"

"I'm never bitchy," she returned.

"Me neither."

They exchanged smiles and went back to watching their movie.

As much as Ellen tried to concentrate on the television, her mind unwillingly returned to Derek's announcement. "Do you think you should call Danielle?" Her lashes fluttered downward, disguising her discomfort. Having Reed with her these past few hours had been like an unexpected Christmas gift, granted early. But she felt guilty that it had been at the other woman's expense.

Impatience tightened Reed's mouth. "Maybe I'd better. I didn't mean to offend her or her family by leaving early." He seemed to measure his words as he spoke. He paused a moment, then added, "Danielle is a little high-strung."

Ellen had certainly noticed, but she had no intention of mentioning it. And she had no intention of listening in on their conversation. "While you're doing that, I think I'll wash up the popcorn dishes and call it a night."

Reed's eyes widened slightly in a mock reprimand. "It's a little early, isn't it?"

"Perhaps," she said, faking a yawn, "but I've got this hot date tomorrow night and I want to be well rested for it."

The front door opened and Pat sauntered in. "Hi." He stopped and studied them curiously. "Hi," he repeated.

"I thought you were staying home for the weekend." Ellen remembered that Pat had said something about being gone for the entire four-day holiday.

"Mom gave my bedroom to one of my aunts. I can't see any reason to sleep on the floor when I've got a bed here."

"That makes sense," Reed said drily.

"Are you two getting along again?"

"We never fought."

"Yeah, sure," Pat mumbled sarcastically. "And a basket isn't worth two points."

Ellen had been unaware how much her disagreement with Reed had affected the boys. Apparently, Reed's reaction was the same as hers; their eyes met briefly in silent communication.

"I'll go up with you," she told Pat. "See you in the morning, Reed."

"Right."

Halfway up the stairs, Pat tossed her the basketball. "Here, catch."

She caught it nimbly and flung it back. "One of these days you're going to discover something more exciting than sports."

"Yeah?"

"Yeah." She laughed and left him on the second floor to trudge her way up to the third.

It shouldn't have been a surprise that she slept so well. Her mind was at ease and she awoke feeling contented and hopeful. Neither of them were making any commitments yet. They didn't know if what they felt would last a day or a lifetime. They were explorers, discovering the uncharted territory of a new relationship. Ellen felt wonderful.

Humming, she bounded down the stairs early the next morning. Reed was already up, sitting at the kitchen table drinking coffee and reading the paper.

"Morning," she offered, pouring water into the tea kettle and setting it on the burner.

"Morning." His eyes didn't leave the paper.

Ellen brought down a mug from the cupboard and

walked past Reed on her way to get the canister of tea. His hand reached out and gripped her around the waist, pulling her down into his lap.

Before she could protest, his mouth firmly covered hers. When the kiss was over, Ellen straightened, resting her hands on his shoulders. "What was that for?" she asked to disguise how flustered he made her feel.

"Just to say good morning," he said in a warm, husky voice. "I don't imagine I'll have too many opportunities to do it in such a pleasant manner."

"No," she said and cleared her throat. "Probably not."

Ellen was sitting at the table, with a section of the paper propped up in front of her, when the boys came into the kitchen.

"Morning," Monte murmured vaguely as he opened the refrigerator. He was barefoot, his hair was uncombed and his shirt was still unbuttoned. "What's for breakfast?"

"Whatever your little heart desires," she told him, neatly folding over a page of the newspaper.

"Does this mean you're not cooking?"

"That's right."

"But—"

Reed lowered the sports page and glared openly at Monte.

"Cold cereal will be fine," Monte grumbled and took down a large serving bowl, emptying half the contents of a box of rice crisps inside.

"Hey, save some for me," Pat hollered from the doorway. "That's my favourite."

"I was here first."

Derek strolled into the kitchen. "Does everyone have to argue?"

"Everyone?" Reed cocked a mocking brow in his brother's direction.

"First it was you and Ellen, and now it's Pat and Monte."

"Hey, that's right," Monte cried. "You two aren't fighting. That's great." He set his serving bowl of rice crisps on the table. "Does this mean...you're...you know."

Lowering the paper, Ellen eyed him sardonically. "No, I don't know."

"You know...seeing each other?" A deep flush darkened Monte's face.

"We see each other every day."

"That's not what I mean."

"But that's all I'm answering." From the corner of her eye, she caught sight of Pat pantomiming a fiddler, and she groaned inwardly. The boys were going to make it difficult to maintain any kind of romantic relationship with Reed. She cast him a speculative glance. But if Reed had noticed the activity around him, he wasn't letting on, and Ellen was grateful.

"I've got a practice game tonight," Pat told Ellen as he buttered a piece of toast. "Do you want to come?"

Flustered, her gaze automatically sought out Reed. "Sorry...I'd like to come, but I've got a date."

"Bring him along."

"I...don't know if he appreciates basketball."

"Yeah, he does," Derek supplied. "Charlie and I were talking about it recently and he said it's one of his favourite games."

She didn't want to tell an outright lie. But she would save herself a lot of aggravation if she simply let Derek and the others assume it was Charlie she'd be seeing.

"What about you, Reed?"

His gaze didn't flicker from the paper and Ellen marvelled at his ability to appear so dispassionate. "Not tonight. Thanks anyway."

"Have you got a date, as well?" Derek pressed.

It seemed as though everyone in the kitchen was watching Reed, waiting for his response. "I generally go out Friday nights."

"Well," Ellen said, coming to her feet. "I think I'll get moving. I want to take advantage of the holiday to do some errands. Does anybody need anything picked up at the cleaners?"

"I do," Monte said, raising his hand. "If you'll wait a minute, I'll get the slip."

"Sure."

By some miracle, Ellen was able to avoid any more questions for the remainder of the day. She busily went about her errands and didn't see Reed until late in the afternoon, when their paths happened to cross in the kitchen. He quickly whispered the time and meeting place and explained that he'd leave first. Ellen didn't have a chance to do more than agree before the boys were upon them, their eyes wide and questioning.

At precisely seven, Ellen met Reed at the grocers car park lot two blocks from the house. He'd left ten minutes earlier to wait for her there. As soon as he spotted her he leaned across the cab of the pickup and opened the door on her side. Ellen found it slightly amusing that when he was with her he drove the pickup, and when he was with Danielle he took the sports car. She wondered whether or not this was a conscious decision. In any event, it told her quite a bit about the way Reed viewed the two women in his life.

"Did you get away unscathed?" he asked, chuckling softly.

She slid into the seat beside him in the cab and shook her head. "Not entirely. All three were curious about why Charlie wasn't coming to the house to pick me up. I didn't want to lie, so I told them they'd have to ask him."

"Will they?"

"I certainly hope not."

Reed's hand reached for hers and his eyes grew serious. "I'm not convinced that keeping this a secret is the right thing to do."

"I don't like it either, but it's better than being the constant brunt of their teasing."

"I'll put a stop to that." His voice dropped ominously and Ellen didn't doubt that he'd quickly handle the situation.

"But, Reed, they're just having a little innocent fun. They don't mean any harm. I was hoping we could lead them gradually into accepting us as a couple. Let them get used to seeing us together before we spring it on them that we're...dating." She used that term for lack of a better one.

"Ellen, I don't know."

"Trust me on this," she pleaded, her round eyes imploring him. This arrangement, with its secrecy and deception, was far from ideal, but for now, she thought, it was necessary.

His kiss was brief and ardent. "I don't think I could deny you anything." But he didn't sound happy about it.

The restaurant to which Reed took her was located in the south end of Seattle, thirty minutes from Capitol Hill. Ellen was mildly surprised that he chose one so

far from home but didn't mention it. The food was
fantastic and the view from the Des Moines Marina
alone would have been worth the drive.

Reed ordered a bottle of an award-winning Char-
donnay that came from a local winery. It was satisfy-
ingly clear and crisp.

"I spoke to Danielle," Reed began.

"Reed." She stopped him, placing her hand over
his. "What goes on between you and Danielle has
nothing to do with me. We've made no promises and
no commitments." In fact, of course, she was dying to
know about the other woman Reed had dated for so
long. She hoped that if she pretended no interest in his
relationship with Danielle, she'd seem much smoother
and more sophisticated then she really was.

He looked a little stunned. "But—"

Swiftly she lowered her gaze. "I don't want to
know." Naturally, she was longing to hear every sordid
detail. As it was, she felt incredibly guilty about the
other woman. Danielle might have had her faults, but
she loved Reed. She must have, to be so patient with
his travelling all these months. And when Derek had
first mentioned the other woman, he'd spoken as
though Reed and Danielle's relationship was a per-
manent one.

Danielle and Ellen couldn't have been more different. Ellen was practical and down-to-earth. She'd had
to be. After her father's death, she'd become the cor-
nerstone that held the family together.

Danielle, on the other hand, had obviously been
pampered and indulged all her life. Ellen guessed that
she'd been destined from birth to be a wealthy socialite, someone who might, in time, turn to charitable
works to occupy herself. They were women with com-

pletely dissimilar backgrounds, she and Danielle. And completely different futures.

"I'll be in Georgia the latter part of next week," Reed was saying.

"You're full of good news, aren't you?"

"It's my work, Ellen," his soft voice accused her.

"I wasn't complaining. It just seems that the minute we come to an understanding, you're off again."

"It won't be long this time. A couple of days. I'll fly in for the meeting and be home soon afterward."

"You'll be here for Christmas?" Her thoughts flew to her family and how much she wanted each one of them to meet Reed. Bud, especially. Recently her brother's letters had revealed a new maturity. Bud would be in Yakima over the holidays and Ellen was planning to take the Greyhound over to spend some time with him. But first she had to get through her exams.

"I'll be here."

"Good." But it was too soon to ask Reed to join her for the trip home. He might misinterpret her invitation, see something that wasn't there. She had no desire to pressure him into the sort of commitment that meeting her family might imply.

After their meal, they walked along the pier, holding hands. The evening air was chilly and Ellen shivered involuntarily. Reed wrapped his arm around her shoulder to lend her his warmth.

"I enjoyed tonight," he murmured.

"I did, too." She bent her arm so that her fingers linked with his.

"Tomorrow night—"

"No." She stopped him, turning so that her arm slid around his middle. Tilting her head back, she stared into the troubled green eyes. "Let's not talk about tomorrow. With us, it can only be one day at a time."

His mouth met hers before she could finish speaking. A gentle brushing of lips, a light exchange. Petal soft and petal smooth. Then he deepened the kiss, and his arms tightened around her, and her whole body hummed with joy.

Ellen was lost, irretrievably lost, in the taste and scent of this man. She felt frightened by her response to him—it would be so easy to lose her heart. But she couldn't let that happen. Not yet. It was too soon. Far too soon.

HER WORDS about taking each day as it came were forcefully brought to Ellen's mind the following evening. She'd gone to the store and noticed Reed's Porsche parked in the driveway. When she returned, both Reed and the sports car had disappeared. Swallowing down the hurt, Ellen acknowledged that Reed was with Danielle.

CHAPTER SEVEN

"WHY COULDN'T I SEE THAT?" Ellen moaned, looking over the algebraic equation Reed had worked out. "If I can fix a stopped-up sink, tune a car engine and tie flies, why can't I understand something this simple?" She was at the end of her rope with this maths class and quickly losing a grip on the more advanced theories they were now studying.

"Here, let me show it to you again."

Her hand lifted the bouncy curls off her forehead. "Do you think it'll do any good?"

"Yes, I do." Reed obviously had more faith in her powers of comprehension than she did. Step by step, he led her through another problem. When he explained the textbook examples, the whole process seemed so logical and simple. Yet when she set out to solve a similar equation, nothing went right.

"I give up." Throwing her hands over her head, she leaned back in the kitchen chair and groaned aloud. "I should have realised that algebra would be too much for me; I had difficulty memorising the multiplication tables, for heaven's sake."

"What you need is a break."

"I couldn't agree more. Twenty years?" She stood up and brought the cookie jar to the table. "Here, this will help ease the suffering." She offered him a chocolate-chip cookie and took one herself. Reed's calm,

assured attitude as he tutored her had been little short
of amazing.

"Be more patient with yourself," he insisted.

"There's only three weeks left in this term. I haven't
got time to mosey around and smell the cherry blos-
soms. I need to understand this stuff and I need to
understand it now."

He laid his hands on her shoulders, massaging
gently. "No, you don't. Come on, I'm taking you to a
movie."

"I've got to study," she protested, but not too stren-
uously. Escaping for an hour or two sounded infinitely
more appealing than struggling with these impossible
equations.

"There's a wonderful foreign film showing at the
Moore Egyptian Theatre and we're going. We can
worry about that assignment once we get back."

"But, Reed—"

"No buts. We're going." He took her firmly by the
hand and led her into the front hall. Derek and Monte
were watching TV and the staccato sounds of machine
guns firing could be heard in the background. Neither
boy noticed them until Reed opened the hall closet.

"Where are you two headed?" Derek asked, peering
around the living-room door as Reed handed Ellen her
jacket.

"A movie."

Instantly Derek muted the television. "The two of
you alone? Together?"

"I imagine there will be one or two others at the
cinema," Reed responded drily.

"Can I come?" Monte had joined Derek in the doorway and he clearly had no qualms about inviting himself along.

Instantly Derek's elbow shoved the other boy in the ribs. "On second thoughts, just bring me back some popcorn, okay?"

"It's yours."

Ellen pulled a knit cap over her ears. "Do either of you want anything else? I'd buy out the concession stand if one of you felt inclined to do my algebra."

"No way."

"Bribing them won't help," Reed commented, reaching for her hand.

"I know, but I was hoping."

It was a cold, blustery night. An icy north wind whipped against them as they hurried to Reed's truck. He opened the door for her before running around to the driver's side.

"Brr." Ellen stuffed her hands inside her jacket pockets. "If I doubted it was winter before, now I know."

"Come here and I'll warm you." He patted the seat beside him, indicating that she should slide closer.

Willingly she complied, until she sat so near to him that her thigh was pressing softly against his. Neither of them moved. Reed's right hand rested on the ignition key. It had been several days since they'd been completely alone together and longer still since he'd held or kissed her without interruption. The past ten days had been filled with frustration. Often she'd noticed Reed's gaze on her, studying her face and her movements, and she'd felt his angry disappointment. It seemed that every time he touched her one of the boys would unexpectedly appear.

Reed dropped his hand from the key and he turned to her. Their thoughts echoed each other's; their eyes locked hungrily. Ellen required no invitation. She'd been longing for his touch for days. With a tiny cry she reached for him just as his arms came out to encircle her, drawing her even closer.

"This is crazy," he whispered fervently into her hair.

"I know."

"I've been wanting to hold you for days." As though he couldn't deny himself any longer, his hands cradled her face and he slowly lowered his mouth to hers. His lips skimmed lightly, tenderly, over hers, torturing her with anticipation.

"You do taste like cotton candy," he whispered.

Ellen was so consumed with longing that his words barely registered in her bemused mind. Her mouth and tongue melted against his like the sweetest of sugars.

"Reed," she groaned, arching closer.

Their lips clung and his tongue sought and found hers in a loving duel, dipping again and again to taste her sweetness. Reed's hand went around her ribs as he held her tight. The kiss was long and thoroughly satisfying.

Panting, he tore his mouth from hers and buried his face in the sloping curve of her neck. "We better get to that movie."

It was all Ellen could do to nod her head in agreement.

When Reed made a move to start the truck, she saw that his hand was trembling. She was shaking too, but no longer from cold. Reed had promised to warm her and he had, but not quite in the way she'd expected.

They were silent as Reed switched on the engine and pulled onto the street. After days of carefully avoiding any kind of touch, any lingering glances, they'd sat in the driveway kissing in direct view of curious eyes. She realised that the boys could easily have been watching them. Nothing made sense anymore.

Ellen felt caught up in a tide that tossed her closer and closer to a long stretch of rocky beach. Powerless to alter the course of her emotions, she feared for her heart, afraid of being caught in the strong pull of the undertow.

"The engineering department is having a Christmas party this weekend at the Space Needle," Reed murmured.

Ellen nodded. Twice in the past week he'd left the house wearing formal evening clothes. He hadn't told her where he was going, but she knew. He'd driven the Porsche and he'd come back smelling of expensive perfume. For a Christmas party with his peers, Reed would escort Danielle. She understood that and tried to accept it.

"I want you to come with me."

"Reed," she breathed, uncertain. "Are you sure?"

"Yes," his hand reached for hers and squeezed. "I want you with me."

"The boys—"

"To hell with the boys. I'm tired of playing cat and mouse games with them."

Her smile came from her heart, radiating through her eyes. "I am too."

"I'm going to have a long talk with them."

"Don't," she pleaded. "It isn't necessary to say anything."

"They'll start in with their insufferable teasing."

"Let them, and then we can say something. I don't want to invite trouble."

He frowned briefly. "All right."

The Moore Egyptian was located in the heart of

downtown Seattle, so parking was limited. They finally found a spot on the street three blocks away. They left the truck and hurried through the cold, arm in arm, not talking much. The French film was a popular one; by the time they reached the cinema, a long line had already formed outside.

A blast of wind sliced through Ellen's jacket and she buried her hands in her pockets. Reed leaned close to ask her something, then paused, slowly straightening.

"Morgan." A tall, brusque-looking man approached Reed.

"Hello, Dailey," Reed said, quickly stepping away from Ellen.

"I wouldn't have expected to see you out on a night like this," the man Reed had called Dailey was saying.

"This film is supposed to be good."

"I've heard that too." Dailey's eyes returned to the line and rested on Ellen, seeking an introduction. Reed didn't give him one. It seemed as though Reed was pretending he wasn't with Ellen.

She offered the man a feeble smile, wondering why Reed would move away from her, why he wouldn't introduce her to his acquaintance. The line moved slowly toward the ticket booth and Ellen went with it, leaving Reed talking to Dailey on the pavement. Resentment flared when he rejoined her a few minutes later.

"That was a friend of a friend."

Ellen didn't answer him. Somehow she didn't believe him. And she resented the fact that he'd ignored the most basic of courtesies and left her standing on the pavement alone, while he spoke with a friend. The way he'd acted, anyone would assume Reed didn't want the man to know Ellen was with him. That hurt.

Fifteen minutes earlier she'd been soaring with happiness at his unexpected invitation to the Christmas party, and now she was consumed with doubt and bitterness. Perhaps this Dailey was a friend of Danielle's and Reed didn't want the other woman to know he was out with Ellen. But that didn't really sound like Reed.

Once inside the cinema, Reed bought a huge bucket of buttered popcorn. They located good seats, despite the crowd, and sat down, neither of them speaking. As the room darkened and the thick curtain parted, Reed placed his hand on the back of her neck.

Ellen stiffened. "Are you sure you want to do that?"

"What?"

"Touch me. Someone you know may recognise you."

"Ellen, listen…"

The credits started to roll on the huge screen and she shook her head, telling him she didn't want to hear any of his excuses. She sincerely doubted that he had one.

Maintaining her bad mood was impossible with the comedy that unravelled before them. Unable to stop herself, Ellen laughed until tears formed in the corners of her eyes; she was clutching her stomach because it hurt so much from laughing. Reed seemed just as amused as she was, and a couple of times during the film, their smiling gazes met. Before she knew it, Reed was holding her hand and she hadn't a thought of resisting when he draped his arm over her shoulder.

Afterward, as they strolled outside, he tucked her hand in the crook of his elbow. "I told you a movie would make you feel better."

It had and it hadn't. Yes, she'd needed the break, but Reed's behaviour outside the cinema earlier had revived the insecurities she was trying so hard to sup-

press. She knew she wasn't nearly as beautiful or sophisticated as Danielle. Nor did she possess the sterling
social background of the other woman.

"You do feel better?" His finger lifted her chin to
study her eyes.

She might have been confused, but there was no de-
nying that the film had been wonderful. "I haven't
laughed that hard in ages," she told him, smiling.

"Good."

FRIDAY NIGHT, Ellen wore her most elaborate outfit—
black velvet trousers and a silver lamé top. She'd spent
hours debating whether an evening gown would have
been more appropriate, but had finally decided on the
trousers. Examining herself from every direction in the
full-length mirror that hung from her closet door, Ellen
released a pent-up breath and closed her eyes. This one
night, she wanted everything perfect. Her sling-back
heels felt a little uncomfortable, but she'd get used to
them. She rarely had any reason to wear heels. She'd
chosen them now because Reed had said there would
be dancing and she wanted to adjust her height to his.

By the time she reached the foot of the stairs, Reed
was waiting for her. His eyes softened as he gazed at
her, taking in everything; from her shining curls to her
elegant shoes. "You're lovely."

"Oh Reed, are you sure? I don't mind changing if
you'd rather I didn't wear trousers."

His eyes held hers in a lengthy, intimate exchange.
"I don't want you to change a thing."

"Hey, Ellen." Derek burst out of the kitchen, and
stopped abruptly. "Wow." For an instant he looked as
though he'd lost his breath. "Hey, guys," he called
eagerly. "Come and look at Ellen."

The other two joined Derek. Pat dropped his basketball to the carpet, where it bounced once and rolled away. "Gee, you look like a movie star."

Monte closed his mouth and opened it again. His Adam's apple bobbed up and down his throat. "You're *pretty*."

"Don't sound so shocked."

"It's just that we've never seen you dressed...like this," Pat mumbled.

"Are you going out with Charlie?"

Ellen glanced at Reed, suddenly unsure. She hadn't dated Charlie in weeks. She hadn't wanted to.

"She's going out with me," Reed explained in an even voice that didn't invite comment.

"With you? Where?" Derek's eyes got that mischievous twinkle Ellen recognised so readily.

"A party."

"What about—" He stopped suddenly, swallowing several times.

"You wanted to comment on something?" Reed encouraged drily.

"I thought I was going to say something," Derek muttered, clearly embarrassed, "but then I realised I wasn't."

"Good." Hiding a smile, Reed held Ellen's coat for her.

She slipped her arms into the satin-lined sleeves and reached for her beaded bag. "Good night, boys, and don't wait up."

"Right." Monte raised his index finger. "We won't wait up."

Derek took a step forward. "Should I say anything to someone...anyone...in case either of you gets a phone call?"

"Try hello," Reed answered, shaking his head.

"Right." Derek stuck his hand inside his trouser pocket. "Have a good time."

"We intend to."

Ellen managed to hold back her laughter until they were on the front porch. But when the door clicked shut the giggles escaped and she pressed a hand to her mouth. "Derek thought he was going to say something."

"Then he realised he wasn't," Reed finished for her, chuckling. His hand at her elbow guided her down the steps. "They're right about one thing. You do look exceptionally lovely tonight."

"Thank you, but I hadn't thought it would be such a shock."

"The problem is the boys are used to seeing you as a substitute mother. It's suddenly dawned on them what an attractive woman you are."

"And how was it you noticed?"

He studied her a moment, his gaze caressing and ardent. "The day I arrived and found you in my kitchen wearing only a bra, I knew."

"I was wearing more than that," she argued.

"Maybe, but at the time that was all I saw." He stroked her cheek with the tip of his finger, then firmly tucked her arm in his.

Ellen felt a sense of warm contentment as Reed led her to the sports car. This night would be one she'd treasure all her life. She realised it as surely as she recognised that somewhere in the past two weeks Reed had made an unconscious decision about their relationship. Maybe she was being silly in judging the strength of their bond by what car he chose to drive. And maybe not. Reed was escorting her to this party in his Porsche

because he viewed her in a new light. He saw her now
as a beautiful, alluring woman—no longer as the independent college student who seemed capable of mas-
tering everything but algebra.

The Space Needle came into view as Reed pulled
onto Denny Street. The world-famous Needle, which
had been built for the 1962 World's Fair, rose 605 feet
above the Seattle skyline. Ellen had taken the trip up
to the observation deck only once and she'd been
thrilled at the unobstructed view of the Olympic and
Cascade mountain ranges. Looking out at the unspoiled
beauty of Puget Sound, she'd understood immediately
why Seattle was described as one of the world's most
livable cities.

For this evening, Reed explained, his office had
booked the convention rooms on the hundred-foot level
of the Needle. The banquet facilities had been a recent
addition, and Ellen wondered what sort of view would
be available.

As Reed eased to a stop in front of the Needle, a
red-coated valet suddenly appeared, opening Ellen's
door, offering her his gloved hand. She climbed as
gracefully as she could from the low-built vehicle. Her
smile felt a little strained, and she took a deep breath
to dispel the gathering tension. She wanted everything
about the evening to be perfect; she longed for Reed
to be proud of her, to feel that she belonged in his
life—and in his world.

Her curiosity about the view was answered as soon
as they stepped from the elevator into the large circular
room. She glanced at the darkened sky that resembled
folds of black velvet, sprinkled with glittering gems.
When she had a chance she'd walk over toward the
windows. For now, she was more concerned with fit-

ting into Reed's circle and being accepted by his
friends and colleagues.

Bracing herself for the inevitable round of introduc-
tions, she scanned the crowd for the man she'd seen
outside the cinema. He didn't seem to be at the party
and Ellen breathed easier. If Dailey was there, he
would surely make a comment about seeing her with
Reed that night, and she wouldn't know how to answer
him.

As they made their way through the large room, several people called out to Reed. When he introduced
Ellen, two or three of them appeared to have trouble
concealing their surprise that he wasn't with Danielle.
But after only a few seconds of embarrassment, the
moment she'd dreaded most had passed. No one mentioned Danielle and they all seemed to accept Ellen
freely, although a couple of people tossed her curious
looks. Eventually, Ellen breathed easier and smiled up
at Reed, her heart in her eyes.

"That wasn't so bad, was it?" he asked, his voice
tender.

"Not at all."

"Would you like something to drink?"

"Please." A drink didn't sound particularly appealing just then, but at least it would give her something
to do with her hands.

"I'll be right back."

Ellen watched Reed cross the room toward the bar,
proud of the fine figure he cut. He wore the suit with
an easy assurance, completely unaware of how splen-
did he looked. Ellen was absurdly proud of him and
made no attempt to disguise her feelings when he returned to her, carrying two glasses of white wine.

"You shouldn't look at me like that," he murmured handing her a glass.

"Why?" she teased, her eyes sparkling. "Does it embarrass you?"

"No. It makes me wish I could ignore everyone in this room and kiss you, right this minute." The slow, almost boyish grin spread across his features.

"That would certainly cause quite a stir."

"But not half the commotion if you knew what else I was thinking."

"Oh?" She hid a smile by taking another sip of wine.

"Are we back to that word again?"

"Just what do you have in mind?"

He dipped his head so that he appeared to be whispering something in her ear, though actually his lips brushed her face. "I'll show you later."

"I'll be waiting."

They stood together, listening to the music and the laughter. Ellen found it curious that he'd introduced her to so few people and then only to those who'd approached him. But she dismissed her qualms as petty, and worse, paranoid. After all, she told herself, she was here to be with Reed, not to make small talk with his friends.

He finished his drink and suggested another. While he returned to the bar for refills, Ellen wandered through the crowd, seeking her way to the windows for a glimpse of the magnificent view. But as she moved, she kept her gaze trained on Reed.

A group of men stopped him, questioning him animatedly. His head was inclined toward them, and he appeared to be giving them his rapt attention. Yet periodically his gaze would flicker through the crowd, searching for her. When he located her by the huge floor-to-ceiling windows, he smiled as though he felt relieved. With an abruptness that bordered on rudeness, he excused himself from the group and strolled in her direction.

"I didn't see where you'd gone."

"I wasn't about to leave you," she told him. Turning, she faced the window, watching the lights of the ferry boats glide across the dark-green waters of Puget Sound.

His hands rested on her shoulders and Ellen leaned back against him, warmed by his nearness. "It's lovely from up here."

"Exquisite," he agreed, his mouth close to her ear. "But I'm not talking about the view." His hands slid lazily down her arms. "Dance with me," he said, taking her hand and leading her to the dance floor.

Ellen walked obediently into his arms, loving the feel of being close to Reed. She pressed her cheek against the smooth fabric of his dark jacket as they swayed gently to the slow, dreamy music.

"I don't normally do a lot of dancing," he whispered.

Ellen wouldn't have guessed that. He moved with an unexpected grace. She assumed that he'd escorted Danielle around a dance floor more than once during the course of their relationship. At the thought of the other woman, Ellen grew uneasy, but she forced her tense body to relax. Reed had chosen to bring her, and not Danielle, to this party. That had to mean something—something wonderful and exciting.

"Dancing was just an excuse to hold you."

"You don't need an excuse," she whispered in return.

"In a room full of people, I do."

"Shall we wish them away?" She closed her eyes, savouring the feel of his hard, lithe body pressing against her own.

He manoeuvred them into the darkest corner of the dance floor and immediately claimed her mouth in a shattering kiss that sent her world spinning into orbit. His fingers sank into the thick curls at her nape, and his tongue chased hers.

Mindless of where they were, Ellen arched upward, Reed responded by sliding his hands down her back, down to her hips, drawing her even closer.

Roughly he dragged his mouth across her cheek. "I'm sorry we came."

"Why?"

"I don't want to waste time with all these people around. We're so seldom alone. I want you, Ellen."

His honest, straightforward statement sent the fire roaring through her veins. "I know. I want you, too." Her voice was unsteady. "But it's a good thing we aren't alone together very often." At the rate things were progressing between them, Ellen felt, for once, relieved that the boys were at the house. Otherwise, it would have been impossible to leave Reed and go up to her room alone....

"Hey, Reed." A friendly voice boomed out only a few feet away. "Aren't you going to introduce me to your friend?"

Reed stiffened and for a moment Ellen wondered if he was going to pretend he hadn't heard. He looked at her through half-closed eyes, and she grinned up at him, mutely telling him she didn't mind. Their private world couldn't last forever. She knew that. They were at a party, an office party, and Reed was expected to mingle with his colleagues.

"Hello, Ralph." Reed's arm slid around Ellen's waist, keeping her close.

"Hello there." But Ralph wasn't watching Reed. "Well, good buddy, aren't you going to introduce me?"

"Ellen Cunningham, Ralph Forester."

Ralph extended his hand and captured Ellen's in both of his for a long moment. His eyes were frankly admiring.

"I don't suppose you'd let me steal this beauty away for a dance, would you?" Although the question was directed to Reed, Ralph didn't take his eyes from Ellen. "Leave it to you to be with the most beautiful woman here," the other man teased. "You attract them like flies."

Reed's hand tightened around Ellen, pinching her waist, but she was convinced he wasn't aware of it. "Ellen?" He left the choice to her.

"I don't mind." She glanced at Reed and noted that his expression was carefully blank. But she knew him too well to be fooled. She could see that his jaw was rigid with tension and that his eyes revealed sharp annoyance at the other man's intrusion. Gradually he lowered his arm, releasing her.

Ralph stepped forward and claimed Ellen's hand, leading her onto the dance floor.

She swallowed tightly as she placed her left hand on his shoulder and her right hand in his. Wordlessly they moved to the soft music. But when Ralph tried to bring her closer, Ellen resisted.

"Have you known Reed long?" Ralph asked then, his hand trailing sensuously up and down her back.

She tensed, holding herself stiffly. "Several months now." Despite her efforts to keep her voice even and controlled, she sounded slightly breathless.

"How'd you meet?"

"Through his brother." The less said about their living arrangements, the better. Ellen could just guess what Ralph would say if he knew they were living in the same house. "Do you two work together?"

"For the last six years," the other man declared, studying her curiously.

They whirled around and Ellen caught a glimpse of Reed standing against the opposite wall, studying them like a hawk zeroing in on its prey before swooping down to make the kill. Ralph apparently noticed Reed as well.

"I don't think Reed was all that anxious to have you dance with me."

"I'm sure it doesn't matter."

Ralph chortled gleefully, obviously enjoying Reed's reaction. "Not if the looks he's giving me are any indication. I can't believe it. Reed Morgan is jealous," he said with another chuckle, leading her out of Reed's sight and into the dimly lit centre of the floor.

"I'm sure you're mistaken."

"Well, look at him."

All Ellen could see was Reed peering suspiciously at them across the crowded dance floor.

Ralph seemed overjoyed at Reed's behaviour. "This is too good to be true."

"What do you mean?"

"There isn't a woman in our department who wouldn't give her eye-teeth to go out with Reed."

Ellen was shocked, yet somehow unsurprised. "Oh?"

"Half the women there are in love with him and he ignores them. He's friendly, don't get me wrong. But it's all business. Every time a single woman gets transferred into our area it takes a week, maybe two, for her to fall for Reed. The rest of us guys just stand back and shake our heads. But with Reed otherwise occupied, we might have a chance."

"He *is* wonderful," Ellen admitted, managing to keep a courteous smile on her face. What Ralph was describing sounded so much like her own feelings that she couldn't doubt the truth of what he said.

Ralph arched his thick brows and studied her. "You too?"

"I'm afraid so."

"What's this guy got?" He sighed expressively, shaking his head. "Is it bottled?"

"Unfortunately, I don't think so," Ellen responded lightly, liking Ralph more and more. His approach might have been a bit overpowering at first, but he was honest and compelling in his own right. "I don't imagine you have much trouble with the ladies."

"As long as I don't bring them around Reed, I'm fine." A smile swept his face. "The best thing that could happen would be if he were to marry. I don't suppose that's in the offing between you two?"

He was so blithely serious that Ellen laughed. "Sorry."

"You're sure?"

Ralph was probably referring to some rumour he'd heard about Danielle. "There's another woman he's seeing. They've known each other for a long time and apparently, they're fairly serious," she explained, keeping her voice calmly detached.

"I don't believe it," Ralph countered, frowning.

"Reed wouldn't be tossing daggers at my back if he was involved with someone else. One thing I suspect about this guy, he's a one-woman man."

Ellen closed her eyes, trying to shut out the small pain that came from the direction of her heart. She didn't know what to believe about Reed anymore. All she could do was hold on to the moment. Wasn't that what she'd told him earlier—that they'd have to take things day by day? She didn't want to read too much into his actions. She couldn't. She was on the brink of falling in love with him...if she hadn't already. To allow herself to think that he might feel the same way was surely asking for trouble. For heartbreak.

The music ended and Ralph gently let her go. "I'd best return you to Reed or he's likely to come after me."

"Thank you for...everything."

"You're welcome, Ellen." With one hand at the back of her waist, he steered her toward Reed.

They were within a few feet of him when Danielle suddenly appeared. She seemed to have come out of nowhere. "Reed!" She was laughing delightedly, flinging herself into his arms and kissing him intimately. "Oh, darling, you're so right. Being together is more important than any ski trip. I'm so sorry. Will you forgive me?"

CHAPTER EIGHT

"ELLEN," RALPH ASKED. "Are you all right?"

"I'm fine," she lied.

"Sure you are," he mocked, sliding his arm around her waist and guiding her back to the dance floor. "I take it the blonde is Woman Number One?"

"You got it." The anger was beginning to build inside her. "Beautiful too, you'll notice."

"Well, you aren't exactly chopped liver."

She gave a small, mirthless laugh. "Nice of you to say so, but in comparison, I come in a poor second."

"I wouldn't say that."

"Then why can't you take your eyes off Danielle?"

"Danielle. Hmm." He dragged his gaze away from the other woman and stared blankly into Ellen's round eyes. "Sorry." For her part, Ellen instinctively turned her back to Reed, unable to bear the sight of him holding and kissing another woman.

"Someone must have gotten their wires crossed."

"Like me," Ellen muttered. She'd been an idiot to assume that Reed had meant anything by his invitation. He'd just needed someone to escort to this party, she fumed, and his first choice hadn't been available. She was a substitute, and a poor one at that.

"What do you want to do?"

Ellen frowned, her thoughts fragmented. "I don't know yet. Give me a minute to think."

"You two could always fight for him."

"The stronger woman takes the spoils? No, thanks. I'm not much into mud wrestling." Despite herself she laughed. It certainly would have created a diversion at this formal, rather staid party.

Craning his neck, Ralph peered over at the other couple. "Reed doesn't seem too pleased to see her."

"I can imagine. The situation has put him in a bit of a bind."

"I admit it's unpleasant for you, but, otherwise, I'm enjoying this immensely."

Who wouldn't? The scene was just short of being comical. "I thought you said Reed was a one-woman man."

"I guess I stand corrected."

Ellen was making a few corrections herself, revising some cherished ideas about a certain Reed Morgan.

"I don't suppose you'd consider staying with me the rest of the evening?" Ralph suggested hopefully.

"Consider it? I'd say it was the best offer I've had in weeks." She might feel like a fool, but she didn't plan to hang around here looking like one.

Ralph nudged her and bent his head to whisper in her ear, "Reed's staring at us. And he doesn't look pleased."

With a determination born of anger and pride, she forced a smile to her lips and gazed adoringly up at Ralph. "How am I doing?" she asked, batting her thick lashes at him.

"Wonderful, wonderful." He swung her energetically around to the beat of the music. "Uh-oh, here he comes."

Reed weaved his way through the dancing couples and tapped Ralph on the shoulder. "I'm cutting in."

Ellen tightened her grip on Reed's colleague, silently pleading with him to stay. "Sorry, old buddy, but Ellen's with me now that your lady friend has arrived."

"Ellen?" Reed's eyes narrowed as he stared intently into hers. The other dancing couples were waltzing around and glancing curiously at the party of three that had formed in the centre of the room.

She couldn't remember ever seeing anyone look more furious than Reed did at this moment. "Maybe I'd just better leave," she said in a low, faltering voice.

"I'll take you home," Ralph offered, dropping his hand to her waist.

"You came with me. You'll leave with me." Reed grasped her hand, pulling her toward him.

"Obviously you made provisions," Ellen countered, "just on the off chance Danielle showed up. How else did she get in here?"

"How the hell am I supposed to know? She probably told the manager she was with me."

"And apparently she is," Ellen hissed.

"Maybe Reed and I should wrestle to decide the winner," Ralph suggested, glancing at Ellen and sharing a comical grin.

"Maybe."

Clearly, Reed saw no humour in the situation. Anger darkened his handsome face, and a muscle twitched in his jaw as the tight rein on his patience slipped.

Ralph withdrew his hand. "Go ahead and dance. It's obvious you two have a lot to talk about."

Reed took Ellen in his arms, his grip rough and almost painful.

"You're hurting," she cried.

His hold instantly relaxed. "I suppose you're furious."

"Have I got anything to be angry about?" Now that the initial shock had worn off, and the anger had dissipated, she was beginning to find some humour in the situation.

"Hell, yes. But I want a chance to explain."

"Don't bother. I've got the picture."

"And I'm sure you don't." His eyes demanded that she look up at him.

Ellen stubbornly refused for as long as she could, but the pull of his gaze was too compelling to resist. "It doesn't matter. Ralph said he'd take me home and…"

"I've already explained my feelings on that subject."

"Wonderful, Reed. Your Porsche seats two. Is Danielle supposed to sit on my lap?"

"She came uninvited. Let her find her own way home."

"You don't mean that."

"The hell I don't."

"You can't do that to Danielle. It would humiliate her." Ellen didn't bother to mention what it was doing to her.

"She deserves it."

"Reed, no." Her hold on his forearm tightened. "This is unpleasant enough for all of us. Don't complicate it."

The song ended and the music faded from the room. Reed fastened his hand on Ellen's elbow, guiding her across the floor to where Danielle was standing with Ralph. The two were sipping champagne.

"Hello again," Ellen began amicably, doing her utmost to appear friendly, trying to smooth over an already awkward situation.

"Hello." Danielle stared at her curiously, obviously not recognising Ellen.

"You remember Ellen Cunningham, don't you?" Reed stated drily.

"Not that college girl your brother invited—" Danielle stopped abruptly, shock etched starkly on her perfect features. "You're Ellen Cunningham?"

"In the flesh." Still trying to keep things light, she cocked her head toward Ralph and spoke stagily out of the side of her mouth, turning the remark into a farcical aside. "I wasn't at my sterling best when we met the first time."

"You were fiddling around with that electrical outlet and Reed was horrified," Danielle inserted, her voice completely humourless, her eyes narrowed assessingly. "You didn't even look like a girl."

"She does now." Ralph beamed her a brilliant smile.

"Yes." Danielle swallowed, her face puckered with concern. "She looks very...nice."

"Thank you." Ellen dipped her head.

"I've made a terrible mess of things," Danielle continued, casually handing her half-empty glass to a passing waiter. "Reed mentioned the party weeks ago and Mom and I had this ski party planned. I told him I couldn't attend and then I felt terribly guilty because Reed's been such an angel escorting me to all the charity balls."

Ellen didn't hear a word of explanation beyond the fact that Reed had originally asked Danielle to the party. The other woman had just confirmed Ellen's suspicions, and the hurt went through her like a thousand needles. He'd invited her only because Danielle couldn't attend.

"There's no problem," Ellen said in a colourless voice. "I understand how these things happen. He asked you first; you stay and I'll leave."

"I couldn't do that."

Reed's eyes were saying the same thing. Ellen ignored him, and she ignored Danielle. Slipping her hand around Ralph's arm, she looked up at him and smiled, silently thanking him for being her friend. "It isn't any problem, I assure you. Ralph's been wonderful."

Reed's expression was impassive, almost aloof, as she swung around to look at him. "I'm sure you won't mind if Ralph takes me home."

"How understanding of you," Danielle simpered, locking her arm around Reed's.

"It's no problem. I'd much prefer this to mud wrestling."

"Mud wrestling?" Danielle clapped her hands with delight. "What a bizarrely fascinating idea."

Ralph choked on a swallow of his drink, his face turning several shades of red as he struggled to hide his amusement. The only one who revealed no sense of humour was Reed, whose face grew more and more shadowed.

The band struck up a lively song and the dance floor quickly filled. "Come on, Reed," Danielle said, her blue eyes eager. "Let's dance." Leading the way, she tugged at Reed's hand and gave a sensuous little wriggle of her hips. "You know how much I love to boogie."

So Reed had done his share of dancing with Danielle—probably at all those charity balls she'd mentioned. Ellen had guessed as much and yet he'd tried to give her the impression that he rarely danced.

But examining the stiff way Reed held himself now, Ellen could almost believe him.

Ralph placed a gentle hand on her shoulder. "I don't know about you, but I'm ready to get out of here."

Watching Reed hold Danielle in his arms was absurdly painful; her throat muscles constricted in an effort to hold back tears and she simply nodded her agreement.

"Did you have dinner? I'm starved."

Ellen blinked. Dinner. She couldn't remember. "No, I don't think... I'm not really hungry," she amended. The afternoon had been spent getting ready for the party, and she hadn't thought about food, assuming they'd have something to eat later in the evening.

"Sure you're hungry," Ralph insisted. "We'll stop off at a nice restaurant before I drive you home. I know where Reed's place is, so I know where you live. Don't look so shocked. I figured it out from what you and Danielle were saying. But don't worry, I understand— impoverished students sharing a house, and all that. So, what do you say? We'll have dinner and get home two hours after Reed. That should set him thinking."

Ellen didn't feel in any mood to play games at Reed's expense. "That's not a good idea."

Ralph's jovial expression sobered. "You've got it bad."

"I'll be fine."

His fingers stroked the back of her neck. "I know you will. Come on, let's get out of here."

The night that had begun with such promise had evaporated so quickly, leaving a residue of uncertainties and suspicions. As they neared the house, her composure gradually crumpled until she was nervously twisting the delicate strap of her beaded evening bag over and over again between her fingers. To his credit, Ralph attempted to carry the conversation, but her responses became less and less animated. She just wanted to get home and bury her head in her pillow.

By the time Ralph pulled up in front of the Capitol Hill house, they were both silent.

"Would you like to come in for coffee?" she offered. The illusion she'd created earlier of flippant humour was gone now. She hurt, and every time she blinked, a picture of Danielle dancing with Reed came to her mind. How easy it was to visualise the other woman's arms around his neck, pressing her voluptuous body against his. The image tormented Ellen with every breath she drew.

"No, I think I'll make it an early night."

"Liar," she teased affectionately. "Thank you. I couldn't have done it without you."

"No problem. Listen, if you want a shoulder to cry on, I'm available."

She dropped her gaze to the tightly coiled strap of her bag. "I'm fine. Really."

Gently he patted her hand. "Somehow I don't quite believe that." Opening the door, he came around to her side and helped her out.

On the top step of the porch, Ellen softly kissed his cheek. "Thanks again."

"Good night, Ellen."

"'Night." She took out her keys and unlocked the front door. Pushing it open, she discovered that the house was oddly dark and oddly deserted. It was still relatively early and she'd have expected the boys to be around. But not having to make excuses to them was a blessing she wasn't about to question.

As she removed her coat and headed for the stairs,

she noticed the shadows bouncing around the darkened living room. She walked over to investigate and, two steps into the room, caught the sound of soft romantic music drifting from the stereo. A flicker of candlelight could be seen from the formal dining room.

Ellen stood there paralysed, taking in the romantic scene before her. A bottle of wine and two glasses were set out on the coffee table. A gentle fire blazed in the brick fireplace. And the soft violin music seemed to assault her from all sides.

"Derek," she called out.

Silence.

"All right, Pat and Monte. I know you're out there somewhere."

Silence.

"I'd suggest the three of you do away with this... stuff before Reed returns. He's with Danielle and not in any mood for games." With that, she marched up the stairs, uncaring if they heard her or not.

"With Danielle?" she heard a male voice shout after her.

"What happened?"

Ellen pretended not to hear.

THE MORNING SUN sneaked into her window, splashing the pillow where Ellen lay awake staring sightlessly at the ceiling. Sooner or later she'd have to get out of bed, but she couldn't see any reason to rush the process. Besides, the longer she stayed up here, the greater her chances of missing Reed. The unpleasantness of facing him wasn't going to vanish with time, but she might be able to postpone it for a morning. Although she had to wonder whether Reed was any more keen on seeing her than she was on seeing him. Anyway she could always kill time by dragging out her algebra books and studying for the exam—but that was almost as distasteful as facing Reed.

No, she decided suddenly, she'd stay in her room until she was weak with hunger. Checking her wristwatch, she figured that would be about another five minutes.

Someone knocked on her bedroom door. Sitting up, Ellen pulled the sheets over her breasts. "Who is it?" she called out, not particularly eager to talk to anyone.

Reed threw open the door and stalked inside. He stood in the middle of the room with his hands on his hips and barked, "Are you planning to stay up here the rest of your life?"

"The idea has distinct possibilities." She glared back at him, her eyes flashing with outrage and ill humour. "By the way, you'll note that I asked who was at the door. I didn't say, 'come in.'" Her voice rose to a mockingly high pitch. "You might have walked in on me when I was dressing."

A smile crossed his boyish mouth. "Is that an invitation?"

"Absolutely not." She rose to a kneeling position, taking the sheets and blankets with her. She pointed a finger in the direction of the door. "Would you kindly leave? I'd like to get dressed."

"Don't let me stop you."

"Reed, please," she said, irritably. "I'm not in any mood to exchange witticisms with you."

"I'm not leaving until we talk."

"Unfair. I haven't had my cup of tea and my mouth feels like the bottom of Puget Sound."

"All right," he agreed reluctantly. "I'll give you ten minutes."

"How generous of you."

"Considering my frame of mind since you walked out on me last night, I consider it most charitable of me."

"Walked out on you!" She flew off the bed. Her mouth dropped so wide open, she felt as though her chin had lost its support. "That's rich."

"Ten minutes," he repeated, his voice dropping low in warning.

The whole time Ellen was dressing, she fumed. Reed had some nerve accusing her of walking out on him. He obviously didn't have any idea what it had cost her to leave him at that party with Danielle. He was thinking only of his own feelings, showing no regard for hers. He hadn't even acknowledged that she'd swallowed her pride to save them all from an extremely embarrassing situation.

Four male faces met hers when she appeared in the kitchen. "Good morning," she said with false enthusiasm.

The three boys looked sheepishly away. "'Morning," they droned. Each found something at the table to occupy his hands. Pat examined the grooves on his basketball as though seeking some insidious leak. Monte read the back of the cereal box and Derek folded the front page of the paper, pretending to read it.

"Ellen and I would like a few minutes of privacy," Reed announced, frowning at the three boys.

Derek, Monte and Pat stood up simultaneously.

"I don't know that there's anything we have to say that the boys can't hear," she contradicted.

The three youths reclaimed their chairs, looking with bright-eyed expectancy first to Reed and then to Ellen.

Reed's scowl deepened. "Can't you see that Ellen

and I need to talk?'' He pointedly directed his comment to the boys.

"There's nothing to discuss,'' Ellen insisted, pouring boiling water into the mug and dipping the tea bag in the water several times before tossing it in the bin.

"Yes, there is,'' Reed countered.

"Maybe it would be best if we did leave,'' Derek hedged, noticeably uneasy with his brother's anger and Ellen's feigned composure.

"You walk out of this room and there will be no packed lunches next week,'' Ellen cried softly, leaning against the counter and sipping her tea.

"I'm staying.'' Monte crossed his arms over his chest as though preparing for a long standoff.

Ellen knew she could count on Monte; his stomach would always take precedence. Childishly, she flashed Reed a saucy grin. He wasn't going to bulldoze her into any confrontation.

"Either you're out of here *now*, or you won't have a place to *live* next week,'' Reed flared back. At Derek's smug expression, Reed added, "And that includes you, little brother.''

The boys exchanged shocked glances. "Sorry, Ellen,'' Derek mumbled on his way out of the kitchen. "I told Michelle I'd be over in a few minutes anyway.'' Without another moment's hesitation, Reed's brother was out the door.

"Well?'' Hands placed on his hips, Reed approached Monte and Pat.

"Yes, well...I guess maybe I should probably...'' Pat looked to Ellen for guidance, his resolve wavering.

"Go ahead.'' She dismissed them both with a wave of her hand.

"Are you sure you want us to go?" Monte asked anxiously, glancing at Reed and back at Ellen again.

Ellen smiled her appreciation at this small display of mettle. "I'll be perfectly all right."

The sound of the door swinging back and forth echoed through the emptiness of the large kitchen. Ellen drew a deep, calming breath and turned to confront Reed, who didn't look all that pleased to have her alone now, though he'd certainly gone to some lengths to arrange it. His face was pinched, and fine lines etched his eyes and mouth. Either he'd had a late night or he hadn't slept at all. Ellen decided it must have been the former.

"Well, I'm here within ten minutes, just as you decreed. If you've got something to say, say it."

"Don't rush me," he snapped.

Crossing her arms over her chest, Ellen released an exaggerated sigh. "First you want to talk to me—then you're not sure. This sounds amazingly like someone who asked me to a party once. First he wanted me with him—then he didn't."

"I wanted you there last night."

"Was I talking about you?" she asked in mock innocence.

"You're not making this easy." He ploughed his fingers through his hair, the awkward movement at odds with the self-control he usually exhibited.

"Listen," she breathed, casting her eyes down. "You don't need to explain anything. I have a fairly accurate picture of what happened."

"I doubt that." But he didn't elaborate.

"I can understand why you'd prefer Danielle's company."

"I didn't. That had to be one of the most awkward moments of my life. I wanted you—not Danielle."

Sure, she mused sarcastically. That was the reason he'd introduced her to so few people. She'd had plenty of time in the past twelve hours to think. If she hadn't been so blinded by the stars in her eyes, she would have figured it out sooner. Reed had taken her to his company's party and kept her shielded from the other guests; he hadn't wanted her talking to his friends and colleagues. At the time, she'd been highly complimented, assuming he wanted her all to himself. Now she understood the reason. The others knew he'd invited Danielle; they knew that Danielle usually accompanied him to these functions. The other woman had an official status in Reed's life; Ellen didn't.

"It wasn't your fault," she told him. "I understand what happened. Unfortunately, it was unavoidable."

"I'd rather Danielle had left instead of you." He walked to her side, deliberately taking the mug of tea from her hand and setting it on the counter. Slowly his arms came around her.

Ellen hadn't the will to resist. She closed her eyes as her arms reached around him, almost of their own accord. He felt so warm and vital.

"I want us to spend the day together."

Her earlier intention of studying for her algebra exam flew out the window at the mere mention of being with Reed. Despite all her hesitations, all her doubts and fears, she couldn't refuse this chance to be with him. Alone, the two of them. "All right," she answered softly.

"Ellen." His breath stirred the curls on the crown of her head. "There's something you should know."

"Hmm."

"I'm flying out tomorrow morning for two days."

Her eyes flew open. "How long?"

"Two days, but after that, I won't be leaving again until the Christmas holidays are over."

She answered him with a nod. Traveling was part of his job, and any woman in his life would have to accept that. She was touched that he felt so concerned for her. "That's fine," she whispered. "I understand."

Ellen couldn't fault Reed for the remainder of the weekend. Saturday afternoon, they went Christmas shopping at the Tacoma Mall. His choice of shopping area surprised her, since there were several in the immediate area, much closer than the forty-five-minute drive to Tacoma. But they had a good time, wandering from store to store. Before she knew it, Christmas would be upon them and this was the first opportunity she'd had to do any real shopping. With Reed's help, she picked out gifts for the boys and her brother.

"You'll like Bud," she told him, licking a chocolate ice-cream cone. They found a place to sit, with their packages gathered around them, and took a fifteen-minute break.

"I imagine I will." A flash of amusement lit his eyes, then he abruptly looked away.

Ellen lowered her ice-cream cone. "What's so funny? Have I got chocolate on my nose?"

"No."

"What, then?"

"You must have forgiven me for what happened at the party."

Her eyes narrowed. "What makes you say that?"

"The way you looked into the future and claimed I'd like your brother, as though you and I are going to have a long, meaningful relationship."

The ice cream suddenly became terribly important and Ellen licked away at it with an all-consuming energy. "I told you before that I feel things have to be one day at a time with us. There are too many variables in our...relationship." She waved the ice cream in his direction. "And I use that term loosely."

"There is a future for us."

"You seem mighty sure of yourself."

"I'm more certain of you." He said it so smoothly that Ellen wondered if she heard him right. She would have challenged his arrogant assumption, but just then, he glanced at his wristwatch and suggested a movie.

By the time they returned to the house it was close to midnight. He kissed her with a tenderness that somehow reminded her of an early-summer dawn, but his touch was as potent as a sultry August afternoon.

"Ellen?" he murmured into her hair.

"Hmm?"

"I think you'd better go upstairs now."

The warmth of his touch had melted away the last traces of icy reserve that the party had built around her fragile heart. She didn't want to leave him. "Why?"

His hands gripped her shoulders, pushing her apart from him, putting an arm's length between them. "Because if you don't leave now, I may climb those stairs with you."

At his straightforward, honest statement, Ellen swallowed and blinked twice. "I enjoyed today. Thank you, Reed." He dropped his arms and she placed a trembling hand on the railing. "Have a safe trip."

"I will." He took a step toward her. "I wish I didn't have to go." His hand cupped her chin and he drew her face toward his, claiming her mouth with a hunger that shook Ellen to the core. It took all her strength not to throw herself against him and wrap her arms around him again.

MONDAY AFTERNOON, when Ellen walked into the house after her classes, the three boys were waiting for her. They looked up at her with peculiar expressions on their faces, as though she were someone they'd never seen before and they couldn't understand how she'd wandered into their kitchen.

"All right, what gives?"

"Gives?" Derek asked.

"You've got that guilty look."

"*We're* not the guilty party," Pat announced.

"All right, you'd better let me know what's happened so I can deal with it before Reed gets back."

"You'll need to," Monte said, his hand on the kitchen door. He swung it open so that the dining-room table came into view. In the centre of the table was the largest bouquet of red roses Ellen had ever seen.

Her breath got trapped in her lungs as the shocked gasp slid from the back of her throat.

"Who…who sent those?"

"We thought you'd want to know so we took the liberty of reading the card."

Their prying barely registered in her numbed brain as she walked slowly into the room and removed the small card pinned to the bright red ribbon. It could have been Bud—but he didn't have the kind of money to buy roses. And if he did, Ellen suspected he wouldn't get them for his sister.

"Reed did it," Pat inserted eagerly.

"Reed?"

"We were as surprised as you."

Her gaze fell to the tiny envelope. She removed the

card, biting into her bottom lip when she read the message. *I miss you. Reed.*

"He said he misses you," Derek added.

"I see that."

"Good grief, he'll be back tomorrow. How can he possibly miss you in this short a time?"

"I don't know." Lovingly her finger caressed the petals of a dewy rosebud. They were so incredibly beautiful, but their message was far more dear.

"I bet this is his way of telling you he regrets what happened the night of the party," Derek murmured.

"Not that any of us actually knows what happened. We'd like to, you understand, but it'd be considered bad manners to ask," Pat explained. "That is, unless you'd like to share with us why he'd take you to the party and then come back alone."

"He didn't get in until three that morning, either." Monte said accusingly. "You aren't going to let him off so easy are you, Ellen?"

Bowing her head to smell the sweet fragrance, she closed her eyes. "Roses cover a multitude of sins."

"Reed's feeling guilty, I think," Derek said with authority. "But he cares, or else he wouldn't have gone to this much trouble."

"Maybe he just wants to keep the peace," Monte added as an afterthought. "My dad bought my mom flowers once for no apparent reason."

"We all live together. Reed's probably figured out that he had to do something if he wanted to maintain the status quo."

"Right," Ellen agreed tartly, scooping up the flowers to take to her room. Maybe it was selfish to deprive the boys of the flowers' beauty, but she didn't care.

They had been meant for her, as a private memento from Reed, and having them close was a comfort.

THE FOLLOWING DAY, Ellen cut her last morning class, knowing that Reed's flight arrived around noon. She could ill afford to skip algebra, but it wouldn't have done her any good to stay. The entire class time would have been spent thinking about Reed—so it made more sense to hurry home.

She stepped off the bus a block from the house and even from that distance she could see his truck parked in the driveway. It was the first—and only—thing she noticed. She sprinted toward home and dashed up the front steps.

Flinging open the door, she called breathlessly, "Anyone home?"

Both Reed and Derek came out of the kitchen.

Her eyes met Reed's from across the room. "Hi," she said in a low, husky voice. "Welcome home."

He took a step toward her, his warm gaze holding hers.

Neither spoke as Ellen threw her books on the sofa and advanced toward him.

He caught her around the waist as though he'd been away for months instead of days, hugging her fiercely.

Ellen savoured the warmth of his embrace, closing her eyes to the overwhelming emotion she suddenly felt. Reed was becoming far too important in her life. But she no longer had the power to resist him. If she ever had.

"His plane was right on time," Derek was saying. "And the airport was hardly busy."

Irritably, Reed tossed a look over his shoulder. "Little brother, get lost."

CHAPTER NINE

"I'VE GOT A PRACTICE GAME today," Pat said, his fork cutting into the syrup-laden pancakes. "Can you come?"

Ellen's eyes met Reed's in mute communication. No longer did they bother to hide their attraction to each other from the boys. They couldn't. "What time?"

"Six."

"I can be there."

"What about you, Reed?"

Reed wiped the corners of his mouth with the paper napkin. "Sorry, I've got a meeting. But I should be home in time for the victory celebration."

Ellen thrilled to the way the boys automatically linked her name and Reed's. It had been that way from the time he'd returned from his short trip. But then, they'd given the boys plenty of reason to think of her and Reed as a couple. He and Ellen were with each other every free moment, the time they spent together was exclusively theirs. And Ellen loved it that way. She loved Reed, she loved being with him...and she loved every single thing about him. Almost. His reticence on the subject of Danielle had her a little worried, but she pushed it to the back of her mind. She couldn't bring herself to question him; she'd just have to assume that the earlier relationship was over now. As far as she knew, Reed hadn't spoken to Danielle since the night of the Christmas party. Even stronger evidence was the fact that he drove his truck every day. The Porsche sat parked in the garage, gathering dust.

Reed stood up and delivered his breakfast plate to the sink. "Ellen, walk me to the door?"

"Sure."

"For Pete's sake, the door's only two feet away," Derek scoffed, feeling noticeably brave. "You travel all over the world and all of a sudden you need someone to show you the way to the back door."

Ellen didn't see the look the two brothers exchanged, but Derek's mouth curved upward into a knowing grin. "Oh, I get it. Hey, guys, they want to be alone a minute. If we were a bit more into this romance thing we would have recognised it sooner."

"Just a minute." Monte wolfed down the last of his breakfast, still chewing as he carried his plate to the counter.

Ellen was mildly surprised that Reed didn't comment on Derek's needling, but she supposed they were becoming accustomed to it.

One by one, the boys left the kitchen. Silently, Reed stood by the back door, waiting. When the last one had departed, he slipped his arms around Ellen.

"You're getting mighty brave," she whispered, smiling into his intense green eyes. Lately, Reed seemed almost to invite the boys' comments. And when they responded, the teasing rolled off his back like rain off a well-waxed car.

"If you knew what I was thinking you'd be in the other room with Derek and the others." He slid a hand around the back of her neck and into her hair.

"Oh?" Despite her efforts not to blush, Ellen felt her face grow warm.

"It's torture being around you every day and not touching you," he said as his mouth inched closer to hers. "But it's a sweet torment," he concluded just before his mouth descended on hers in an excruciatingly slow kiss that seemed to melt Ellen's very bones.

Reality seemed light-years away as she clung to him, and she struggled to recover her equilibrium. "Reed," she pleaded, "you've got to get to work."

"Right." But he didn't stop kissing her and his grip seemed to tighten, arching her closer and closer.

"And I've got class." If he didn't stop soon, they'd both reach the point of no return. Each time he held and kissed her, it became more and more difficult to break away.

His hand cupped the throbbing fullness of her breast. His thumb teased her nipple to a hard peak and Ellen moaned. "Reed…"

"I know. I know." His throaty voice echoed through the fog that held her captive. "Now isn't the time or the place."

Her arms around his middle tightened as she burrowed her face against the hard muscles of his chest. With one heartbeat, she was telling Reed they had to stop and with the next, she refused to release him.

"I'll be late tonight," he murmured into her hair.

"Okay." She remembered that he'd told Pat something about a meeting.

"Let's go out to dinner." His warm breath fanned her temple. "Just the two of us, alone. I've come to love being alone with you."

Ellen wanted to cry with frustration. "I can't. Exams start next week and I've got to study."

"Need any help?"

"Only one subject." She looked up at him and sadly

shook her head. "I don't suppose you can guess which one."

"Aren't you glad you've got me?"

"Eternally grateful." Ellen would never have believed that algebra could be her greatest downfall and her greatest ally. If it weren't for that one subject, she wouldn't have had the excuse to sit down with Reed every night to sort through her homework problems. But then, lately, she hadn't needed an excuse.

"We'll see how grateful you are when grades come out."

"I hate to disappoint you, but it's going to take a lot more than your excellent tutoring to rescue me from my fate this time." The exam was crucial. If she didn't do well, she would probably end up repeating the class. The thought filled her with dread. It would be a waste of her time and, even worse, a waste of precious funds.

Reed kissed her lightly before reluctantly releasing her. "Have a good day."

"You, too." She stood at the door until he'd climbed inside the pickup and waved to him when he backed out of the driveway.

Knowing she'd best get the stars out of her eyes before she had to confront the boys, Ellen loaded the dirty dishes into the dishwasher and cleaned off the counter, humming as she worked.

One of the boys knocked on the door. "Is it safe to come in yet?"

"Come on in. I'm waiting."

All three innocently strolled into the kitchen. "You and Reed are getting a little thick, aren't you?"

Running hot tap water into the sink, Ellen nodded. "I suppose."

"Reed hasn't seen Danielle in a long time."

Ellen didn't comment, but she did feel encouraged that Derek's conclusion was the same as hers.

"You know what I think?" he asked, hopping onto the counter so she was forced to look at him.

"I can only guess."

"I think Reed's getting serious about you."

"That's nice."

"*Nice*—is that all you can say?" He gave her a look of disgust. "That's my brother you're talking about. He could have any woman he wanted."

"I know." Coyly, she smiled at him as she poured soap into the dishwasher, then closed the door and turned the dial. Instantly the sound of rushing water could be heard, drowning out Derek's next comment.

"Sorry, I've got to get to class. I'll talk to you later." Still humming, she sauntered past Pat and Monte, offering them a friendly smile.

"She's got it bad." Ellen heard Monte comment. "She hardly even bakes anymore. Remember how she used to make cookies and cakes every week?"

"I didn't know love did that to a person," Pat grumbled.

"I'm not sure I like Ellen in love," Monte flung after her as she stepped out the door.

"I just hope she doesn't get hurt."

The boy's remarks echoed in her mind as the day wore on. Ellen didn't need to hear their doubts; she had more than enough of her own. Sudden qualms assailed her heart when she least expected it—like during algebra class, or during the long afternoon that followed.

But one look at Reed that evening and all her anxieties evaporated. As soon as she entered the house, she walked straight into the living room, hoping to find him there, and she did.

He folded the newspaper when she walked in. "How was the game?"

"Pat scored seventeen points and is a hero. Unfortunately, the Huskies lost." Sometimes, that was just the way life went: winning small victories yet losing the war.

"Something smells good." Monte followed her into the kitchen, sniffing appreciatively.

"There's a roast in the oven and an apple pie on the counter," she answered him, trading her coat for a terry-cloth apron. She'd bought the pie in hopes of celebrating the Huskies' victory. Now it would soothe their loss. "I imagine everyone's starved."

"I am," Monte announced.

"That goes without saying," Reed called from the living room, picking up the newspaper again.

Ellen checked the oven, shocked to discover that her hands were trembling. It was unfair that just seeing Reed would have this effect on her. As Monte had declared earlier in the day, she had it bad.

The evening was spent at the kitchen table, poring over her textbooks. Reed came in twice to make her a fresh cup of tea. Standing behind her chair, he glanced over her shoulder at the psychology book.

"Do you want me to get you anything?" she asked. This was the second time he'd strolled into the kitchen. She was studying there, rather than in her room, just to be close to Reed. Admittedly, her room offered more seclusion, but she preferred being around people—one person, actually.

"I don't need a thing." He kissed the top of her head. "And if I did, I'd get it myself. You study."

"Thanks."

"When's the first exam?"

"Monday."

He nodded. "You'll do fine."

"I don't want fine," she countered nervously. "I want fantastic."

"Then no doubt you'll do fantastic."

"Where are the boys?" The house was uncommonly silent for a weekday evening.

"Studying. I'm pleased to see they're taking exams as seriously as you are."

"We have to," she mumbled, her gaze dropping to her notebook.

"All right. I get the message. I'll quit pestering you."

"You're not pestering me."

"Right." He bent his head to kiss the side of her neck as his fingers sensuously stroked her arms.

Shivers raced down her spine and Ellen closed her eyes, unconsciously swaying toward him. "Now...now you're pestering me."

He chuckled, leaving her alone at the kitchen table when she would so much rather have had him with her every minute of every day.

THE FOLLOWING MORNING, Ellen stood by the door, watching Reed pull out of the driveway.

"Why do you do that?" Pat questioned, giving her a glance that said she looked utterly foolish standing there.

"Do what?" She decided the best reaction was to pretend that she didn't have the foggiest notion what he was talking about.

"Watch Reed leave every morning. He's not likely to have an accident pulling out of the driveway."

Ellen didn't have the courage to confess that she watched so she could see whether Reed drove the pickup or the Porsche. It would sound so asinine to admit she gauged their relationship by which vehicle he chose to drive that day.

"She watches because she can't bear to see him go," Derek answered when she didn't. "From everything I hear, Michelle does the same thing. What can I say? The woman's crazy about me."

"Oh, yeah?" Monte snickered. "And that's the reason she was with Rick Bloomingfield the other day."

"She was?" Derek sounded completely shocked. "There's a logical explanation for that. Michelle and I have an understanding."

"Sure you do," Monte teased. "She can date whoever she wants and you can date whoever you want. Some 'understanding.'"

To prove to the boys that she wasn't as badly smitten as they assumed—and maybe to prove the same thing to herself—Ellen didn't watch Reed leave for work the next two mornings. It was silly, anyway. So what if he drove his Porsche? He had the car, and she could see no reason for him to not drive it. Except for her unspoken insecurities. And there seemed to be plenty of those. As Derek had claimed earlier in the week, Reed could have any woman he wanted. And why he would want her was still a mystery to Ellen.

She was the first one home that afternoon. Derek was probably sorting things out with Michelle, Pat had basketball practice and no doubt Monte was in someone's kitchen.

Gathering the ingredients for her special spaghetti

sauce, she arranged them neatly on the counter. She was busy reading over her recipe when the phone rang.

"Hello," she greeted cheerfully.

"This is Capitol Hill Cleaners. Mr. Morgan's evening suit is ready."

"Pardon?" Reed hadn't told her he was having anything cleaned. Ellen usually offered to pick up his dry cleaning because it was no inconvenience to stop there on her way home from school. And she hadn't minded at all. As silly as it seemed, she'd felt very wifely doing that for him.

"Is it for Reed or Derek?" It was just like Derek to forget to mention something like that.

"The slip says it's for a Mr. Reed Morgan."

"Oh?"

"Is there a problem with picking it up early? He brought it in yesterday and told us he had to have it this evening."

This evening? Reed was going out tonight?

"From what he said, this is something special."

Well, he wouldn't wear a suit to a barbecue. "I'll let him know."

"Thank you. Oh, and be sure to mention that we close at six tonight."

"Yes, I will."

A strange numbness overpowered Ellen's mind as she replaced the receiver. Something was wrong. Something was very, very wrong. Without even realising it, she moved rapidly through the kitchen and then outside.

Repeatedly, Reed had told her the importance of reading a problem in algebra. Read it carefully, he always said, and don't make any quick assumptions. It seemed crazy to remember that now. But he was right.

She couldn't jump to conclusions just because he was going out for the evening. He certainly had every right to do so. She was suddenly furious with herself. All those times he'd offered information about Danielle and she'd refused to listen, trying to play it so cool, trying to appear so blithely unconcerned when on the inside she was dying to know what he had to say.

By the time she reached the garage she was trembling, but it wasn't from the cold December air. She knew without looking that Reed had driven his sports car to work. The door creaked as she pushed it open to discover the pickup, sitting there in all its glory.

"Okay, he drove his Porsche. That doesn't have to mean anything. He isn't necessarily seeing Danielle. There's probably a logical explanation for this." Even if he was seeing Danielle, she had no right to say anything. They'd made no promises to each other.

Rubbing the chill from her bare arms, Ellen returned to the house. But the kitchen's warmth did little to chase away the bitter cold that cut her to the heart. Ellen moved numbly toward the telephone and ran her finger down the long list of numbers that hung on the wall beside it. When she located the one for Reed's office, she quickly punched out the seven numbers, then waited, her mind in turmoil.

"Mr. Morgan's office," came the efficient voice.

"Hello...this is Ellen Cunningham. I live, that is, I'm a friend of Mr. Morgan's."

"Yes, I remember seeing you the night of the Christmas party," the voice responded warmly. "We didn't have a chance to meet. Would you like me to put you through to Mr. Morgan?"

"No," she said hastily. "Could you give him a message?" Not waiting for a reply, she continued, "Tell him his suit is ready at the cleaners for that…party tonight.''

"Oh good, he wanted me to call. Thanks for saving me the trouble. Was there anything else?''

Moisture welled in the corners of Ellen's eyes, wetting her lashes. "No, that's it.''

Being reminded by Reed's secretary that they hadn't met the night of the Christmas party forcefully brought to Ellen's attention how few of his friends she did know. None, really. He'd even gone out of his way *not* to introduce her to people.

"Just a minute,'' Ellen cried, her hand clenching the receiver. "There *is* something else you can tell Mr. Morgan. Tell him goodbye.'' With that, she severed the connection.

A tear rolled down her cheek, searing a path as it made its way to her chin. Her mind was buzzing. She'd been a fool not to have seen the situation more clearly. Reed had a good thing going, with her living at the house. She was a hair's breadth from falling in love with him. Hell, she was already there and anyone looking at her knew it. It certainly wasn't any secret from the boys. She cooked his meals, ran his errands, mended his clothes. How convenient she'd become. How handy and useful she'd been to the smooth running of his household.

But Reed had never said a word about his feelings. Sure, they'd gone out, but always to places where no one was likely to recognise him. And the one time Reed did see someone he knew, he'd pretended he wasn't with her. And when he *had* included her in a social event, he'd only introduced her to a handful of people, as though…as though he didn't really want others to know her. As it turned out, that evening had been a disaster, and apparently, he'd decided to take Danielle with him this time. The other woman was far more attuned to the social graces.

She'd let Reed escort Danielle tonight. Fine. But she was going to quit making life so pleasant for him. How appropriate that she now used the old servants' quarters, she thought bitterly. Because that was all she meant to him—a servant. Well, no more. She would never be content to live a backstairs life. If Reed didn't want to be seen with her, or include her in his life, that was his decision. But she couldn't…she *wouldn't* continue to live this way.

Without analysing her actions, Ellen punched out a second set of numbers.

"Charlie, it's Ellen," she said quickly, doing her best to swallow back tears.

"Ellen? It doesn't sound like you."

"I know." The tightness in her chest extended all the way to her throat, choking off her breath until it escaped in a sob.

"Ellen, are you all right?"

"Yes…no." The fact that she'd called Charlie was a sign of her desperation. He was so sweet and she didn't want to do anything to hurt him. "Charlie, I hate to ask, but I need a friend."

"I'm here."

He said it without the least hesitation, and his unquestioning loyalty caused her to weep all the louder. "Oh, Charlie, I've got to find a place to live and I need to do it today."

"My sister's got a friend looking for a roommate. Do you want me to call her?"

"Please." Straightening, she wiped the tears from her face. Charlie might have had his faults, but he'd recognised the panic in her voice and immediately assumed control. Just now, that was what she needed—a friend to temporarily take charge of things.

"How soon can you talk to her?"

"Now. I'll call her and get right back to you. On second thoughts, I'll come directly to your place. If you can't stay with Patty's friend, my parents will put you up."

"Oh, Charlie, how can I ever thank you?"

The sound of his chuckle was like a clean, fresh breeze. "I'll come up with a way later." His voice softened. "You know the way I feel about you, Ellen. If you only want me for a friend, I understand. But I'm determined to be one hell of a good friend."

The back door closed with a bang. "Is anyone home?"

Guiltily, Ellen turned around, coming face to face with Monte. She replaced the telephone receiver, took a deep breath and squared her shoulders. She'd hoped to get away without having to talk to anyone.

"Ellen?" Concern clouded his youthful face. "What's wrong? You look like you've been crying." He narrowed his eyes. "You have been crying. What happened?"

"Nothing." She took a minute to wipe her nose with a tissue. "Listen, I'll be up in my room, but I'd appreciate some time alone, so don't come get me unless it's important."

"Sure. Anything you say. Are you sick? Should I call Reed?"

"No," she fairly shouted at him, then instantly regretted reacting so harshly. "Please don't contact him...he's busy tonight anyway." She rubbed a hand over her eyes. "And listen, about dinner—"

"Hey, don't worry. I can cook."

"You?" This wasn't the time to get into an argument. How messy he made the kitchen was no longer her concern. "There's a recipe on the counter if you want to tackle spaghetti sauce."

"Sure. I can do that. How long am I suppose to boil the noodles?"

One of her lesser concerns at the moment was boiling noodles. "Just read the back of the package."

Already he was rolling up his sleeves. "I'll take care of everything. You go lie down and do whatever it is women do when they're crying and pretending they're not."

"Right," she returned evenly. "I'll do that." Only in this case, she wasn't going to lie across her bed, burying her face in her pillow. She was going to pack up everything she owned and cart it away before Reed even had a hint she was leaving.

Sniffling as she worked, Ellen dumped the contents of her drawers into open suitcases. A couple of times she stopped to blow her nose. She detested tears. At the age of fifteen, she'd broken her leg and gritted her teeth against the agony. But she hadn't shed a tear. Now she wept as though it were the end of the world. Why, oh why, did her emotions have to be so unpredictable?

Carrying her suitcases down the first flight of stairs, she paused on the boys' floor to shift the weight of the heavy load. Because she was concentrating on her task and not watching where she was going, she walked headlong into Derek. "Sorry," she muttered.

"Ellen." He glanced at her suitcases and said her name as though he'd unexpectedly stumbled into the Queen of Sheba. "What...what are you doing?"

"Moving."

"Moving? But why?"

"It's a long story."

"You're crying." He sounded even more shocked by her tears than by the fact that she was moving out of the house.

"It's Reed, isn't it? What did he do?"

"He didn't do a thing. Stay out of it, Derek. I mean that."

He looked stunned. "Sure." He stepped aside and stuck his hand in his side pocket. "Anything you say."

She made a second trip downstairs, this time carting a couple of tote bags and the clothes from her closet, which she draped over the top of the two suitcases. There wasn't room in her luggage for everything. She realised she'd have to put the rest of her belongings in boxes.

Convinced she'd find a few empty cardboard boxes in the garage, she stormed through the kitchen and out the back door. Muttering between themselves, Monte and Derek followed her. Soon her movements resembled a small parade.

"Will you two stop it," she flared, whirling around and confronting them. The tears had dried now and her face burned red with the heat of anger and regret.

"We just want to know what happened," Monte interjected.

"Or is this going to be another one of your 'stay tuned' responses?" Derek asked.

"I'm moving out. I don't think I can make it any plainer than that."

"But why?"

"That's none of your business." She left them

standing with mouths gaping open as she trooped up the back stairs to her rooms.

Heedlessly she tossed her things into the two boxes, more intent on escaping than on taking the proper care to ensure that nothing broke in the process. When she got to the vase that had held the roses Reed had sent her, Ellen paused and hugged it to her breast. Tears burned for release and with a monumental effort she managed to forestall them by taking in deep breaths and blinking rapidly. Setting the vase down, she decided to leave it behind. As much as possible, she wanted to leave Reed in this house and not carry the memories of him around with her like a constant, throbbing ache. That would be hard enough without taking the vase along as a constant reminder of what she'd once felt.

The scene that met her at the foot of the stairs was enough to make her stop in her tracks. The three boys were involved in a shouting match, each in turn blaming the others for Ellen's unexpected decision to move out.

"It's your fault," Derek accused Monte. "If you weren't so concerned with your stomach, she'd stay."

"My stomach? You're the one who's always asking favours of her. Like baby-sitting and cooking meals for you and your girlfriend and—"

"If you want my opinion…" Pat inserted.

"We don't," Monte and Derek shouted.

"Stop it. All of you," Ellen cried. "Now, if you are the least bit interested in helping me, you can take my things outside. Charlie will be here anytime."

"Charlie?" the three echoed in shock.

"Are you moving in with him?"

The suggestion was so ridiculous that she didn't

bother to respond. Lugging the suitcases, the bags, two boxes and all her clothes on hangers onto the front porch, Ellen sat on the top step and waited.

She could hear the boys were pacing back and forth behind her, still bickering quietly. When the black sports car squealed around the corner, Ellen covered her face with both hands and groaned. The last person she wanted to confront now was Reed. Her throat was already swollen with the effort of not giving way to tears.

He parked in front of the house and threw open the car door.

She straightened, determined to appear cool and calm.

Abruptly Reed stopped in front of her suitcases. "What the hell is going on here?"

"Hello, Reed," she said with a breathlessness she couldn't control. "How was your day?"

He jerked his fingers through his hair as he stared back at her in utter confusion. "How the hell am I supposed to know? I get a frantic phone call from Derek telling me to get home quick. On the way out the door, my secretary hands me a message. Some absurd thing about you saying goodbye. What the bloody hell is going on? I thought you'd half killed yourself."

"I'm sorry to disappoint you."

He stalked the area in front of her twice. "Ellen, I don't know what's happening in that overworked little mind of yours, but I want some answers and I want them now."

"I'm leaving." Her hands were clenched so tight that her fingers ached.

"I'm not blind," he shouted, quickly losing control

of his obviously limited patience. "I can see that. I'm asking you why."

Pride demanded that she raise her chin and meet his probing gaze. "I've decided I'm an unstable person," she told him, her voice low and quavering. "I broke my leg once and didn't shed a tear, but when I learn that you're going to a party tonight, I start to cry."

"Ellen." He said her name gently, then shook his head as if clearing his thoughts. "You're not making any sense."

"I know it. That's the worst part."

"In the simplest terms possible, tell me why you're leaving."

"I'm trying." Furious with herself, she wiped a tear from her cheek. How could she explain it to him when everything was still so muddled in her own mind? "I'm leaving because you're driving the Porsche."

"What!" he exploded.

"I told you I'm an unstable person."

He rubbed a hand along the back of his neck and exhaled sharply. "I'm beginning to believe you."

"All right," she burst out. "You tell me. Why did you drive the Porsche today?"

"Would you believe that my truck was low on fuel?"

"I may be unstable," she cried, "but I'm not stupid. You're going out with Danielle. Not that I care, mind you."

"I can tell." His mocking gaze lingered on her suitcases. "I hate to disappoint you, but Danielle won't be with me."

She didn't know whether to believe him or not. "It doesn't matter."

"None of this is making sense."

"I don't imagine it would. Really, I apologise for acting like such an unreasonable woman, but that's exactly the way I feel. So, I'm getting out of here with my pride intact."

"Is your pride worth so much?"

"It's the only thing I have left," she said simply. She'd already given him her heart.

"She's moving in with Charlie," Derek inserted in a concerned voice. "You aren't going to let her go, are you, Reed?"

"You can't," Monte added.

"He won't," Pat stated confidently.

For a moment, the three of them stared intently at Reed. Ellen noticed the way his green eyes hardened to points of steel. "Yes, I can," he said at last. "If this is the way you want it, then so be it. Goodbye, Ellen." With that, he marched back into the house.

CHAPTER TEN

"I'M SWEARING OFF MEN for good," Ellen vowed, taking another long swallow of the pink Chablis.

"Me, too," Darlene, her new roommate, echoed. To toast the promise, Darlene bent forward to touch the rim of her wineglass against Ellen's and missed. A shocked moment passed before the two broke into hysterical laughter.

"Here." Ellen replenished their half-full glasses as tears of mirth rolled down her face. The world seemed to spin off its axis for a moment as she straightened. "You know what? I think we're drunk."

"Maybe you are," Darlene declared, slurring her words, "but not me. I can hold my wine as well as any man can."

"I thought we weren't going to talk about men anymore."

"Right, I forgot."

"Do you think they're talking about us?" Ellen asked, putting a hand to her head in an effort to keep the walls from going around and around.

"Naw, we're just a fading memory to those bums."

"Right." Ellen pointed her index finger toward the ceiling in emphatic agreement.

The doorbell chimed and both women stared accusingly at the door, as though it were the source of all their problems. "If it's a man, don't answer it."

"Right again." Ellen staggered across the beige carpet. The floor seemed to pitch under her feet and she put a hand on the back of the sofa to steady herself. Facing the door, she turned around abruptly. "How do I know if it's a man or not?"

The doorbell sounded again, in short irritated beeps.

Darlene motioned languidly with her hand to show that she no longer cared who was at the door. "Just open it."

Holding the knob in a death grip, Ellen pulled open the door and found herself glaring at solid male chest. "It's a man," she announced to Darlene.

"Who?"

Squinting her eyes, Ellen studied the blurred male figure who dominated the doorway, and she recognised Monte. "Monte," she cried, instantly sobering. "What are you doing here?"

"I...I was in the neighbourhood and thought I'd stop in and see how you're doing."

"Come in." She stepped aside to let him enter. "What brings you to this neck of the woods?" She hiccuped despite her frenzied effort to look sober. "It's a school night. You shouldn't be out this late."

"It's only ten-thirty. You've been drinking." He made it sound as though she were sitting in the middle of an opium den.

"Me?" She slammed her hand against her chest. "Have we been drinking, Darlene?"

Her roommate grabbed the wine bottle from the tabletop and hid it behind her back. "Not us."

Monte cast them a look of utter disbelief. "How'd your exams go?" he asked Ellen politely.

"Fine," she answered and hiccuped again. Embarrassed, she covered her mouth with her hand. "I think."

"What about algebra?"

"I'm making it by the skin of my nose."

"Teeth," both Darlene and Monte corrected.

"Right."

Looking uncomfortable, Monte added, "Maybe I should come back another time."

"Okay." Ellen wasn't about to look a gift horse in the mouth. If she was going to run into her former housemates, then she'd prefer to do it when she looked and felt her best. Definitely not when she was feeling…tipsy and the walls kept spinning. But on second thought, she couldn't resist enquiring about the others. "How's…everyone?"

"Fine." But he lowered his gaze to the carpet. "Not really, if you want the truth."

A shaft of fear went through her, tempering the effects of several glasses of wine. "It's not Reed, is it? Is he ill?"

"No, Reed's fine, I guess. He hasn't been around much lately."

No doubt he was spending a lot of his time at parties and social events with Danielle. Or with any number of other women, all of them far more sophisticated than Ellen.

"Things haven't been the same since you left," Monte added sheepishly.

"Who's doing the cooking?"

He shrugged his shoulders dramatically. "We've more or less been taking turns."

"That sounds fair." She hoped that in the months she'd lived with them the three boys had at least learned their way around the kitchen.

"Derek started a fire yesterday."

Ellen struggled to conceal her dismay. "Was there any damage?" As much as she tried to persuade herself that she didn't need to feel guilty over leaving the boys, this news was her undoing. "Was anyone hurt?" she gasped out.

"Not really, and Reed assured us the insurance would take care of everything."

"What happened?" Ellen was almost afraid to ask.

"Nothing much. Derek forgot to turn off the burner and the fat caught on fire. Then he tried to beat it out with a dish towel, but that burst into flames, too. But the real mistake was throwing the burning towel into the sink because when he tossed it, the towel lit the curtains."

"Oh, good grief." Ellen sank her head into her hands.

"It's not too bad, really. Reed said he wanted new kitchen walls anyway."

"The walls too?"

"Well, the curtains started the wallpaper on fire."

Ellen wished she hadn't asked. "Was anyone burned?"

Monte moved a bandaged hand from behind his back. "Just me, but only a little."

"Oh, Monte," she cried, fighting back an attack of guilt. "What did you do—try and pound out the fire with your fist?" Leave it to Monte. He'd probably tried to rescue whatever it was Derek had been cooking.

"No, I grabbed a hot biscuit from the oven and blistered one finger."

"Then why did you wrap up your whole hand?" From the size of the bandage, it looked as though he'd been lucky not to lose his arm.

"I thought you might feel sorry for me and come back."

"Oh, Monte." Gently, she reached up to brush the hair from his temple.

"I didn't realise what a good cook you were until you left. I kept thinking that maybe it was something I'd done that caused you to leave."

"Of course not."

"Then you'll come back and cook dinners again?"

Good ol' Monte never forgot about his stomach. "The four of you will do fine without me."

"You mean you won't come back?"

"I can't." She felt like crying all the more. But she struggled to hold back the tears that were stinging her eyes. "I'm really sorry, but I can't."

Hanging his head so low that his chin touched his collarbone, Monte nodded. "Well, have a merry Christmas anyway."

"Right. You, too."

"Bye, Ellen." He turned back to the door, his large hand gripping the knob. "You know about Pat making varsity, don't you?"

She'd read it in the *Daily*. "I'm really proud of him. You tell him for me. Okay?"

"Sure."

She closed the door after him and leaned against it while the regrets washed over her like a torrent of rain. Holding back the tears was difficult, but somehow she managed. She'd shed enough tears. It was time to put her grief behind her and to start facing life again.

"I take it Monte is one of the guys," Darlene remarked. She set the wine back on the table, but neither seemed interested in indulging in another glass.

Ellen nodded. "The one with the stomach."

"But he's so skinny."

"I know. There's no justice in this world." But she wasn't talking about Monte's appetite in relation to his weight. She was talking about Reed. If she'd held any hopes that he really did care for her, those had vanished in the past week. He hadn't even tried to get in touch with her. She knew he wouldn't have had any problem locating her. The obvious conclusion was that he didn't *want* to see her again. At first she thought he might have believed the boys' ridiculous claim that she was moving in with Charlie. But if he'd loved her half as much as she loved him, even that shouldn't have stopped him from coming after her.

Apparently, presuming that Reed cared for her was a basic mistake on her part. She hadn't heard a sound from him all week. Exam week, at that. Well, fine, she'd decided. She'd wipe him out of her memory— just as effectively as she forgot every algebraic formula she ever learned. A giggle escaped and Darlene tossed her a curious look. Ellen carried their wineglasses to the sink, ignoring her new roommate, as she mused on her dilemma. The trouble was, she wanted to remember the algebra, which seemed to slip out of her mind as soon as it entered, and she wanted to forget Reed, who never left her thoughts for an instant.

"I think I'll go to bed," Darlene said, holding her hand to her stomach. "I'm not feeling so great."

"Me neither." But Ellen's churning stomach had little to do with the wine. "'Night."

"I'll see you in the morning."

Ellen nodded. She was fortunate to have found Darlene. The other woman, who had recently broken up with her fiancé after a two-year engagement, understood how Ellen felt. It seemed natural that they drown their sorrows together. But damn it all, she missed the boys and...Reed.

One thing she'd learned from this experience was that men and school didn't mix. Darlene might not have been serious about swearing off men, but Ellen was. She was through with them for good—or at least until she obtained her degree. For now, she was determined to bury herself in her books, get her teaching credentials and then become the best first-grade teacher around.

Only, she couldn't close her eyes without remembering Reed's touch or how he'd slip up behind her and wrap her in his arms. Something as simple as a passing glance from him had been enough to thrill her. Well, that relationship was over—ruined. And just in the nick of time. She could have been hurt. Really hurt. She could be feeling terrible. Really terrible. Just like she did now.

SIGNS OF CHRISTMAS were everywhere Ellen looked. Huge weatherproof decorations adorned the streetlights down University Way. Store windows were painted in a variety of Christmas themes, and the streets were jammed with holiday traffic. Ellen tried to absorb some of the good cheer that surrounded her, with little success.

The following morning she planned to leave for Yakima. But instead of feeling the pull toward home and family, Ellen's thoughts drifted to Reed and the boys. They had been her surrogate family since September and she couldn't erase them from her mind as easily as she'd hoped.

As she walked across campus, sharp gusts of wind mussed her hair and caused her to cast her eyes downward. Her face felt numb with cold. All day she'd been debating about what to do with the Christmas gifts she'd bought for the boys. Her first inclination had been to deliver them herself—when Reed wasn't home, of course. But just the thought of returning to the lovely old house had proved so painful that Ellen abandoned the thought. Instead, Darlene had promised to deliver them the next day, after Ellen had left for Yakima.

Hugging the books against her chest, Ellen trudged toward the bus stop. According to her watch, she had about ten minutes to wait. Now her feet felt as numb as her face. She frowned at her open-toed pumps, cursing the decrees of fashion and her insane willingness to wear "cute" shoes at this time of year. It wasn't as though a handsome prince were likely to come galloping by only to be overwhelmed by her attractive toes. Even if one did swoop Ellen and her frozen toes onto his silver steed, she'd be highly suspicious of his character.

Swallowing a giggle, she took a shortcut across the lawn in the Quad.

"Is something funny?"

A pair of men's leather loafers had joined her fashionable grey pumps, matching her stride step for step. Stunned, Ellen glanced upward. Reed.

"Well?" he asked again in an achingly gentle voice. "Something seems to amuse you."

"My...shoes. I was thinking about attracting a prince...a man." Oh heavens, why had she said that? "That is," she mumbled on, trying to cover her embarrassment, "my feet are numb."

"You need to get out of the cold." His hands were thrust into his pockets and he was so compellingly handsome that Ellen forced her eyes away. If she stared at him long enough, she feared, she'd give him whatever he asked. The way his face had looked the last time she'd seen him was seared into her memory for all time. She remembered how steely and cold his eyes had become the day she'd announced she was moving out. One word from him and she would have stayed. If only he'd explained. Hell, the ''might-have-beens'' didn't matter anymore. He hadn't asked her to stay and so she'd gone. Pure and simple. Or so it had seemed at the time.

Determination thickened her trembling voice as she finally spoke. ''The bus will be at the corner in seven minutes.''

Her statement was met with silence. Together they reached the pavement and strolled toward the sheltered bus area.

Much as she wished to appear cool and composed, Ellen's gaze was riveted on the tall, sombre man at her side. She noticed how straight and dark Reed's brows were and how his chin jutted out with stubborn male pride. Every line of his beloved face emanated strength and unflinching resolve.

Abruptly, she looked away. Pride was no stranger to her, either. Her methods might have been wrong, she told herself, but she'd been right to let Reed know he'd hurt her. She wasn't willing to continue being a victim of her love for him.

''Ellen,'' he said softly, ''I was hoping we could talk.''

She made a show of glancing at her wristwatch. ''Go ahead. You've got six and a half minutes.''

''Here?''

''As you so recently stated, I need to get out of the cold.''

"I'll take you to lunch."

"I'm not hungry." To further her embarrassment, her stomach growled and she pressed a firm hand over it, commanding it to be quiet.

"When was the last time you ate a decent meal?"

"Yesterday. No," she corrected, "today."

"Come on, we're getting out of here."

"No way."

"I'm not arguing with you, Ellen. I've given you a week to come to your senses. I still haven't figured out what went wrong. And I'm not waiting any longer for the answers. Got that?"

Stubbornly she ignored him, looking instead in the direction of the traffic. She could see the bus approaching, though it was still several blocks away. "I believe everything that needed to be said—" she motioned dramatically with her hand "—was already said."

"And what's this I hear about you succumbing to the demon rum?"

"I was only a little drunk," she spat out, furious at Monte's loose tongue. "Darlene and I were celebrating. We've sworn off men for life." Or at least until Reed freely admitted that he loved her and needed her. At the moment it didn't appear likely.

"I see." His eyes seemed to be looking all the way into her soul. "If that's the way you want it, fine. Just answer a couple of questions and I'll leave you alone. Agreed?"

"All right."

"First, what the hell were you talking about when you flew off the handle about me driving the Porsche?"

"Oh, that." Now it just seemed silly.

"Yes, that."

"Well, you only drove the Porsche when you were seeing Danielle."

"But I wasn't. It's been over between us ever since the night of the Christmas party."

"It has?" She realised that the words came out in a squeak.

Reed dragged his fingers through his hair. "I haven't seen Danielle in weeks."

Resolutely Ellen dropped her gaze to the pavement. "But the cleaners phoned with that business about the suit. You were attending some fancy party."

"So? I wasn't taking another woman."

"It doesn't matter," she insisted stubbornly. "You weren't taking me, either."

"Of course not," he shouted, his raised voice attracting the attention of several passersby. "You were studying for exams. I couldn't very well ask you to attend an extremely boring business dinner with me. Not when you were spending every available minute hitting the books." He lowered his voice to a calm, even pitch.

The least he could do was be more unreasonable, Ellen thought irritably. She simply wasn't in the mood for logic.

"Did you hear what I said?"

The sheer force of his will demanded that she nod. She did.

"There is only one woman in my life. You. To be honest, Ellen, I can't understand any of this. You may be many things, but you're not the jealous type. I've wanted to talk about Danielle with you. Any other woman would have loved hearing all the details. But not you." His voice was only slightly raised. "Then when you throw up these ridiculous accusations about the truck and the Porsche, I'm at a loss to understand you."

Oh, lord, now she felt even more of a fool. "Then why were you driving the Porsche?" Her arms tightened around her books. "Forget I asked that."

"You really have a thing for that sports car, don't you?"

"It's not the car."

"I'm glad to hear that."

Squaring her shoulders, Ellen decided it was time to be forthright and honest, time to face things squarely rather than skirt around them. "My feelings are that you would rather not be seen with me," she said bluntly.

"What?" he exploded.

"You kept taking me to these out-of-the-way restaurants."

"I did it to be alone with you."

"Ha! You didn't want to be seen with me," she countered.

"I can't believe this." He took three steps away from her, then turned around sharply.

"Don't you think the Des Moines Marina is a bit far to go for a meal?"

"I was afraid we'd run into one of the boys."

More logic, and she was in no mood for it. "Try to deny not introducing me to your friend the night we went to that French film."

His eyes narrowed. "You can damn well bet I wasn't going to introduce you to Tom Dailey. He's a lecher. I was protecting you."

"What about the night of the Christmas party? You only introduced me to a handful of people."

"Of course. Every man in the place was looking for

an excuse to take you away from me. I was keeping you to myself. If you'd wanted to flirt with the others, you should have said something.''

"I only wanted to be with you.''

"Then why bring up that evening now?''

"I was offended.''

"I apologise,'' he shouted.

"Fine.''

The bus arrived, its doors parting with a swish. But Ellen didn't move. Reed's gaze commanded her to stay with him, and she was torn. Her strongest impulse, though, was not to board the bus. It didn't matter that she was cold and the wind was cutting through her thin coat or that she could barely feel her big toe. Her heart was telling her one thing and her head another.

"You coming or not, miss?'' the driver called out to her.

"She won't be taking the bus,'' Reed answered, slipping his hand under her elbow. "She's coming with me.''

"Whatever.'' The door swished shut and the bus roared away, leaving a trail of black diesel smoke in its wake.

"You are coming with me, aren't you?'' he coaxed.

"I suppose.''

His hand was at the small of her back, directing her across the busy street to a coffee shop, festooned with tinsel and tired-looking decorations. "I wasn't kidding about lunch.''

"When was the last time *you* had a decent meal?'' she couldn't resist asking.

"About a week ago,'' he grumbled. "Derek's cooking is a poor substitute for real food.''

They found a table in the back of the café. The waitress handed them each a menu and filled their water glasses.

"I heard about the fire."

Reed groaned. "That was a comedy of errors."

"Is there much damage?"

"Enough." The look he gave her was mildly accusing.

The guilt returned. Trying to disguise it, Ellen made a show of glancing through the menu. The last thing on her mind at the moment was food. When the waitress returned, Ellen ordered the special of the day without knowing what it was. The day was destined to be full of surprises.

"Ellen," Reed began, then cleared his throat. "Come back."

Her heart melted at the hint of anguish in his low voice. Her gaze was magnetically drawn to his. She wanted to tell him how much she longed to be...home. She wanted to say that the house on Capitol Hill was the only real home she had now, that she longed to walk through its front door again. With him.

"Nothing has been the same since you left."

The knot in her stomach pushed its way up to her throat, choking off her breath.

"The boys are miserable."

Resolutely she shook her head. If she went back, it had to be for Reed and not on account of the boys.

"Why not?"

Tears blurred her vision. "Because."

"That makes about as much sense as you being angry because I drove the Porsche." His clipped reply conveyed the depth of his irritation.

Taking several deep, measured breaths, Ellen shook

her head. "If all you need is a cook, I can suggest several who—"

"I don't give a damn about the cooking."

The café went silent as every head turned curiously in their direction. "I wasn't talking about the cooking *here*," Reed explained to the room full of shocked faces.

The normal noise of the café resumed.

"Good grief, Ellen, you've got me so tied up in knots I'm about to get kicked out of here."

"Me, tie you in knots?" She was amazed Reed felt she had that much power over him.

"If you won't come back for the boys, will you consider doing it for me?" The intense green eyes demanded a response.

"I want to know why you want me back. So I can cook your meals and—"

"I don't give a damn if you never do another thing around the house. I want you there because I love you, damn it."

Her dark eyes widened. "You love me, damn it?"

"You're not making this any easier." He ripped the napkin from around the silverware and slammed it down on his lap. "You must have known. I didn't bother keeping it secret."

"You didn't bother keeping it secret…from anyone but me," she repeated hotly.

"Come on. Don't tell me you didn't know."

"I didn't know."

"Well, you do now," he yelled back.

The waitress cautiously approached their table, standing back until Reed glanced irritably in her direction. Hurriedly the teenaged girl set their plates in front of them and promptly moved away.

"You frightened her," Ellen accused.

"I'm the one in a panic here. Do you or do you not love me?"

Again, it seemed as though the entire customer population paused, awaiting her reply.

"You'd best answer him, miss," the elderly gentleman sitting at the table next to theirs suggested. "Fact is, we're all curious."

"Yes, I love him."

Reed cast her a look of utter disbelief. "You'll tell a stranger but not me?"

"I love you, Reed Morgan. There, are you happy?"

"Overjoyed."

"I can tell." Ellen had thought that when she admitted her feelings, Reed would jump up from the table and throw his arms around her. Instead, he looked as angry as she'd ever seen him.

"I think you'd better ask her to marry you while she's in a friendly mood," the older man suggested next.

"Well?" Reed looked at her. "What do you think?"

"You want to get married?"

"It's the time of year to be generous," the waitress offered. "He's handsome enough."

"He is, isn't he?" Ellen agreed, her sense of humour restored by this unexpected turn of events. "But he's a little hard to understand at times."

"All men are, believe me," a woman customer from across the room shouted. "But he looks like a decent sort. Go ahead and give him another chance."

The anger washed from Reed's dark eyes as he reached for Ellen's hand. "I love you. I want to marry you. Won't you put me out of my misery?"

Tears dampened her eyes as she nodded wildly.

"Let's go home." Standing, Reed took out his wallet and threw some money on the table.

Ellen quickly buttoned her jacket and picked up her purse. "Goodbye, everyone," she called with a cheerful wave. "Thank you—and Merry Christmas!"

The amused customers broke into a round of applause as Reed took Ellen's hand and pulled her outside.

She was no sooner out the door when Reed hauled her into his arms. "Oh, lord, Ellen, I've missed you and your cotton-candy kisses."

Revelling in the warmth of his arms, she nuzzled closer. "I've missed you, too. I've even missed the boys."

"As far as I'm concerned, they're on their own. I want you back for myself. That house was full of people, yet it's never felt so empty." Suddenly he looked around, as though he'd only now realised that their private moment was taking place in the middle of a busy street. "Let's get out of here." He slipped an arm about her waist, steering her toward the campus car park. "But I think I'd better tell you something important."

"What?" Her eyes glowed with an inner sparkle as she glanced up at him.

"I didn't bring the truck."

"Oh?" She swallowed down the disappointment. She could try, but she doubted that she would ever be the Porsche type.

"I traded in the truck last week."

"For what?" Her eyes widened with dismay.

"Maybe it was presumptuous of me, but I was hoping you'd accept my marriage proposal."

"What's the truck got to do with whether I marry you or not?"

"*You're* asking me that? The very woman who left me—"

"All right, all right, I get the picture."

"I traded it in for a station wagon. A family wagon that's waiting to be filled with children."

"Oh, Reed." With a small cry of joy, she flung her arms around this man she knew she would love for a lifetime. No matter what car he drove.

Boardroom Bridegroom
Renee Roszel

CHAPTER ONE

JOSHUA RAVEN rested an elbow on the antique mantel, half listening to the gushy blonde socialite, who was spilling out of her gown. Tonight he couldn't be bothered with simpering coquettes. Tonight was the beginning of the end of his quest to own Maxim Enterprises. All he had to do was marry Gower Isaac's daughter. What was her name again? Mindy, Sandy? No. Wendy. That was it. He must not forget.

Smiling at appropriate moments in the blonde's conversation, he scanned the elegant living room. Decorated in shades of peach and rust reds, the Georgian-style salon seemed to be eternally bathed in sunset.

Josh's scowling host, Gower Isaac, met his gaze and shrugged. Clearly the head of Maxim Enterprises was as distressed by his daughter's tardiness as Josh.

With another noncommittal murmur toward the buxom socialite still babbling at his elbow, he glanced at his watch. Almost half-past eight. Gower's daughter was over an hour late, and Josh was growing bored.

Ordinarily he would make a brief appearance at inane corporate functions like this, then leave with an excuse about "pressing business matters." But tonight was different. Tonight, he was being presented to the Maxim Enterprises's executives as their next CEO. The only remaining element, vital to the deal, was the tardy Miss Wendy Isaac. She didn't know it, but she was about to meet her future husband—*if* she ever arrived.

A bit "odd" Gower had called his only child. *Odd.* Josh closed his eyes in a grimace of resignation. Loveless marriages were sometimes necessary in negotiating multimillion-dollar deals. He only hoped the Odd-Miss-Isaac would arrive soon. He wanted to get on with the chore of wooing her.

Gower had grimly presented the stipulation of Josh's marriage to his daughter, obviously believing it would be a hard condition to swallow. But Josh was a pragmatist. He knew the ways of the world. People married for many reasons, only one of which was love.

For years, gaining control of Maxim Enterprises had been his dream. Nothing was going to stand in his way. *Nothing.* Especially not one odd-little-duck of a woman—who apparently had the notion she must be adored by the man she married.

He heard a loud cough and his gaze shot to Gower. The older man headed toward the room's double-doored entrance where a woman stood. In jeans and a voluminous sweatshirt, she looked laughably out of place among the tuxedos and spangled gowns. The woman waved at Gower and took a step backward, as though just checking in to let him know she was either coming or going. It didn't appear that she had any intention of joining the gathering.

Josh watched as Gower Isaac took the woman's arm, thwarting her escape. His ruddy face grew redder, and though his comments were whispered, it was clear the rotund little man was agitated. The woman smiled, and gave him a hug. If this was the tardy, Odd-Miss-Wendy-Isaac, Josh had to give her points for not being intimidated by her scowling father. She and Josh seemed to be the only two people at the cocktail party who weren't cowed by the little dictator.

His glance shifted from Isaac to scan the woman's face. She wasn't a beauty. Her features lacked the fleshy lushness current high fashion considered elegant. Her hair was muddy brown, straight and pulled back in a ponytail. Displaced strands danced about her face. Yet, when she smiled at her father, Josh decided she had a nice mouth. The friendly expression lit up her face, and his lips quirked in response. She might be odd, tardy and woefully underdressed, but she had an infectious grin.

He was surprised when she turned to look at him. Her smile faded slightly, and she squinted as though in concentration as her father spoke, his manner unmistakably agitated. With a quick glance back at the bald man, she tweaked his thin nose and began to wend her way toward Josh.

He noticed she had on jogging shoes, and recalled the slogan for that brand. *Go for it!* He had a feeling not only the shoes, but Wendy Isaac herself, lived by that philosophy.

As she advanced on him like a general leading troops, he wondered what her father had said. *Wendy, dear, this man is helping me avoid a hostile takeover by purchasing Maxim Enterprises as my White Knight. To keep control of the company in the family, I'm forcing him to marry you. Now go make nice.*

Josh didn't believe Gower said anything like that. The older man had warned him that Wendy had vowed she didn't intend to be a pawn in any business deal the way her mother had been. She would marry for love or not at all. Besides, as the young woman marched his way, she was smiling. He didn't think her expression would be particularly amicable if her father had told her the truth.

Josh found himself turning to face her as she came up to him. The poor blonde at his side stopped chattering, apparently realizing she was being openly ignored.

Wendy thrust out a hand. "Hello, Mr. Raven." When he grasped her fingers, she shook his hand. Actually shook it—quaintly unsophisticated for a woman of her breeding. "Dad tells me we should meet. I'm sorry I don't have time to chat. I just dropped by to pick up some stuff. I'm on my way out."

Josh watched her animated face, noting her eyes were bigger than he'd first thought. They were an unusual shade of blue, more like neon purple. Pretty eyes, actually, and they smiled at him with a guileless quality he hadn't expected from the offspring of a cunning tyrant like Gower Isaac.

"I teach adult literacy classes on Tuesday, Thursday and Saturday night," she was saying. "Dad always forgets. I'm sorry I have to run, but the man I'm tutoring—well, he's forty and he was so ashamed when he started class—I mean having lied all his life about not being able to read. But he's trying hard. I wouldn't cancel on him for the world. Dad's horribly angry with me."

She shrugged as though accustomed to being a disappointment to her father, but her grin exhibited an undaunted quality he found commendable. "Dad tells me you're the White Knight who rode in to save Maxim from those raiders. That's wonderful. I do hope we'll have a chance to chat sometime." She flicked up her wrist to check her watch. "Wow, eight-thirty. I really must go."

She dropped his hand, gave him one more genuinely friendly second of eye-to-eye contact, and spun away on those go-for-it shoes. An instant later she was gone.

"Nice to meet you, too, Wendy," he murmured with a wry chuckle. Mentally he surveyed his ego. Just the tiniest puncture wound. He would heal. But it was clear that Odd-Little-Wendy-Isaac didn't find Joshua Raven as irresistible as the tabloids continuously suggested. He had a feeling this purple-eyed dynamo might not be the easy conquest he'd expected her to be. He'd have to lay it on thick.

"I'm embarrassed, my boy." Josh felt a heavy paw on his shoulder. "Damned girl has a mind of her own."

Josh turned to see Gower, his face a wrinkled portrait of aggravation. Still experiencing ironic amusement at being brushed off so thoroughly, he grinned at the older man. "You warned me she was odd, Gower. To be honest, I thought she was refreshing."

Gower's frown didn't ease. "You're a gentleman, my boy." He brightened. "Say, what if I invite you to dinner tomorrow?"

Josh slipped his hands into his tux pants' pockets. "Does your daughter teach anybody to do anything on Sunday nights?"

Gower grunted in disgust. "I don't think so." He shook his head. "No, I remember a charity open house last month. She went with me, but it was like pulling teeth. That was on a Sunday night."

Josh forced himself to hold on to his smile. The man was an arrogant son of a gun. The only downside to their alliance, besides the demand that Josh marry his daughter, was Gower's other deal-breaker requirement—that the older man be installed on Josh's board of directors. Since Josh had no choice if he was to realize his dream, he had acquiesced. Ironically, agreeing to the concession that Gower Isaac be underfoot had been harder to accept than the prospect of marrying a woman he'd never met.

"I'll make sure she's home—even if I have to tie her to a chair," Gower vowed, teeth gritted.

Josh's brows dipped for an instant, before he restored his grin. "Fine."

"Then you can start your seduction."

Josh felt an unpleasant twinge. As Gower glanced away to wave at someone across the room, he stared at the shorter man. How could any father talk about his own flesh and blood like she was a brood mare, to be sold to the highest bidder? Unfortunately, he could hardly cast stones. After all, he was the *buyer* in this bargain, and Wendy Isaac was just another piece of merchandise exchanging hands. When Gower turned back, he patted Josh on the shoulder. "All right, my boy, we'll see you tomorrow night. Six-thirty."

Nodding, he shoved all thoughts from his mind except his ultimate goal. Maxim Enterprises—the plum of plums—when combined with his own company, would make him one of the wealthiest men in America.

To that end, wide-eyed Wendy Isaac would soon be swept off her feet by an adoring Joshua Raven—at least that's what she would believe.

Wendy liked the butler's quarters on her father's estate. Cluttered with books and smelling of pipe tobacco, it was cozy and welcoming, just like the man who resided there. She'd known Millville all her life. He was like a grandfather to her. She missed him and his dog, Agnes, more than she missed her father—a sad commentary on her family.

She squatted on the woven rug to pet the old Irish setter. "How are you doing, Aggie, girl?"

The dog lifted her head and licked Wendy's hand. "We've missed you, too. That's why I brought Al to see you." She stroked her albino crow on the head. The bird was perched atop a magazine stand, beside the coffee table. Wendy glanced at her pet. "What do you say, Al? Aren't you happy to see Aggie?"

The crow was pure white, from the tip of her beak to her snowy claws. The only color she could boast was the light pink of her eyes. Lifting a foot as though in a wave, the bird squawked, "Al loves Aggie. Al loves Aggie."

Wendy laughed. "Yes, and Aggie loves—"

"What do you think you're doing, *girl?*"

Accustomed to her father's growling, Wendy hardly flinched. But Agnes crawled beneath the coffee table with a whimper. Al flapped from her perch with a high-pitched screech, a second later thudding down hard on Wendy's head. In panic, the crow's claws scraped at her scalp, not quite breaking the skin. *"Ouch!"* Wendy yelped, thanking heaven she'd just clipped Al's claws.

She fumbled to stand, grimacing at her father. "Dad! Look what you've done! You've scared Al." She tried to pry her crow's talons from the curls she'd painstakingly created with her curling iron, but the bird pecked at her fingers. *"Ouch.* Drat." The three-pound bird an unwieldy crown, Wendy narrowly eyed her father. "You really have a way with animals."

She watched his steely eyes scan her where the crow held her hair in a death grip. With his most imposing scowl, his gaze trailed down her body to her feet. He was making it painfully clear he didn't think her green, cotton sundress and sandals were appropriate for tonight's dinner party.

"Is that what you're wearing?"

She shook her head at his attitude, then winced as the move caused Al to clutch tighter. "Dad, why do you want me at this dinner? I'm sure you and Mr. Raven have business to discuss. Usually you tell me my chattering gives you a headache."

"I thought you and Josh should get to know each other, that's all." He indicated her with a wave. "Did you leave any clothes here after you moved out? Surely there's something you could change into."

Trying to hold her temper, she moved up to him and patted his cheek. "This isn't nineteen fifty-five when women wore girdles and white gloves. Mr. Raven is buying the *business,* not me. I'm sure he won't care what I'm wearing."

Her father crossed his arms over his ample paunch. Dressed in a navy silk suit, he looked impeccable. "Dammit girl, take that ridiculous bird off your head. I don't want him to think you're insane." The melodious sound of a doorbell intruded, and a look that seemed almost fearful crossed Gower's features. "There he is, now."

Wendy was confused by his nervous demeanor. Her father never got rattled. She watched, concerned, as he glanced through the door into the kitchen. "There goes Millville." When he faced her again, he grimaced. "Do something about that damned bird!"

"Shhhh!" she admonished as Al let out a screech

and clutched tighter. "Shouting only makes it worse. Unless you want me to cut a big bald spot on the top of my head, she'll be there until she calms down." Wendy took her father's hand. "You know when Al's upset she can't be forced to do anything. If you're very quiet for fifteen or twenty minutes, I can probably coax her down."

He moved with her most of the way through the kitchen, then halted, dragging her to a stop. She noticed the staff had frozen in an amusing tableau, clearly unaccustomed to seeing albino crows attached to women. "You don't mean to tell me you're going to meet Mr. Raven with that—that thing on your head?"

She smiled impishly. The only time he really paid attention to her was when he was outraged at her. It felt good to be noticed. "Why shouldn't Mr. Raven meet Al? With a name like his, they already have a lot in common. They'll want to chat."

"Wendy!" Gower shouted, but when the bird scolded, he ran a beefy hand over his face. "Where did I go wrong?" he muttered. "You're not a child any longer. You're a twenty-five-year-old woman. Women don't greet guests with wild fowl in their hair!"

She felt a tinge of pity. Pathologically correct and infinitely self-centered, the poor man would never understand how much of his distress he brought on himself. She reached out to hug him but he brushed away her hands. "Don't do that! You know how I hate gush."

She sighed, struggling to remain positive, but refusing to be cowed. "Just remember whose fault it is that Al is in my hair, Dad." Wendy took his arm. "Besides, haven't you already apologized to Mr. Raven about me—being eccentric? I thought that was the first thing you told people.''

His frown was grim and vaguely sheepish.

''See!'' She was only slightly insulted that her father felt it necessary to apologize for her, accustomed to it by now. ''You've brilliantly prepared him, already.''

''Nevertheless, I *forbid* you to see Mr. Raven with that monstrosity on your head!''

''You forbid me?'' Wendy might not be much like her father in most ways, but she *was* his daughter. And like her father, she did not allow herself to be dictated to. She met his disapproving eyes without flinching. ''You're mistaking me for my mother,'' she said quietly. Taking his elbow, she tugged. ''Come on.''

Though Gower was stiff as a board, she coaxed him toward the front door. If she were totally honest, she didn't relish meeting Mr. Raven with a crow in her hair any more than she relished sitting through a stuffy business dinner. Deciding she might as well give them both a break, she offered, ''On the other hand, I could sneak out the back and go home.''

''No, I—'' he began roughly, then seemed to think better of his tone. ''I want you to join us this evening.'' He glanced at her as they headed down the hall to the foyer, his gray eyes narrowed on the crow. ''Why did you bring that bird over here, anyway?''

''Al was depressed. I've been gone a lot. I figured she'd enjoy seeing old Agnes and Millville.''

His expression dubious, he growled, ''Depressed? How can a bird be depressed?''

''Al was barking. She always barks when she misses Agnes.''

Gower shook his head, looking befuddled, and Wendy could hardly keep from laughing. Feeling concern for anybody or anything that didn't affect *his* bottom line was an utterly foreign concept for her father.

She tried to love her father, crusty old bully that he was. After all, he was the only family she had. He'd made her mother's life miserable, but sadly her mother hadn't had any backbone. Wendy had learned how *not* to handle her dad by watching her mom continually knuckle under to his demands. She'd tried many tactics over the years, and finally found it best to simply ignore his tantrums, be as kind and attentive as she could, but refuse to lose herself in the force of his intimidating presence.

Her attitude of affectionate insubordination drove him batty. She didn't mean for it to, but that seemed to be the only way to handle him. She refused to be swallowed up by the man—by his selfish demands— the way her poor mother had been. So she became an individual to be reckoned with, on her own terms.

As they entered the foyer, their heels tapped out a staccato rhythm on the marble floor, the domed ceiling echoing their steps. The oval room, complete with a majestic, winding staircase, was white on white, from the classical columns to the Georgian moldings and cornices that embellished the place. Wendy thought wryly that in all this fancy white decoration, Mr. Raven might not notice Al cleaving to her head.

When Millville, their aging butler, stepped back from the double doors to allow their guest entry, Wendy couldn't help but take singular notice. Dressed in black, Joshua Raven was a sharp contrast to the surroundings. Though his attire was casual, trousers and a polo shirt, he was every inch as striking today as he had been in his tuxedo.

She vividly recalled her first sight of him. Standing there, tall and elegant across the room, his black eyes trained on her. She'd felt an electrical shock when their glances met, as though she'd been in the cross-hairs of a rifle. She'd shaken off the irrational thought, but she hadn't forgotten how it made her feel. She supposed any man who clawed his way up from poverty to reach such extraordinary success at his age, probably looked at everybody as potential prey.

She watched as his gaze fell on her—and her crow. Those ebony eyes widened a fraction. She sensed the tiny reaction was quite a show of emotion for a man accustomed to keeping his own counsel. Waving broadly, she urged her balky father forward. "Hello, Mr. Raven. Welcome."

Their guest seemed to have difficulty pulling his glance from her headgear. When their eyes met, she smiled. "If you're wondering, this is Al." She reached up and stroked the bird along its wing and was promptly pecked for her trouble. "Ouch!"

"Miss?" Millville asked in his sedate way. "Shall I take her?"

"Millville, I'd love it, but Daddy *shouted*." She shrugged.

The butler nodded in understanding. "I'll fetch the persuader."

"Oh, what a wonderful idea," Wendy said. "I'd forgotten about that."

"What is it?" Josh asked, his lips curling. "A sling-shot?"

Wendy laughed. "No. Al likes Twinkies. Sometimes it works."

"Ah." Josh's perusal lingered on the crow for another moment before he peered at Gower. Wendy noticed her father's face was a shade of red she'd never seen before. "Dad would rather I didn't wear Al to dinner," she teased. "Actually, I think he'd like to *have* Al for dinner."

Josh Raven's husky laugh echoed in the cavernous room. "Eat crow? Gower Isaac? I know people who'd pay big money to see that."

Startled by his wit, she giggled. Reaching up, she stroked Al's soft feathers and was relieved when the bird didn't peck at her. "I like Mr. Raven, Al. What's your opinion?"

"You're a pretty boy," the bird blurted. "Kiss me, pretty boy."

"Oh, lord," Gower muttered.

Josh laughed, and once again the room rumbled pleasantly with his mirth. "A white crow that talks and doubles as a hat. I'm impressed." His glance shifted to Wendy. "By the way, please call me Josh."

"Thank you—Josh." Wendy found their guest to be unlike anything she'd expected. Oh, she'd known he was handsome, even before last night. Anybody who'd lingered in the checkout line in a supermarket knew his face. He was quite the lady's man, according to the tabloids—naturally, she only *scanned* the stories. Cameras loved him, making him look darkly seductive in every grainy photo she'd seen.

As she examined his face, she had to rethink that notion. Cameras didn't do justice to that cleft chin or the shadowed hollows beneath his strong cheekbones. And those deep-set eyes. Sparkling with vitality, they were surrounded by lashes so thick and long they looked artificial. It was widely known that Joshua

Raven had been born with a double set of eyelashes—
a rare birth defect any woman in her right mind would
commit murder for.

"Kiss me, pretty boy!" Al repeated, drawing
Wendy out of her musings.

"I'm not into feathers, Al, old buddy," Josh said
with a crooked grin. "But thanks anyway."

Deciding he'd passed a test she hadn't been aware
she was giving, she reached up and stroked the crow's
soft breast. "Okay, Al, you've made your point." She
met those darkly sexy eyes. "Al's short for Alberta.
She's a shameless flirt. We think her former owner
was a lady of the evening."

"Alberta has clearly made a change for the better."

She experienced a flutter of admiration. No wonder
he was so popular with women. If he could make her
feel as though having a crow on her head was perfectly
proper dinner attire—even as it shrieked off-color
propositions at him—then he deserved his reputation
as a charmer.

The sound of footfalls attracted their attention. "Oh,
good, the cavalry's coming." She turned to see
Millville approach. Looking starched and professional
in his dark uniform, he carried a shaft of sponge cake.
"Come to Uncle Millie, Alberta," he cooed. "You
and I and Agnes shall have a Twinkies pig-out in my
quarters."

With a squawk, Al fluttered off Wendy's head, pulling out reluctant strands of hair in the process.
Landing on Millville's outstretched arm, the crow tore
into the cake.

"Thanks, Millville." She ran her fingers through
her ruined curls in an attempt to minimize the damage.
"I'll pick her up before I go."

"No hurry, miss," the old man offered. "Agnes and I have missed this naughty girl."

"Millville," Gower said in an unusually restrained tone. "Get rid of that refugee from a corn field, and tell Cook our guest would like to eat."

As Millville exited the foyer, Al squawked, "Pretty boy—*kiss* me!" spraying Twinkies crumbs into the air. The crow's high-pitched plea snapped Wendy from an odd trance, and it struck her that she'd been staring at Josh with an inane grin on her face.

Though she was positive he was accustomed to women gaping longingly at him, she hadn't thought of herself as the type of ninny to be drawn in by a playboy's charisma. Chagrin heated her cheeks. *How superficial!* Turning toward her father, she forced an offhand tone. "I'm starving, Dad. Let's eat."

She was starting to have major regrets about meeting this man with a crow on her head. But it was too late to alter his impression. The best course was to get this dinner over as quickly as possible and hope that Joshua Raven would be charitable and forget he ever met her.

The multitiered stone patio was one of Wendy's favorite spots, and one of the very few things about her mother's ancestral home she missed. Located in Kennilworth, a suburb on the North Shore of Chicago, Wendy had grown up in one of the most affluent communities in the country. Hers had been a beautiful if cheerless home. Fighting a bout of melancholy at the memories, she gazed out over the calm waters of Lake Michigan. Sunset-tinged sailboats skimmed along its glassy surface. The lake was so vast, it looked like an ocean, flowing out beyond the horizon as far as the eye could see.

The cool breeze off the lake grew nippy as the sun sank low in the evening sky. She shivered, rubbing her arms.

"Are you cold?"

She faced Josh. Her father had excused himself sometime ago, saying he'd forgotten an appointment. So here she was, left to entertain Joshua Raven. *Alone*. Gower Isaac rarely left her to entertain his business associates. But she blessed him for choosing this time, and this man.

Josh was smiling at her as though he thought she was quite wonderful to behold. She couldn't help but smile back. The setting sun did eerie things to his dark hair, making it gleam with subtle fire.

Meeting his gaze, she had the strangest sensation. His eyes glittered with a light that was almost predatory. The thought flashed through her mind that a raven was sometimes thought of as a bird of ill omen. *How silly.* Anything ominous she'd imagined in his glance had to be a caprice of the sunset. Josh Raven was their White Knight, for heaven's sake. Certainly not an enemy. She mentally shook herself, trying to hold on to the subject at hand. "It—it gets chilly very quickly when the breeze is off the lake."

"Let me get you a sweater." He rose to his feet.

Just then Millville came outside to clear away the dessert plates and bring more coffee. The darling man had a shawl draped over his arm. She accepted it gratefully. "You read minds, Millie?"

He nodded, loading the remainder of the dishes on a tray. "More coffee, miss?"

"No, I'm fine."

Millville shifted to look at Josh. "Sir?"

Josh shook his head.

"Then, I'll leave you two to enjoy the evening," the butler murmured before silently disappearing into the house.

Wendy was adjusting the shawl when she felt a hand on her shoulder. "Let me."

She glanced up to see Josh smiling down at her. With a nod, she released the white crocheted fabric. After he placed the shawl about her, he skimmed a finger along her shoulder. The brief touch was astoundingly sensual, sending a ripple of excitement through her. "There." He moved to her side and held out a hand. "Why don't we walk down to the water? I love the lake."

Her brain went foggy as she watched herself accept his hand. This was not how she'd expected the evening to go at all. She'd anticipated sitting in the big, impersonal dining room playing hostess with a plastered-on smile, keeping her mouth shut per her father's usual orders.

Gower Isaac had made it no secret that he'd been immensely displeased that his only child was a girl, and worse, one who preferred volunteer work to making money. He usually allowed her to forgo hostess duties, grousing that he never knew what she might say to embarrass him—from cajoling business associates into investing in Project Literacy or the Society for the Prevention of Cruelty to Animals, to brazenly counseling them to quit smoking.

After disappointing her father last night she'd decided not to turn him down, and had consented to be his hostess. However, because of her past experiences with strained dinner parties, she had dreaded tonight.

For once in her life, the experience was delightful. Her father had hardly spoken, allowing the conversation to flow, with business barely intruding at all. Josh proved to be a fascinating conversationalist. Wendy had been enthralled and the meal she'd expected to drag, simply flew. Then, as dessert was about to be served, Gower Isaac abruptly withdrew.

She didn't understand it, but she wasn't looking a gift horse in the mouth. She liked Josh Raven. She liked him as a person, something she hadn't expected to do. And his drop-dead good looks didn't hurt. Every time he grinned, her pulse went into a jig as mad and thrilling as the footwork in the musical extravaganza "Riverdance."

"You have a lovely home, Wendy," he said, drawing her back.

They ambled along a stone path winding through the lavish gardens toward a retaining wall, where a stone stairway led down to the lake.

She clasped her hands before her as they walked. "It is nice. But I don't live here."

She could feel his eyes on her. "Really? Why not?"

She smiled, but didn't glance his way. "If Gower Isaac were your father, would you?"

His low laughter was mellow.

"It's not that I don't love him," she said, feeling the need to explain.

"You don't have to tell me." His pause drew her gaze. "Just between us, I wouldn't want to live with your father, either."

"But it's not that you don't *love* him," she quipped.

His lips quirked. "I love him like the father I never wanted."

She burst out laughing, elated by their mutual opinion of her father, and even more, the fact that he wasn't afraid to say so. "I can tell you didn't let

Daddy browbeat you in this deal,'' she said. ''For once old Growling Gower met a man he couldn't make dance to his tune. You should be proud.''

Some rueful emotion skittered across his features. Or did it? The light was fading and she couldn't be sure. The breeze picked up, ruffling her hair. She pulled the shawl closer about her, but it was too thin to do much good.

''Maybe this will help.'' Josh draped an arm about her, drawing her close.

She was amazed by her melting reaction. But then, Josh Raven wasn't one of those pathetic conformists she usually dated, who were more interested in currying favor with her father than in being with her. Josh was a successful, tough-minded man who had galloped in on his white charger and saved her father's company.

Now it was her father who was nervous in *Josh's* presence. That realization made her smile. Instead of stiffening and drawing away, she found herself nestling into the crook of his arm. His aftershave wafted about her, a sultry scent of summer nights and cedar. She inhaled deeply, enjoying the aroma.

What's going on, here? her brain cried. Something rosy-pink was clouding her mind. Why did she feel she'd known Joshua Raven all her life? What was it about his touch, his nearness, that made her want to know him—very, very well—for the rest of her days?

''Is that better?'' His warm breath stirred the hair at her temple.

She glanced up, struck again by the staggering beauty of those eyes. Her voice deserted her, and all she could do was nod.

"Good." He grinned, a crooked slash of straight, white teeth.

He shifted to gaze out at the lake, growing indistinguishable from the sky in the dimness. As they strolled, he continued to hug her to him. The only sound in the growing dusk was the pleasant lapping of water on sand, and the distant buzzing of a motorboat far out on the water.

They reached the end of the lawn and Josh turned to face her, propping a hip against the stone rail of the retaining wall that separated them from the beach ten feet below. "Would you like to walk on the sand?"

She hadn't done that in years. "I think I would."

He took her arm and helped her down the steep staircase. At the bottom step she sat down and tugged off her sandals. He pulled off his loafers and socks, then rolled up his trouser legs. With a sidelong glance, he said, "If it were warmer, we could swim."

She laughed. It had been eighty-nine degrees that afternoon. Warm for the first day of June. But the lake would be too cold for swimming for at least a month.

She indicated her dress. "I couldn't swim in this."

"You're right." His grin was sexy. "The dress would definitely have to come off."

As his gaze held hers, a rush of heat invaded her body. Oh, gracious! What was wrong with her? Why wasn't she slapping his face? Why did she have a scary feeling that if it were July, she'd be tearing off her clothes? "What a shame it isn't warmer," she finally managed, hoping she was kidding.

"Damn shame." He took her hand and pulled her up to stand.

As they strolled along, she couldn't help but ask, "Do you skinny-dip a lot?"

"Never have."

She peered at him. "Oh, *please*."

"No. Really."

She smirked, unconvinced. Some unruly imp inside her took the conversational reins. "And you've never made love, I suppose." She was surprised at herself. She didn't talk like this to a man she'd hardly met. Actually she didn't talk like this at all!

"Never made love?" His eyes twinkled. "Let me think."

She grinned, warming to the flirting game, unfamiliar though it was. "I bet you've never even kissed a woman."

"How did you guess?"

"We are now entering the Twilight Zone, folks," she said with a laugh.

His irresistible grin did insidious things to her insides. Needing a break from the lure of those eyes, she forced her gaze away.

He tugged on her hand and she realized he'd come to a halt. When she turned, his expression had lost all humor. "What?" she asked, strangely breathless, wondering at his mood change.

He inclined his head, the gesture unmistakable. He was telling her to come to him, though he was only a step away. "What do you want?" Her heart tripped over itself with womanly knowledge. She knew. And she was shocked to discover she wanted it, too.

He reached out, cupping her nape with gentle fingers. His thumb caressed the underside of her jaw, the sensation wildly erotic. She grew weak—and utterly willing—as he drew her face to his.

CHAPTER TWO

JOSH sat at his massive desk in his massive office, fighting off a massive headache. With a raw curse, he pushed up from his leather chair and stalked to stare out the window wall, overlooking Lake Michigan. Damn he felt like a worm, kissing the woman the way he had, leading her on.

But hadn't that been the point? Wasn't that the reason for the whole evening—to begin the "Wooing of Wendy"? When he'd made his deal with Gower Isaac he simply hadn't realized what a lousy taste the underhanded sham would leave in his mouth.

Not her kiss, he realized. There had been nothing lousy about the taste of her kiss. The odd little woman who wore crows in her hair was certainly compatible enough in that area. And she wasn't all that odd-looking, either. In that green sundress, with her hair curling around her face, there was an innocent sexiness about her. Another bit of compatibility he hadn't expected from Isaac's lackluster description of his daughter. Of course Gower would have no inkling of anything like that about his Wendy. The old man saw her as his useless non-son. Well, useless except for manipulating her into unknowingly helping to keep company control in the family.

A stab of pity made him wince. Hell, he didn't want to pity the woman, he wanted to marry her. No. In truth, he wanted to get the marriage behind him so he could get on with running what would now be called Raven-Maxim Enterprises.

He was proud that his consumer software publishing company had grown to be one of the largest in the United States. Combined with Gower Maxim's holdings, consisting of newspapers, television and radio stations as well as several national magazines, Josh would have wealth and power beyond his wildest dreams. The debts Isaac had incurred over the past few years didn't bother Josh. All Maxim Enterprises needed was a revitalization. That would come with innovative business techniques, along with trimming corporate fat. The challenge excited him. He was in his element.

Only one thing put a damper on his enthusiasm— the obligatory wedding. Nevertheless, didn't he know that nothing truly valuable came without sacrifice? Didn't he learn from his struggle up from meager beginnings, with parents who'd married more from need than desire, that life was not a bouquet of thornless roses?

"A man has to do what a man has to do," he muttered, repeating the tired phrase he'd heard his father say more times than he cared to remember. "So get on with it, Raven," he ground out. Pivoting away from the million-dollar view, he returned to his huge chrome-and-glass desk and punched his intercom. "Miss Oaks, get me Miss Isaac."

After her brisk "Yes, sir," he started to release the button, then thought better of it. "No—send her a dozen roses with an invitation to dinner."

"Where shall I send them, sir?" his secretary asked.

He closed his eyes, weary irritation rushing through him. "I don't know. Call Gower's office. Somebody there can track her down."

There was a pause, then, "Yes—sir. Should I say you'll be by to pick her up?"

He bit off a curse. "Of course I'll pick her up. Make it eight o'clock and get me that address."

"Yes, sir." Another pause. "Did you want to look over the stock prospectus now, sir?"

"Hell—I forgot. Yes. *Now,*" he barked, then realized what an ass he was being. This was totally unlike him. "Miss Oaks," he added more gently. "I'm sorry for snapping. It's been one of those days."

"No problem, sir." She sounded relieved. "We all have them."

"Thanks, Miss Oaks." He managed to sound less aggravated than he felt. "That will be all."

Releasing the button he flung his hand through his hair, hoping the Odd-Miss-Isaac would be as pleasantly disposed toward a quick marriage as her crow apparently was to Twinkies. He wanted to get this wedding business over.

Pressing his knuckles against throbbing temples, he sagged back in his chair. "Good lord, Raven, you've turned *yourself* into a blasted Twinkie!"

That evening, a few minutes before eight, Josh's chauffeur pulled to a stop in front of a brick apartment building in Evanston, a north Chicago suburb. Josh templed his hands before him, eyeing the place with diffidence. Though Evanston had its share of palatial lakefront homes, this apartment house was not in the most affluent section of town. Or even the middle class section. She certainly lived frugally, if her residence was any indication.

"Are you sure this is the right address, Mr. Raven?" his chauffeur asked.

Josh tapped his pursed lips with templed index fingers, fighting an ironic grin. "I'm afraid so, Higgins."

"Would you like me to go get the lady for you, sir?"

Josh cleared his throat to hide a chuckle. Obviously Higgins wasn't aware that in his childhood, this modest, aging building would have seemed like a palace. No doubt his chauffeur thought Josh feared catching something from the great unwashed masses. "No, Higgins, I'll retrieve the lady myself."

"What if there's no elevator, sir?"

Josh worked at keeping his expression serious. "Let's not be negative, Higgins." He opened the door, stepping onto the sidewalk, then remembered something and tapped the chauffeur's window. When the young man lowered the glass Josh held out a hand. "Give me that sack."

Higgins's small features were already drawn down in a perplexed frown—an expression that became even more perplexed as he picked up the brown paper sack and handed it through the window.

"Thanks."

"Yes, sir." As the darkened window glass rose, Josh watched in amusement as his chauffeur shook his head, clearly dumbfounded.

When Josh turned away, he had to grin. He didn't think Higgins had ever been more confused than a few minutes ago when Josh asked him to pull into a nearby Quick-And-Go store and buy the box of Twinkies.

Dim yellow light from a street lamp illuminated a dandelion in his path, its yellow head poking through a crack in the walkway. Stepping around it, he followed an uneven cement walk to the front steps, eyeing the thin strip of yard in the gloom. The grass could use mowing.

He bounded up two cracked and chipped steps. Inside a peeling green door he found himself in a narrow hallway, the walls papered with green cabbage roses from some long bygone era. It didn't take more than a glance to determine that there was no elevator. Just four doors labeled 1A, B, C, and D.

Drawing a slip of paper from his suit coat, he confirmed his suspicion—5A. "Naturally."

He scowled at the staircase dividing 1A and B from C and D. The steps were steep and well-worn. "Miss Isaac-the-Odd," he muttered under his breath, "I salute your cardiovascular fitness."

With a determined set of his jaw, he started up the creaky stairs, reminding himself this was a small price to pay for the realization of his life's goal.

Wendy Isaac answered his knock with unsophisticated speed. The woman didn't seem to know the meaning of the term "feminine wiles," at least not the one about keeping a gentleman cooling his heels outside her door.

"Hello, Josh," she said with that contagious grin. Though a bit winded, he grinned back as he scanned her from head to toe. She wore a basic black dress that hugged her slim waist, giving her an appealing hourglass look. Her scent was light, like fresh air after a rain. He had a feeling it was soap rather than cologne. Nice, though, and refreshing, after some of the perfume-drenched debutantes he'd known.

Her brown hair was swept up in a casual pile, stray wisps framing her face. Though Josh knew such artful disarray was all the rage in woman's coiffures these days, he sensed that with Miss Isaac it was more due to her breezy lifestyle than a fashion statement.

She stepped away from the door to allow him entry, indicating a bouquet on an oval dining table. Though the piece of furniture was polished to a bright sheen, it looked as though it had come from a thrift shop. "The roses are lovely Josh." Her cheeks grew pink. "I'm so sorry about the lovely vase." She peered at him sheepishly. "I'm afraid Alberta knocked my best one over and broke it. I had to borrow a mayonnaise jar from next door, and then I had to trim the stems to make them fit." She shook her head, looking pained. "In Illinois, I think it's a felony to trim long-stemmed roses to fit into a mayonnaise jar."

He found himself chuckling, his dour mood lifting somewhat. "Only a misdemeanor, but we'll keep it just between us." He contemplated the small apartment, wondering why she lived like this. Surely she had a trust fund or an inheritance from her mother. The place was neat and clean, but everything had the look of secondhand stores and flea markets. As he surveyed the place, his glance once again fell on Wendy. She'd moved silently across the worn carpet to a green and brown plaid couch. Across one arm lay a black jacket that matched her sleeveless dress.

She picked it up and handed it to him.

As he helped her into it he heard a rustling sound. "Kiss me, pretty boy!" came the familiar challenge. Josh looked up in time to see a flurry of white feathers swoop in from another room.

The crow landed on the tabletop and gave the roses a piercing look. If Josh hadn't known better, he'd have thought the bird was finding fault with them. Suddenly he remembered the sack. "Oh, I brought something for Alberta."

Wendy looked at him, her expression one of surprise. "Really?"

He held out the paper bag. "You do the honors."

Wendy took the sack and opened it, her astonished expression changing, softening into a lovely smile. "Why, Josh…" She shook her head as though in awe. "That's so sweet." Lifting the box out, she wagged it at her crow. "Look, you naughty girl. Josh brought you a present, too."

Like a shot, Al was airborne, landing heavily on Wendy's outstretched sleeve. Ripping at the cardboard, Al squawked, "Take it off, pretty boy! Take it all off!"

With a laugh, Wendy tossed the box to the couch and Al quickly fluttered after it. She faced Josh, those neon eyes shining. "I think I'd better rescue all but one of those or she'll make herself sick."

Intrigued by the bird's comical antics, Josh relaxed against the wall, crossing his arms before him. "Who did you say owned Al before you did? The Happy Hooker?"

Though her back was to him, Josh watched her neck go red with embarrassment as she detached the box and its contents from Al's talons—all but one Twinkie, already mutilated beyond recognition. "We're not sure who her first owner was. One day Millville found her perched on Daddy's patio table singing that song 'Bad to the Bone.' You know the one? Anyway, Millville loves animals so he tried lots of things to coax her to him." Wendy disappeared around a corner and Josh assumed she was putting the Twinkies away in a kitchen cabinet. When she returned, she smiled shyly. "Anyway, what finally worked was a Twinkie."

She shrugged. "When Al's spicy vocabulary began to come out in dribs and drabs, we started having misgivings about her previous owner. We advertised in the lost and found section of the paper for a month, but nobody answered the ad." She stopped by the couch and lovingly stroked the crow's head. "Al's so smart and funny. I couldn't leave Daddy's house, and not bring her with me. I love her—vocabulary and all."

Josh glanced at the bird, perched on the sofa in the middle of shredded cellophane and Twinkies crumbs. Al eyed him back, her head cocked jauntily to one side, a glob of cream filling on her beak.

He grinned at the cocky little vixen. "What? No 'thank you,' young lady?"

Al inclined her head the other way, as though considering his request. Then with what looked like a wink of one pink eye, she squawked, "Cash. No checks!"

Josh felt a surge of absurd amusement and laughed. "You're welcome, you little hussy."

"Now, be good, Al," Wendy admonished. "If anybody tries to get in, you bark like Aggie and scare them away."

The crow flapped her wings threateningly and gave off a startling impression of a bloodthirsty Doberman. "Whoa." Josh grinned at Wendy. "Remind me never to cross that female."

As he smiled down at her, quiet seconds ticking by, Wendy lowered her gaze and fidgeted with her jacket as though straightening it. To Josh it looked more like a nervous gesture than a need to adjust her clothing. When she lifted her gaze to meet his once again, her cheeks were that bright peach color they seemed to be every time she made direct eye contact with him. "You don't have to worry about Al," she murmured. "She has a crush on you."

Placing his hand in the small of her back, he steered her out of the apartment. "How many men can say that about a crow they've just met?" he kidded.

Though he kept his grin in place, he thought cynically, *Good going, Josh, you've won the damn bird's affections, now you'd better get the woman's—and fast!*

The restaurant on the ninety-fifth floor of the Hancock building served a variety of the best in international cuisine that Chicago had to offer. Unfortunately, Wendy couldn't taste a thing. Her whole body, taste-buds and all, were focused on the fact that she was actually out on a real live date with one of the most eligible bachelors in the country—and his attention was riveted to her every word.

He smiled all the time, laughing at her smallest funny story, appearing vitally interested in her passion for Project Literacy. How perfect could one evening be?

Perhaps another kiss? No, that would be too perfect. Nobody in the history of the world had ever experienced an evening *that* perfect. Under the cover of the table, she'd actually pinched herself several times to make sure she wasn't dreaming all this. She feared she'd have a good size bruise tomorrow.

Josh gazed into her eyes, smiling, his craggy features splendidly male in the candlelight. She found herself harking back to last night and the kiss they shared. His lips had been warm, masterful, yet beautifully sensitive. She'd learned a terrible and wonderful truth with that kiss.

It had been all too clear—a truth she hadn't wanted to form into a full-blown, rational thought. And that truth was, the instant Josh Raven smiled at her last night—with Al stuck to her head—she'd fallen hopelessly, irrevocably in love with him. She'd recognized that fateful moment somewhere on a subconscious level, but the protective part of her brain had tried desperately to keep it buried.

But Josh's kiss had released that truth from its captivity and she was forced to face it head-on. *She loved him.* What an awful thing to discover about a man who could get any woman he wanted—and according to the tabloids—*did*. When the roses and his dinner invitation came today, she'd almost died of both terror and joy. She didn't dare believe that he had been moved by their kiss, too. But she hadn't been strong enough to refuse his invitation.

In the companionable silence she ran her tongue along her upper lip as her thoughts drifted with warm, delicious memories of his kiss. Strains of something soft and classical served as a romantic backdrop while they sat there, communicating with their eyes. He sipped his coffee but his glance remained on her.

When he put his cup down, he smiled and she had to quell a tremor at the intimate beauty of it. She felt a prick of sadness, wishing she hadn't accepted for this evening. Being so near Josh Raven was cruel torture. This man could never think of her as anything but "the peculiar daughter of Gower Isaac," so why did she have to put herself through this? No doubt this evening was his way of ingratiating himself to "the family." She swallowed hard. It would have been kinder if he'd sent the Twinkies by courier and kept his distance.

"Wendy?" The sound of her name, spoken in a husky whisper, sent a delightful quiver skittering along her spine.

She nodded. "Hmmm?"

His big, warm hand slipped over hers and squeezed. "Let's get married."

She had been smiling at him. Dreamily indulging her schoolgirl fantasies. But with his touch and the softly spoken request, she blinked. Surely he'd said something completely ordinary, like "Pass the sugar," and her lovesick brain had garbled the request.

She picked up the china sugar bowl and lay it beside

his coffee cup. His glance shifted with her movement to the bowl, then returned to her face. His brows dipped in what appeared to be puzzlement.

Wondering at her bizarre brain malfunction, she cast her gaze around the table. What could he have possibly asked for? There were only the salt and pepper shakers left to choose from, since he couldn't have asked her to pass him the candle. But did he really want salt or pepper on his black walnut cake? She stared at him, bewildered. "I'm sorry. I'm afraid I didn't hear you."

His expression eased into another charming smile. "There goes my ego. I ask a woman to marry me and she's not even paying attention." He squeezed her fingers. "Do I have your attention, now?"

She gaped. He'd said absolutely nothing about sugar, salt or pepper. He'd said something about *marriage*.

He leaned around the table and lightly kissed the shell of her ear. "Wendy." His breath caressed her cheek. "Say something." When he drew back so their glances could meet, his gaze was intense.

She felt her hand being squeezed again, and managed to shake herself out of the pleasant stupor the touch of his lips against her ear had induced. Her heart turned over with a mixture of excitement and mystification. He couldn't mean what it sounded like he meant, could he? Gorgeous men of the world didn't actually fall in love with blunt, headstrong oddballs like her. And they certainly didn't propose marriage on the first date. She was simply going to have to make a doctor's appointment to have her ears checked—or get herself committed—or both.

She shook her head, trying to clear whatever it was that was blocking her ears. "Forgive me, Josh, but—"

"I know this is sudden," he cut in. "But I have to tell you, Wendy. No other woman has made me feel this way before. I need you in my life."

She blinked, staring into his eyes. They were amazing eyes. And they seemed to have nothing more pressing to do than gaze lovingly in her direction. "Wendy?" Her name came quietly, this time with a hint of—of *what?* Desperation? Longing? Or possibly—dare she even think it—hurt?

"Yes, Josh?" High-pitched and feeble, her voice didn't sound like her at all.

His gaze never leaving her face, he lifted her hand and brushed a kiss across her knuckles. "Do you think you could care for me, Wendy?"

Her hand tingled from the stroke of his lips and lingering touch of his fingers. Her ear still sizzled from his kiss. Her body was hot all over, and she knew her face must be flaming, though she prayed the candlelight masked her blush. Flustered and timid, she lowered her glance to her neglected crème brûlée. "I—I…" Her throat closed and she couldn't squeeze any words past the lump that formed there.

"Wendy, Wendy," he whispered urgently, leaning nearer until their lips were hardly an inch apart. "I realize what I've said may frighten you away. Still, I can't help it. I'm a man of action. I don't know any other way than just to say what I feel."

She met his gaze, wide-eyed in her amazement. He couldn't actually be proposing marriage. She didn't have that kind of effect on men. Sure she'd had boyfriends, but never had she known any man who radiated such potency, was so ragingly sensual or so unabashedly male. And never in a million—no make that a trillion—years, would she have held out any foolish hope that such a man would look twice at her.

Let alone propose marriage!

He reached out with his other hand, curling gentle fingers about her nape, drawing her just close enough to lightly tease her lips with his. "I have frightened you." He drew away, but only far enough to speak.

She sucked in a shaky breath. "Yes," she admitted, pulling out of his touch. "This doesn't make sense. You can't possibly be in love with me. You've known me for little more than twenty-four hours."

He took her hand, refusing to let her pull away. "Haven't you heard, darling? It happens that way, sometimes."

She swallowed spasmodically. Yes, of course, she'd heard of love at first sight. She'd even experienced it—with Josh! But it couldn't have happened to him! He couldn't have fallen for her. This was a dream. She pinched herself again, and winced. No, she felt awake. Her pulse beat pounded so furiously in her brain, she feared for her skull. But this simply couldn't be real. He couldn't possibly mean it. "This is a very bad joke, Mr. Raven," she said, trying to sound stern.

His smile faded and he released her hand. Sitting back in his chair, he mouthed a curse and looked away. "I'm sorry, Wendy, I just—" His jaw bunched and flexed in agitation as he jerked out his wallet, retrieving a platinum charge card. "I was a fool to speak my mind. Of course, now I see my feelings are all one-sided. Forgive me for embarrassing you."

Though he was no longer touching her, her head still reeled and throbbed, her body trembled. She hesitated, staring, baffled. His eyes seemed to shimmer with sadness. What was going on here? Had what he'd proposed been honest? Had he meant it from the heart? She vacillated, floundering in conflicting emotions. There was nothing she wanted more than to spend the rest of her life at this man's side, bearing his children, being his loving wife.

He lifted a hand to signal the waiter who seemed to appear from nowhere to relieve him of his card. When the employee was gone, Josh faced her, his expression solemn. "Do you forgive me for my rashness?" He reached out as though intent on taking her fingers in his, but seemed to think better of it and lay his hand on the table. "I'm an impulsive fool."

His dark eyes exhibited a bleakness that was hard to witness and she had to suppress a scream of frustration at the back of her throat. *What had she done?* Had this been a real proposal—from a man she'd fallen so hopelessly in love with that she couldn't believe it when she heard it? Had she actually turned him down? Did this sort of crazy miracle happen to ordinary people like her?

He cleared his throat. "Well, what should we talk about?" he asked, sounding as though he was working at being nonchalant.

"*Yes,*" she blurted. What good did it do to try and analyze the vagaries of falling in love? That was as fruitless and pointless as allowing this magnificent man to slip through her fingers. "I don't understand how it all happened so quickly, but *yes,* Josh. I'll marry you."

Reaching out, she lifted his hand from the tabletop, kissed his palm, then scanned his handsome face. "I didn't want to admit it even to myself..." she murmured through a tremulous sigh. "But when you kissed me last night, I knew, Josh. I knew I was in love with you."

His eyes, those marvelous, expressive dark eyes widened the smallest fraction, then narrowed slightly, and she wondered what flinty emotion flashed in their depths. Or was the rush of tears that blurred her vision responsible for the mysterious distortion?

"Darling," he said, his voice low. "My darling, Wendy."

She smiled through trembling lips. "Oh—Josh."

He took her face between his hands. They seemed so cool, so steady. "You'll never know how happy this makes me."

Her heart flew away, soared and dived in the heavens as tears of joy slid down her cheeks. "How—how…" Working at collecting her emotions she smoothed back a lock of his hair, loving the silk feel of it beneath her palm. She relished the thought of knowing this amazing man *much* more intimately—of loving him for the rest of her life as he so clearly loved her.

"Oh, Josh—" Her voice breaking with happiness, she began again. "Oh, Josh—darling—what have I done to deserve you?"

CHAPTER THREE

LIKE shooting fish in a barrel, Josh thought grudgingly. He was engaged, just like that. Exactly as he'd planned—to a woman he hardly knew. A woman who had professed to love him.

He walked out onto the balcony of his apartment, two floors above his suite of offices in one of Chicago's most prestigious high-rises. The view of Lake Michigan was beautiful, with city lights defining graceful undulations of the shoreline. Sometimes after a hectic day the view helped Josh relax. But not tonight. He'd returned his new fiancée to her apartment and left her there with one, chaste kiss. Closing his eyes, he slumped against the railing. "Well, Gower, it looks like you've bartered yourself a son-in-law."

The chiming of his doorbell brought his head up with a start. He glowered at his watch. "Midnight?" he muttered. "Who the hell could be dropping by at this hour?" He reentered a living room that reeked of classic richness and unhurried grace. At least that's what a recent article in *Architectural Monthly* had stated. He gave the room's low slung modern furnishings and distinctive artwork a disgruntled look. As far as he was concerned it looked like a pretentious interior designer's waiting room. He heard a sound and glanced toward the entryway in time to see his butler hurriedly donning a black suit coat. "I'll get it, Nelson." He waved off the portly man. "You go on to bed."

Nelson stifled a yawn and nodded his thanks, withdrawing silently to his quarters. Josh's shoes made a clipped rat-a-tat across the black granite foyer to the double-doored entry. One quick look through the peephole told him who was there. "This is all I need," he grumbled under his breath. Opening the door, he manufactured a smile. "Hello, Evelyn. You're looking well."

The tall brunette swept past him, leaving a trail of designer fragrance in her wake. Once inside, she twirled around to face him. Her slim column dress of iridescent red organza was slit up one side to mid-thigh, showcasing a long, shapely leg.

Shiny, black hair swirled with her, falling into perfect order about her shoulders. Her smile was brilliant, expectant. "You look like you're getting ready to go to bed." Her bright blue eyes narrowed speculatively as her glance slid over him. "No tie, no jacket?"

He lifted a brow to indicate his doubt that she dropped in on many men at midnight to find them totally primed for an evening out. "I don't know what came over me," he said, his tone purposely sardonic.

She gave Josh what he had come to think of as "her best pout." "I thought we might go dancing." She smiled slyly. "Or—something."

He closed the door and leaned against it, crossing his arms before him. "You did, did you?" He smiled at her, but didn't bother to keep the impatience from his voice. "It's midnight, Evelyn. Tomorrow's a workday. Just because you can sleep until noon doesn't mean I can."

She moved toward him and began to toy with his shirt collar. "Don't be silly, Josh, dear. You're the boss. You can do anything you want."

He gave her a level stare. "Perhaps I want to get to work before noon."

She skimmed a long fingernail over his lower lip. "What else do you want to do, sweets?" Her question was highly suggestive. Only a stone or a dead man could miss her meaning.

Here was another complication to his upcoming marriage. *The girlfriend.* His gut clenched, even though Evelyn Jannis wasn't technically his girlfriend. They'd merely gone out several times over the past few weeks. That was it. He'd made no promises and she'd asked for none. Nevertheless, Evelyn seemed to be broadly hinting she wanted to take their relationship to a higher level—or, more likely, she was feeling lusty. He reached up and took her wrist. "Evelyn, you're a lovely woman, and we've—"

"We certainly have," she cut in with a sultry laugh, lifting her free hand to run her fingers through his hair. "Come on, Josh, I'm not in the mood for chatting."

Pressing against him, she lifted her chin, giving him a "kiss me" look. He smiled without enthusiasm, firmly setting her away. "Listen to me, Evelyn." His sternness made her blink and stare.

"What?" she asked, her expression going wary. "What's so serious?"

He didn't think there was any point in beating around the bush. "I'm getting married."

She didn't move for a few seconds, then her lips parted in a stunned "Oh." "Married," she echoed, with barely any sound. Quickly, she seemed to gather her wits, and straightened her shoulders. "Who?" Her tone was hard, her pupils all but disappearing. "When did this happen?"

"Tonight. I'm marrying Gower Isaac's daughter."

She frowned for a second, then her face cleared. "Oh—it's *business.*" She smiled, looking relieved. "You had me worried for a moment." Her arms came up to skim along his shoulders, then curl behind his neck, as she drew herself against him once more. "That needn't affect us, sweets. I'm a big girl. I know about these things."

He gritted his teeth. She was *definitely* feeling lusty! It was too bad the woman knew how to move her body to do the most damage to his resistance. Her nudging and rubbing was subtle, but ripe with erotic innuendo. "Josh," she prodded, lifting her lips toward his, "let's play."

He inhaled, the male animal in him battling with his promise of marriage to another woman. He may have set about this wedding scheme knowing he didn't love Wendy Isaac, but he had also set about it with honorable intentions—well, as honorable as the situation allowed.

He believed in the institution of marriage. His parents may have come together out of mutual need, but they'd come together with the belief that the vows they'd taken were sacred. Through poverty and hardship, they'd struggled together, trusted and depended on each other. Their union had been honest and upright.

Nostrils flaring with a determined inhale, he pulled her arms from about his neck. "I mean for this marriage to work, Evelyn. I won't be playing around."

Evidently not expecting to be set away for a second time, Evelyn stumbled a step, and Josh had to take her arm to steady her. She stared in visible disbelief. "Work?" She sounded incredulous. "What do you mean *work?* You aren't saying you love this woman, are you? I've never even heard you mention her. You haven't even said her name!"

"Wendy," he murmured, not completely convinced it was the best idea to reject a warm, willing female he knew to be an appealing bed partner, for no other reason than the fact that he'd promised to marry someone he hardly knew. His future bride was a naive young thing who lived like a destitute college student. Not only that, she'd adopted a bird that had unquestionably witnessed more about satisfying a man than her owner could even imagine. "Wendy Isaac," he repeated, noting with regret that his tone was less than elated.

The brunette tapped her foot, her elegantly arched brows dipping in consternation. "Okay, you've said her name. What does that prove?" She planted her hands on her hips. "Tell me this marriage is *not* business, that you love her *wildly. I dare you!*"

He lifted his gaze away from his guest's damning expression. His glance fell on a brass-and-granite table across the room. Atop it, before the window wall, stood a carved wooden stallion, quarter life-size, cantering majestically in a silver stream of moonlight. It crossed Josh's mind that he liked that piece—he supposed—as much as anything in the place. After a moment, his gaze fell once again to the woman before him. Interestingly, he didn't feel as much emotion for Evelyn as he felt for the chunk of wood.

As he looked into angry green eyes, another thought came to him. He liked Wendy Isaac—at least she could make him laugh, and she cared about something besides herself. That had been refreshing to discover about anybody in this day of cynicism and "me first" mentality.

"I'm fond of Wendy Isaac," he stated truthfully. "I'm going to try to be a good husband." He reached for the doorknob, turning it, though his eyes remained on his frowning companion. "Now, if you'll excuse me, Evelyn, I have an early meeting."

The latch clicked and her gaze skittered to the knob. Josh stepped away, opening the door wide. She stared as though in disbelief, then glared at him. "What was *I*, then?" she demanded.

His polite smile faded as she scowled at him, a mixture of dread and helplessness sparking in her eyes. She looked as though he was holding a gun to her head, and he found himself experiencing a twinge of guilt. She was good at dredging up blame, he had to give her that. The truth was, Evelyn knew what she was to him—and he knew he meant exactly the same thing to her. A diversion. A brief dalliance to satisfy sexual needs. However, he supposed, being the one dumped, she had the right to play "injured party."

"Evelyn," he began as gently as he could, "You're a lovely woman, but we both knew—"

A hard slap across his face cut him off. "Don't you dare say it, Josh!" Her features contorted with rage. "Don't tell me what we both *knew!*" Stalking by, she spun on him at the threshold, and lifted her chin belligerently. "I never want to see you again," she shouted. "Don't call me!"

Once she'd flounced out of his line of vision, he closed the door. Frowning, he wondered if her theatrics had been overheard by anyone at this late hour. With a rush of resignation and pity, he stuffed his hands into his trouser pockets. If her face-saving act helped soothe her ego, allowing even one person to think she had broken it off, it was little enough to grant her. After all Evelyn was as much a victim as Wendy, he supposed. He only hoped his new fiancée would never discover how he'd callously manipulated her into a promise of marriage.

He retraced his steps across the living room's plush carpet, heading onto the patio. A shimmering trail of moonlight on the lake caught his eye. Lifting his face to the moon, he scowled. The pale orb stared down at him, its ancient features eerily accusing. "Don't look at me like that," he muttered, rubbing his stinging jaw. "Didn't I turn down a sure thing and get slapped in the bargain, just to remain *honorable?*"

A half dozen tense seconds slipped by as the word "honorable" ricocheted inside his head. Wincing, he turned his back. "Shut up, old man," he snarled. "Who asked you?"

With a despondent sigh, Wendy realized she should have made something easier for dinner, like hot dogs. This menu wasn't working out well. The beef Roulade called for dill pickles. Unfortunately, her shopping list got smudged in the rain, so she'd neglected to buy them. Consequently, she'd been forced to use pickled okra, reasoning that once the thin slices of beef were rolled up around the other ingredients who would know?

But now, witnessing the steaming results of her labors, they didn't look much like the picture in the cookbook. Some of the toothpicks had come out, and their innards lolled on the gravy like shipwreck flotsam in a brown sea.

One of the salad tomatoes ruptured when she stuffed it and looked in need of emergency surgery. Its guts of cooked vegetables poked out the rip in an excruciating-looking display.

At least the apple pudding smelled good. And she'd remembered to buy lemon ice cream for a topping, just as the recipe suggested. She crossed her fingers that the rest of the dinner would taste as good as the apple pudding smelled. She'd been assured by Josh's chef that these were some of his favorite foods. If she was to be his wife, she wanted to show him she cared about such things. She wanted to make him happy he'd chosen *her* over all the women he could have married.

A knock on her door set her heart to beating at the rate of a hummingbird's wings. Hurriedly, she checked her face in the shiny blade of a butter knife. With a self-deprecating giggle she thumped it down on the tile countertop, hoping the rest of her face was as smudge-free as the half-inch strip she'd been able to see.

Nervously she smoothed her yellow cotton dress, fiddling with the collar as she dashed to the door.

"Let's scram! It's the cops!" squawked Al.

Wendy frowned at the crow on her perch as Al flapped her wings and caw-cawed. "Oh, hush," she admonished in a whisper. "Be a good girl, tonight. I have *plans!*" She took a deep breath and threw open the door.

There he was. The man she loved. Every time she saw him, witnessed his masculine perfection, she was gripped in a pleasant paralysis. She trailed her gaze over him, wishing she could devour him, take him completely inside her to keep and hold, to cherish, forever. Dressed casually in beige trousers and a burgundy polo, he looked recklessly elegant, no—he looked too sexy to bear.

"Hi," he said with a grin, his voice releasing her from her immobility.

"Hi, yourself," she echoed breathlessly, running into his arms. His kiss was warm and welcome and she held him close, relishing the feel of his hard chest against her breasts, his subtle scent beneath the tang of cedar-spiced cologne. "I missed you, yesterday," she admitted shyly, her smile and her voice overflowing with love.

He took her hand and drew her inside, closing her door. "Whose fault was that?"

She nuzzled his jaw. "Mine. But it was my day to read stories in the children's ward at the hospital. As for last night, I can't abandon my literacy students, now can I?"

He drew her to the sofa and pulled her down to sit beside him. "Of course not." Releasing her hand, he rested an arm along the back of the sofa. "Besides, I had to meet with—"

"I know," she interrupted with a laugh. "Daddy."

He nodded. "Not my favorite Isaac." He squeezed her shoulders and she reveled in his show of affection. Looking away, he sniffed the air. "What smells so good?"

She took a deep breath. "That's your favorite dessert."

He glanced at her, his brows dipping in incredulity. "Apple pudding?"

She smiled. "I've fixed all your favorites." Unable to help herself, she touched his chin, coaxing him to lower his face. "Because I love you." She lightly kissed his lips, but continued to watch his eyes. They were wonderful eyes, dark, framed by wickedly thick lashes. Yet, something in their depths—

She sat back, suddenly unsure. "Is something wrong, Josh?"

His eyebrows knit for an instant before he recovered, grinning. "Not a thing—except I'm starving." Pushing up, he held out a hand. "Let's eat."

She placed her fingers into his. "Forgive me, sweetheart. Of course, you've had a long day. I'm being selfish."

"Not at all," he countered. "And you shouldn't have gone to all this trouble. My chef could have done this for us. I hope you don't want me to put the poor man out to pasture after we're married. He's only thirty-three."

"Of course not." Wendy curled an arm about his waist. "But he'll have a day off, won't he?"

"There's the slight chance," he kidded.

She laughed. "And didn't you tell me we'd spend our honeymoon alone at your cabin in the Adirondacks?"

"That's true." He glanced down at her, his features amused and curious.

"So, do you cook?" she teased.

"Actually, I do." He chuckled at her surprise. "So, what are your favorite foods?"

She shook her head. "Oh, no, a girl has to keep *some* secrets until after the wedding."

He gave a mock grimace. "That bad, huh?"

"Certainly not! They're all easy and tasty, but— cholesterol city." When they reached the table, she moved his latest bouquet to the side and indicated his place opposite hers. "You sit and relax. I'll serve."

Twenty minutes later, Wendy was pleased at how smoothly dinner was going. Josh didn't seem to notice the substituted okra, or at least didn't mention it. And even though his rolled-up beef Roulades all unrolled with an uncharitable lack of consideration for Wendy's painstaking work, they tasted good.

She listened attentively as Josh told her about his day and his plans for rejuvenating her father's company. She watched him dreamily. Could he possibly be even more handsome when he spoke so enthusiastically about the work he loved?

Al landed on Josh's shoulder and nabbed a slice of

beef off his fork. After the crow made a fluttery get-away with her booty, Wendy fought a grin at Josh's reaction. For a second he appeared stunned, his fork poised at his mouth. But soon enough his expression eased into a smile. "I realize crows will eat just about anything, but right off my fork?" he quipped. "Is this one of the secrets you were keeping from me until after the wedding?"

"We women of mystery have all kinds of secrets, darling," Wendy joked. "Actually, I think Al wanted a souvenir from you. Be glad she didn't nip out a lock of your hair." Wendy made a pained face. "Trust me. I know what I'm talking about."

He chuckled, and the rich sound sent renewed waves of happiness through Wendy's body. This man, Josh—this love of her life—had a wonderful, deep, sincere laugh. She knew she would never tire of hearing it, not if she lived to be two thousand years old.

Dabbing her lips with her napkin, she inhaled, attempting to slow her heart rate. Every time she looked at him, heard his voice, experienced again that dazzling smile, she went a little batty, wanting to cry out her joy, run madly from housetop to housetop yelling out her bliss.

She'd always been a passionate person—passionate about jumping in and helping people and animals in need—but she'd never felt particularly passionate about a man before. Probably because none of them had been the *right* man. None of them had been Joshua Raven.

Now she knew what her girlfriends meant when they went on and on with gushy exuberance about the special men in their lives. Now she understood how loving a man truly felt. It was one of the most marvelous miracles to be imagined—the divine connection that happened between the right man and the right woman. She felt blessed and humbled to be so fortunate.

Clearing a lump of weepy thankfulness from her throat, she managed evenly, "Are you ready for dessert? Coffee?"

He winked at her. "You read my mind." He pushed up. "But I'll help. You cooked the whole dinner."

She started to protest, but the woman inside her squelched the urge. She wanted to be near him, to brush against him, to spontaneously kiss and hold the man she loved. To be embarrassingly honest, she was dying for him to sweep the dinner dishes to the floor, grab her up in his arms, throw her on the table and make wild love to her right there.

"What are you looking at?" Josh asked, sounding very near.

She blinked, unaware that she'd slipped into a lewd daydream, lingering there like a demented fool, staring longingly at the table, envisioning their bodies entwined in the act of....

She cast her glance away, unable to look him in the eye for fear he'd see her desire. "Nothing—nothing at all." She flinched at the squeaky sound of her voice, and barreled into the kitchen.

"Something's wrong, Wendy," he insisted, following her.

"No, please." She grabbed a couple of pot holders and opened the oven. Carefully she withdrew the apple pudding, chagrined to see her hands shaking. "I'm being foolish."

When she placed the dessert on the counter, she felt Josh's hands on her shoulders, coaxing her to face him. "Foolish?"

She didn't meet his gaze, but smiled wanly. "Very."

With a finger, he tipped her chin up and she had to look him in the eye. "What could be that foolish?"

She swallowed. She didn't dare tell him she wanted him to ravish her. It was his place to start the seduction, wasn't it? Or was it okay for a woman to ravish her fiancé if she decided to? She'd never been engaged before. Still, from what she knew of relationships today, men and woman didn't need to be engaged—or even know each other well—to indulge in a little consensual ravishing. Did they?

"What is it, Wendy?" Josh's features closed in confusion. "Have I done something?"

She shook her head at the irony of his question. "No—" She forced a smile, but her cheeks burned. "You haven't done anything...." Those few words were the absolute crux of the problem, yet she sensed Josh wouldn't grasp it. She was being too vague, drat her! Why couldn't she simply grab him by his shirtfront and demand, "Kiss me!" like Al did with such mortifying frequency?

"You're a pretty boy! Kiss me!" Al screeched, right on cue. Wendy jumped as though her own thoughts had come to life and been bellowed out to humiliate her. Blood thundered in her temples and she was helpless to staunch the flood of emotions that seared through her.

Josh's close scrutiny made her shudder, fearful that he might read her thoughts and think less of her for allowing her feelings to fall to such a base level. She was so ashamed! She'd never had erotic thoughts like this before. It was just—just that she loved him so much. Maybe she was going a little crazy.

Before she knew what was happening she'd thrown

herself into Josh's arms and was crying, sobbing. He
enfolded her in a tentative embrace, as though perplexed about what was going on, and afraid she might
panic if he held her too tightly.

Suddenly it was all too nutty, too surreal, and she
had to laugh. Why should she be ashamed of wanting
the man she loved to make love to her? Her laughter
mixed with shuddery sobs, making her look completely insane, she knew. But she couldn't help it. She
merely clung to Josh, sobbing and hiccuping.

After a minute she was lifted off the ground and
carried out of the kitchen. "Wendy, you're overwrought. It's my fault," he assured softly, lowering
her to the couch. "I'll go."

When he lifted himself away, she grabbed his wrist.
"*No!* I'm not overwrought." She clutched his wrist
with both hands. "I'm not crazy, either. I'm just—I
just want you to…to…" She swallowed, aware that
what she wanted, what she needed from him, was right
there for him to see—in her eyes.

He watched her for a moment, his expression bewildered, then compassionate, then cautious. Then uneasy. Anxiety charged through her. Uneasy? Why
would a man known as a rake and a playboy be uneasy
with the idea of making love to his own fiancée? It
made no sense. "Josh?" she cried, frightened, and not
sure why.

With her uncertain tone, he blinked, his expression
easing into a gentle smile. "I'm sorry, darling. I didn't
understand." Lifting her hand he kissed the sensitive
pulse point on the inner side of her wrist, murmuring
against her skin, "I want you, too, you must know
that."

He leaned toward her, bracing a hand beside her
head on the cushion. Brushing her hair away from her

face, he kissed her cheek, then each eyelid. The touch of his lips was tender, and in its tenderness, unbelievably erotic. "You're the one woman in my life," he vowed softly, his lips trailing sensuously to her mouth. "I want you to be happy." He kissed her then, and the beauty of it brought a hot ache to the back of her throat. She raised her arms to encircle his neck. But all too soon the kiss was over, and a soft cry of longing escaped her lips as he lifted himself away.

"I have something for you, darling," he whispered, taking one more lingering taste of her mouth before he sat up. "I was going to give it to you later this evening, but..." He paused, his expression serious.

All she wanted from him was the gift of his lips on hers, his hands on her bare skin, bringing her alive with his loving. Yet, she couldn't voice her need, could hardly see him. Her eyes were filled with thankful tears—tears that he had read the desire in her eyes, and now knew what to do.

He withdrew something from his trouser pocket and held it out to her. A small black velvet box. "I hope you like it." He lifted her hand, limp and unresponsive, her body still staggered from his kiss.

"A ring?" she asked, startled. *Oh, had she spoiled his romantic seduction with her silly fit?* She hitched up on one elbow. "Open it for me, sweetheart," she urged, in a murmur of wonder.

When he did, she blinked away more tears. Could any woman be this happy? First he would present her with an engagement ring, and *then* he would show her in a very physical way how much he adored her. She stared at the ring, then smiled up at him. "I—I've never seen such a beautiful thing." The diamond was pear-shaped, and nearly as large as her thumbnail. Having been acquainted with many wealthy women over the years, Wendy had seen her share of magnificent diamonds. Even so, this exquisite stone shimmered and flashed with such splendor, it would shame all but a handful of the most spectacular gems.

"May I slip it on your finger?" Josh asked.

She lifted her left hand. "It's lovely," she whispered, though she would have preferred something less splashy. She'd turned her back on her father's showy lifestyle several years ago in favor of a simpler, fuller existence, and such a huge ring made her uncomfortable.

"You don't like it?" he asked.

Wendy's gaze shot to his face. He was more intuitive than she'd imagined. She held it up to look at it, sparkling there on her finger. "Well—it's a little heavy." She gave him a sheepish look. "But—it's from you, Josh, so I love it."

He smiled wryly. "You hate it."

She pushed up to sit, hugging him to her. "I love *you*." She pulled back to look into his face. "But I'd love you every bit as much if you gave me a simple gold wedding band."

He eyed her curiously. "Are you sure?"

She laughed, loving this vulnerable side to him. "Am I sure I'd love you?" she teased. "Of course, silly. What a question."

"I meant are you sure about the ring?"

"Oh." She stroked his cheek. "I'm sure. Don't be mad."

"Your father might be," he muttered, or at least that's what she thought he said.

"My father?" She shifted to better see him. "Why should we care what he thinks?"

"We don't." He pulled her against him, snuggling her in the crook of his shoulder. "Not at all." He kissed her temple. "One plain, gold band it is." He slid the diamond ring off her finger.

Teasing his throat with her lips, she murmured, "Thank you, sweetheart." She kissed his warm flesh, nipping lightly. His scent was stimulating, arousing her, heightening her senses. Her body fairly hummed with need for him, every fiber of her being eager for the lovemaking to come. "You're perfect," she whispered through a sigh.

He rested his chin on the top of her head, and she wondered what his expression was—if he smiled with anticipation, too. He held her against him, yet the hand that had removed the ring lay idly by his side, fisted around the jewelry.

"I'm going to leave now, Wendy," he said at last.

She blanched, stiffening, not believing what he was saying. Tilting her head back, she stared into his eyes. "What?"

He removed his arm from around her and stood. Wendy felt cold, though the apartment windows were open, allowing the warm evening breeze inside. She blinked, bewildered. Had she hurt his feelings by refusing his gift? Reaching out, she took his hand. "Josh, don't go."

He squeezed her fingers affectionately, but stepped away. "Things have been moving quickly. I'm to blame. I see now you need a little space." He pressed a brief kiss on her forehead. "I'll call you tomorrow."

Before she could react, he was gone.

She stared blankly at the door. She *had* hurt him! That little speech about giving her space had been a transparent excuse if she'd ever heard one. Tears welled and overflowed. How stupid could she be? How could she have rejected his ring so bluntly the way she had? She'd called it *heavy* of all things.

He'd taken it as a personal rejection.

Flinging herself down on the couch, she wept into the cushion, calling herself every name she could think of and making up a few, to make sure she didn't misunderstand what a callous ignoramus she was. She'd ruined Josh's beautifully planned seduction, and she'd managed to wound him in the process. No woman in the history of accepting engagement rings could have been as clumsy and unfeeling as she was tonight.

Something poked her in the back as Al hopped to a landing between her shoulder blades.

"Roll me over in the clover!" came a singsong shriek, as the crow sauntered around on her back. "Roll me over in the clover, pretty boy!"

"Oh, Al..." she moaned. "Don't rub it in!"

CHAPTER FOUR

JOSH wasn't accustomed to leaving a woman when she had that "take me" look in her eyes. He wasn't accustomed to driving home with sweat beading his forehead, his knuckles clamped on the steering wheel in sexual frustration. And he wasn't accustomed to taking cold showers while cursing himself for thinking of this marriage as a means to an end—visualizing Gower Isaac's daughter as merely a hostess for business dinners and the mother of his two-point-five children.

He'd never considered how his scheme would affect a flesh-and-blood woman, a woman he was beginning to know as both caring and vulnerable. Yes, all in all, last night had been an evening full of experiences he wasn't accustomed to having, and feelings he wasn't accustomed to feeling.

"Damn."

"Did you say something, Mr. Raven?"

His gaze snapped up to see his secretary pause in the act of laying out his mail. He hadn't heard her come in. He scowled, unable to shake his foul mood. "No. Nothing." He bent over the profit and loss figures he'd been studying, shading his eyes from the young woman. "That will be all for now, Miss Oaks. Just leave the mail."

"Yes, sir."

Though his secretary was an attractive blonde, he made it a point never to get involved with employees. Never to even look at them funny. In today's business climate, if he had an affair with an employee and then dumped her, he would either end up being sued for sexual harassment or he'd come to work one day to find honey and catsup poured in his files. No, thanks. He didn't need female problems at work. That kind of trouble was easy enough to find without asking for it.

He heard the door to his office close and glanced up with a frown. Right now, he was having enough trouble with his fiancée.

Wendy wanted sex.

Maybe it was more correct to say she wanted to be made love to by the man who'd expressed a desire to spend the rest of his life with her. And *blast it,* she had every right to expect that.

He shoved a hand through his hair, slumping back. But he wasn't the man to show her. His one great love had always been his work. That's where he used up his passions every day. Oh, he knew how to seduce a woman and he knew how to please, but to show love? *That,* he didn't know how to do.

Marrying Wendy Isaac under the conditions Gower had outlined was dishonorable enough, without adding insult to injury. Sure, it would be pleasant to have sex with her. She was an attractive woman and he sensed that with the right guidance, she could be an extraordinary lover.

Since she was inexperienced, there was every possibility he could fool her into believing his feelings were more than superficial. But even if he did, taking her to bed before the wedding would be contemptible. She was a decent kid. She deserved to be treated decently.

According to his bargain with Gower, until the wedding vows were spoken, the final papers wouldn't be signed and the stock wouldn't be transferred. So before Wendy was his legitimate bride, there would be no messing around. He felt like a big enough pile of dirt as it was.

What if something happened and the merger fell through at the last minute? He damn well wouldn't go through with any marriage. And if he walked out, what would it do to an innocent like Wendy to discover she'd given herself so completely to a man who'd been lying to her? A hard fist of disgust twisted his gut, and he tasted bile. *No!* He would not indulge himself sexually simply to satisfy baser needs. Maybe he was a business shark, but he wasn't completely without scruples.

"Okay, smart guy," he grumbled, "how do you plan to keep her in her clothes for the next two months?" Here was yet another experience he was totally unfamiliar with—the *preservation* of a woman's virtue.

Sucking in a quick breath, like someone about to dive into icy water, he closed his eyes. His exhale was slow, through gritted teeth. It was going to be a long two months.

Josh realized with relief that he needn't have worried about keeping Wendy in her clothes. As soon as the news broke in the paper the next morning, it seemed the entire state of Illinois decided to host parties, dinners and showers to celebrate the upcoming nuptials.

Of course most of them were business affairs, and Josh could see that Wendy was only putting up with all the pomp and circumstance for his benefit. She could be a game kid, he mused, watching her smile and chat with the governor and his wife. He lounged against the wall of the country club ballroom where this latest fete was being hosted. Finding a quiet spot amid all the grandeur, glitter and gossip, he simply observed his bride-to-be.

She wore a conservative beige linen dress. The sleeves were short, the hemline falling midway between her knees and ankles. The simple dress had a scooped neck, but not scooped low enough to show cleavage. Her hair was pulled away from her face, not a strand out of place. Her only jewelry was a pair of tiny freshwater pearl earrings. She looked like a young girl at her commencement—a debutante in training.

He had a feeling she'd changed her hairstyle and her mode of dressing for him. It wasn't something he would have asked of her, yet, like learning his favorite foods, she must have assumed he would want her to look more like the cookie-cutter social butterfly her father clearly wanted her to be.

It was odd, but seeing her now, he realized he didn't care for the debutante look on Wendy. She was a "crow in her hair" type of woman, and he found nothing wrong with that. Maybe the world needed more people who weren't afraid to be a little different. He made a mental note to mention that she didn't have to dress for him. Though she was unaware of it, she was doing enough, simply by consenting to be his bride.

He crossed his arms and scanned her face as she laughed. It seemed to him, that even with a string quartet playing Mozart in the background, and the buzz of a hundred guests, he could hear the ring of her laughter. It sounded genuine, and she looked radiant, but Josh knew that deep inside she was upset about having to miss another tutoring session. She'd missed quite a few in the past weeks, not to mention several afternoons reading in the children's ward or taking her turn behind the cash register of the Animal Rescue Thrift Shop.

Still, she never complained. With a sweet smile, she'd said she would make do. She understood the necessity of these things, and after all, it meant so much to Gower. "Daddy," she'd said with a laugh, "would have a stroke if we declined a single invitation. For once in my life he's proud to call me his daughter."

Josh dropped his gaze at the memory, clenching his fists in his trouser pockets. Gower didn't deserve Wendy. Neither did he.

"Hey, there, Josh, old man, why are you hiding in the shadows?"

Shifting, he noticed one of his vice presidents grinning at him. "Just watching my future bride," he said, honestly.

"I don't blame you." The older man turned to scan Wendy, his expression appreciative. "She's about as lovely as they come, Josh." He shifted back, looking playfully skeptical. "How'd you ever talk her into marrying a good-for-nothing, workaholic, bum like you?"

Josh grinned wryly at his friend's kidding. "Luckily, I didn't send you to speak on my behalf, Pete." He clamped a hand on the man's shoulder, trying to appear the carefree bridegroom. "I think I'll go snatch her before the governor says something to make her regret her decision."

Pete snickered. "Yeah, weren't you two in college together?"

"That's what I mean." Josh pushed away from the wall. "I was a bit of a womanizer back then."

"A *bit?*" Pete chortled. "Back *then?*"

Josh had taken a step away, but turned back, arching a wry brow. "I trust your résumé is polished and up to date?"

Pete's laughter didn't fade with the threat. He just waved his boss off.

A moment later Josh joined Wendy. Governor Perry acknowledged him with a nod, but continued with his story. Since it was one that Josh had heard many times before, he absently observed the crowd. Tucking his fiancée beneath an arm, he tried to communicate his assurance that he understood how hard all this was for her. She responded to his touch with a smile, her bright purple eyes aglow with soft emotions. When she turned back, he watched her profile for a moment before realizing the governor had directed a comment to him. "What?" he finally said, glancing up.

Ben Perry shook his head at his old school friend. "Lovesickness looks good on you, Josh."

He stared at Ben, put off by his analysis. It was interesting how thoroughly people could delude themselves. Just because he'd proposed to Wendy, and because he smiled at her and held her close, people assumed such asinine things. Then again, Ben was easy to bluff. He'd never won a poker game from Josh in his life. Chuckling as though caught, he said, "I could never hide anything from you, could I?"

Ben's grin widened. "Look, it's late. Why don't you two sneak on out? I can tell you'd like to be alone."

Josh sensed Wendy's eyes on him. He glanced at her, feeling trapped. "Would you like to leave, darling?"

She smiled. *Of course she would. Stupid question.*

He smiled down at her, though it wasn't easy. He knew what she wanted. *Damn.* Two more weeks until the wedding, and each one of the past six had been tougher than the one before, concocting ways to keep her at arm's length. What was he going to use for an excuse tonight? It was too late for her to believe he was expecting a conference call. Maybe, a headache? He'd tried about everything else. "Well, then...." He glanced at the governor and held out a hand. "Thanks, Ben. It was nice of you both to do this for us."

Ben winked. "It was worth every penny it cost, not to mention the trip up from Springfield. I have to say, I never thought I'd witness the taming of Joshua Raven." He took Wendy's hand. "But then, I'd never met this refreshing woman."

Wendy flushed. "Thank you, Governor. And you'll be hearing from me about that literacy legislation when the time comes."

"I'll look forward to your call."

The governor stepped away as Mrs. Perry, a petite redhead, gave Wendy a hug. "Best wishes. I know you two will be very happy."

Wendy returned the hug, and then faced Josh. "Ready?" Her pretty eyes sparkled with anticipation, making Josh more uneasy.

He took her arm, wondering how to stall, yet not appear to be stalling. "Should we find your father and say goodbye?"

She shook her head. "He's having a wonderful time. He won't even notice we're gone."

That was true. Josh had never known any man more egotistical than Gower Isaac. If he could have managed to do the merger and the wedding alone—with neither Josh nor Wendy along to steal any of his thunder—he would have.

The trip to the front door of the country club took ten more minutes, with well-wishers stopping them to visit. Then the parking valet took a few more moments to retrieve Josh's car. *Not nearly enough time,* Josh mused. By one-thirty they were on the road.

Weeks ago, Josh opted to leave his chauffeured limo at home and drive his stick-shift, BMW sports car, for obvious reasons—no back seat, no free hands and a gearshift between their seats, discouraging potential intimacy.

The drive began pleasantly enough, in companionable silence, but that agreeable quiet didn't last long. "Josh?" Wendy asked, her tone sending a jolt though him.

He cast her a quick look. "Yes?"

"Maybe we should spend the night at your place. You have that early meeting, and if you drive me all the way to my apartment, it'll add an hour to your trip.

He watched the highway, trying not to look like he knew this might happen and wasn't crazy about it. If he said he had a headache, she'd definitely not want him to drive all the way to her place. Blast! After a pause, she added, "I've barely seen your apartment— just those two evenings we dropped by between parties. I'd love to spend some time there." She touched his arm, and he stiffened. "Isn't that where we're going to live? At least at first?"

He peered her way, hoping his smile wasn't as stiff as it felt. "I thought we might." Maybe if he avoided the "let's go there and spend the night" part of her question, they'd be beyond the point of no return before it came up again. "I'd think it would be good to stay there for the first year or so. Then, we could look for something in the suburbs, once we decide to start trying to have children.''

''I want to start trying right away.''

He gritted his teeth and glared at the road. He had to open up *that* can of worms! Where had he thought that remark would lead? Why was he suddenly turning into a mush-brained idiot?

''Josh, please,'' she said, quietly. There had been no whining in her request, just the tone of a fiancée who wanted to spend some quality time—naked—with the man she loved. ''Here's the exit for downtown.''

He took the turn, but his brain was working on all cylinders. Was he going to have to burn down the darned high-rise to keep her out of his bed?

She squeezed his arm. ''Good,'' she whispered, and lay her head back. He cast her a surreptitious glance. She'd closed her eyes, and was smiling.

He scowled as he merged into traffic. *Hell, Raven, are you going to be a weak, greedy jerk and take her virginity, or are you going to be strong—reject her again with heaven only knows what excuse—and be a chivalrous, if sexually frustrated, bastard?*

Once inside the apartment, Josh dismissed his butler for the evening. Determined to delay the inevitable, he looked at his fiancée. ''Would you care for anything to drink?''

She shook her head. ''No.'' Coming close, she hugged his middle, lifting her face to invite a kiss. ''I just want you.''

He flinched inwardly, but gave her the kiss she wanted. She held him so tightly he could feel her tremble, her whole body telling him of her need, her passion. He had no problem with the message—at least no problem with the way it was conveyed. She had a nice way with her kisses—innocent, yet full of erotic promises she didn't even know she was making. Yes, she would be an exciting lover.

Oh, no! This was not the way he was supposed to be thinking! His control slipping, he tugged her against him, groaning against her mouth. It had been a hell of a long time between women, and she felt so good. Up to now, he'd been careful with Wendy, very much the gentleman. But it was starting to wear him down. He wasn't accustomed to weeks and weeks of abstinence. And, it seemed, his little fiancée had no plans to make him wait a minute longer.

She drew a handbreadth away and whispered, "Take me to bed, darling."

He wasn't surprised by her request, but he was disheartened by her there-will-be-no-backing-out-tonight expression. If she only knew how badly they both wanted the same thing. He scanned her face, so lovely in expectation.

He hesitated, his physical need battling his wish to be fair. After a few seconds, she surprised him by sliding her arms from around his middle. Almost before he could take a breath, she was standing there in a puddle of linen. He swallowed hard at the sight. She wore nothing but a camisole and tap panties. Pink silk and lace cried out to be slipped lovingly from her comely body.

With a sinking feeling, he gaped at her, so ripe and ready, so willing to be loved. His mouth felt like old parchment. She stood, proud, vulnerable, with her heart wide open to him. *Oh, Lord!* He closed his eyes. A groan of frustration, like the growl of a wounded beast, escaped his lips.

"Where's your bedroom?" He felt her hand grip his with determination. "Show me."

He stared at her, so exquisite, so resolved to have her virginity taken away. Wasn't this scenario every man's fantasy? Her eyes remained on his, innocently questioning, coaxing, and once again he was assailed by weakness and yearning. Inclining his head he indicated the direction. "Back there," he rasped.

She smiled, drawing him along in her wake. She was all pale skin and liquid grace, the pain in Josh's gut was so severe he had trouble walking upright. Hellfire, was he sure waiting was a good idea, after all? Maybe it would be better to.... *Damn!* He shook off the rationalization. *If you do this, Raven, you're nothing but a lecherous predator!*

They entered his bedroom, made golden by hidden accent lighting. A king-size bed dominated the masculine room. Sheers covered the window wall, giving them gauzy access to a sky full of stars and the vast Lake Michigan, forty stories below.

Wendy led him to the bed, where she sat down, kicking off her high-heeled sandals. "I like the room. It even smells like you." Her smile seemed exactly like that of the Mona Lisa—vaguely sensual, yet shy.

A deep ache wrenched his belly as she drew him down to sit beside her. He felt guilty and selfish—all too aware that he was losing the last remnants of control. He faced the fact that he had to do something drastic, right now, or Wendy would find herself flat on her back beneath him, her underwear ripped from her, their bodies writhing with pent-up desires.

He pushed himself off the bed, jamming his hands into his pockets. He couldn't stand to look into those big, hopeful eyes. "Wendy," he began roughly, "this is hard for me, but I have to tell you…'' He had no idea what he was going to say. Maybe he could make up something about how it was a family tradition not to touch his fiancée before marriage. Would she swallow that, knowing his reputation? Would she believe it if he assured her that some women were worthy of marriage and some only for playing around, and she was… *No, blast it!* He didn't even believe that one. Perfectly saintly women lost their virginity before they were married, every day. So what the hell was he going to—

"I know everything, Josh," she cut in so quietly he wasn't sure he heard her say it.

He frowned, facing her. "What?"

She pulled up on her knees and took his hand, forcing him to sit. "I said, I know everything." She took his face between her hands.

He eyed her with caution. *She knew everything?* "You do?" he asked, warily. If she knew everything, then why was she wearing pink, lacy underwear, holding his face tenderly? Why wasn't she driving a stake through his heart?

Wendy nodded, looking solemn. "I began to suspect that night I fixed you dinner in my apartment, but I didn't want to believe it."

He became increasingly apprehensive under her grave scrutiny, even though there was no place in her skimpy attire to conceal a weapon. He decided he'd better go along and try to figure out what she thought she knew. "You didn't?" he stalled, fishing for clues.

She nodded again, drawing up and kissing his lips with great care, as though she feared he might break. "And since I volunteer at the library once a week, I've been reading up on it."

It? What the hell was *it?* He had no idea what she could have been reading up on—unless it was *The Scheming, Manipulative Male Monster and How To Make Him Suffer?* If so, she was off to a fantastic start in that outfit. "You have?"

She sat back on her heels, her expression tender. "And don't you worry, impotence is nothing to be ashamed of."

He heard her, but he couldn't believe his ears. "Impo—*what?*"

She leaned forward and hugged him, her breasts soft against his back. "It's the stress—of the merger. You're working so hard—seven days a week, ten hours a day—and then you have to put up with all these social things at night." Her breath caressed his ear. "I, above all people, know how Daddy can be. Darling, I'm not surprised you're—having problems."

He eyed the ceiling. Lord! Impotence? This was an excuse he never would have thought of. Men didn't even like to be in the same room with *that* word. The idea was so ludicrous it was funny. He pursed his lips, trying to squelch a wayward grin.

When he turned to look at her face, tears trembled on her lower lashes. Good Lord, had she been that upset? Evidently, she'd been worrying silently for weeks. About him. All thoughts of laughter drained away. He couldn't recall ever seeing anyone look at him like that. Not since he was eight years old. He'd been riding a rickety old bike and was hit by a drunken driver. His arm had been broken in three places and he'd had a bad concussion. When he woke up in the hospital, his mother's eyes had glimmered with tears just that way.

Unable to think of a thing to say, he kissed her

cheek. The act was spontaneous, and he wasn't sure what brought it on. Possibly it was because she'd come up with this justification for not taking her to bed—however bizarre. Or possibly it was because the whole idea that she'd been reading up on such a delicate topic—trying to help—was extraordinarily kind.

She lifted up and forward enough to reach his lips with hers and kissed him back. The sweet sensuality of the act reawakened his male ardor, and he was grateful she was pressed against his back. "I'm sure when we're off by ourselves on our honeymoon I can get you all relaxed and you'll be fine," she whispered.

He exhaled heavily. *You keep kissing me like that and the last thing I'll be is relaxed,* he groused inwardly.

When he realized she was about to kiss him again, he looked away in self-defense. "It's good of you to take it this way, Wendy." He hated to have to go along with this, but he had to admit, it was a godsend, and just in time.

"Let me lie next to you tonight, Josh. Hold you." She wrapped her arms about him again, her breasts burning cruelly into his back. "I don't want to put any pressure on you. Just be with you. Okay?"

He stirred restively, trying to overcome his arousal. He cleared his throat. "Of course—that would be nice." What could he say? No? After all her worry, her *study*—on his behalf? The word "impotence" forced its way into his mind and he winced, wondering if other volunteers at the library noticed her area of interest.

She released him with a brief kiss above his shirt collar. "I'll let you get ready for bed, darling."

He felt the bed move. When he turned to look at

her, he saw the flash of a shapely leg as she slipped beneath the covers. When she smiled at him, he lifted his chin in a half nod and got up before he did something really stupid and counterproductive.

Since he didn't wear pajamas, and under the circumstances suspected nudity was not the best idea, he scrounged up a pair of baggy cotton shorts. Once he crawled into bed, she was immediately cuddling in the crook of his arm, hugging him close. "Good night, sweetheart," she said. "I love you."

He kissed her, but just barely, not wanting to start anything he couldn't keep himself from finishing. "Good night," he whispered, staring up at the ceiling.

Hours later Josh still stared at the ceiling. She didn't want to put any pressure on him, he mused ironically. Her body rubbing against his was certainly no pressure. *No pressure at all.* Yeah, right! He had a meeting with his board of directors in two hours and he'd done nothing but stare at the ceiling trying not to feel her soft curves molded against him, trying not to inhale the sweet scent of her hair.

The hand that hugged his chest for hours had slipped lower, and was now below the waistband of his shorts. Any further slippage and Wendy would awaken with a very big shock, and the realization that her fiancé was not quite the stress-impaired man she thought he was.

Gently, he lifted her hand to a safer spot on his chest. Stroking her fingers absently, he wondered how he'd gotten himself into such a weird situation. Wendy Isaac was a unique little bird. He'd never run across a woman like her. She threw herself into everything she did with her whole being—including loving a man, it appeared. She seemed to love him, completely,

uncompromisingly, even when she thought he was—
well, amorously impaired. He didn't know any women
who would do what she was doing—just hold him as
though the strength and depth of her love could heal
him.

He looked at her, sleeping so soundly and peace-
fully.

So trusting.

She was nice, dammit. He nuzzled her hair, then
found himself kissing the top of her head.

She stirred, a fragile sigh warming his throat, and
he drew her closer. When he realized he'd instinctively
folded her into his arms, he frowned. Confused, he
lifted his gaze to the ceiling.

Was it possible, he pondered, *that pure, unqualified
love, given so selflessly, might be a little bit catching?*

CHAPTER FIVE

JOSH agreed completely with Wendy about her father's absurd idea of what her wedding should be. Ostentatious was the mildest adjective that came to mind for the ceremony that included every fatuous excess imaginable, from twelve trumpeteers, costumed like palace guards, to the harp quartet, decked out to resemble angels.

Wendy had wanted to be married among a few close friends on the patio of her mother's ancestral home, but Gower put his foot down. His daughter's marriage to the wealthy and powerful Joshua Raven would be the event of the season. How dare Wendy even consider depriving him of this social opportunity?

Josh had wanted to flatten the man then and there, but he'd kept silent. The wedding ceremony was the bride's family's domain. Besides, Josh had enough on his plate running his own company as well as finalizing plans for refurbishing Gower's holdings—once he was officially CEO.

Still, no matter how surreal and absurd the wedding was, Josh didn't think Wendy had been tainted by the excesses. As she stood beside him, in flowing white, before the minister, he thought she looked—well, like a fairy princess. Her huge, purple eyes glimmered engagingly as she repeated her vows.

When his turn came, Josh faced the minister to hear the holy words that spoke of loving, honoring and cherishing his bride—until death. His "I do" rang clearly, echoing in the cavernous cathedral. Inwardly, he winced, hoping his pledge to love her would not prove to be a lie. Closing his eyes, he silently swore he would try his best.

"You may kiss the bride." The minister's voice broke through Josh's grim contemplation, startling him. The end of the ceremony? So soon? It was amazing how few moments it took to bind two people to each other for life. Grateful for the small favor of short Protestant weddings, he turned toward his new wife. Lifting her veil, he gave her the traditional kiss. Her lips trembled, and he tasted salty tears. Confused, he pulled slightly away. "Are you all right?"

She smiled. "I'm so happy."

A jolt shot through him. She was crying with *happiness*? Even after all the browbeating her father had put her through in order to use her wedding for his own selfish purposes? Genuinely touched by her forgiving nature, he grinned. If it had been left up to him, he would have told the old goat to go to Hades and let Wendy get married the way she wanted to.

Josh leaned down, kissing her again, this time with greater fervor. He could feel her fingers tentatively touch his waist and he knew she wanted to squeeze him hard, hold him tightly. Love him. And dammit, he had the same urge.

She'd taken to sleeping beside him every night, hugging his middle. It had been a rough two weeks, but he'd managed to suffer her gentle touch without so much as an audible groan of lust. By now he was teetering on the edge of sanity, his desire to drag her to the floor and take her right there, difficult to deny.

Fortunately, decorum prevailed. After enjoying the taste of her kiss for a few more seconds, he ended it.

Then, accompanied by traditional organ music, Josh escorted his bride down the isle and out of the packed sanctuary.

A million pictures and a trillion handshakes later, they made it to the site of the reception and dinner. Gower had rented the ballroom in one of Chicago's most palatial country clubs, where he had been a long-time member. Josh had never joined any clubs. Since he didn't play golf or care that much for society life, he'd opted to restrict his associations to work.

Accompanied by background music of a twenty-piece orchestra, the festivities seemed to grind on forever. Gower played the effusive master of ceremonies, everlastingly popping up to make wordy toasts, or pontificate about the meaning of life and the importance of love. Considering what Josh had learned from Wendy about the man's loveless marriage to Wendy's mother, Josh knew Gower's indulgence into pseudo-philosophic prattle was wholly for the sake of hearing his own voice.

Josh ground his teeth. He should have sensed Gower would milk the occasion for every scrap of attention he could get. Compared to that old tyrant, he felt like a novice in the art of manipulation. Which was ludicrous, considering the major-league tampering he'd done to Wendy's life.

After the congratulatory speeches were finally over, Wendy leaned close, drawing Josh from his irascible thoughts. "How are you?" she whispered.

Though his mood was far from cheerful, he couldn't help but smile. She was obviously concerned about his physical problem, or what she *thought* was his problem. Could he blame her? After all, she was about to leave on her honeymoon. He covered her hand with his and squeezed. "I'm only anxious about one thing—and that's how long it will be before I can get you alone."

Her cheeks flushed. Strange, but he never seemed to tire of seeing that. As the orchestra switched from classical selections to a more danceable tune, Josh looked at his watch, wondering how much longer this silliness would go on. They had a long trip ahead of them if they were going to get to his place in the Adirondacks tonight. "Our flight's in two hours," he said in an aside to Wendy. "We need to go fairly soon."

Wendy smiled. "You won't get any arguments from me, darling."

Gower came up to his daughter, his features florid. He looked puffed up with pride, but Josh didn't think Wendy was fooled. He was only full of himself—portraying the devoted daddy with melodramatic zest. "It's time to get the dancing started, daughter." With a flourish he took her hand. "I believe the first dance is traditionally mine."

Gower squeezed Josh's shoulder, drawing his gaze. The older man briefly nodded, murmuring something. With the swell of the melody, Josh couldn't hear. He felt a prick of misgiving and wondered if Gower had been affirming that the wedding made their merger a done deal. He frowned, appalled, as the fairy princess was led away by the egocentric old troll. "Don't say anything, you idiot," he grumbled. "Especially not in front of your daughter."

Gower's self-absorption was disgusting. Didn't the man ever spare a thought to Wendy's feelings? Didn't he remember or care that his daughter wasn't supposed to know about the marriage deal? One wrong word at the wrong time, and she would be shattered. Josh might not be in love with her in the head-over-heels sense, but he cared about her. The last thing he wanted was to see her hurt.

Gower swirled his daughter onto the dance floor, showing himself off as Mr. Perfect-Father-And-Expansive-Host. It was all Josh could do to look pleasant. Unfortunately, Gower's self-importance wasn't the only thing making him irritable. Evelyn Jannis was there, sitting a table away. He felt a tug of regret but not surprise when she stood and wriggled his way. He smiled politely but eyed her as though she were a coiled rattlesnake.

She placed a hand on his. "Hello, sweets."

"I didn't expect to see you, Evelyn," he said with as little edge to his voice as he could manage.

"I came with Daddy." She lifted a shoulder in a casual shrug. "Surely you knew he and Gower are old poker buddies."

"I didn't know." When her smile broadened—a clear indication she thought he was lying, that she believed the wedding invitation meant *he* wanted her there—his grip on politeness slipped to dangerous levels. "Well, Evelyn," he began, thin-lipped, "it's been nice seeing—"

"You look yummy in that tux, sweets," she broke in, her grin sly. "I could eat you up."

He pursed his lips, biting back an unchivalrous remark. "I know what you can do, Evelyn." Removing his hand from hers, he went on. "However, this is hardly the time or place to—"

"Okay, sweets," she interrupted, perching a hip on the table. "Call me when you get back. We'll find a time and place." She cast a glance at Wendy and her father, the sole couple on the dance floor. "You know my number."

He scanned her, ravishing, sleek and completely amoral. Evelyn Jannis was any lecherous bachelor's idea of a great date. "I'm trying to forget your number," he muttered, unsettled that he'd responded with such naked honesty.

Her expression grew cunning. "Trying?" She trailed a fingernail across his knuckles. "That's the most interesting remark I've heard in ages." She stood, but leaned down, displaying ample cleavage. "You keep *trying,* sweets." With a shrewd twitch of her lips, she added, "And when you fail, I'll be there."

She walked away, but her perfume lingered. Josh felt an absurd guilty twinge, as though he'd been caught with lipstick on his collar. Blast! He didn't want to be attracted to Evelyn, or any old girlfriend. He wanted to be attracted to his wife. And he was.

But would he still be after his lust was satisfied? Was what he felt for Wendy anything more substantial than frustrated animal need? Could he keep his promise to be the husband she deserved? He exhaled long and low, recalling with a stab of guilt all he was gaining with the marriage. After a few moments of internalized counseling—reminding himself that today he had made a commitment to Wendy, in good faith—he looked up to see his wife and her father finish their dance. He felt almost slime-free.

Almost.

After the music ended, Gower swaggered back with Wendy displayed on his arm like a prize cockatoo, handing her over to Josh. "Your dance, I believe— *son.*"

Josh stood. Taking Wendy's hand, he led her onto the dance floor then drew her into his arms as another waltz commenced. "After this, we're out of here," he grumbled near her ear. "I've had all I can stomach."

"I'm with you. Five more minutes of being paraded around like a prize sow at the state fair and I'll start screaming."

He chuckled. "Speaking of screaming and calling out, are you sure you want to take Al along?"

Wendy's smile dimmed. "Why—don't you?"

He felt like a rat. He hadn't meant to toss cold water on any of her plans. She'd had enough of that done to her by her father. "It's fine with me. I just thought she'd be happier with Millville."

Wendy shook her head. "She's been lonely a lot lately—barking herself hoarse. I hate to leave her where Daddy might upset her."

Josh lifted a knowing brow. "Right. We wouldn't want to come back and find her stuffed and mounted in your father's den."

Her big eyes grew bigger. "Horrors." Recovering her smile, she added, "She's waiting at my apartment. I've never seen her so excited. And we have to go there to get my bags and change, anyway."

He laughed. "Okay, okay. I'd hate for it to get out that I refused my bride's request to take an extra female on my honeymoon. Very kinky, but for *you*, I'll do it." He led her in a spin as the music faded. "I'll race you to the car."

She squeezed his hand, lovingly. "Let me say good-bye to my friends."

He allowed her to lead him to the table where her volunteer cronies and literacy students had been seated. If it bothered her that they'd been hidden away at a faraway table near the kitchen, she didn't show it.

Josh had been introduced to them in the reception line, but he couldn't recall which ones volunteered where—except for a couple of library volunteers, whose sympathetic looks had made him want to grab them by the shoulders and insist he was *not* having manhood problems. Nevertheless, considering the circumstances, he simply smiled and gritted his teeth.

As they approached the table, Josh realized this small group of ten people were subtly dissimilar from the rest of the guests. Dressed suitably, but unlike so many of the other guests, these people lacked gaudy pretensions. Not a ten-carat diamond ring or tie tack in the bunch. Yet, Josh recognized the names of one or two, and knew them to be quite well off. These people were fundamentally different from most of the people he knew. No doubt the difference was that they cared for things other than themselves. And it showed. That difference showed in their eyes and their smiles. That was what set the table apart, really. An aura of basic goodness.

This friendly, caring band of individuals would have been nearly all the wedding guests, if Gower had given his daughter her way. And considering what they had been put through today, Josh would have preferred that, too. These people might not make headlines on the society pages, but they were every bit as genuine and worthy as Wendy. He was sorry he hadn't had more time to get to know them. He had a feeling they were the sort who would be there for a friend in need. Like Wendy had been there for him these past few weeks—giving her all and asking nothing in return.

Josh watched his wife as she gave each one at the

table a hearty hug, promising to see them in two weeks. Taking Wendy's cue, Josh shook the men's hands and accepted brief hugs from the women. The two library volunteers seemed to squeeze harder, as though trying to dispense strength—so he could perform his husbandly duties. Or was it a stupid impression he'd conjured up in his own head? *He damn well hoped so.*

After making his own farewells to a few close buddies, Wendy tossed her bouquet to a writhing knot of squealing females. An attractive mahogany-skinned literacy volunteer caught the bouquet.

"Karen Ann!" Wendy cried.

Squealing with joy, Karen Ann sprang into the air, wriggling and high-kicking, like a quarterback doing a victory dance in the end zone after a touchdown. Her impromptu performance was so free-spirited and whimsical, even Josh joined in the laughter and clapping.

"I gather she's happy," Josh shouted over the noise.

Wendy grinned. "I don't see her live-in boyfriend remaining single much longer," she shouted. "If Karen Ann aims one of her high kicks at him, he'll either instantly promise to marry her or she'll put him in a coma."

As the melee died down, the newlyweds were free to make their escape. Josh noticed that Gower hadn't advanced to receive a kiss from his daughter, or to offer a goodbye hug. She lingered by the door, watching him. When he made no move to come to her, she gave a tentative wave.

It was apparent that Gower was so busy glad-handing with the governor, he hardly had time to ac-

knowledged their departure. His answering wave was
more like an impatient dismissal. The old man had
gotten all he wanted from both his daughter and son-
in-law, and had more important social and political
fish to fry.

With a stab of aggravation, Josh took Wendy's arm
and pulled her outside. Though she smiled at him, he
bore witness to the flash of distress in her eyes. That
tiny melancholy shimmer made it clear that she'd
thought her acquiescence to Gower's every wish might
have softened him towards her. Oh, she was good at
hiding her hurt. She covered well, making jokes about
her father. Still it was painfully evident that, like most
daughters, Wendy would have loved to be close to the
man who had given her life.

Josh forced from his mind pleasant visions of dis-
membering Gower and murmured, "Come on—Mrs.
Raven."

The happy flush of her cheeks charmed him so
much he kissed the tip of her nose. Closing her door,
he strode around the car to get in on the other side.
He might not be "in love" the way the songs described it, but Wendy Isaac Raven was a sweet, passionate woman. And by heaven, he swore by all the
work he'd done to secure this merger, that *nothing*
would screw up this honeymoon!

Wendy didn't quite know what she thought would
happen when she and Josh got to her apartment—
maybe a quick, fiery bout of lovemaking on her rug,
quenching their thirst for each other so they could relax on the flight to New York.

As it all too frequently happens with fantasies, that's
not the way it worked out.

When they reached Wendy's apartment, her neighbor, Judy Sawyer, was waiting for them. Judy was a quiet young woman, a single mother struggling to make a life for herself and her five-year-old son, Seth. The thin, sweet-faced woman wore faded jeans and a green tank top. Looking bashful, she held out a brightly wrapped package.

"I hated to miss the wedding," Judy said. "Seth has that stomach flu that's going around. But rather than pout about missing your wedding, I spent the time working on my court reporter skills. I have that job interview coming up." She grinned shyly. "It wasn't as much fun as the wedding, I'm sure."

Wendy liked Judy and her son, and knew that becoming a court reporter would give them a more secure financial footing. Even if Seth weren't sick, Wendy would have understood if Judy had missed the wedding to study. "I understand." Wendy smiled, accepting the gift. "When I get the pictures back, I'll come by. Okay?"

Judy nodded, appearing grateful. "You look so beautiful," she murmured, her glance shifting to Josh.

He grinned. "Thank you. I don't think I've ever been called beautiful before."

Judy blushed. "Well, you're beautiful, too, but I was talking to Wendy."

"Story of my life," Josh kidded, with a laugh.

As he unlocked Wendy's door, Judy began to gather up the flowing train. "Your dress is so wonderful," she said in awe. "It must have been like a fairytale." She followed them inside the apartment, then lovingly spread out the train, gazing at it like a little girl in the presence of royalty. Wendy noticed a wistful sheen in Judy's blue eyes. No doubt she was thinking about her own husband, who died when Seth was two. Silently Wendy wished Judy well—that she would get the job as a court reporter and find another man to love as thoroughly and completely as Wendy loved Josh.

It suddenly occurred to Wendy that she was still holding Judy's gift. It would be impolite not to open it while Judy was there. "Oh—your present." She untied the ribbon, glancing at Josh. He watched her, his eyes twinkling. She smiled, wondering if he'd had the same fantasies of a torrid indulgence before catching the plane. From his expression it seemed he had, and he, too, could see the chance of that happening quickly disappearing. At least he took the realization with gracious good humor. Josh Raven was a wonderful, gallant, giving man!

Wendy tore away the silver wrappings and set the box on the sofa. Lifting the lid, she found a quart jar amid the tissue.

"It's an old family recipe for marshmallow mint sauce," Judy explained. "Tastes wonderful on ice cream or chocolate pudding." Her thin cheeks glowed red. "It may not seem like much of a gift, but in my mother's family it's become a wedding tradition. For good luck. If you eat it on your honeymoon, you'll have a deliriously happy married life." Her smile grew melancholy. "If Seth's daddy hadn't gotten sick and…" She swallowed hard. "Well—we were deliriously happy, Jerry and I. For the six years we had together."

A lump formed in Wendy's throat, and her nose tickled, a sure sign she was going to cry. Handing the jar to Josh, she hugged Judy. "How sweet of you," she whispered. "That's the most thoughtful gift I can think of. Thank you." With a sisterly kiss on Judy's cheek she backed away.

When she focused on Judy's face, her neighbor was blinking back tears, too. "You'll let me know the instant you get that court reporter job, you hear?" Wendy insisted, her voice shaky with emotion. "I'll be holding a good thought."

Judy nodded, wiping away a tear. "Yes—and, well…" She cast a shy glance at Josh. So did Wendy. He watched Judy with compassion, his smile gone. "I wish you both all the happiness in the world," Judy went on, backing away. "I—I guess you need to get ready, huh?"

Josh nodded and held up the jar. "While Wendy changes, I'll pack this." He winked. "Thanks."

Tall and lean in his tux, Josh looked more princely at that moment than she could ever remember. His expression genuinely sympathetic, his eyes gentle, Wendy's heart swelled with love.

With a wave, Judy made a quick exit. The young woman was dear, and her son was a sweet, timid child. Wendy would miss being their neighbor.

"I'll have Higgins put this in my duffel," Josh said, drawing her back.

Going up on tiptoes she kissed his jaw. "You're sweet to want to take it along."

His brows came up as though in surprise. "What? And fly in the face of tradition?"

She giggled, slipping her arms about him. "I love you so much, darling."

He tenderly drew her against him. With a sigh that sounded as ripe with frustration as she felt, he kissed her temple. "Go get changed—before I do something rash."

She knew what he meant. She had an urge to act very rashly, too, but she reluctantly withdrew from the harbor of his embrace. "I'm going." This was best—not succumbing to something rushed and fevered. It was terribly chivalrous of Josh to want her first experience to be wonderful, meaningful—with plenty of time to linger and savor each other, without impediments like time schedules or—or chauffeurs! Even though they could draw the curtain in Josh's limousine, she would feel uncomfortable with Higgins up front *knowing!* She imagined Josh felt that way, too, for the problem had never come up.

"I'll change out here." He indicated the bag he'd brought containing his travel clothes. "I don't trust myself to keep my hands off you otherwise."

With great effort she turned away from the delicious man she'd married. "I'll hurry," she said, taking extra care to keep her voice even. "We wouldn't want to miss the plane and ruin our honeymoon."

His hearty laughter chased her into her room. It wasn't until she'd closed her door that she realized what his laughter meant. The steamy vision that slammed into her brain made her body go hot with anticipation. He was telling her that even if they ended up *walking* to the Adirondacks their honeymoon would be a blissful success. Joshua Raven—her fully functional husband—would see to that!

Nothing—absolutely *nothing* on this earth or in heaven could spoil the perfection of her happiness.

. . . he should have told them to order, but then
later . . . he wouldn't ring. Josh grew forgetful when
frozen. Well, it was her fault. Worry aside, she now . . .
Shifting back, he noticed Wendy was watching him.
He smiled as he . . . *then the moon above hidden slowly
softly* . . .

CHAPTER SIX

JOSH could see the lights of Raven's Roost from the
cruiser's cabin. At last. He checked the illuminated
dial of his wristwatch. Nearly two in the morning. The
trip, by plane, hired car, then boat, to his isolated hideaway in the Adirondacks, had been long and tiring.

He glanced at Wendy. She was curled up on a cushioned bench, her face turned toward the bulkhead.
She'd fallen asleep almost as soon as the cabin cruiser
left the dock. He smiled at her, leaning down to touch
her shoulder. "Darling, we're here." He watched her
profile as she stirred.

When she shifted to look up at him, she blinked as
though she wasn't sure she was awake. Then she
smiled. "Hi." The greeting sounded charmingly
sleepy, and had a sensual effect on him.

He put out a hand in a wordless offer to help her
to her feet. "Ready?"

Her shy smile said it all.

Moments later their bags and Al's covered cage had
been removed from the boat by the two-man crew and
placed inside the door to their honeymoon retreat. The
pine log dwelling had been stocked with food and
readied for them, per his secretary's instructions. An
array of lights had been left on, emitting a welcoming
glow. As Josh and his bride hurried hand in hand up
the winding granite-slab path toward the house, Josh
heard the boat's motor rev. He glanced back to watch
it set about for a return trip to civilization, wondering

if he should have told them to check back next Saturday, rather than leaving them alone for two whole weeks. Well, it was too late to worry about that now. Shifting back, he noticed Wendy was watching him. He smiled at her, hoping his hesitation hadn't shown on his face.

After they mounted the stairs that led to a broad covered porch, Josh stepped inside, holding the door for Wendy. Her dawdling made him glance at her face, puzzled. "What's wrong?"

Her smile was bashful and she cast her gaze down. "I thought—I thought you might carry me over the threshold."

He felt like a fool. He was married, after all, and carrying one's new bride inside their honeymoon home was a time-honored tradition. With a quick grin, he quipped, "Already bossing me around, hmmm?" He winked to make sure she realized he was joking.

Before she could respond, he lifted her into his arms, carrying her into the rustic entry hall. "Your neighbor Judy doesn't have the only family with venerated honeymoon traditions."

Wendy hugged his neck and giggled. "And this one doesn't even have calories."

"We aim to please," Josh teased.

"Promises, promises." She nuzzled his cheek. "And don't think I won't hold you to that."

He gazed fondly at her. Those big, purple eyes were wide now. Not a trace of sleep in them. He inclined his head and she met him halfway. Her lips were warm against his, a tantalizing invitation, as she clung to him. The small sound of desire that issued up from her throat had its effect, and he lost any urge to joke around. When the kiss ended, he was no longer smiling. "There's another tradition that takes place on honeymoons—hopefully on the wedding night—that's venerated, too."

She met his glance steadily. "Really?"

He nodded. She was cute, looking so flushed and wide-eyed. He had an impulse to sweep her straight up the stairs and into bed. But he fought it. Honeymoons with inexperienced brides shouldn't be rushed. He didn't want to scare her.

She snuggled against him. "Would you like me to guess what that other tradition is?"

"Go ahead." Her kittenish seductiveness caused a new swell of heat to rush through him. He could dive into those lovely eyes and cheerfully drown.

"I have no idea," she teased with a smile. "But if you'll put me down, I'll show you what I *think* it might be."

Visions of the night two weeks ago surged in his memory—when she'd stepped out of her dress, all willing and vulnerable. That time he'd been bound by honor not to touch her, but nothing would keep him from enjoying her charms tonight. He set her on her feet. "Show me," he said, his voice strangely hoarse.

Her smile was teasing as she walked to his duffel. Her loafers pit-a-patted almost coquettishly across the parquet.

"What are you doing?" he asked, knowing she couldn't possibly tug anything sheer and sexy from *his* bag.

"You'll see." She slipped the latches. "Be patient."

I've been patient for two months! he said inwardly, grinning at her playful tantalizing. For an inexperienced young woman, she knew how to titillate.

"Here." She turned to display her prize. "Marshmallow mint sauce!"

He stared. This wasn't what he'd had in mind at all. "You're kidding."

She stood and moved to him, taking his arm. "Show me the kitchen. We must have some for luck. Remember?"

He chuckled. "I don't think we were required to eat it the instant we got here."

She eyed him with impish determination. "Kitchen?"

He shook his head, grunting out a low laugh. "I suppose we get no further with this honeymoon until we've had some?"

"You suppose correctly, Mr. Raven."

He indicated the living room ahead of them. "Through there, Mrs. Raven." They descended two steps to a large room with walls of whole pine branches and big windows. As they wended their way around cushioned, log furniture, he said, "I don't think we have any ice cream or pudding."

"Minor details." She passed him a sweet smile. "Besides, I'm not that hungry."

They reached another foyer, this one smaller and devoid of furniture. A sliding-glass door gave access to an interior courtyard with an enclosed shade garden. A bubbling central fountain was subtly lit.

Josh led Wendy on around a corner into a beamed dining room, the wood ceiling fitted with tongue-and-groove pine. Skirting the oval table, he directed his wife through a pantry bulging with food stuffs. At last, they entered an airy, picturesque kitchen, constructed of more natural pine. Above a work island, in the center of the room, hung a wrought-iron pot-hanging rack, overflowing with polished copper cooking vessels.

"Will this do?" he asked, releasing her arm.

She scanned the place, her expression filled with wonder. "The whole house is amazing! Beautiful!" Facing him, she added in hushed awe, "I thought you said it was a cabin. This is huge."

He felt a strange sense of gratification at her compliment. Somehow her approval made the house seem more appealing than he'd ever thought before. The simmering passion in his belly leaped to flame and he battled down a mighty urge to toss her to her back onto the table. Instead, he took the sauce jar from her fingers and with one mighty twist removed the lid. "Now what?"

She looked at the jar he held out, then at his face. Her expression of love was encouraging, yet a blush colored her cheeks—a devilishly arousing combination. He wondered if her belly sizzled, too. He doubted it. Virgins didn't sizzle until they learned what to sizzle about.

Reaching into the jar with two fingers, Wendy scooped at the beige stuff, then surprised him by holding them up to his lips. "You first."

He cocked his head, eyeing her. "This isn't what I had in mind for two in the morning."

She pressed her sauce glazed fingers to within an inch of his mouth. "*Eat.* I want to be made love to."

Her blunt addendum surprised and tickled him. He didn't plan to argue *that.* Taking her fingers into his mouth, he sucked the sweet, minty sauce from her, teasing her flesh with his teeth. With her startled inhale, he grasped her wrist so she couldn't reflexively remove her hand. With deliberate thoroughness, he licked away sauce that had dripped along her palm.

"Ummm." Pulling her two fingers back into his mouth, he suckled, watching her face as she stared. Barely suppressing a grin, he followed another dribble down her palm, kissing and licking as he went. All the while, he eyed her face. Her lips sagged open in a small "oh."

He nibbled and stroked, casually indulging himself with the sweet taste of her skin until he reached the inside of her wrist. Sliding his tongue back and forth, back and forth, in a light caress, he ended his pilgrimage by kissing the sensitive flesh.

When he released her arm, she didn't move. Didn't drop her hand, and her breathing had become rapid and faint. Apparently his uninitiated little bride had never been made aware of the erotic potential of food. She simply gaped at him, her arm bent upward, hand flopped forward.

Suddenly there were no shadows across his heart. He was extremely gratified that he was here—on his honeymoon.

With her.

He burned to make love to her, to teach her the earthly, intimate pleasures a man and woman could share. Scooping up a finger full of sauce, he held it to her lips, still sagging open in the astonished "oh." "Your turn."

She blinked, then blinked again, seeming to return slowly from her dazed state. "What?"

Leaning close, he waved the marshmallow-mint-sauced finger in front of her eyes. "For luck, remember?" he murmured, charmed by her struggle to recover.

When she only stared, he touched her upper lip with the gooey stuff and observed the pleasant sight as she licked it away with her tongue.

As he watched, her lips curved into a smile. She grasped his wrist and pressed his finger inside her mouth. Her gaze holding his, she licked his finger as he'd done, then teased with her teeth.

He swallowed as her mouth moved against his palm to catch a few droplets, her tongue stroking. She nipped at the fleshy part of his palm, below his thumb, teasing and exciting with her tongue.

He cleared his throat. She was doing fine, this inexperienced bride of his. "Wendy," he groaned, tugging from her grasp. "It's time we satisfied that *other* tradition."

"I'm glad..." Her eyes bright with desire, she drew up on tiptoe and kissed him, hugging his neck and pressing against him. "Where's our bedroom, darling?"

Hunger, powerful and white-hot, coursed through him, the communication of her body wanton, even in its innocence. "I thought you'd never ask," he murmured, surprised by the huskiness in his voice.

Lifting her in his arms, he whisked her back to the entry hall, and up the darkened stairs.

Josh felt good this morning. Not just physically sated—which he was. But good. He'd awakened late, around nine, to find Wendy sleeping beside him. She looked almost too tempting not to touch, with her hair tousled across her pillow, her body sleek and nude beneath the sheet, her lips pursed slightly as though in invitation. It seemed criminal to slide from the bed without another small taste.

But he knew one taste would lead to another and another, and very soon...

He shook the provocative vision from his brain as he quickly pulled on a pair of jeans, padding out of the bedroom and down the stairs. He wasn't a sex maniac, for Pete's sake. He could control himself. After all, Wendy was new to all this, and she would be a little uncomfortable today. He needed to give her time to become accustomed to the more intimate aspects of married life.

At the bottom of the stairs he spied Al's covered cage and decided to take the crow into the kitchen with him. He could use some company.

Once he had the coffee going and bacon frying, he went to the refrigerator and took out a carton of eggs. Turning he noticed Al, perched on the back of a chair. "Does she like her eggs scrambled or fried?" he asked.

The crow cocked her head and winked one pink eye. "Pretty boy, *kiss me!*"

He grinned. "'Fraid I'm a little tired, old girl."

He ambled to the range and set down the carton. "Scrambled," he said aloud. "I'm pretty good at that."

"You're pretty good at a lot of things."

Josh turned at the sound of Wendy's voice. She stood in the pantry entrance, leaning against the door-jamb. He looked her up and down, and grinned. She wore his polo shirt. Its four buttons were undone, showing off a nice glimpse of soft, pale flesh. She wore nothing else but his beige cotton socks, squished down around her ankles. No wonder he hadn't heard her.

"Hi." He turned his back on the stove and took her

in. She was damned cute in his cast-off clothing, her hair mussed and her gaze drowsy from sleep. "I was about to scramble eggs. Is that okay with you?"

She pushed away from the wall and began to walk toward him, her approach soundless and surprisingly sexy. Though his shirt hem hit her at mid-thigh, he didn't think he'd ever seen any sight quite so erotic. Those slender, well-proportioned legs were smooth and pale, yet subtle muscle flexed beneath her skin, reminding him of how those legs had clasped him to her last night, so possessively, so passionately.

Heat rushed through him, warming his blood and clenching his gut. When she reached him, she slid her arms around him and kissed his chest. "I want you for breakfast," she murmured, her lips tickling his bare skin.

He chuckled at her fetching wantonness. *Oh, Lord, keep me focused,* he pleaded inwardly, trying to maintain control. "We need to eat," he said. "To keep up our strength."

"*Cash!* No checks!" Al squawked.

Wendy laughed, lifting her face to look into her new husband's eyes. "Al's a romantic fool."

Josh grinned, hugging her. "She propositioned me before you came in."

"Oh?" Wendy's eyebrows rose playfully. "And what did you do?"

"I told her I was tired."

Her cheeks flushed prettily and he would have bet anything she was thinking about the explosive abandon of their lovemaking. Stepping back from him she took his hand. "Tired, hmmm?" Leading him to the small kitchen table, she pulled out the chair nearest the window and across from Al. "You sit. I'll scramble the eggs."

"I don't mind," he said, but she nudged his hip with hers. "Sit. I'll bring you coffee."

He obliged, enjoying the sight as she filled a mug, returning with it and a brief kiss on his cheek.

He sipped and relaxed, watching her as she cracked eggs and scrambled them over the butane flame. The coffee was good, if he did say so himself. The kitchen smelled great. He inhaled, lounging back. The air had been nippy when he'd gotten up, but with the stove going and the sun shining in the window, it was nice in here.

Watching Wendy was nice, too. He was a little surprised at how much he enjoyed this. He didn't know what he'd expected to feel the first morning after his wedding. Sexually satisfied, he supposed. And he did—but not like all the other mornings with other women, when he'd left without breakfast, looking forward to escaping to his office.

His glance trailed over Wendy as she stirred the eggs. The beige polo shirt had slipped off one pale shoulder, and he experienced a strong urge to kiss the flesh revealed there. It was odd, he mused, but he felt strangely contented this morning. It was almost like coming home after a long, dreary trip.

She turned around, returning his smile. "Toast?"

He picked up his orange juice glass. "To you."

She laughed, a tinkling sound that warmed his belly.

"Thank you, kind sir." She curtsied. "Let me rephrase. Would you like some toast with your eggs?"

"Oh," he teased. "I'm game if you are."

"Wild man," she kidded.

As she busied herself at the toaster, Josh laced his

fingers behind his head and observed her. The way she separated slices of bread and then stuck them into the four-slice mechanism gave him a rush. Making toast had never seemed like a sexually explicit activity before, but the way she did it was making him hot.

She went back to stir the eggs, then turned off the burner. "More coffee?" she asked.

"No, thanks." He inclined his head in a silent request that she join him.

"But the toast."

He grinned. "I need a kiss."

Her cheeks went all peachy. Lord, he loved that.

She padded over to him complaisantly, then startled him when she straddled his lap and draped her arms loosely about his neck. "You need a kiss, hmmm?"

He closed his eyes, collecting himself. Unfortunately, his strangled groan of desire made itself known. When he peered at her, she was watching him with eyes that seemed a lot more knowing than they had twenty-four hours ago. And they were twinkling. Yes, his bride had learned a few things about men recently. "Is a kiss *all* you want, Mr. Raven?"

He swallowed, she was making it rough for him to keep his vow to take things slowly with her.

She smiled slyly. "There's something else, isn't there?" She didn't wait for him to respond. Her lips touched his, whisper-light at first, her arms curling tightly around him. Then suddenly her kiss became urgent, hungry.

He crushed her to him, his body growing aroused, his control and his interest in breakfast fading fast. He wondered if she was ready for the lesson about making love on the kitchen table, and was about to fling her on her back, when she ended the kiss, with a giggle.

Her eyes were alight with feminine wiles. "I thought so," she said.

She slid off him, and he could only stare as she walked calmly away. How could she do that when he felt like he'd touched a live wire and his body buzzed and sputtered from the shock. What in the hell was she doing? "Where..." It came out sounding like a rusty gate. He cleared his throat. "Where are you going?"

She didn't respond until she'd opened the refrigerator and retrieved something. When she turned, her face held a triumphant grin. "I bet you want some of this on your toast," she said softly, almost tauntingly, as she displayed a jar of gooseberry jam. *Hellfire! She'd certainly learned a thing or two about driving a man crazy.* Had he been that good a teacher, or did she have the tiniest little sadistic streak in her?

He sat forward, his second choice to doubling over in frustrated lust. But he was a man after all, and men didn't roll to the floor moaning in front of women if they could help it. "I don't want gooseberry jam," he said as evenly as he could.

With a loud "pop," the toaster sprang to life, displaying four pieces of toasted bread. "No jam?" Wendy asked, the twinkle in her eyes never brighter. "Well, then, I can't imagine what you might possibly want."

He rested his elbows on the table and gave her a you're-gonna-get-it smirk. Crooking a finger at her, he growled softly, "Come here, Mrs. Raven."

Her look of confusion had no more validity than a six dollar bill. "But the eggs are ready and so is the toast."

"To hell with 'em."

She set the jam on the counter, then eyed him coyly. "But, Josh, didn't you say we needed to eat to keep up our strength?" Crossing her arms before her, she went on. "And didn't you say you were tired?"

Her prim act was amusing, but he was in pain. His lips quirked, in spite of himself. "Do you write down *everything* I say?" He sat back. "Come over here."

She grinned, and with a saucy turn, disobeyed him. "I'll get the toast."

"You're gonna *be* toast if you don't get over here, wife."

She stopped in the act of reaching for the first piece. "Oh?" Pointedly turning her back on him, she went on with her toast gathering. "Joshua Raven, I'd hate to think you're trying to boss me around."

"Young lady, if I could get up from this chair, I'd— I'd...."

She twisted back. "Fall to the floor into a writhing wad of seething lust?" Her lips quirked impishly.

"That's not funny—*correct* but not funny!" Josh shook his head at her, fighting a grin. "You know what you've done to me, you vixen."

She shoved a strand of hair behind her ear, her expression earnest. "I've done no more to you than you did to me weeks ago, with only a smile."

Her soft admission did something strange to his insides. He grew serious and sat back, feeling less playful. *Lord, she loved him.* He'd allowed himself to forget that, as he'd selfishly reveled in their shared gratification. Last night she'd shown him how much she cared, giving herself freely, taking his coaching on how to please and how to receive pleasure. She'd done things to him—with him—earthy, brazen things that had been, on her part at least, pure, unselfish devotion.

His old pal Guilt swooped down to peck at his eyes. With a grin he hoped didn't look too rueful, he murmured, "On second thought, maybe we'd better eat." He pushed up to stand, stifling a groan as he forced his body to straighten. "I'll serve the eggs. You butter the toast."

When he brushed past her, she hugged his waist. "Are you okay?"

He kissed the top of her head. "I'm fine."

"Did I do something wrong?"

His chuckle was dark and ironic. "No, Wendy. Don't even think that." With his hands on her upper arms, he pressed her away. "We shouldn't waste the food, that's all."

"It wouldn't go to waste." She looked perplexed and disappointed. "Al would eat it."

He smiled down at her. "Al's already too fat."

The bird squawked on cue, and Josh was glad to see Wendy's lips curl upward.

"We'll eat, then we'll—think of something else to do." Unable to help himself, he kissed her rosy cheek.

"But won't we get stomach cramps?"

He burst out laughing. Slinging an arm around her, he scooped up the skillet and carried it to the table. "Maybe. But just between us, I'm not planning to make love to you in the lake this morning. So I don't think we'll drown."

"Oh..." He could feel her self-deprecating laughter in their close contact.

Five minutes later, with sun shining in the kitchen window, warming Josh's back, Wendy jumped up, toast in hand. "Oh, I forgot! I want to try that gooseberry jam." She scooped up the jar from the tile countertop and skimmed out a half teaspoonful, dumping it on what was left of her piece. "I gather it's one of your favorites, since it's here."

He eyed her with amusement, accepting the jar. He liked gooseberry jam, but he was in the mood for something much warmer and sweeter at the moment.

"Wow," Wendy said, chewing. "It's tangy." She glanced his way and Josh noticed her eyes were watering.

He spread some on his slice. "Tangy, huh? Is that a nice way of saying you hate it?"

She giggled, swallowing. "No, it's really pretty good."

More to indulge her than in any real interest in food, he took a bite. "I don't insist you learn to love gooseberry jam just because you married me."

"I love it. And I love you." She smiled. "I'm so happy." Her tender expression sent a shaft of renewed desire through him.

"You know what I want to do, Josh?"

He had no clue, and shrugged. But he hoped she wanted to straddle him again so he could get on with his lesson about making love to her on the kitchen table. He set down his toast, just in case. "What?"

She stood, and his heart rate shot up. This was a good sign.

"I'm going to call Judy and tell her how wonderful her sauce is."

He looked at her in disbelief, experiencing a slight let-down. "You want to call your neighbor and talk about marshmallow mint sauce—on our honeymoon?"

She grinned at him, her expression impish. "Why not? Do you have urgent plans?"

"You bet I have urgent plans," he said, mock reproach in his tone. "You're trying to kill me, aren't you?"

She walked over to him and put his face between her hands, kissing him, her lips sweet and full of promises. "It's such a little thing and she'd be so thrilled."

When she drew away, he forced himself to sit back. Damn, why was he suddenly jealous of her fondness for a bashful, well-meaning neighbor? This was stupid. Wendy had an urge to do a nice thing. What was wrong with that? He counted to ten and smiled. "Fine. Good idea."

"I knew you'd agree. I'll tell her hello for you, too." She kissed her fingertips then brushed his cheek with them. "Where's the phone, sweetheart?"

"My briefcase in the entry hall."

"Your briefcase?" She cocked her head in question. "Don't tell me you plan to conduct *business* on our honeymoon."

Another stab of guilt made him wince inwardly. How did he explain to her that this honeymoon was business—that he hadn't foreseen enjoying her, being with her, wanting her...

He lifted a skeptical brow. "Who's making the calls?"

She laughed and blew him a kiss. "Finish your breakfast. I'll be right back."

He crossed his arms, looking as stern as he could. "Two minutes."

"One and a half." She turned away, then looked over her shoulder. "Guess what I'm thinking."

He grinned. "You can't remember Judy's phone number?"

She laughed. "No, silly, I love you."

She was suddenly and silently gone. His gaze remained trained on the pantry door for a full minute. Finally, he shook his head. "I haven't guessed right once." Facing Al across the table, he grinned at the bird. "She's pretty cute."

Al flapped her wings. "Roll me over in the clover!" she shrieked, sidestepping along the chair left and then right. *"Kiss me!"*

Josh picked up his fork. "Not a chance, kid. I'm hot for your mom."

Intent on proving to himself—and to his playful, seductive bride—that he was a man of boundless control, a man who couldn't be twisted around a comely finger—he finished his bacon and ate a couple of bites of toast and jam.

Attempting to take his mind off his need to charge after her and christen the entry hall with reckless lovemaking, Josh watched Al do a perky little side-to-side dance on the chair edge. He chuckled as the bird wriggled her tail feathers in what looked like a blatant come-on. "You're bad, Alberta."

"Bad to the bone!" she chirped, executing another thoroughly bawdy wiggle.

Josh roared with mirth, curiously contented, in light of his situation. Honeymoons—even with clowning crows—were damn nice, he decided. Wendy was better than nice. He had a feeling these next two weeks were going to be more rewarding than he'd imagined—and in ways that had nothing to do with his corporate bottom line.

Something warm and wet splattered his chest. At the same time he heard a loud clank. His glance shot to his plate where he noticed a swath had been cut through the middle of his meal. Globs of egg were scattered across the table and all up and down his belly and chest.

Another crash, this one louder, drew his gaze to the far kitchen wall. A small dark chunk of plastic lay on the floor amid yellow bits of egg. He looked closer, realizing the mangled casualty had once been his cell phone.

"What the hell…" Jerking around, he saw Wendy framed in the pantry door. Her body was rigid and she looked—

"You—you *snake!*" she hissed.

CHAPTER SEVEN

JOSH grew wary. Something was very wrong with Wendy. He'd never seen her angry, but if he didn't miss his guess, she was homicidal. Her features were hard as her gaze bored into his. She looked like she planned to draw blood.

In her hand she held—or rather wadded—a sheet of paper. "Wendy—honey?" he asked softly, cautiously. "Is something wrong?"

With his quiet question, her body stiffened further, her gaze flinging bolts of killer lightning. "Don't *honey* me, you belly-crawling *weasel!*" she shot in a curt, explosive salvo. "You mud-wallowing *pig!* You—you lying *bastard!*"

She flung the crumpled document at him, smacking him squarely in the center of his chest. "I never want to see you again—as long as I live!" The last came out splintered and broken. As she spun away, Josh heard a strangled sob.

In a confused trance, he took a step to follow her, to ask what had happened to make her so furious. But an instant later, his brain caught on the fact that the mangled page at his feet might hold his answer. He bent to retrieve it. Standing, he smoothed out the sheet. It startled him to notice the page held Gower Isaac's familiar, silver letterhead. Beneath it, a short note was scrawled in Gower's hand.

Josh frowned, perplexed. He'd never seen this letter before. Had Gower slipped it into his briefcase sometime after the wedding, yesterday? Why? He scanned the message. *Josh, my boy, you've held up your part of our bargain by marrying my daughter. Now, I'll do mine. The stock transfer will be complete by the time you return from your honeymoon. Congratulations. I don't have to tell you that you've made yourself a good deal.*

A good deal!

Josh experienced a rush of murderous rage. How could Gower have done such a thing—when it had been Gower, himself, who'd made Josh swear Wendy must never know she was part of the merger?

He sucked in a breath, then blew it out between clenched teeth. Fury coursed through him and his body began to shake with it. "Damn the man to a bottomless pit in hell for this!" His glance snapped toward the empty door where Wendy had stood a moment before. He recalled the sound of her sob, the tortured look of betrayal in her eyes, and felt sick. *Lord, what was he going to do? How was he going to fix this?* A hot wave of blood rushed up his neck and his world turned crimson. "*Damn* you, Gower," he thundered. "What have you done—what have *we* done—to your daughter?"

He heard a crash, and it brought him back to the here and now. She'd said she never wanted to see him again. What did she mean? With a stab of fear, he sprinted out of the kitchen. He reached the bottom of the staircase, but had to jump back to dodge the bouncing approach of her suitcase. "What the..." When it landed, he leaped over it and started up the stairs. "Wendy? Let me explain."

She stalked into his line of sight, looking as though she'd dressed hurriedly. She wore jeans, a pink T-shirt and sandals. Her hair was every bit as tousled as when she'd gotten up. She looked like a kitten—a furious kitten. "What's to explain?" she shot. "You made a great *deal!*"

The accusation was like a fist in his gut.

"Listen to me," he pleaded, taking the stairs two at a time. "Please—I didn't mean for you ever to know—"

"Don't you come near me, you—you—"

"I don't blame you for what you think of me," he broke in, wanting to pull her into his arms, soothe her misery, wipe away the hurt he'd done. "I know what I am, Wendy. I'm so sorry."

Her gaze shimmered and sparked, a dazzling mix of loathing and heartache. He reached for her, but she ducked, avoiding him. "Don't touch me!" She vaulted down the stairs. "I'm leaving you!"

"How?" he called, his voice tight and troubled. "We're in the middle of nowhere."

She stilled, turned, her face a study of anguish. "I—I'll call somebody." With the heel of her hand, she scrubbed away a tear. "I'll send for a boat."

She looked so stricken, so violated. So lost. Squeezing his eyes shut, he pinched the bridge of his nose, attempting to thwart a headache that had begun to pound between his ears. "We don't have a phone." He made himself look at her, to endure the spectacle of what he'd done. "Cell phones tend to disintegrate when used as torpedoes."

A flicker of realization dashed across her face. For a moment, her gaze grew bleak, but after a second her jaw hardened. "I'll get out of here. Mark my words, Mr. Raven..." Her voice rang with rebellion. "You can make all the dirty deals with my father you want.

But I won't be a part of them.'' Whirling away, she grabbed her suitcase and wrenched open the door. ''Put Alberta in her cage and bring her down to the dock for me.'' The door slammed, echoing in Josh's brain, already hammered with guilt.

He grimaced. Shaking his head, he slumped against the banister. He was completely in the wrong, here, with no words to explain himself, no excuses she would ever accept. She'd been horribly deceived by her only living relative and her husband—the two people in the world she should have been able to trust. Opening his eyes, he peered at his chest, almost surprised he saw no gaping wounds. Her stare had fired off purple spikes of resentment so hostile, their stabs caused him physical pain.

Dammit, Raven, save the postmortem for later. Right now you have to stop your wife before she does something reckless and kills herself! With fresh resolve, he plunged down the staircase and out the front door. Off to his right, he caught movement and realized Wendy had dragged a canoe away from the side of the house. She'd made it to the sandy beach and was almost down to the water. ''Wendy, stop!''

She looked up, her features cast in defiance. He winced at the fire he saw there. She said nothing, but went on with her work. With one huge tug, she dragged the canoe the rest of the way to the lake's edge. Hurrying around the craft, she pushed it halfway into the water. Josh headed toward her, running down the granite walkway. ''Listen to me, Wendy. That damn thing will sink.''

She had to have heard him, but she was making it clear she no longer gave a fig about anything that came out of his mouth. As she heaved the canoe into the water, she slid inside and grabbed the paddle.

"Wendy! It's got a hole in it!" Josh cried, padding barefoot to the water's edge. Stiff-backed, she settled in the bottom and paddled with all her might, out of his reach. The boat wobbled, and skewed slightly off to the right, but she got it under control. "Wendy, don't be a fool!" he pleaded gruffly.

Wendy had never been in a canoe before, but she'd seen the movie, *The Last of the Mohicans.* She knew you paddled on one side and then the other. Shifting to her knees, she leaned against the canoe's center thwart. The fact that she had no idea which way she should be going put a crimp in her escape plan, but she figured she would run into somebody—another house along the shoreline, a boat. *Something!*

She paddled, ignoring Josh's shouts. How dare he tell her there was a hole in the boat. There was no hole. She gritted her teeth and took another hard swipe with her paddle. Josh was a liar through and—through. She faltered, looking down. A little water sloshed around in the bottom. She hadn't noticed it before. She frowned, but discounted it. No doubt it had been there all the time, it just hadn't lapped against her knees until now.

She paddled furiously. Unable to help herself she glanced over her shoulder and was horrified to discover she had paddled and paddled and was only a stone's throw from shore. Josh wasn't where he had been the last time she looked. She scanned the shoreline, appalled to see her suitcase sitting on the dock where she'd set it before spying the canoe. Darn! The sight of Josh racing toward her had unsettled her so she'd forgotten all about it in her mad dash to escape.

Noticing movement, she shifted to spot her conniving husband, standing at the end of the pier. He was only about two canoe lengths from her. She wished she had a stone right now! Or a brick, or an African blow pipe. He made a big stationary target, standing there, his legs braced, his fists planted on trim hips, looking far from happy. "Dammit, Wendy, turn around while you still have time."

She stared at him—at his tall, lean good looks. Her heart fluttered with unruly disregard for the slime he was. Spinning away, she paddled like a crazed woman. When her small craft tottered in her efforts, water lapped further up her jeans. In the kneeling position, the lower half of her legs were definitely wet, now.

Her stomach lurched and she cast a worried glimpse down. A couple of inches of water had accumulated. *Oh, no! There is a leak, after all.* Josh hadn't been lying about this. Probably the first true statement he'd made since they'd met, the bum! She bit down hard on her lower lip and vacillated, halting her frantic paddling. Did she really want to be further out in the lake when the canoe sank?

"Wendy!" came Josh's gruff call. "Jump out and swim toward me."

She shifted. He was holding a life preserver tied to a rope. She didn't know where he'd come up with that. Apparently he could conjure life-saving equipment out of thin air. She swallowed hard around the lump in her throat, trying to hold back another sob. Too bad he couldn't conjure up a way to talk her out of hating his guts.

He'd made such beautiful love to her last night.

Tears welled as she recalled how very, very believable his lovemaking had been. She'd never experienced anything so wondrous. She didn't even know such intimate bliss could exist between a man and a woman. A tear escaped, and she angrily wiped it away. Why did Joshua have to be such a lying rat? She'd been so happy only an hour ago, thinking she had what every woman dreamed of. And now—she had nothing.

"Wendy!" Josh called again, lifting the life preserver, perhaps thinking she hadn't noticed it. "Jump. I promise I'll get you."

The canoe was at a standstill, sluggish and riding low in the water. When she moved and the boat wobbled, the rolling water made her have to struggle to remain upright. She could feel her backside taking the first cold pats of the encroaching lake. In a moment she'd be swimming whether she jumped or not.

She'd be darned if she would go anywhere near Josh and his life preserver. She was a strong swimmer and making the beach from there was a piece of cake. Pushing up to stand, she faced the shore and dived. As she plunged into the murky depths, she become aware that the water not far under the surface was very cold—liquid ice. The shock of such stunning coldness made her expel the air in her lungs, and she paddled to the surface where the temperature wasn't quite so body-numbing. As she swam, her sandals fell away, but there was nothing to do about it. The lake was too frigid for lingering in search of discount store shoes.

Pumping her arms and kicking hard, she aimed for shore. Every so often she caught sight of Josh. Darn the man. He'd realized she wasn't heading toward him, so he loped back along the dock and leaped to the beach. With a sinking feeling, she knew she would have no choice but meet him when she made shore.

When her foot smacked sandy lake bottom, she shoved up to stand. Soaked to the skin and teeth chattering, she walked out of the lake as proudly as she could.

When Josh waded out to take her hand she jerked from his touch and took a mighty swing at his jaw. Unfortunately, she missed, and the force she put into her attempt to knock him flat ended up tipping her off balance. She sprawled headfirst back into the water.

Sputtering, she propelled herself up to stand, batting sopping hair from her eyes. Still blinded by water, she heard him mutter a low oath. An instant later, she found herself in his arms, being lifted into the air. "You—let me go!" She wriggled and kicked, pushing against him. *"I hate you!"*

"Quit fighting me, Wendy. You'll have pneumonia if you don't get out of those wet things."

"Good," she retorted, "I want pneumonia!" Her voice broke, and a bone-rattling shudder forced a delay in her struggle to get free.

"No, you don't," Josh said, more softly. "You need your strength to murder me."

She eyed him with scathing animosity. "You think that's *not* my major goal?"

"I'm sure it is," he said, his expression bleak. "I don't blame you."

Wendy felt like she was breaking open, spilling pieces of herself—her heart, her mind, her soul—into a ruthless, chaotic wind. She doubted she could ever be whole again after what Josh had done. Her body quaked, her teeth banged against each other so hard she feared they would crumble. Tears flowed as though a dam had burst inside her heart.

Impotent from loss and sadness, and too cold to resist, she went limp in his arms. But the worst thing of all was how much it hurt to realize something inside still craved him, still loved him. With effort she battled down a stupid urge to cling to him, to beg him to love her back.

How could she have been so wrong about him? He was a man so devoid of feelings that he could manipulate her into making her fall in love with him. At least her mother had had the option of going into her business marriage with her eyes open.

It was all so horribly clear, now. Joshua Raven had used his abundant charisma to pull her into his trap, and being the naive fool that she was, she'd followed willingly. He must have found it hilarious to discover how easily she succumbed to his line of bull.

And her father. How could he have done this to her? His had been the first betrayal, but Josh had gone along willingly, uncaring, his blind greed dictating his every calculated move.

Well, Wendy Isaac Raven—she felt a stab at the realization that she shared his name—would *not* be Joshua Raven's possession, to shrivel and die the way her mother had. A cry of anguish tore from her throat, and her fight came back with a fury. She rammed an elbow in Josh's chest and was rewarded with a grunt of pain. She would not allow herself to be used this way. "Get your hands off me, Mr. Raven!"

She was surprised when he lowered her to her feet. Doubly surprised to discover she was back in the upstairs bedroom. "Strip, Wendy."

Her gaze flew to his. "G—get out-t-t of here!" Her

teeth chattered so badly she could barely get the words out.

"Hell." He grabbed the hem of her shirt and yanked it up. "You're taking that thing off, *now*."

She gasped as he forced the wet T-shirt over her head. When he tossed it aside, she instinctively covered her breasts. "What do you think…"

"Now the jeans."

He took hold of the waist snap and yanked it open. When he reached for the zipper, she slapped his hand away. "You have no right to touch me!"

Jaw working, he peered at her, his eyes dark, determined. "I'm your husband. I've touched you much more intimately than this." Brushing away her restraining fingers, he yanked the zipper tab down. Grabbing the jeans, he tugged. "Step out."

She'd dressed so hurriedly, she wore no underwear. Mortified, she attempted to hide herself, but it was impossible to screen everything his ungentlemanly behavior exposed. "I won't!" She stooped to reach for her jeans.

Before she could make good on her attempt, Josh swung her into his arms, one hand jerking the soggy denim off her feet. "While you soak in a hot bath, I'll start a fire." Wendy found herself settled into an empty bathtub. She scrambled to her knees, but he grasped her shoulder, pressing her down. "I'm not getting in, if that's what you're worried about. Sit still."

His rugged features were closed in firm resolve. His dark eyes dared her to disobey, very clearly communicating she was no match for his strength—if he chose to use it.

His macho tactics on the heels of his treachery,

skewered her heart. But she knew brute strength would win out in the long run, and decided to save her energy for when she could better use it. "If you leave me alone," she retorted, grimly. "I'll take the bath."

His expression altered slightly, from resolute to dubious. "There's nowhere for you to go, Wendy. Outside that window is a long drop. Don't be a fool and try anything crazy, again."

Gritting her teeth, she dropped her gaze.

She heard movement, then the sound of water pouring from the tap. Warm and rejuvenating, it streamed across her frigid toes. "Promise?" he demanded, over the gurgling sound.

She closed her eyes, hating the fact that he was lounging on the edge of the tub, staring at her trembling nudity. This thuggish attitude toward her was no doubt his true one. He spoke no soft words, whispered no sweet lies about her loveliness, made no move to brush his fingertips or his lips along sensitive, secret places. She swallowed hard, working on building a healthy hatred worthy of such an egotistical lowlife. He was a morally corrupt beast, allowing her a glimpse of paradise, then snatching it away.

She bit back stinging accusations she wanted to spew at him. Instead, she nodded submissively. She was too mentally and emotionally exhausted to even dredge up the fortitude to look at him. At this moment, she needed sanctuary from his towering, unfeeling presence more than she needed retribution. *But that would come!*

Drawing herself into a protective ball, she covered her face with her hands. "Just go."

A snake. That's what Josh felt like as he stacked wood in the bedroom fireplace. A slithering viper. Ironically, he'd begun to feel less like one only this morning, when he'd awakened next to Wendy. She'd been lovely in the morning light, her lips parted in vague, oblivious invitation. He'd smoothed a strand of hair from her face, and almost given in to the urge to kiss the spot where the tendril had grazed her cheek. He'd felt almost whole, clean, lying there next to her. But now he felt like he'd been drilled in the belly with a load of buckshot.

Needing to keep busy, he got the fire going, and spread her wet jeans and T-shirt on the stones of the outer hearth. He stilled, staring down at the pink shirt, recalling how the sight of Wendy rising from the lake had affected him. Soaked, the cotton knit plastered to her body, brazenly displayed the outline of her breasts. He'd found himself frozen—gaping. A rush of raw lust came to life in his gut. The sight had incapacitated him, and he'd been incapable of defending himself when she'd taken a swing at his jaw. He was lucky she'd missed.

Dragging a hand through his hair, he pulled his gaze from the T-shirt. "Raven, get a grip." Satisfying his lust was not on Wendy's agenda. Homicide was. For the sake of his mental health he'd better keep her out of wet T-shirts for the duration. And, for his physical well-being, he'd be smart to hide all sharp objects. It was crystal-clear his new wife despised him. Fury and pain sparked in her gaze like volcanic eruptions. He closed his eyes, releasing a store of pent-up and confused emotions in a drawn-out sigh.

He heard the bathroom door click, and glanced around. When his gaze locked with Wendy's, he detected an urge to retreat flicker in her gaze, but a second later, with the lift of her chin, it disappeared. "I—I need my clothes." She didn't quite meet his eyes.

He scanned her. She wore his oversize terry robe that had been hanging on a hook in the bathroom. Her hair was wet and slicked back. Her eyes were red and puffy. She looked so small, so fragile. So tragic. He experienced a jolt of self-disgust, a sensation that was beginning to feel all too common these days. With a nod, he left the room to fetch her things from the dock.

Bounding back up the stairs with her suitcase, Josh decided Wendy was going to hear his side whether she wanted to or not. It wasn't as black as she thought. After all, he'd married her honorably, hadn't he? Slinging open the door, he caught sight of her, huddled in the rocker facing the fire. Her feet were tucked beneath her. His white robe enveloped her completely to the tips of her fingers.

Only her dipped head was visible in all that soft terry. When he closed the door, she didn't seem to register his presence. That worried him. She hadn't gone into some sort of shock, had she? There wasn't any post-traumatic syndrome for finding out your husband lied about loving you, was there? He felt nausea churn his belly. "Look, Wendy," he began gently. "In this world, people sometimes marry for reasons more pragmatic than notions of infatuation. Lots of these couples stay married. My parents didn't marry for love, and they were happy."

Slowly she lifted her head and peered at him. Her glance ripped through him like talons. A heartbeat later she turned away. He felt the slash of her rejection, but forged on. "I want our marriage to work. I plan to be good to you." He lifted his hands in a beseeching gesture, though she wasn't looking in his direction.

"I stopped seeing other women. That should prove I mean to be honorable."

She stared into the crackling fire. After a tension-filled minute, she looked at him. "How big of you." A tear materialized, trembled for an instant, then skimmed down her cheek. "Then again, what are a few sexual rendezvous more or less, compared to a multimillion-dollar business deal?" Turning away, she whispered tartly. "I *loathe* you, Joshua Raven."

The tone in her voice caused a heavy dullness to constrict his chest. He couldn't allow himself to accept that. Setting down her suitcase, he strode to stand before her. Kneeling, he slipped a hand into her robe sleeve to take her fingers. "Wendy, I care for you. I really do."

Her recoil bordered on violence as she wrenched from his grasp. "I don't want to hear any more of your lies." She jumped up, scurrying to place the rocking chair between them. The robe sagged wide, displaying pale, soft flesh. She yanked the lapels together and marched further out of reach. "I've decided I'm going to camp out for the duration of the two weeks. Bird-watch."

He stood, frowning at this new twist. "Do *what?*"

She cast a savage glance his way. "I saw a sleeping bag in the closet and some binoculars in the dresser. *I'm going to bird-watch!*" she repeated, slowly and distinctly, as though gritting it out through clenched jaws would frighten him away from disagreeing with her.

Fat chance! He took a step toward her, but with her shuffling retreat to the far side of their bed, he gave it up. She was having nothing to do with him, so he might as well face it. "Have you ever camped out in your life?" he asked, trying to be the voice of reason.

"That's none of your business."

"But, Wendy—"

"Get out of here and let me dress. If I can't leave you by water, I'm going to at least put some acreage between us."

"There are wild animals out there," he coaxed. "Bears. Even a moose in a bad mood could kill you."

Uncertainty skittered across her features, and Josh felt a surge of progress. "What if you get lost?" he pressed. "You can't eat off the land. You're a city girl."

She swallowed visibly, opened her mouth to speak, but no words came. He almost smiled. Success! Victory! He decided to add icing to the cake of her growing misgivings. "Not to mention poisonous snakes."

"*Snakes?*" she spat. Cinching the robe's belt tighter, as though the word had struck a painful cord, she scowled at him. "There can't be any snakes out there that are more dangerous than the one in here!"

He flinched at her harshness. "I never meant to hurt you, Wendy," he murmured, meaning it. "Honestly."

Her lips trembled and her eyes brew bright with new tears. "I'm going." Her stance unyielding, her teary glare damned him to hell. "I'd rather be eaten by a bear than share this house with you."

He was so frustrated he wanted to bash the stick-work rocker against the wall and turn it into high-priced kindling. Clenching his jaw and his fists, he battled to hold his temper. "You're my wife, and you're *staying*."

Lifting a stubborn chin, her eyes shot defiant sparks.

CHAPTER EIGHT

THE first day Josh ever saw Wendy he'd sensed she was the type to act on her feelings—a "Go for it!" kind of woman. For once, he was sorry he was right.

Wendy had made it excruciatingly clear she had no intention of breathing the same slime-polluted air he breathed. She would not be deterred in her crazy scheme to camp out in the woods. His only alternative, short of binding and gagging her, was to let her go. The binding and gagging idea held merit—especially since he knew she'd be in less danger that way. Unfortunately, in her current mood, he had a sinking feeling she would simply gnaw through the ropes and escape.

He managed to get her to compromise, thank heaven. She would make camp on a rise within sight of the house. That way, if there was trouble she could run to safety. Not to mention that food and logs for her campfire were nearby.

He exhaled, worried. She wasn't exactly Dr. Livingstone. *And why should she be?* he chided inwardly. She hadn't intended to get her Girl Scout camping badge on this trip. She'd expected to share a romantic honeymoon hideaway with her husband.

Josh trekked up the wooded incline a few paces ahead of Wendy, leading her to her campsite. This had been another hard-fought compromise, being allowed to show her the way. His wife wasn't much in the mood for negotiating. Getting this far with her had been as formidable a task as any business transaction he'd ever won in a boardroom. He didn't dare presume it was a step forward, but if he set up camp, himself, at least he could make sure she didn't wander too far astray.

The late morning air was brisk and thick with the clean scent of pine. Not far off the trail, an effervescent waterfall flowed over a granite shelf. Sparkling even in shadow, it collected in a crystal-clear pool of smooth, gray rock below. Josh breathed deeply of the pristine woods and found himself experiencing an unexpected burst of optimism. How could the beauty and calm of this vast, uninterrupted wilderness not assuage Wendy's bruised heart? Maybe a little time exposed to the idyllic splendor of the Adirondacks wasn't a bad idea.

He checked over his shoulder to see how she was keeping up. Their glances clashed for an instant before she turned pointedly away. She carried the bedroll she'd found; the binoculars dangled around her neck— as though she had the faintest idea what to do with them. He'd bet his last dollar that Alberta was the only bird she'd ever watched in her life.

The white crow clung to Wendy's head, visibly distressed at being dragged out into the wilds. Wendy had been stubborn about that, too. She wanted Alberta with her. What exactly did she think he planned to do to her precious crow—eat it?

The path he led her over was moss-covered, and had a pleasant texture—solid, yet spongy—a living carpet. When he reached the crest of the rise, he dropped an armload of firewood and his shovel. He settled the basket of food he'd brought on a large rock. Straightening, he scanned the clearing. This was nice, just as he remembered. Through the trees to his left he could see a rocky ledge overlooking the lake. At least nothing could attack her from that side.

The clearing was about the size of an average bedroom, with a dense growth of pines, maples and birch trees serving as the bower's woodland walls.

He heard Wendy enter the clearing and turned. With a nod, he indicated the center of the campsite. "I'll build your fire there."

She dropped the bedroll. "Don't bother. I can do it." She sounded vaguely breathless from the steep trek.

"Sure you can, Dan'l Boone," he muttered cynically. Grabbing his shovel, he went about clearing away dead leaves and pine needles. "This is a bad idea, Wendy." He eyed her as she unrolled her bed.

"You're a fine one to talk about bad ideas!" With an accusing stare, she lowered herself to sit. Alberta fluttered and squawked, attempting to maintain purchase on Wendy's head. "Go back to the house. I can make my own fire."

He tossed aside the shovel and retrieved some firewood. "Once I get it started you can keep it going." He arranged the cut wood in the cleared area, using dry leaves as kindling. Once the fire was going good, he stood and peered at her. Neither she nor Al looked very relaxed. The sight roused a surge of helpless irritation. "Wendy, you don't even have a tent. This is crazy."

Her gaze brimmed with fire and pain. "I'll be fine," she countered, each word fired like a bullet.

Cold fingers of contrition tightened around his belly. Dammit, she wouldn't be fine! Why didn't she see that? *Lord, please don't let it be that she doesn't care what happens to her!* At his wit's end, he shook his head, trying for composure. "At least let me take Alberta back. She's scared stiff."

Wendy made a pained face, an indication Al's claws were yanking at her hair. *"Ouch!"* She lifted her hands to the bird's talons, attempting to loosen her grip. "Al, you're hurting me."

"Hide me!" Al screeched. *"Let's scram! It's the cops!"*

"She doesn't sound pleased," Josh prompted. He held out a hand. "Come here, Alberta, honey. We'll go back and have a Twinkie."

Al flapped her wings and crowed. *"Kiss me,* pretty boy." Two seconds later she lit on Josh's head. *"Let's scram! Caw—caw!"*

Josh surveyed Wendy with compassion. She was hunched on the bedroll, her arms hugging her knees. Her posture spoke eloquently of her anxiety. "It's best if Al stays inside. Deep down, you know that." Crossing his arms before him, he exhaled tiredly. "Would it do me any good to tell you again that you're better off in the house, too?"

She shifted to her knees and crossed her arms over her binoculars, mirroring his disapproving stance. *Blast it,* she was one stubborn woman!

"Just take my crow and go," she bit out, sounding as obstinate as ever. Yet, a new, forlorn note tinged her words. Josh sensed she felt she'd been betrayed by everyone and everything she cared about—and now even her pet had deserted her.

Facing away, she fumbled for the field glasses and put them to her eyes. Josh glanced in the direction she'd turned, and frowned, suspecting the abrupt move was an effort to disguise a new bout of crying.

Whatever else she intended by the move, there was no mistaking her dismissal.

"Okay, okay," he mumbled. "I can take a hint." He turned to go, then shifted back. This time he caught the flash of a tear on her cheek as it reflected firelight. Guilt assailed him and he bit back a curse. "If you need me, Wendy—I'll—just call out."

She didn't turn, didn't act as though she'd heard. She merely held that stupid pair of binoculars to her eyes. Another tear blazed with reflected firelight. The sight put a mean torque on the knife in his belly.

Clenching his jaws against the ache, he lurched out of the clearing and trudged toward the house.

Hours later the knife still twisted mercilessly as he hid in the shadows, watching Wendy cry. He had no intention of allowing her to stay out there all by herself, a naive city girl, weeping in the wilderness. She was so lost in her sorrows, a bear could have lumbered into her camp and had her half devoured before she'd even notice.

Only moments after depositing Alberta safely in her cage, Josh stealthily returned, clambering into a nearby spruce. His elevated perch gave him an overview of the area, just in case some wild, deadly animal roamed too close. He'd be damned if he would break Wendy's heart, then let physical harm come to her, too. He liked her—a lot.

His lips lifted in a sneer of self-loathing, and he muttered, "So, this is how you treat the people you like, Raven?" He scanned his wife, lying facedown on the bedroll, her face tucked into one elbow. Every so often, between the twitter of birds and the rustle of a breeze, he could detect her muffled sobs. "You're a fine man," he muttered. "I'm proud all to hell of you, buddy."

His mind drifted to last night, of her kisses, how her mouth had set fire to his blood, made him forget he wasn't in love with her. He'd thought of nothing but pleasing her, teaching her things she learned so willingly—so exquisitely.

He bit back a curse, snatching his mind from thoughts of Wendy's lips, Wendy's sweet, soft sighs, Wendy's yielding body and her unschooled, yet exhilarating touch. And those neon, angel eyes, glistening with an otherworldly light that stole his breath. He groaned, then snapped his glance back to focus on his wife. She didn't move, didn't react. She hadn't heard him. Good. Leaning back against the tree trunk, he clutched hard at the branch under his left arm. What was his problem? He wasn't a man disposed to drift off into daydreams.

A snap of a branch off to his right drew him up, alert. He craned around to see what made the sound, visions of a six-foot bear exploding in his brain. Quietly, he drew up his shotgun, prepared to shoot to kill if Wendy's safety was threatened.

Then he saw it, a doe, lapping from the brook. Close by her side, her fawn sniffed the air, then dipped its tawny head for a drink. Josh sank back, his body prickling with the rush of adrenaline. He inhaled deeply, grateful for this reprieve, at least. Closing his eyes, he lolled his head against the rough bark. "Lord..." He sucked in another breath, working to get his thudding heart under control. "Don't make me spend the next two weeks in a tree."

The wedding had been last Saturday. Today was Wednesday, or was it Thursday? Josh was so brain dead he was no longer sure. And he'd spent so much time in a tree he felt "Raven" was more than just his name. He was afraid he might get a sudden urge to fly south for the winter.

He chuckled, then clamped his jaws together. Running a hand across his eyes, he squinted in a futile attempt to clear his vision. He was too tired to be much good to Wendy. He had to get some sleep. The short catnaps he'd taken when he went back to the house to bathe and eat, hadn't been enough. He was getting addled from fatigue, laughing out loud at his own twisted thought processes.

With a weary groan, he picked his way down the now familiar branches of the spruce. The night was pitch-black, low-ceilinged, silent and perfect for sleep. Jumping silently to the ground, he crept to the edge of the clearing. Wendy was curled in the sleeping bag, her back to him. The fire had dwindled to coals. Soundlessly, he made his way to the stack of wood and fed the ebbing campfire. A breeze swept through, chilling him through his wool shirt.

As the fire licked at the new logs, Josh observed Wendy's face. There was little peace in her expression. Even in sleep, her features were pinched and sad. The dull ache that seemed to have ridden his chest forever grew sharp and he ran both hands through his hair. "Oh, Wendy," he moaned. "What can I do?" The question came out in a melancholy whisper that vanished on a cold breeze before it could reach her ears—as ineffective as he felt.

Suddenly he didn't give a damn about anything. He was too exhausted to think. Besides, what good had all his thinking done him? He had a strong need to comfort her, even if it meant she would spit and kick and bite and defy the overture with all her strength. He was too tired to care what physical blows she might inflict on him. He was emotionally beaten, so what was a little blood and a few broken bones?

In two steps he was beside her, lowering himself to the ground. He was so tired he couldn't bother about the right or wrong of it, and pressed against her back. He encircled her protectively with one arm. "Good night, my little spitfire," he murmured into her hair. He inhaled her scent, then smiled at the gentle memories it conjured.

That was Josh's last thought until peachy fingers of dawn stretched into the glade, waking him.

It was weird how his spirits seemed lighter today, and it had nothing to do with sleep. It had been Wendy's nearness, he knew—and sheltering her in his embrace.

As he returned to the shadows, a rush of satisfaction completely out of proportion to the situation lightened his step.

Wendy stirred and rubbed her eyes. She didn't want to wake up. She'd been dreaming about Josh—about how it felt to be held in his arms, to be gathered close against his big, solid body. She'd known this feeling of belonging, of being cherished, for only one night, but the memory was so strong it almost seemed as though...

She forced herself to open her eyes. There was no sense dwelling on a foolish dream. Another day of misery and loneliness had begun, and she might as well get on with it. She realized now she'd done a stupid thing by insisting she camp out. She should have taken Josh up on his offer to sleep out here, yielding the house to her. At least, if he was the one camping out, she would have—what? A roof over her head to cry under? Yes—but it was *Josh's* roof. Everything in that house belonged to Josh. She didn't intend to become one of *Josh's* things. One of *his* purchases. In one of *his* houses.

Heaving a sigh, she clambered out of the bedroll. Her glance caught on the basket sitting nearby. It was different from the one that had been there when she'd gone to sleep. Her attention flicked to the bonfire, blazing away. That was impossible—unless. She pushed her hair off her face, reluctant to think of Josh so near, attempting to make amends in small ways.

She knew he was suffering, too. But his suffering had to do with being found out, not heartbreak. His suffering had to do with figuring out a way to get back into her good graces so he could keep his corporation. His suffering involved corporate survival, not emotional demise. She supposed, if she allowed herself to be objective, his suffering—considering what he truly *loved* in this world—was as acute as hers.

She bit down on her lip until it throbbed with her pulse. Pressing her hands to her face, she gulped down a whimper of despair. She had to get over this thing! Be strong! Joshua was only a man—and not a very nice man, at that. She must put this behind her and move on. She must grow whole again. It might take time, but she couldn't let the treachery of her father and one unscrupulous corporate shark get the better of her.

Imposing iron control over her emotions, she made herself reach for the basket. She was so sick at heart she wasn't hungry, but she had to eat—even if the breakfast was an offering from her two-faced husband. There was no sense in being any more childish about this mess than she'd already been.

She lifted the basket lid to spy a thermos. Coffee. That would taste awfully good. The morning air was nippy. And muffins. Oranges. She unscrewed the lid of the thermos, using it as her coffee mug. The steaming brew smelled strong and delicious. Sipping she munched on a bran muffin.

How sweet life could have been if she were only inside the house, sharing this breakfast with a man who loved her. Such seemingly small things were what made life a paradise on earth. Not fame or fortune. Just a good cup of coffee and a muffin, and the right man smiling at you from across the breakfast table.

A new rush of tears stung her eyes, but she choked them back. *She would not cry about him any longer.* She'd spent all the tears she ever wanted to spill over that—that shifty, diabolical con artist! She would bide her time. The first boat she saw that came close enough to the inlet that led into their secluded cove, she'd wave and make such a screaming racket, they'd have to come check on her.

Then there was the mail boat. You'd think somebody would write them a letter. One letter! Unfortunately the U.S. mail didn't seem to know they were there, since the mail boat hadn't come to check for outgoing posts. She had to hope somebody—*anybody*—would send them a letter. And soon.

Pushing up to stand, she took her breakfast to the ledge overlooking the inlet. These past four days, the peaceful view had helped fortify her battered soul. The unruffled water shone like sterling silver at this time

of day. In the afternoons it turned a rich blue-green.
Deep and calm and full of peace.

Across the water lay boundless forested hills. The
lush terrain rose and fell, rose and fell, again and again
and again, until the distance became so great their
vivid hues dissolved and blurred.

Though immersed in great sadness, Wendy couldn't
help but be touched by the grandeur of this protected,
eastern wilderness. She sat simply staring for so long,
time seemed to disappear. But the ache in her heart
remained, her only constant in a world of deceit and
ruined dreams.

She didn't see Josh all day. The time Wendy spent
in the house, bathing, changing clothes and visiting
Al, her senses were fine-tuned for the sound of a door
opening. The whole place smelled of him, and she
inhaled, taking his essence deep inside her. Imbecile
that she was, she faced the hard truth that it wasn't
only his scent she missed. Her heart seemed bent on
craving his nearness, her eyes pined for a glimpse of
his face. Even her arms ached to hold his head against
her breast once more, her fingers caressing the silky
bliss of his hair.

Where is he? her mind cried. He couldn't have left
her all alone at his secluded home. There was no way
out. Or did he know of a secret road? Had he hiked
to some woodland hamlet where he was now on the
phone, scheming with her father about ways to salvage
their mutually profitable deal? Ways to get Wendy under control again? Or was he salving the wounds of
this business setback in some convenient woman's
arms? She felt a twinge with the picture that evoked.
She hated feeling anything. She didn't want to be jeal-

ous. Why, oh, why did she have to be? She wanted to hate the man. He deserved her hatred.

Where was he? Okay, so she'd made it blisteringly clear she'd rather be devoured by wild beasts than see him again, but...*but she wanted to see him again, drat her witless hide!*

Deep in the night, Wendy was hunkered down in her bedroll. Though emotionally exhausted she slept fitfully. Finally, so tired she felt drugged, she managed to drift off. Somewhere in her dreamy reverie, she fastened onto the fact that she was no longer chilled. The fire crackled, shooting sparks toward heaven, while she lay there, secure within the haven of loving arms. *What a wonderful dream.*

The fire smelled nice. She inhaled. Along with wood smoke, she detected Josh's unmistakable scent. She smiled, sucking in another draft of fragrant air. Nobody smelled as nice as Josh. She drifted happily along in her private oblivion, willing the manifestation to stay, to comfort and complete her—if only for tonight.

Turning, she snuggled in the crook of her dream lover's arm. Her lips brushed the hollow of his throat and she impulsively kissed him, his pulse beat registering against her lips. Releasing a contented sigh, she slipped an arm about his waist, hugging him close. Her unruly behavior didn't trouble her. After all, you couldn't control your dreams, could you? Besides, when she woke up, she probably wouldn't remember any of it.

A pity.

His breath feathered her hair, warm and sweetened with his essence. His lips brushed her temple in a light kiss. Josh was such a gentle, caring man—in her dreams.

Wendy heard a hissing sound. Hissing?

Hiss. Hiss.

What was it? She frowned. No! She didn't want her dream to change. She didn't want a snake to be in her dream. Something cold hit her on the forehead. Then again, but this time the strange cold thing splatted on her cheek.

"Wendy, darling—it's raining."

She fought this mutation in her fantasy. She didn't want snakes or rain right now. She wanted Josh! She wanted his kisses, his—

"Wendy, wake up," a deep, male voice whispered. "It's raining."

She fought encroaching consciousness, but her brain conspired against her. The fog began to lift and she squinted, rubbing her eyes. As she did, the back of her hand was smacked by a large, cold raindrop.

"We'd better go inside," the voice coaxed.

She stilled. Sliding her hand away from her eyes, she was startled to see a face looming above hers. *Josh's face?* Another gaggle of hisses caught her attention. Befuddled, she shifted to stare at the fire. Raindrops popped and sizzled as water met flame. Wood smoke rode heavy in the air, and she coughed. It *was* raining; that was real enough. But the part about Josh—that had been a dream.

Hadn't it?

Her groping mind cleared in a rush. She jerked around to assure herself that her dream had vanished, as it should have, or... Oh, dear! He hadn't been a dream. Josh was there. *Lying beside her.*

He pushed up on an elbow and gazed down at her.

He wasn't smiling, but his eyes held such gentleness, she had to will her anger to rise up and shatter a surge of desire. Defensively, she pressed him away. "What are you doing here?"

"Sleeping."

"Sleeping?" She scrambled to sit, putting distance between them. "What does that mean—*sleeping?*"

He came up on one knee, taking her arm. "We'll talk about it inside. It's raining."

She tugged from his grasp. "I know it's raining! Now answer my question."

He stood. With the toe of his boot, he scattered burning logs, kicking dirt over the fire. "You get the basket." He plucked up the bedroll, shaking leaves and dirt from it. "The forecast calls for rain for the next several days. You have to come inside."

He flung the bedroll over one shoulder and took her arm. "Basket?" he reminded.

In an odd daze, she did as he softly commanded. Part of her wanted to fight him, to plunk herself down in the rain, like a boulder, and stay until she grew moss. But the other part of her—the part that sang with the touch of his fingers on her arm, the part still tingling from the kiss on her temple, the part dizzy from his scent—*that* part kept her from shouting out denials and rejections.

That disobedient, perverse, moronic, lovesick part coerced her into putting one foot in front of the other, one foot in front of the other, shuffling after him, like a zombie, as he drew her toward the house.

Halfway back the rain got serious, and Wendy snapped out of her trance.

CHAPTER NINE

WENDY'S feline growl startled Josh. She wrenched from his grasp, the hasty move almost upending her on the mossy slope. When he made a grab for her arm, she slapped his hand away. "Oh, no, you don't!" She stumbled a step backward.

Soaked to the skin, her hair plastered around her crimson face, she wagged a finger at him. "You're not using your charm to hypnotize me back under your spell!"

Needles of rain pelted his head and shoulders. He lifted the bedroll like a hood, extending one end in her direction. "Get under here with me. This is no place to discuss it."

She eyed him with abhorrence. "I'm not slipping under any more covers with you, Joshua Raven!" She poked his chest. "Let me put it in a way a tough businessman like you can understand." She swiped rain from her eyes. Or were they tears? "That scheme you and Daddy cooked up—that marriage gimmick— it's a *deal-breaker*, buddy." She poked again. Hard. "Nothing—*nothing* you can do or say will ever change that. You might as well face that fact and deal with it!"

The repeated stabs of her finger caused him little physical pain. The pain came from the necessity of witnessing her sadness. She tried to mask it with anger, which was probably healthy. But he wasn't fooled.

He felt helpless, at a loss for what to do. He was a son of a bitch; he knew that. But he was a weary son of a bitch. He was weary from thinking about what he'd done and continually cursing himself. He'd been weary for days. And *yes,* he was angry, too. He was angry at Gower and angry at himself. And he was starting to get mad at Wendy. She was too pigheaded for her own good, standing there in the cold, dawn rain, shaking violently as her body fought the loss of heat.

Something in him snapped, allowing his fury, his helplessness, and his frustration to break free, take charge. He grabbed her poking hand and growled, *"Enough!"* An instant later, his rebellious wife was slung over his shoulder, her derrière wriggling next to his face. Casting a glance at her fidgety bottom as though in conversation with it, he shouted, "You're the most obstinate woman I've ever had the misfortune to marry!"

She slapped ineffectually at his backside. "Put me down, you *ape.*" With his arms wrapped around her legs, she was fairly well hobbled, but that didn't stop her from trying to kick and flail. "I've—*oof!*—never been manhandled in my life!"

"It's a first for me, too, sweetheart!" he yelled over the driving rain. "But if it makes you feel better, it looks like you're going to get carried over the threshold a second time."

She squirmed. "I won't! *Oof!* Not by you!"

"Who's going to stop me?"

She beat at his back with her fists. "Put me down. I'm going to throw up!"

He mounted the stone patio steps with a less jarring stride. Her ride over his shoulder wasn't the most comfortable mode of transportation in the world, and he didn't want to make her ill.

"I said, put me down!"

Walking to the door, he swung it wide and stepped into the narrow foyer that opened onto the central courtyard. After setting her on her soggy tennis shoes, he grabbed her fists so she couldn't put them to use. "Settle down," he ordered, his hands clutching hers an effective deterrent.

For now.

He had a suspicion that when he finally let her go, she'd grab the wood ax and split his skull. "Listen, Wendy," he began as gently as his exasperation would allow. "You have to change out of those wet clothes. You're shivering. Then you need to get warm and you need to eat." He kept his expression, his tone, calm, as he worked to inject reason into this bizarre honeymoon. "We both need to keep our heads. We're alone here. You might as well face *that* fact and deal with it."

Her eyes blazed when he threw her own admonition back at her, but her expression exhibited more hopelessness than anger. She knew he was right. Like him, her days and nights alone in the woods, had taken their toll on her bravado. He could tell she was heartsick about having to make compromises with someone she considered lower than a worm's belly, but she wasn't stupid.

Expelling a ragged sigh, she nodded. Her arms relaxed within his grasp, and he sensed that if he let her go, she wouldn't fight. "Go upstairs and soak in a warm bath. I'll fix breakfast." He released her and her arms fell loosely to her sides.

Her jaw worked, but she made no move to strike

out. He searched her eyes for some hint of softening, some rudimentary sign of tolerance. After a tension-filled minute, she spun away, dashing through the living room, toward the front stairs.

Dark irony curled his lips. "Congratulations, Raven. You found out what you wanted to know," he muttered. "Those eyes could cut diamonds."

By the time she came downstairs, dressed in a sweatshirt, jeans and a pair of bulky socks, Josh had bathed and changed in a downstairs bathroom. Coincidentally, he, too, wore a sweatshirt, jeans and bulky socks. Odd how their choice of rainy-day attire was so simpatico, but as a couple they were as far apart as the North and South poles.

She'd pulled her damp hair back into a ponytail, and she wore no makeup. He wondered what he'd expected—that she'd doll herself up for him? Was the sack of guilt he'd been lugging around making him delusional? "Hi." He smiled, hoping their cease-fire might be extended to civility. "How's pancakes for breakfast? I have a batch ready, if you're hungry."

She padded to the table and began to stroke Al on the head. The bird perched on the back of the chair nearest the window. "How are you, my little traitor?" Wendy murmured.

Thunder rumbled and Al *caw-cawed,* fidgeting sideways in a little hop-slide dance. "I love *Josh!*" the crow shrieked. "I *love* Josh!"

Josh didn't turn, but continued to tend the pancakes. He'd already heard the newest addition to Alberta's repertoire. The first time the bird screeched the declaration, Wendy had been bathing after her aborted attempt to escape in the canoe. Alberta's timing had been as superbly faulty then as it was now.

With a melancholy hitch of his breath, he pictured Wendy, eyes alight, singing out that proclamation over and over during their two month engagement. Sadly, Al had picked it up with every melodious nuance of Wendy's speech patterns. By the time the crow displayed her newest mimic, Josh could take no pleasure in it. His emotions were too steeped in guilt, and hearing those words only worsened his burden.

He couldn't imagine what the sound of Al's fervent pronouncement must be doing to Wendy. He had a feeling her emotions ran heavily toward humiliation and homicide.

He cleared his throat. "Coffee's ready."

She didn't respond, so he glanced over his shoulder.

She stood at the window, shoulders stiff, staring out at the driving rain.

"Would you like a cup?"

She shook her head.

He experienced a twinge of aggravation. "Look, Wendy, you have to—"

"I want a divorce," she cut in quietly.

He heard it, and couldn't say he was surprised. Even so, it slugged him hard in the gut. Shifting to face the stovetop he shut his eyes and rubbed at his lids.

"Did you hear me?" she asked.

Reluctant to answer, he grimaced.

"Josh?"

"I heard you," he muttered.

Silence stretched into a slim, frayed thread. After a time, Josh pulled himself together, flipping the pancakes he no longer had any appetite for. A lot of things were going down the tubes with those four, blandly spoken words.

I want a divorce.

"I love *Josh!*" Alberta screeched in bird-brained disregard of the tension choking the room. "I *love* Josh! Roll me over in the clover, pretty boy."

"I'm going to roll you in breadcrumbs, bird, if you don't button your beak," Josh mumbled under his breath.

He heard the flutter of wings, felt talons grip his shoulder. "I love *Josh!* I *love* Josh!" the bird repeated in what sounded disturbingly like Wendy's voice. "*Kiss me,* pretty boy!"

Scowling at the bird, he removed her from his shoulder and set her on top of the refrigerator. "Do you understand the phrase 'barbecued bird'?" he ground out.

Flapping and cawing, Al hop-hopped around the surface, plainly unconcerned by the threat.

When Josh turned around, he was startled to see Wendy pouring herself a cup of coffee. She looked composed. When their eyes met, he saw nothing in the purple depths. No emotion at all. Not sadness, not anger, nothing. It was as though she'd stuffed everything in some deep, dark mental closet—anesthetizing her heart for the duration.

He stared, shaken. This dearth, this void of feeling, from such a vital woman, was utterly incompatible with the Wendy he knew. He swallowed the bile that had risen in his throat. "Wendy?"

She walked casually to the table and took a seat before glancing his way. "Yes?"

He shrugged to hide growing apprehension. "I just…" He moved to take the chair next to hers. "Are you feeling okay?"

Her big eyes remained on him, but they didn't draw him in the way they used to. Where there had been loving invitation, he saw only blankness—an emotional wall—blocking access to her heart and mind. He was an outsider, now, a non-being in her world. It was simply her bad luck to be trapped with him in his isolated home in the woods.

He had a ferocious urge to pound his fists against that wall. He wanted back in, dammit! In there, with her, the world was decent and giving and loving. He didn't want to be shut out. He didn't want to be alone.

Bitter despair swept over him as his future without her loomed before his mind's eye—meaningless, cold and full of shadows. Wincing, he forced back the vision he didn't want to see, didn't want to believe.

In the flash of an instant came Joshua Raven's moment of truth. It struck him like the flat of a hand, hard, vicious, slapping him to wake to a new reality—one that completed him and made him whole.

All at once he understood why he'd allowed himself to go through with this crazy marriage conspiracy. He'd known it from the first moment he'd looked into those damn beautiful purple eyes, but he hadn't wanted to believe anything so sappy about himself. He'd always been Mr. Hardnose. Mr. Rational. Mr. There's-No-Such-Thing. Nothing so illusory as love could ever wield power over him.

Good Lord! What a fool he'd been! What a superficial, lost fool!

Instinctively he took her hand in both of his. "Don't shut me out, Wendy," he implored, a throb in his voice. "I love you."

Joshua Raven had to be the cruelest man on earth. Those three words fell like burning coals on Wendy's heart, searing painful gashes she was hard-pressed to conceal. How dare he resort to such brutal tactics. She gulped down a sob and willed her eyes not to overflow with her misery. She would not listen to his lies, not be affected by him in any way—not the feel of his big, warm hands tenderly holding hers, and certainly not the stricken look in those lush, dark eyes. He was not only a dangerous corporate shark, he was a consummate actor. He actually looked distressed!

Her breath became a solid mass in her throat, and she couldn't breathe. Unable to bear the sweet torment of his touch an instant longer, she dragged her hand from his. "So you love me, now." Her voice was remarkably steady. Pushing herself to stand, she gripped the chair back to support wobbly legs.

With effort, she controlled the spasmodic shiver of loss and longing rushing through her. She knew if she didn't get out of his sight immediately she would explode into a wailing, shattered mess. Summoning a bland expression, she lifted a courageous chin. "It's fascinating how your love can be turned on and off like a faucet."

"Wendy." He reached again for her hand, but she side-stepped, moving out of range.

"Turn off the faucet, Josh." Incapable of meeting his gaze any longer, she whispered the bitterest lie of her life. "I—I don't love you anymore." Managing a stately grace only royalty or those determined not to collapse in anguish can achieve, she swept from the kitchen.

At the pantry entrance, Alberta lit on Wendy's shoulder. The bubble of gratitude that billowed inside her short-circuited her ability to remain composed, and tears flooded down her face. Hating the thought that Josh might discover how much she suffered, she fled to the master bedroom, locking herself and her pet inside.

Rain continued to fall long after the gloomy day died. Josh sat in darkness on the rough-hewn sofa in the living room. The rustic piece of furniture wasn't long enough for him to lie on, so he simply sat, listening to the rain, the thunder, and the creak of wood as Wendy paced the floor above his head.

She wasn't getting any sleep, either. Lolling his head back on the knotty-pine support, he willed her to come downstairs. He closed his eyes and concentrated. *Come to me. Look me in the eyes and tell me you don't love me.* He'd be damned if he'd let her out of his life now.

Wendy had become more than a minor obstacle in reaching his professional goal. Over the past two months she'd wangled her way into his heart to become a richly rewarding part of his life. A clean, pure presence, taming the gluttonous fire-breathing dragon of his soul. She'd given him so much—openly, honestly, trusting him with her gentle heart. And how had he repaid her? By stomping all over those delicate gifts with the hobnailed boots of his greed. He'd betrayed her trust, destroyed her faith.

How was he going to convince her he loved her, after all the harm he'd done?

He heard a click, and tensed. She was coming. She'd opened her door and was actually coming downstairs. Immobilized with surprise, he listened, tense and alert, following her progress in the darkness by sound alone. He sank back and drew in his feet, making him harder to detect in the blackness of the unlit house.

She reached the bottom of the stairs and turned toward the living room. He held his breath, barely able to make her out as she took the two steps down into the room. Without hesitation, without a glance in his direction, she turned toward the back of the house.

The kitchen. That's where she was going. She hadn't eaten all day. He knew she had no idea he was sitting there. No doubt she believed he was asleep in one of the three downstairs bedrooms. Evidently she had never peeked into any of them, or she would know they were completely unfurnished. The only bed in the place was in the master bedroom.

Once she disappeared through the back foyer, he stood and followed. When he reached the dining room, he detected light filtering through the pantry. He padded into the storeroom and moved soundlessly to the kitchen door, which stood ajar. Movement caught his eye and he located her as she opened the refrigerator. She wore the same sweatshirt and jeans she'd put on that morning. In the shaft of light, he checked his watch. Two o'clock. It seemed neither of them was getting much sleep. If the truth be told, he'd gotten more rest in the tree.

She took out the plate of sandwiches he'd made and set it on the countertop. After pouring a glass of milk, she padded to the table and sat down with her back to him. He experienced a tug of disappointment. He wanted to watch her face.

Stepping back, he leaned against the pantry counter, waiting as impatience gnawed at him. She needed to eat as much as he needed to find a way to convince her of his love. It was hard to stand there doing nothing after all the hours of waiting and listening, waiting and wanting. He burned to take her in his arms, beg her forgiveness, to show her the depth of his love in the world's most ancient and intimate form of communication.

What seemed like a year dragged by before Josh allowed himself to check on Wendy. She sat motionless, her hand clutching the glass of milk. He frowned at her lack of progress. *Please eat, darling.* He threw the thought at her, hoping the force of his will would prod her into action.

She lifted the glass to her mouth and his lips twitched with melancholy humor. If it were only that easy, his telepathic commands for her to believe him, to forgive him and love him, would have had her leaping into his arms hours ago, crying out, "I love *Josh!*" with the same fervor as Alberta's spirited rendition.

He heard the glass clank to the table. It was empty. Good. Usually, Wendy emptied her glass after finishing her food. Deciding it was as good a time as any, he pushed open the door and went into the kitchen.

Wendy was rising from her chair when she seemed to sense him and turned. She stilled, holding her plate and glass. Her expression registered surprise for a heartbeat, before that damnable mask of indifference settled over her features.

Without a word, she spun away, hurrying to the sink. She turned on the water and rinsed her plate, making it grimly obvious she intended to ignore him. When she lifted the dinner plate to transfer it into the dishwasher, he was beside her, taking hold of it. "Did I ever tell you about the man I bought this place from?"

He plucked the wet dish from her grip. Instead of answering his question, she went about rinsing the glass.

"He was a Texas oil millionaire. Actually I bought it from his estate lawyer," Josh went on, refusing to allow her snub to discourage him. "As the story goes, the Texan built this place as a retirement home for himself and his wife. They'd moved in and were still decorating the place when she suddenly died." Josh took the glass from her hands, though she was still diligently scrubbing it beneath the spray of water. "He left the place exactly the way it was when his wife died. Never did another thing. Never built a boathouse, never bought a boat. I understand he stayed here, all alone, nursing his broken heart until the day he died." Josh stuck the glass in the dishwasher and closed it. "This place hasn't known much happiness, Wendy. I hope—"

"What sort of provision did Daddy put in your contract about divorce?" Wendy interrupted, her voice cool.

Her dogged single-mindedness on the subject of divorce irked him. He gritted his teeth and counted to ten. "There was no provision made in our deal about a divorce."

She met his gaze, her big eyes displaying disbelief. "Come now. In this day and age? You don't expect me to swallow that. What do you have to give up if I leave you?"

He inhaled a quick breath, then let it out with a slow shake of his head. "Nothing," he said, truthfully.

She frowned, scoffing, "I wouldn't believe that in a million years!"

"Your mother didn't divorce your father, and I had no reason to believe you would divorce me."

Her expression grew incredulous. "You had no reason—*how vain can you be?* Did you really assume you were so perfect no woman could ever want to leave you?''

Her taunt stung. Over the years, he'd had quite a bit of experience with women, and never once had anyone dumped him. Perhaps there had been a touch of conceit in the oversight. Clearly Gower's raging ego, and his history with his own wife, had blinded him to how different his daughter was from her mother. At the time the bargain was made, Joshua hadn't even met the lady.

In truth, when Gower made no mention of a divorce clause, Josh had been surprised, but elected not to mention it. After all, as the contract stood, divorce or no, the company was his. So why make problems for himself? Besides, his intentions had been honorable even if their deal hadn't been. Josh's plans were to make a home with Wendy, start his overdue family, and get on with his greatly enhanced corporate life.

''It seems I was wrong to think you wouldn't want to leave me,'' he murmured, deciding to keep explanations to a minimum.

''It *seems* you were wrong? *Ha!*'' Her facade of indifference cracked as anguish edged her voice. ''You should have that carved on your tombstone!''

''Perhaps,'' he said. ''But I'm being honest with you, Wendy.''

''Honest!'' Her eyes glistened, and he felt a rush of exhilaration. She was giving him back her emotions, at least. Lord, he wished he could get her trust and her sweet kisses back as readily. But he was no fool. He knew it would take time to prove himself. Honesty was the path back.

''A divorce won't do me any harm,'' he admitted. ''Besides, you don't want to leave.'' He couldn't stop himself from taking her hand. "You love me and we both know it."

She yanked free and shoved at his chest. "I don't believe you about the business. You're saying that to trick me, make me think you have nothing to lose."

A hot current of blood swept up his neck and burned his face. His gaze locked with hers. *I have a lot to lose, darling,* he vowed with his eyes. *I'll lose you.* He knew it would do no good to repeat his pledge of love. Not now. She couldn't believe anything he said at present. Only time and patience would disclose if he could ever win back her confidence. And though he knew, deep in his soul, that she loved him, he also knew she would never again give herself to him, freely and openly—not without complete, uncompromising trust.

"I'm going to bed." She headed for the pantry exit.

"Good idea." He fell in step behind her.

She cocked her head to peer around. "Don't follow me."

He shrugged his hands into his jeans pockets. "Do you expect me to sleep in the kitchen?"

She scowled and spun away. "I don't care where you sleep!"

With a surge of wry amusement, he murmured, "I have a feeling you will."

"Ha!" She marched through the dining room, the back foyer and living room. When she reached the foot of the stairs, she wheeled on him. "I told you not to follow me! Where are you going?"

"To bed." He put a hand on the pine rail and smiled. "Ignore me."

"No problem!" With a haughty toss of her head, she stomped up the steps.

She reached the master bedroom, storming inside, but his hand on the door kept her from slamming it. "What do you think you're doing?"

He slipped inside and closed the door at his back. "Are you having trouble with your memory, darling?" He indicated the bed with a nod. "I told you twice."

Apparently it didn't take a brick to fall on her to figure out what he meant, because her lips sagged open. "Not in *my* bed, you're not!"

He lounged against the door. "*Your* bed?"

Even in the darkness, he could see her throat go into a spasm of swallows. "Okay—you're too big for me to stop you. I'll take one of the others."

"Others?" Speculating on how long it would take her to grasp the significance of the word, he let it linger in the stillness. While he waited, he crossed his arms before him.

"What do you mean?" She looked unsure.

"Remember, I told you about the Texas oil millionaire? How his wife died and how he stopped decorating the house?"

There was another taut pause. "He never furnished the other bedrooms," she mumbled as though stating a very unpalatable fact.

"Right."

"But—but you could sleep on the couch."

"Nope. I tried."

"Then, I will."

He didn't enjoy the resolve in her voice. "Of course, you may," he stated, his manner deliberately arrogant.

She had cast her gaze away, but at his supercilious tone, her head jerked up. "I—what?"

He lifted a brow, projecting a thoroughly overbearing attitude. He knew he was manipulating her as completely now as at any time in their past, but he prayed his motives would excuse him. How could he show her his love if they were never in the same room? He wanted her within arm's length, touching distance, so that deep in the night he could take her into his arms.

He wanted her to remember what they'd so briefly shared, to see that she didn't want a divorce. No matter how underhandedly she'd become Mrs. Joshua Raven, their marriage was right. She had to see that. He had to make her see. "You have my permission to sleep on the couch," he told her with as much masterful impertinence as he could stomach.

"I have your *permission*, huh?" She glared at him for a split second before she whirled away. Yanking her sweatshirt off over her head, she hurled it to the floor. She wore nothing underneath and even though her back was to him, Josh felt an immediate physical effect. Yanking open the snap at her waist, she unzipped her jeans and shimmied out of them. Though she wore panties, the sight, even in darkness, was disturbing.

She reached for something draped over the log footboard and dragged it on. "Thank you very much, Mr. Raven!" she jeered. "But as far as I'm concerned you can march your egotistical patoot downstairs and sleep on the couch, even if you have to bend yourself into a pretzel. You don't have any right to give me orders! As long as I'm Mrs. Raven, I can sleep anyplace in this back-country mausoleum I want!"

He was glad he was resting against the door, because the sight of her slim, pale body made him light-headed. He hadn't expected nudity. Even that brief flash in the darkness had done him damage. *Hell,* the woman knew how to punch a guy right where it hurt.

Suffering behind his carefree pose, he sucked in a restorative breath. As he gradually released it, Wendy scrambled under the covers and flipped to face away from him.

For a long moment, his gaze lingered on the mound of covers that outlined his bride. With a certain amount of melancholy, he considered his latest handiwork, far from proud of himself. But he hadn't gotten where he was in life without being able to read people, to correctly judge how they would react when steered into certain positions. If there was one thing he'd learned about Wendy, it was the fact that she couldn't abide being told what she could and couldn't do. By giving her his lordly permission to sleep on the couch, he'd pushed a hot button that wouldn't allow her to do it—even if it meant she would be sleeping with him.

He knew his superior attitude would so enrage her that she wouldn't be able think the thing through. He knew she expected him to go downstairs and sleep on the couch.

"Not likely, sweetheart," he whispered.

CHAPTER TEN

JOSH knew Wendy wasn't asleep. She lay there, motionless, waiting for him to leave. *Well, sweetheart, you're going to have a long wait.* Pushing away from the door, he walked to the side of the bed and sat down. He had shrugged out of his sweatshirt before he felt movement.

"What are you doing?" Wendy's voice was high-pitched and worried.

He undid the button fastener at his waistband before shifting to look at her. She had drawn up on one elbow and was clutching the covers to her breast like a shield. Turning away, he continued to unfasten his jeans, slipping one brass button at a time. *Don't get up! He commanded mentally. Don't leave me! Please!*

"I'm going to bed," he said at last, then cleared his throat. His voice sounded a little husky to be convincingly offhand. Deciding he'd better tack on something to appease her, he added, "It's a big bed, Wendy. I just want to get some sleep, okay?"

She made no move, said nothing, so he decided the situation was as tolerable as it was likely to get. Standing, he slipped out of his jeans then slid under the covers, careful to make no abrupt or aggressive moves. He wanted her there, beside him. He needed her there.

Facing away from her, he settled in, listening. She hadn't moved, but that didn't necessarily mean things were going well. She must still be poised on one elbow. Probably trying to decide what to do.

"I can use the bedroll." She didn't sound as resolved as she had before.

He closed his eyes and petitioned the heavens to give him a break he didn't deserve. "The bedroll's outside, Wendy." He opened his eyes. "Don't be afraid of me. I would never hurt you."

Thunder burst around them like raucous applause. Josh frowned, positive she'd begun to speak before her words were obscured by the noise. "What?"

He felt movement, and his breathing seized up in his chest.

"I said, you've already hurt me."

The movement stopped, but she was still in bed. Was it possible she'd merely lay back down? Did he deserve his luck?

"You've done a lot of nasty things, Josh, but I don't believe you would take a woman against her will." Her despondent sigh filled the room. "I'm not happy about this, but I'm too exhausted to fight."

Powerful relief filled him and he could breathe again. "Thank you."

"Just stay where you are!"

The beginnings of a smile twitched at the corners of his mouth.

Wendy knew she was a sick puppy. At least when it came to Joshua Raven, she was anything but sensible. She'd lain there as still as a stump for hours, unable to sleep. His scent filled her head; his radiant heat reached out, warming, beckoning.

At least she'd been wise enough to turn her back on him. She didn't know what the added onslaught of seeing him in repose might do to her—forced to stare at those wide, tanned shoulders, to witness the sinful thickness of his lashes fanned out across high, handsome cheekbones. And a mere glimpse at those big, gentle hands made her melt. Memories flooded back of those hands, so skilled in pleasure-giving. She squeezed her eyes shut, attempting to block out visions, sensations she feared would not fade, even with the largess of time.

Somewhere in the night, he reached for her. Whether waking or sleeping, she didn't know. He had drawn her against him, taking her into his embrace— but nothing more. If he had begun to fondle her or make undue advances, she might have gathered enough outrage to resist, to push him away. But he did nothing but hold her, enfolding her within the hollow of his body.

The night was cold, the fire long dead. His touch was bracing, ironic succor to her battered soul. She knew she should pull free, dash away to safety, but her heart would have none of it. To her foolish heart, this man represented a safe haven, all the shelter she needed from life's storms.

Oh, why was her heart so fallible, so easily taken in? Why had her naive, silly heart given her over to him, body and soul, leaving her no escape? Why did she lie in his arms, delighting in the feel of his hard, male body pressed against her back? And why did her fingers seek out the wedding ring he wore, her spirit soaring in gladness at the feel of that flesh-warmed band of gold.

How was she going to convince her heart that everything she'd thought was real between them had been a lie? The ring he wore had nothing to do with loving her. The reasons he'd asked her to marry him had nothing to do with who Wendy Isaac was—as a person. Only as a bloodless stepping stone to his goal.

Held in his arms this way, Wendy could conjure up no anger, just wave after wave of sadness. As crazy as it seemed, she kissed the ring, snuggling her cheek against his hand. How long she dared stay in his arms, she didn't know. She only knew she didn't have the courage or will to break free—yet.

His breath feathered her hair in slow, regular intervals; his heartbeat resounded through her, its tempo solid and unchanging. Cuddling her in his embrace, Josh slept like an innocent, as though he didn't have a care in the world.

She wished desperately sleep would come to her, too—untainted, immaculate, sleep—without disturbing thoughts and haunting memories. She wished she could loathe Josh. And she wished she could drive him out of her heart and her mind. Yet here she was, a stupid, lovesick ninny, snuggled within the harbor of his body, reluctant even to drive him from her bed.

Josh woke slowly, his first groggy observation was that it was daylight. The second—he was alone. That realization brought him fully awake. His last conscious thought before falling into the first restful sleep he'd had in days was that Wendy was in his arms.

He stared at the side of the bed where she had been, experiencing a sharp snap-kick to the gut. Pushing up, he was about to throw off the covers when he saw her. She was curled in the rocking chair, wearing his robe and staring into the flames of a revived fire.

"Good morning." He shifted to lounge on one elbow, his mood lifting measurably. She was still there. "Nice fire."

She cast him a narrowed glance. "I was cold."

He watched her with a masculine hunger that astonished him. She sat there, made rosy by the firelight, looking cuddly and exciting all at once. She was so beautiful he was shocked that he hadn't seen it right away. He'd been a fool in a lot of ways until his Odd-Miss-Isaac slipped unnoticed into his heart. Unable to help himself, he smiled. "I'm sorry you're cold. You felt warm to me."

She jerked around to stare at him. Correction, it was more of a glare—if a frightened doe could glare. "What do you mean, I felt warm to you?"

He watched the sparks of indignation brighten her gaze, and struggled to master the impulse to make love to her right there on the rug. "Are you sure you want to go there, darling?" he murmured. "You're not the best liar in the world."

She stiffened and one slender leg shot from the bundle of white terry. Only her toes touched the floor, but he could tell she was poised for flight. "Lying is something you know plenty about, isn't it!"

Her accusation sliced deep, but he knew he deserved it. The impulse to reach out and touch her face, smooth away the sadness, was almost palpable. Knowing she wouldn't stand for physical contact, he crushed the bedcovers in his fist.

"Anyway, I—I wasn't awake!" she insisted haltingly. "I mean, I don't know what you're talking about."

He pushed up to sit, trying to keep his expression composed. But he was sure the look in his eyes told a different story. All she need do was meet his gaze

to see how much her nearness staggered him.
Something subtle, yet wonderful, had happened to her
in the past few days. The dormant sexuality of her
body had been aroused, and now she fairly radiated a
sensuous aura.

If he hadn't known her as well as he did, he would
surely believe she was playing the hard-to-get game
with purpose—to turn him into a blubbering, broken
fool. He wondered if she had any idea what degree of
power a woman had over the man who loved her.

Slipping his legs from beneath the covers he
reached for his jeans and pulled them on. Fastening
all the buttons except the waistband, he glanced her
way again. She was eyeing him with uncertainty. He
experienced absurd humor at that. She was uncertain.
He was downright whipped.

Cautiously he entered her personal space, kneeling
beside the rocker and placing a hand near hers on the
arm of the chair. "Thank you for last night," he whispered. "For whatever reason—awake or asleep, fluke
or fate—thank you." He grazed her hand with his
thumb, but she jerked away.

She pulled her leg back up into the cocoon of terry
and pointedly faced the fire. Her body language told
him one thing, but the fact that she was still there, still
curled like a kitten so close, told him something else.
She was fighting her attraction. He prayed she was
losing. She loved him, dammit! And he loved her.
They could make this marriage work. If she would
only let herself see that.

"Wendy, what can I do?" he asked, his body throbbing with male hunger. He wanted her and he wanted
her to want him.

"Get me out of here."

Her request was like the flick of a whip, splitting flesh. In the electric silence that followed he cast his gaze toward the fire, powerless. "I can't," he whispered.

She jumped up. "I can *not* believe all the stupid things I did for you!" His gaze shot to hers. Puzzled at her meaning, he stared as she glowered at him. "I wore that stupid black dress. I went to all those insufferable parties! I turned myself into a vapid little twit for you. I neglected my literacy students, my duties at the animal shelter gift shop. And the library! I—I even held you close when I *thought* you had your—your problem! And all the time you just didn't want—*couldn't stand the idea of making love to me!*" Her vehemence, and the deep wound he could see in her eyes, chilled his blood.

"Lord, Wendy, it wasn't like that. I hated those parties, too, and I never asked you to change for me. As for not sleeping with you, I thought it would be more honorable to wait."

"But you were fine with it, weren't you!"

He shook his head. Hating this. "I didn't think—"

"Don't give me that!" she spat. "You were thinking all the time! You were manipulating and plotting and fast-talking! I was happy as a lark being a blind, stupid idiot. I'm ashamed to say I let my heart do all my thinking." Her voice broke and Josh looked on helplessly as she pulled herself together. "Knowing you has taught me an important lesson, Mr. Raven," she charged. "I won't make the mistake of falling for a handsome face, *ever again.* I won't be so quick to believe any old line just because it's honey-coated and pleasant to swallow."

She plunked her hands on her hips. "See? Our little

association hasn't been a total waste.'' Her voice wavered, but her eyes remained locked with his in open warfare. ''I'd be curious to know what you've learned, if anything?'' She cocked her head and smiled at him, but murder lurked beneath that show of teeth.

He slowly stood, holding her gaze. ''I learned about love.''

''*Ha!*'' she shrieked.

Shoving both hands through her hair she mussed it further. In the fire's brilliance, Wendy became the image of a siren gone mad, a sexy nymph bent on man's destruction—not with the mythical lure of love, but with the total eradication of it. She had the power. All she need do to turn him into pulp was open that robe. Display for him all the beauty and sweetness he couldn't have.

''I know I don't deserve it, Wendy, but please believe me.''

She laughed, an unsettling hysterical note dancing around the edges. ''Sure, why not?'' she scoffed. ''I believe you love me, Josh. Just like I believe my father will win the Miss America pageant.'' She flounced around to face away from him, throwing up her hands theatrically. ''I believe Sylvester Stallone is really an eighty-five-year-old grandmother with a good makeup man. And I believe every time a husband says *'Sure I'm listening, honey,'* to his wife, he really is!'' She laughed again. ''Unfortunately for you, I'm a naive lunatic!''

''Wendy, don't—''

''Don't what?'' she cut in, wheeling on him. ''Don't rain on your parade? Don't do this to you? Don't screw up the best deal you ever made in your life?'' she charged, tightly. ''Don't *what?*''

"Don't put yourself down," he said quietly. "You're a beautiful woman. Any man would be lucky to have you."

She stared, eyes narrowing. Her anger fairly sizzled in the air, singeing him. *"Don't..."* she began, but her sentence died, and she spun away. "You're not being fair," she cried weakly, as though trying to catch her breath. "Take your medicine like a man. Your trick didn't work and you've lost. Now just leave me alone."

Her plea came out barely above a whisper. Josh sensed she was on the verge of breaking down, and he wanted to hold her. But he'd already told her he wasn't losing anything if she left him. She was deep into denial. She wouldn't let herself see that she loved him and she wouldn't believe he loved her, even if he burned the words into his chest with a fireplace poker.

He swallowed to ease the ache in his throat. "Okay." Turning away, he grabbed his sweatshirt. "Have it your way. I'm a pig and a liar." He headed toward the door. When he got there he turned back. "So what do you want for breakfast?"

She flicked him a glance and he could see tears shimmering on her lower lashes. "Is that all you have to say? You're a pig, and what do I want for breakfast?"

His options exhausted, at least for now, he lounged against the door and shrugged. "You heard me."

"I see." A tear escaped down her cheek, yet she managed to lift her chin in defiance. "In that case, I want *pork* for breakfast."

Josh separated the bacon slices in the skillet, concentrating on the delicious smell and the sizzle. He'd done everything he could think of to convince Wendy of his feelings. He exhaled, startled by how much like a groan it sounded. All he had on his side was time. This was Friday. He had just over a week left alone with her to get her to change her mind about a divorce.

A sound that had nothing to do with cooking bacon drew his attention. A fluttering. The noise was followed swiftly by the bite of talons in his left shoulder. He cast his feathered companion a sidelong smirk. "And a painful good morning to you, Alberta." He stabbed a limp piece of bacon with his cooking fork and lifted it. "Would you care for pork for breakfast, too?"

The crow nipped at his ear.

"Hey, bird!" he groused. "I meant the pork in the *pan*."

"I love *Josh!*" Al crooned. "I *love* Josh!"

"Yeah? Well, you're the only one," he muttered. A sudden thought hit, and he squinted at the bird. "Al, ol' girl, could you do something for me?"

"*Kiss me,* pretty boy!"

"Not in this life, sweetcakes." He angled his head around to better see the bird. "Repeat after me—Josh loves Wendy," he whispered softly. "Josh loves Wendy."

Al whispered back, "Kiss me, pretty boy."

Eyeing the ceiling with a mixture of frustration and wry humor, Josh repeated, "Josh loves Wendy."

"I love *Josh!*"

"No. Josh loves Wendy."

"Let's scram!" Al said in a hushed mimic of Josh's whisper. "It's the cops."

He couldn't help himself, and laughed. "You birdbrain."

"You birdbrain—*caw-caw!*"

Josh shook his head. "I give up."

"You birdbrain!" Al screeched. "Roll me over in the clover you birdbrain!"

"Now I'm a pig and a birdbrain. That's just great." Josh grumbled, absently tending the bacon. "They're both suitable, but would you mind shutting up about it?"

"Josh loves Wendy," Al whispered.

Josh stilled. "You did it!" Laying aside his fork, he dislodged the bird from his shoulder and brought her around to look squarely into her little pink eyes. "Say it again. Say, 'Josh loves Wendy.' But louder."

"Louder, you birdbrain!"

He grimaced, eyeing the obstinate fowl with disapproval. "You're hopeless." Setting Al on top of the refrigerator, he muttered, "You belong in a pie with twenty-three other crows."

"*Louder,* you birdbrain!"

Josh turned back to the stove, contrary laughter rumbling in his chest. He was about the least happy man in the universe, but that blasted bird brought such an absurd twist to his world, he couldn't help being distracted by it.

His smile died when he realized Wendy did much the same thing. She brought a uniqueness into his existence—a warmth, an off-beat humor. Traits he'd discovered he needed. He'd lived in a bloodless, grasping world much too long. Almost too long to be saved. If Wendy left him, he feared his last hope of salvation might disappear with her.

"Let's scram. It's the cops," Al whispered. The warning drew Josh's attention because it sounded awkwardly like a seduction—in his own voice.

"Birdbrain," he said. "If you can't get it right, just shut up."

"If she can't get what right?"

Josh hadn't heard Wendy come in. She must be wearing those blasted, quiet socks again. He removed the last strip of bacon to a plate covered with a paper towel for draining off the grease. "Nothing," he gritted. "How would you like your eggs?"

"I can cook my own eggs."

"That's not what I asked," he said, growing annoyed. Why couldn't the woman slack off for a single minute?

He knew she had walked up beside him before he saw her; her fresh-from-the-tub scent filled his nostrils, a tastier aroma, by far, than the bacon. He turned, taking her in, but she refused to look in his direction. Instead, she plucked the fork from his hands. "Or would you rather cook yours first?"

Irritated by her bull-headedness, he ran a hand over his mouth to keep from saying something that would make him more *persona non grata* than he already was. "I'll make coffee."

Once he got the percolator perking, he walked back to where she stood before the stove. His glance at the skillet gave him pause. It was full to overflowing with frying eggs. He counted. "Eight? That should clog an artery or two."

She blinked, seeming to come out of a trance. "What?"

He indicated the pan. "Your breakfast. You must have a thing for cholesterol."

Frowning in what appeared to be confusion, she looked at the pan. Josh watched as her cheeks grew peachy. He felt a tug of desire at the sight. "Oh..."

She flicked him a brief, almost guilty look. "I guess I lost track."

"I guess." He suppressed a wry grin. "I'd better get these out before they turn into roofing tiles. Move, sweetheart." He gently nudged her with his hip. "If you don't mind I'll have some of yours."

She cast him a quick glance. "I suppose we shouldn't waste food." She took a couple of plates down from a shelf.

"No, we've got another week here." Taking up a spatula he scooped the eggs onto a platter. "Too many roofing tiles and we might start to get hungry."

"I suppose you're blaming me for all this." Petulance wrinkled her brow. "I broke the phone, so we're stuck! Is that what you're saying?"

"No, Wendy." He took the plates from her, laying them aside. "I don't blame you for anything."

She glowered at him for a few seconds, opening her mouth and closing it. Finally, in a drawn-out groan, she cried, "Why won't you fight with me?" She lifted her fists, shaking them under his nose. "Fight with me, Josh. Say hurtful, nasty things to me. I want to leave here hating you with all my heart!"

"Are you saying you don't hate me that way, now?"

With a wail of frustration, she pounded his chest. "I do! I do hate you!" Her voice became a faulty whimper. "I hate you—oh, I *want* to…" Suddenly her hands were no longer fisted. Her arms slid about his neck. She pressed against him, her trembling lips brushing his throat as she pleaded, "Make me hate you! I've tried—I've tried so hard!"

Icy self-loathing twisted around his heart, and he gathered her in his arms. "I'm sorry, darling."

"No—*no!*" She lifted her face to snag his gaze. "No—say something cruel. Tell me you don't love me. Tell me all the reasons why! Tell me you think I'm silly and strange and you'll be glad to get rid of me." She buried her face in his chest as a sob burst from her throat. Her body trembled with anguish.

He locked her within his embrace. "I love you, Wendy," he whispered, ruffling her sweet-smelling hair. "I can't do what you ask. It would be a lie."

Laughter gurgled in her throat, sad and overwrought. "You're a fiend! Holding on to me this way!" She lifted her face again, looking so distraught a wave of nausea swept through him. "Be kind. For once in your selfish life, Joshua Raven," she begged brokenly, "be—be kind. *Please.*"

Her suffering was so intense, it did him physical harm. His heart constricted, crushed in the vise of her tearful plea. But he couldn't say those things about her. They weren't true. It was wrong. Wrong for both of them.

She loosened her deathgrip, and he realized she was looking at him again. He sensed she could see in his eyes that he had no intention of helping her hate him. "No, sweetheart." His arms tightened about her and he wished he could pull her inside himself. Keep her safe, make her the most important part of him. "No." He gazed down at her, his resolve unshakable. "Never."

Refusing to consider the right or wrong of it, he claimed her lips with his, hungrily covering her mouth. He moved his lips across hers, devouring, exploring. The velvety soft, sweet coupling sang through his veins, warmed his insides, made him whole.

He groaned, wanting more, wanting all. Gently

coaxing, he parted her lips, eager to deepen the physical expression of his love.

Victory seemed within his grasp when he heard a feral cry. Wendy wrenched her face from his, pressing impotently against his chest. "Let me go!" she implored feebly. "You—you have no heart!"

Disoriented by her sudden, violent invective, he released her, his body weak and on fire. Sagging against the counter, he stared at her. In bizarre slow motion he watched her fists batter impotently at his chest, felt the dull thud-thud-thud as she acted out her bitter frustration. It seemed unreal, far away. He was incapacitated, numb, an outsider witnessing as his world spun perilously out of orbit.

Like an automaton, he grasped her wrists, halting her ineffectual attack. She was saying something—probably shouting it by the look on her tear-stained face. He couldn't hear her. It seemed he'd gone deaf, too.

He frowned, trying to make out her words. But did it really matter? He knew what she was saying. Maybe, by some ironic quirk of fate, this last bit of lunacy—his kiss—had pushed her over the edge. Maybe now, she truly did hate him.

But hate between them wasn't for the best. Hate was all wrong. He knew it in his soul, yet there was nothing he could do to fix it. He'd screwed up his chance at happiness. All he had now was his work, which suddenly seemed like a barren, lonely destiny.

He hardly registered the fact when she wrenched her wrists from his grasp. An instant later something blinded him, snapping him out of his paralyzed stupor. By the smell and greasy feel, he realized he was covered with lukewarm eggs. Peeling one of the slimy disks away from his eyes, he could see that Wendy was gone.

"Josh loves Wendy," Al whispered.

Leaning heavily against the counter, Josh looked at the bird, murder and a little yolk in his eye.

On the one-week anniversary of his wedding day, Josh woke up alone in his big bed. He opened his eyes to an overcast, gray day, perfect for his mood. Last night Wendy had adamantly announced that she planned to sleep on the couch—*alone*. He'd made a fire for her in the living room hearth, then left her to her privacy.

Blast it! Without her beside him he'd slept badly when he'd slept at all. Why did he have to be holding Wendy in his arms to get any real rest? He knew exactly why. *He had it bad*. Lying on his back, he slipped his hands beneath his head and glared at the ceiling. He had it bad, all right. Love was an insidious condition. It crept up on a man and had him in a stranglehold before he knew what the hell was wrong with him.

Considering Wendy's attitude lately, he hoped there was a cure. But as far as his stubborn, purple-eyed little bride was concerned, he had serious doubts. Which was okay, too. Josh had never been a man to accept defeat. He had a week left on this honeymoon, and *by heaven*, he didn't plan to squander it.

He heard a scratching sound and eyed Al's covered cage. The darn bird had whispered "Josh loves Wendy" several times yesterday, but, naturally, *never* when Wendy was within earshot. "Darn bird," he muttered.

Another sound invaded the stillness, but it didn't

register. He frowned. Al scratched again. "Okay, okay," Josh mumbled. "I'll let you out in a minute."

He concentrated on the sound. A low whirring—no a rumbling. Like a faraway engine.

His eyes went wide and he bolted up to sit. "A boat." But it sounded like it was leaving. Leaving? Vaulting from the bed, he grabbed his jeans and struggled into them, hopping and stumbling out of the room. *The mail boat, he'd bet anything on it.* It must have been delivering a letter from somebody.

When he reached the bottom of the stairs, the door stood ajar. Skidding to a halt, he glanced toward the living room. Wendy wasn't there. The bedcovers had been tossed on the floor, as though in haste.

Alarmed, the truth exploded in his brain. "Oh, my lord," he breathed, sprinting out the door. He saw it off in the distance. The motorboat employed by the U.S. mail—leaving the inlet.

He tore down the granite walkway, waving and shouting, but the vessel was too far away for him to be heard over its engine. When he reached the dock, he ran all the way to the end, knowing it was futile, but unable to stop.

A letter lay there. More out of reflex than interest, he picked it up. It looked like a greeting card. The envelope was blue and it was addressed to Mr. and Mrs. Joshua Raven. The return address held the faintly scrawled name "Judy Sawyer." She must have gotten that job. Hadn't Wendy insisted Judy let her know immediately? It was somehow fitting that Wendy's kindness and selfless interest in others had come to her aid in her escape from the husband she loathed.

Loathed! his mind jeered. *The woman you love be-*

yond all else in the world loathes you! Congratulations!

Despair welled up in his throat like a fist. His breathing shallow and labored, he lifted his gaze, staring as the motorboat disappeared around an outcropping of rock. *His Wendy, his love, his heart, was leaving on that boat.*

Misery slammed into his gut with the force of a combat boot. Unsteady, he sat down. Blankly, he looked out over the calm waters. Only the barest traces of the mail boat's wake were visible now.

Gone. Wendy was gone. Time was no longer on his side. She had run away from him, taking nothing with her but the clothes on her back. She hadn't even dared fetch her beloved Al. That's how desperately she'd wanted to get away.

He swallowed, his throat scratchy dry. He'd read somewhere that in times of extreme crisis, the body shuts down all unessential functions in its fight for survival. The throat going dry was one sign. He gritted his teeth at the insight. Evidently his entire body knew how fundamental Wendy was to his emotional survival. He'd shut himself down, investing all his energy, funneling his attention, into his mad, headlong race to stop her.

He looked at his hands. They trembled badly. He coiled them into fists as memories surged back—of how her skin warmed in the throes of passion, of the simple, loving touch of her fingers entwined with his. How could he have known two months ago that he would fall so deeply in love with a young woman who wore a crow like an Easter bonnet and believed that a person who couldn't read was one of life's greatest tragedies?

How could he have guessed that losing her—just as he discovered the precious gift she was—would be *his* greatest tragedy?

CHAPTER ELEVEN

"THERE you are, girl!"

Wendy's heart dropped as her father loomed at the top of the staircase in her apartment building. His face was so red he looked in danger of blowing the top of his head into outer space. She faltered on the step. She'd spent the last two weeks avoiding him, hiding in the library basement compiling information on donated books into the computer. She knew she should have confronted her father right away, but she also knew it would only turn into a shouting match. She didn't have the energy yet. Her wounds were still too raw to charge into another battle.

"When Josh got back to town he phoned to tell me you'd run away!" Gower shouted, his tone heavy with accusation.

Gathering her courage, Wendy made quick work of the rest of the steps. "Let's go inside, Daddy. The whole world doesn't need to hear this."

"I don't care who hears, girl," he bellowed. "You just march yourself back to your husband, do you understand me?"

She kept her jaws clamped to keep from shouting at her father. How dare he suggest she go back to a man who'd bought her as part of a package deal! Digging around in her purse, she located her keys. Her fingers didn't seem to want to cooperate, and she dropped the key ring twice before successfully unlocking her door.

Tugging her father inside, she turned on him, her temper flaring. "I won't go back! You know how I feel about marriage for profit, Dad. But you tricked me, anyway—you and—and Joshua Raven! I won't be a piece of property like my mother!"

A vein pulsed in Gower's temple, and his jowls clumped as though he were gnashing his teeth. "Raven proposed to you in good faith."

"Good faith to you, not to me!" She spun away, tossing her purse on the couch, then turned back, hurt bubbling to the surface. "*Why* Daddy—why did you leave that note in his briefcase? Was it because you couldn't stand not being absolutely sure I understood I'd been manipulated? Did your ego require that I know? That I *suffer?* What shameful, Machiavellian reasoning made you write that down? Can't you stand to see anybody happy—even if it's nothing but a self-deluded happiness?"

"What are you talking about?" he growled. "How dare you make me out some kind of a sadistic creature."

"You are—you *and* Joshua Raven. You're greedy killer sharks, and I wish you both all the happiness and success you deserve." She pointed toward the door. "Now get out. I'm tired of trying to make a family out of the two of us. To be honest, Daddy, I don't care if I ever see you again!"

His florid face went purple and his eyes bulged. "I won't have you giving me orders. I can cut off your funds, like that." He snapped his squat fingers. "You may live like an urchin, giving all your money to those sentimental charities, but you still need to eat!"

"I'll eat." She stared him down. "I have a standing

offer to run the Literacy Center. That's a paid position. I don't need mother's inheritance.''

He harrumphed. ''You're a stiff-backed headstrong neophyte. You have no idea who you're dealing with. I'll crush you for your treachery. Don't think I won't!''

''*My* treachery?'' She couldn't hold back a harsh, forlorn laugh. ''How can you say that with a straight face? Get out of my home!'' Stomping to the door, she threw it wide. ''Now.''

He stormed by her swathed in a cloud of pungent cologne. She made a face at the spicy-sweet stench, slamming the door after him. She felt ill and pressed her hand to her stomach. Woozy, she clung to the doorknob to keep from stumbling. After a minute, she staggered to the couch and sank down, wondering what had come over her. Fights with her father had never made her light-headed and sick, before. Hunching forward, she dropped her face in her hands, biting back a sob.

Why couldn't her father love her? Why did he idolize the gods of wealth and power over everything and everyone else? And why did she ache with longing for Josh—a man as flawed and superficial as her father?

The ringing of the phone made her jump. She lifted her face from her hands, sniffling. She didn't want to answer, but out of habit she leaned over to the end table and picked up the receiver. ''Hello?'' She was gratified she only sounded tired.

''Mrs. Raven?'' came a businesslike, female voice.

Her heart lurched at the reminder that she was still Josh's wife—though in name only. ''Y-yes.''

''I'm Faith Hanfield, an attorney on Mr. Raven's

legal staff. I called to see if you're free tonight. There are some papers he would like you to sign.''

She closed her eyes and slumped back. She hadn't been able to bring herself to initiate divorce proceedings. Apparently Joshua felt no similar reluctance. "Of course—the divorce."

"Well—yes." The lawyer sounded both apologetic and businesslike. "Would eight o'clock be convenient?"

"Tonight?" Panic rushed through Wendy, and that surprised her. Divorce was what she wanted.

"If that's not convenient—"

"No—no, it's fine," she broke in, telling herself it was time to face reality. A one-sided love was worse than no love at all. "I'll expect you at eight. Do you need the address?"

"Mr. Raven gave it to me."

"I see." Wendy felt empty. Her head swam and she rubbed her eyes. "Fine—fine. I'll look forward to it." She grimaced. How lame! How absurdly untrue.

The phone went dead as the attractive-sounding attorney hung up. Listlessly, Wendy replaced the receiver in its cradle. "Goodbye, Miss—whatever," she mumbled.

Leave it to Josh to have a pretty lady lawyer serve her with divorce papers!

The knock at her door startled Wendy awake. She lay on her couch with an ice pack on her head. She didn't feel well. Lifting her arm, she checked her watch. Seven forty-five. The attorney, Faith Hanfield, was more than punctual. "Just a minute." She dropped the ice pack on the coffee table. When she sat up, it took her a few seconds to clear her head. Obviously she was coming down with some kind of flu bug.

Pushing herself up, she went to the door and opened it, startled to see Judy Sawyer standing there. Her neighbor smiled, but Wendy could see concern in her eyes. Judy was as broken up about Wendy's situation as she was—well, almost. Clearly Judy took it as a personal defect that her marshmallow mint sauce had failed.

Judy's pleasant expression faded. "Oh—dear…" she said. "You don't look good."

Wendy smiled wanly, unable to argue the truth. "I think I might be coming down with something. Maybe it would be better if you didn't come in."

"Don't be silly." Taking Wendy's arm, Judy helped her to the couch. "Seth gets everything under the sun, and I never get sick. I tell you what…" Judy sat down beside Wendy and lay the back of her hand against Wendy's forehead. "I've just made some chicken soup. I'll bring over some warm broth."

Wendy's stomach churned, and she swallowed hard. "I—I—thanks, but—"

"At least try to eat," Judy insisted. "You don't feel like you have a temperature. I bet a little broth and some crackers would perk you right up." She patted Wendy's hand. "You've been through a lot these last weeks. I bet you haven't been eating right, that's all."

Wendy shrugged, not knowing what to say. If she told the truth, she supposed she hadn't done much more than pick at her food lately. "I've felt fine— really," she said, staring at her lap. "This came on suddenly, tonight. I had an argument with my father and, I felt sick and dizzy. Probably stress."

"Oh?"

When Judy didn't say more, Wendy lifted her glance to meet her neighbor's pensive expression. Judy squeezed Wendy's knee affectionately. "I'll get you some of that broth. Be right back."

"Thanks." Another bout of dizziness made her woozy. Squeezing her eyes shut, she slumped back.

In a short a time Judy reappeared with a quart jar of golden liquid and a box of crackers. "The broth's still warm. Let me put it in a bowl for you."

Pulling her lips between her teeth, Wendy tried not to gag. But the groan that issued up from her throat couldn't be completely stifled.

Judy came over and sat beside Wendy, laying the jar and cracker box on the coffee table. She touched Wendy's hand. "I know this is none of my business, but do you think you might be—"

"Knock, knock?"

Wendy and her companion looked toward the open door. A tall, slender brunette in a chic black business suit smiled at them. A slim leather briefcase hung from her shoulder. Wendy's heart plummeted a ridiculous distance, considering Josh was no longer her concern. But why did his attorney have to be so gorgeous?

"Miss Hanfield?" she asked hesitantly, clutching at the hope that the beauty in black was selling bibles or makeup, or giving away puppies, and wasn't actually one of Josh's legal eagles.

"Yes, I'm Faith Hanfield." She indicated the apartment with a nod. "May I come in?"

"Oh, you've got company." Judy stood. "I'll go." Glancing back down at Wendy, she said, "Try to eat some broth."

Disconcerted by the beautiful lawyer's presence and

the well-meant interference of her neighbor, Wendy was momentarily speechless. "Well—I—"

"Are you ill, Mrs. Raven?" the attorney asked, her expression changing to one of kind concern. "Would you rather I come back another time?"

"She was a little dizzy earlier and her stomach is upset," Judy volunteered, walking to the door. With a friendly touch on the lawyer's arm, Judy said, "Try to get her to eat something."

"It's just a cold, I'm sure," Wendy called after Judy. "Thanks for the broth and crackers."

At the door Judy turned and waved. "I'll check on you before I go to the court house tomorrow." A moment later, Judy was gone, leaving Wendy and the striking lawyer to stare at each other.

After a heartbeat of silence, Faith indicated the couch. "May I?"

Wendy felt like a fool—a dizzy, nauseous fool. "Oh—I'm sorry." She patted the sofa. "Please join me."

Faith moved silently and gracefully across the rug, taking a seat beside Wendy. "You're sure you're feeling all right?"

"Just stress or—lack of sleep or—or something," Wendy mumbled. "I hope I'm not contagious."

The lawyer laughed. "My six-year-old has brought home so many germs from school, I'm sure I'm immune."

Wendy smiled in spite of her mood. The woman had a friendly way about her, even if she was beautiful, and—at the very least—Josh's confidante. Faith's expression grew somber. "We really could postpone this. I know how stressful this sort of thing can be."

Wendy sucked in a fortifying breath, feeling slightly less ill. "No—let's get it done."

"If you say so." All business now, Faith opened her briefcase. She drew out a sheaf of official-looking documents. "Here are the divorce papers. Please read them, then sign where I've indicated."

Wendy took the papers, willing her hands not to shake. Unable to focus on the words that would end her marriage, she flipped listlessly through the pages. "It looks very legal." Another wave of nausea hit her and she pressed her lips together.

"That's what I do—make things very legal."

Wendy scanned the legalese feeling utterly worn down. Discarded.

Faith fished inside her briefcase. "And here are the papers turning over the company. Once again, I've denoted the places requiring your signature."

Wendy nodded absently. She scanned the last page of the divorce papers, deciding there was no need to read them. It was best to get it over. "If you have a pen, I'll…" Something in what the lawyer just said niggled at her brain and she glanced up. "What did you say about the company?"

Faith hefted a second sheaf of papers, this one thicker. She handed it to Wendy. "As I said, the company will be yours as soon as you sign the places I've indicated. You will have complete autonomy to place anyone in charge that you feel—"

"*Mine?*" Wendy was confused. "What do you mean, the company will be mine? What company?"

Faith glanced at Wendy, her brow furrowing as though she assumed Wendy had been appraised of this transaction. "Well—naturally I'm referring to all of Joshua's holdings. Including everything he gained in the merger.'' The attorney studied Wendy, her expression inquiring. ''You didn't know he's giving you Raven-Maxim Enterprises?''

Wendy shook her head, broadsided by this turn of events. ''Has—has he lost his *mind?*''

Faith smiled without humor. ''I've known Mr. Raven for a lot of years, and I've never met a more intelligent, generous employer.'' She shook her head. ''To answer your question, he hasn't lost his mind, Mrs. Raven.'' She held out a golden pen. ''No—his mind is *not* what he's lost.''

Wendy felt as though she'd been struck by lightning. ''But—but does he have the right to give me the company? I mean, since I left him, doesn't the deal fall through?''

Faith pressed the pen into her hand. ''No. Whatever gave you that idea?''

''But—but he tried so hard to make me stay. It couldn't have been—I mean, he didn't really....'' Her sentence died as the impossible began to penetrate. She hardly noticed when Faith took a business card from her briefcase and lifted the golden pen from Wendy's limp fingers, scribbling something on the back of the card.

''Mrs. Raven,'' Faith said quietly, drawing Wendy from her crazy imaginings.

''Hmmm?'' she asked, dazed.

Faith placed the pen into her briefcase. ''Why don't I leave the documents with you? When you've signed them, I'll send one of our paralegals to fetch them.'' She placed her business card on the coffee table, facedown. ''I think I'll send Mark. He's a nice young man, and I have a feeling he might like to meet your neighbor.''

"Judy?" Wendy asked, startled by the change of subject.

Faith smiled, nodding. "I have a sense about people. If I send Mark, will you introduce him to Judy?"

Wendy nodded. Judy could certainly use a nice man in her life. "Of course. It would be my pleasure."

"That's fine." Faith held out a hand and Wendy accepted it. "Goodbye, Mrs. Raven. Take care of yourself."

After a few seconds or a thousand light-years, Wendy couldn't be sure, she realized her apartment door was closed and the lawyer was gone. Disoriented, her senses spinning, she leaned forward, pressing the flat of her hands against her temples. She was so dizzy, so confused. Josh was giving her a divorce—but he was also giving her *everything* he'd worked for all his life? That didn't make any sense—unless he really did—unless he meant everything he'd....

Her glance caught on Faith's business card. Something scrawled there caught her eye. "Dr. John Morris, Obstetrics." Underneath, the lawyer had penned, "I have a sense about people, Mrs. Raven. Make an appointment."

Wendy read the word aloud. "Obstetrics." She stared at it. But wasn't that the type of doctor who cared for women who were pregnant?

Pregnant!

The truth slammed into her brain, and she stopped breathing.

CHAPTER TWELVE

Josh shrugged out of his shirt and tossed it on the pile of firewood he'd already chopped. He didn't need the blasted wood. He'd already chopped enough to last him through two years of continuous blizzards. But he had to do something to work off his restless energy.

He'd spent only a few days in Chicago after the disastrous honeymoon, just long enough to draft the documents turning over the company to Wendy. He hadn't been able to concentrate on anything, and even in the crowded city, he'd felt terribly alone. He preferred the seclusion of Raven's Roost, and had returned nearly two weeks ago. At least, here, he had his memories of the wedding night he'd shared with Wendy.

Wrenching his ax blade out of the stump, he grabbed another section of log and stood it on the tree trunk. With a mighty chop, he split it in two, then tossed the pieces on the growing mountain of firewood. Shifting to get another log, he stopped, listening. A motorboat? He glanced at his watch. A little late in the day for the mail, but he didn't care. He had no interest in what the post might bring. If the truth be told, he had little interest in anything these days.

Drawing in a long breath, he went back to work. Physical exhaustion was his only consolation of late. During this past month, since Wendy ran away, he'd learned how little gratification the acquisition of money and power had ever given him. How many times had he laughed at the old saying "Money can't buy happiness," thinking it sentimental and silly?

These days, alone here in his woodland hideaway, he'd learned how right that adage was. He couldn't conjure up a shred of desire to be the wealthiest man in America anymore. For the first time in his life, Josh felt rudderless, lost, caring for nothing, wanting nothing—but Wendy.

He marked time by driving himself to his physical limits. He might not get much satisfaction out of the sweat of his brow, but at least he got so worn out he could finally fall asleep. It was probably his due that Wendy haunted him even then. He had an ironic thought, wondering if this mountain home was doomed to forever house heartbroken men.

Taking a powerful swing of his ax, he halved another cedar log, taking his frustrations out on hapless wood. Movement out of the corner of his eye caught his attention. Wiping his brow, he turned toward the lake.

Someone was coming up the granite walkway. He straightened, his ax thudding to the ground. Could it be? He sucked in a sharp breath, staring at the figure slowly ascending the distant path.

He began to move toward her. It could be Faith Hanfield with the divorce papers. He hadn't signed them. Couldn't. Not until he actually saw Wendy's signature there. But surely Faith would have mailed them.

He rounded the side of the house. By the time he reached the top of the walk, she was halfway up.

Wendy! His nerves grew taut, his heart rate quickening like an engine running at full throttle.

He hadn't dared hope, but there she was. Walking toward him.

He could barely control himself. *Hold on there, brother,* he counseled inwardly. *She might be here with an altogether reasonable, unromantic question about the business. Don't go grabbing her and kissing her again like a blasted fool!*

Forcing a calm facade, he waved. "Hi, stranger." He grimaced. *Don't remind her that she ran away, idiot!*

She waved back. She carried no suitcase, and she held only a thick manila envelope. Disconcerted, he scanned the dock. No suitcase. But the boat was gone. What did this mean? Maybe the motorboat was supposed to return for her—soon. And the envelope she carried? *Hell.* Had she brought the divorce papers, herself? Why? Revenge? He kept the smile on his face, though he wanted to throw something—his fist through a wall, to be exact.

"It's good to see you," he said honestly. She was only a few steps away now. With great unwillingness, he stuffed his hands into his jeans' pockets.

"It's good to see you, too, Josh." She came to a stop on the slab where he stood—only an arm's length away. She smiled, but it was indefinite, not the full, sweet I-love-you smile he longed for.

She wore a pink sundress. She looked so beautiful. He'd never realized she had a cruel streak. This was torture. Hell on earth. He could detect her scent and inhaled guiltily. Blast! It would be better to get this over before he did something stupid. "Is that for me?" He nodded toward the envelope.

"Yes." She didn't hand it to him, just looked at his face, her expression serious. "Could we—go inside?"

He felt like a jerk—not a particularly unique experience lately. "Sure." Against stern orders, his hand slid from his pocket and took her elbow. He cursed himself, but once he touched her, he couldn't let her go.

She didn't pull away, but she was probably merely being polite. He cleared his throat, opening the door for her to precede him. "Al will be glad to see you," he offered, deciding inane conversation was better than strained silence.

Wendy's expression eased, and almost became a smile, but not quite. "I've missed her. How is she?"

Flapping wings heralded a new presence in the entryway. Talons dug into Josh's bare shoulder. "*Caw-caw!* I love *Josh!* I *love* Josh!"

He winced from the embarrassing reminder of their disastrous past. "I'm sorry about that," he murmured. "She doesn't unlearn things very easily."

It startled him when Wendy took his fingers and led him into the living room. "Let's sit down, Josh."

He frowned at her serious manner. Apparently she wasn't happy to be reminded of their marriage—or the soft feeling she'd once had for him. When they were seated on the couch, he extended a hand. "I presume you want me to sign those?"

She handed him the packet. "Yes, if you don't mind."

He gave the envelope a black look. With a heaviness in his belly, he dumped the contents on the pine coffee table. A pen clattered out with the papers. He forced back a curse. "You thought of everything, I see."

"I hope so."

He lifted the sheaf of papers and scanned the cover

page. "These aren't the divorce papers," he said, confused. "These are for company ownership." He looked at her. "I don't understand."

She picked up the pen and held it toward him. "I've had them drawn up, making you the CEO. You see, I've decided to retire from big business. I'd rather stay home and decorate the nursery—if it's all right with you. Of course we'll have to find a house, first—with lots of rooms for the children."

He listened, baffled, opened his mouth to speak, then stared again. "What?"

She smiled, a real I-love-you smile, and it filled him with a warmth unlike anything he'd ever experienced. Taking his face in her hands, she whispered, "If I'm going to have the baby, darling. You really should do something." She kissed him lightly. "Don't you think?"

Intense pleasure coursed through him, making him go hot and cold and definitely delirious. Had she said what he thought she'd said? "You're pregnant?" he asked, his voice hushed.

She nodded. "Happy?"

"Happy?" he echoed, as the storm clouds that shrouded his heart disappeared. "Happy?" He stood up, sweeping her into his arms. Al squawked and flapped to safety.

Wendy giggled and grasped his neck. "Yes. Are you?"

"Are you?" he whispered, still unable to believe his good fortune.

She nodded, kissing his jaw. "I think it's illegal to be this happy, Josh." Lovely tears shimmered on her lashes.

Lord! He'd missed those big, purple eyes! "If it's

illegal, then we're both going to jail, my love." He carried her toward the staircase, vowing, "I love you."

She snuggled against him. "I know." He felt her brush a kiss against his throat. "By the way, I fired Daddy."

Josh stopped and stared. "You didn't."

She shrugged sheepishly. "Well, I gave him a nice golden parachute. I didn't think you'd mind. I'm sure someday he'll learn to love golf."

Josh couldn't hold back a rumble of laughter. He carried her halfway up the stairs before he halted, suddenly worried. "Say, can you—I mean, are you feeling—er—can we...?"

She touched his cheek, love sparkling in her eyes. "Yes, we can. And if I have anything to say about it, we will for days and days. Why do you think I didn't bring any clothes?"

"Josh loves Wendy," Al whispered from a nearby perch on the banister.

Wendy glanced at the bird, then smiled up at her husband. "I like that, darling."

He kissed the tip of her nose. "Before today is over," Josh promised softly, "that's not all you're going to like."

Eight months later, Josh was reminded of the vital lesson his marriage to Wendy had taught him—about the great and abiding power of love. Neither the lure of wealth nor prominence could begin to rival the glimmering beauty of his wife's eyes as she presented him with their newborn son.

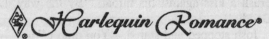
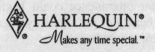

If you enjoyed what you just read,
then we've got an offer you can't resist!

Take 2 bestselling love stories FREE!

Plus get a FREE surprise gift!

Clip this page and mail it to Harlequin Reader Service®

YES! Please send me 2 free Harlequin Romance® novels and my free surprise gift. Then send me 4 brand-new novels every month, which I will receive months before they're available in stores. In the U.S.A., bill me at the bargain price of $2.90 plus 25¢ delivery per book and applicable sales tax, if any*. In Canada, bill me at the bargain price of $3.34 plus 25¢ delivery per book and applicable taxes**. That's the complete price and a savings of over 10% off the cover prices—what a great deal! I understand that accepting the 2 free books and gift places me under no obligation ever to buy any books. I can always return a shipment and cancel at any time. Even if I never buy another book from Harlequin, the 2 free books and gift are mine to keep forever. So why not take us up on our invitation. You'll be glad you did!

116 HEN CNEP
316 HEN CNEQ

Name	(PLEASE PRINT)	
Address	Apt.#	
City	State/Prov.	Zip/Postal Code

* Terms and prices subject to change without notice. Sales tax applicable in N.Y.
** Canadian residents will be charged applicable provincial taxes and GST.
   All orders subject to approval. Offer limited to one per household.
   ® are registered trademarks of Harlequin Enterprises Limited.

HROM99   ©1998 Harlequin Enterprises Limited

A trilogy of warm, wonderful
stories by bestselling author

DEBBIE MACOMBER

Orchard Valley, Oregon

It's where the Bloomfield sisters—Valerie,
Stephanie and Norah—grew up, and it will
always be home to them.

When their father suffers a heart attack, they gather at his
side—the first time in years they've all been together. Coming
home, they rediscover the bonds of family, of sisterhood.
And, without expecting it, they also find love.

ORCHARD VALLEY

MIRA

On sale mid-June 1999 wherever paperbacks are sold!

We'd like to thank you, our reader, for making the past 50 years a success!

Use this coupon and get 50¢ off the purchase of any Harlequin Romance® series book!

50¢ OFF!

when you purchase any  *Harlequin Romance®* book!

RETAILER: Harlequin Enterprises Ltd. will pay the face value of this coupon plus 10.25¢ if submitted by customer for this specified product only. Any other use constitutes fraud. Coupon is nonassignable, void if taxed, prohibited or restricted by law. Consumer must pay any government taxes. Valid in Canada only. Neilson Clearing House customers—Mail to: Harlequin Enterprises Limited, P.O. Box 3000, St. John, New Brunswick, Canada E2L 4L3. Non NCH retailer—for reimbursement submit coupons and proof of sales directly to: Harlequin Enterprises Ltd., Retail Sales Dept., 225 Duncan Mill Rd., Don Mills (Toronto), Ontario, Canada, M3B 3K9.

Coupon expires December 31, 1999. Valid at retail outlets in Canada only.

5 2 6 0 2 7 7 9

PH50CAN

We'd like to thank you, our reader, for making the past 50 years a success!

Use this coupon and get 50¢ off the purchase of any Harlequin Romance® series book!

50¢ OFF!

when you purchase any  Harlequin Romance® book!

RETAILER: Harlequin Enterprises Ltd. will pay the face value of this coupon plus 8¢ if submitted by customer for this specified product only. Any other use constitutes fraud. Coupon is nonassignable, void if taxed, prohibited or restricted by law. Consumer must pay any government taxes. Valid in U.S. only. Neilson Clearing House customers—Mail to: Harlequin Enterprises Limited, P.O. Box 880478, El Paso, TX 88588-0478, U.S.A. Non NCH retailer—for reimbursement submit coupons and proof of sales directly to: Harlequin Enterprises Ltd., Retail Sales Dept., 225 Duncan Mill Rd., Don Mills (Toronto), Ontario, Canada, M3B 3K9.

Coupon expires December 31, 1999. Valid at retail outlets in U.S. only.

5 65373 00050 2   (8100) 1 07013

PH50US

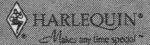